Hearts of a Vanishing City

PREQUEL TO THE KARA MASON STORY

THE ZORIBIATUS CYCLE UNIVERSE

JILL N DAVIES

To everyone holding on to hope during the apocalypse,
I wrote this book so you'll know it's worth keeping on hoping.

And to all my avid readers, we've got to stop meeting like this (in a barely fictionalized dystopian world)

Author's Note

This novel is a dystopian thriller—a love story with zombies. It's not a romance, as the journey to love isn't the focus, but the relationships play a central role.

Hearts of a Vanishing City is a standalone novel. It's also the prequel to the *Kara Mason Story*, which begins with Book 1: *Due North*. Some characters, like Simons, James, and Mora, may be recognizable but you do not need to have read these books in order to appreciate the story within these pages.

The events in *Hearts of a Vanishing City* take place approximately twenty years prior to the beginning of *Due North*.

Content Warnings:

Hearts of a Vanishing City contains violence and gore, body horror, pregnancy, unexpected pregnancy, viral infection, succumbing to a disease, medical trauma and negligence. Please take care of yourself as you read.

CHAPTER

One

ZAYD BABA, CAPITOL CITY STATE

THE ROADS WENT to hell on this side of Main Street. The revitalized cityscape quickly deteriorated into ancient, crumbling buildings, some hastily whitewashed, others still bearing the vitriol of the Resistee movement. Zayd had nearly forgotten how bad it was here, though he'd only been living on the northeast side of the city for three years.

The City Restoration Project would eventually make its way to this area, but by the state of the building exteriors, they were a long way off. During the Damage Control era, the Disease Containment Authorities had hastily blotted out many of the messages scrawled by Resistees leading up to the last outbreak, but traces of their protests still marred the face of the Westside. This was the city Zayd grew up in.

He eased up on the brakes of the oversized transportation vehicle at the intersection of Industrial Avenue and Endgal Boulevard as he passed an old building with *Fear consumes justice* scrawled on its sun-bleached side in ten-story-high lettering. The messages were old and familiar in their raging scrawl, each an outburst stamped in time.

Your vote is your voice
The cure is a lie

Compliance is the only real infection

They reminded him the Resistees had been fighting against the rising political power of Disease Containment.

Fighting and losing.

The vehicle shuddered and jolted as he tried and failed to swerve through a maze of crater-sized potholes dotting the broken asphalt.

"Whoops! Sorry about that!" he said, running his right hand through thick, dark hair, attempting to smooth back the jostled strands.

There was no one else in the driver's compartment to hear him, but he wasn't thinking about a passenger. He was thinking about the cargo...

This was Zayd's first assignment for the boss-man, and he didn't want to mess anything up. Especially since the first credit deposit had already gone through, and the payment was too good to be true. If Johnson was being honest about the payout, then he'd be making almost three times what he made as a floor supervisor at the electronics factory.

He could picture his wife, Anika, marveling at their balance already. "That's quite a promotion," she would say, and he would kiss her on the temple and promise he'd earned every penny working his way up the ranks and impressing Johnson, the city manager for synthetics production and distribution, which was technically true.

But this job wasn't a part of factory production. Technically, this was a transportation job. The way Johnson explained it, transportation was run by this secret group, and if there was a "shortage" of personnel, then the factory had to supply a transporter. Johnson, being in charge of the factory and a member of this secret group, selected the appropriate driver for the task.

Today, Zayd was that guy.

He was still trying to wrap his mind around Johnson's explanation of the whole thing. The folks in the secret group called themselves *dissenters*, which sounded a lot like the Resistees of his childhood, but according to Johnson, they absolutely were not. And since Zayd was interested in helping them, he supposed that made him a dissenter. *Almost.* Johnson was vouching for him for now. All Zayd had to do was keep his mouth shut and do his job. In exchange, he'd get more credits than he could ever earn doing factory work, and hopefully an inside look at the *real* people who didn't believe in the Department of Disease Containment's lies.

Zayd didn't know if the DDC was actually lying, but he was pretty sure the spread of Zoribiatus virus wasn't as big of a deal as everyone made it out to be. He thought the problem likely laid elsewhere—in the overbearing DDC control that was supposed to make everyone feel safe. The factory quota and supply chain problems, the fear that came with the last of the people fleeing the outskirts. Maybe the Resistees had been onto something, and now the dissenters were taking up the torch and pushing back against a government that ruled with fear.

There weren't any people on the roads in the middle of the day. In between school, shift changes and scheduled market time, people kept themselves shut inside. That's just the way things were now. Like everyone else, Zayd wasn't used to being out when the city was silent. It was spooky how everything was so quiet. The dilapidated exteriors of the buildings on the Westside made it look like a ghost town—like it must have looked when everything happened.

The city was, after all, the skeleton of what had been one of the major metropolises before the collapse. This was one of the places where the first outbreak hit the hardest. Just over a hundred years ago, hundreds of thousands of near-dead had converged, destroying civilization and nearly wiping out humanity. There was no disputing the original outbreak—no government could create such a thing, and no government could erase it. Then, just forty years later, there was a second major outbreak. Zayd believed in that one, too, because there were a few people still alive from that time. Again, no amount of government control could make that sort of thing disappear from a society's memory. But the third outbreak, the Resistee incident...

Zayd had been a small child during the protests. He could remember the way people would swarm the streets and then, the next day, entire neighborhoods would be empty. Problem was, he never once recalled seeing someone sick.

It wasn't that Zayd didn't believe in Zoribiatus, the outbreaks, or even the need for the force fields to keep things up and running and the people inside the cities safe. He just didn't believe in the current outbreaks—the ones everyone walked around constantly afraid *might* happen. The outbreaks that didn't exist. People's fear of the disease was a remnant. They were afraid of ghosts.

The DDC was painting over the broken and crumbling exterior of the city's past one building at a time while simultaneously offering people the opportunity to chip away at their fear, one over-priced vial draw and too-hot hand wash at a time. People took all sorts of tests now, but it didn't do anything to make them feel safer. From Zayd's perspective, the DDC wanted people to be afraid of each other. If they were afraid, they wouldn't ask where somebody ended up when they disappeared. They'd just be glad they were gone.

That was why he was a dissenter.

He eased the vehicle to a stop where the road came up against the city limit, lifting his hand so the Department of Disease Containment official manning the boundary could see his acknowledgment and approach. This was the first trial in the gauntlet that would grant Zayd semi-permanent membership into the dissenters' group and give him access to more financial security than he or anyone could ever dream of.

The black-suited official tapped on the transport door. Zayd pressed the button on the wheel, and the window came down.

"I don't have another transport on the roster for departure today," the official said.

Looking down from his mount in the driver's seat, Zayd could barely detect a hint of brownish hair sticking out the sides of the offi-cer's hat. Their facial features were hidden behind the shadow of the hat's rim.

"I don't know much about it, but I'm getting an extra ten percent for bringing this one to 18N by early tomorrow." Like he was instructed, he stuck the folder with the fancy scan code on the cover out the window, angling it down so the officer could easily grab it.

"Be easy and act like an idiot. That's their favorite sort of worker," Johnson had instructed.

Instead of taking it, the officer waved their tablet over the surface. There was a beep, and information filled the DDC official's tablet.

Zayd refrained from saying something stupid and waited for the officer to read through.

"Says you've got six crates of medquip in there?" the officer asked.

"If you say so." Zayd shrugged even though there was no way the officer could see him do it.

"Pull up to the check-bay and open up so I can confirm for sign-off," they said, giving the door another tap before walking toward the border station. As they went, they waved their tablet toward the wide asphalt space, indicating Zayd should follow.

Johnson hadn't said anything about opening the back. Zayd could feel his heart thundering high up in his throat as he eased the transport into the check-bay. When the DDC official banged on the truck a third time, Zayd winced, but he knew what it meant. He needed to comply, quickly and completely, if he expected to get out of this with his ass and his cargo. He unclipped his seatbelt and hopped out of the transport, hurrying to meet the official at the back.

It took him two tries to get his scanner to open the cargo door, but that ended up being alright. It made him look like the idiot he was supposed to be, so when the officer asked him, "Why such a big transport for six crates?" they believed him when he said, "I've got no clue about that. They're just paying me extra to drive."

Only idiots volunteered to leave the cities.

"Let's just open this one in front up and get things moving," the officer said.

Zayd gulped, but said, "Sure thing," fumbling for the right setting on his scanner.

The officer tried not to look impatient as Zayd struggled to get the setting right and pop the lid off the crate. When it beeped and the magnetic locks released, Zayd was pushing so hard that he nearly slammed his head into the side of the transport as the top slid off.

"Careful there, buddy, or you'll get yourself a one-way trip to the clinics with that extra ten percent they're paying you," the official said.

Zayd recovered, brushing the sleeves of his jacket as he stood to peer into the foam-lined crate at a jostled pile of med-chips.

"It's strange how much of this stuff other cities go through in a few months," the officer was saying.

Zayd didn't like the idea of the officer thinking anything about this shipment was strange. He held his breath, waiting for them to ask him to take the tops off the other five crates. That would be a problem.

"But they aren't paying me ten percent more to care, so here you go," the officer said, waving their signature over the virtual form.

The tablet blinked, and Zayd felt the scanner in his back pocket vibrate as the approval went through. The officer climbed back into the border station while Zayd scrambled to get the crate's top back on and engage the magnetic lock. By the time he made his way back into the driver's seat, he was sweaty and flustered, trying to not feel like the idiot he appeared to be.

"You're going to hear a loud buzz, then that overhead light will turn green. That's how you know you're clear to drive through," the official said.

Zayd did his best not to punch it when the light turned green, but still the vehicle lurched when he put his foot on the gas and drove through.

I'm on the other side! Zayd thought as he sped away from the city limits on the old road. He was suppressing a shriek of pure joy until he realized there was no one to hear him. He pressed the window button so the cold, free air assaulted his face and whipped his hair out of place, then let out the most carefree noise he'd ever made.

"Yee-haw!"

It was supposed to be something wild people said in a time even before the old world.

He screamed again and again until his voice was raw and his hands were numb from the cold.

Having spent all the pent-up energy from the encounter, Zayd settled in for the drive. About three hours was what Johnson said to expect. He kept his foot on the gas so the odometer read 80 mph—an important variable in the three-hour equation. All around him, the world whizzed by, a blur of greens, yellows and browns. Ahead of him, the greenery grew dense, appearing to swallow the road as he drove toward a grey horizon.

This was nothing like what he expected on the other side of the force field. It was exactly like what he expected. It was overwhelming.

Most importantly, though, there were no near-dead. That was what everyone was afraid of, wasn't it? The creeping hordes of diseased people clamoring for an unsuspecting populace? That was what the force field was keeping out.

Just like he suspected, just like Johnson had confirmed, the existence of an unfriendly horde was a myth. Sure, Zoribiatus wasn't cured, and sure, there were probably infected people or communities here and there, but now that people knew what the disease was and how to keep it from spreading, there wasn't a real threat. It was all about fear. If the Department of Disease Containment could control people's fear of a disease, then they could control the mob.

The transport vehicle drifted as Zayd's mind wandered. The front wheels hit the rough divots where the asphalt dipped into overgrown woods, drawing his attention forward. He jerked the wheel a little too hard, and the transport jostled. Everything happened fast. The vehicle swerved across the road and into the weed-packed dirt before Zayd regained control. Thick evergreen branches whipped across the windshield, catching on the rearview mirror and dragging against the roof. Zayd applied the brake firmly, easing the transport back onto the road. Then he realized another vehicle was approaching.

He panicked, reversing his direction and sending the transport vehicle the rest of the way off the road and straight into the massive trunk of a fir tree growing too close to the road. The windshield shattered as Zayd snapped forward, saved from the steering wheel by his seatbelt. He saw stars, heard the cargo in back roll and crunch.

Not good.

The world was buzzing all around him, a mixture of insects and raw panic. Zayd sat paralyzed, trying to think of what to do next. He was ruining his first job. He was stranded outside the force field without a vehicle.

Check the cargo.

Another man's life depended on him.

Zayd was already unbuckled and brushing shattered glass from his thick canvas jacket when he realized he wasn't alone. The other vehicle had stopped when he crashed, and the driver was standing outside his door. He was so tall that Zayd could see his head through the window, smooth and bald. Concerned eyes and warm, dark brown skin. The man pulled at the door, wrenching it open despite the protest from the crushed and distorted hinges, which meant he was very strong.

"Hey, man, are you alright?" he asked, reaching in to extract a stunned Zayd from the driver's seat.

"I'm… fine. I'm a dead man after what I did, but I'm fine," Zayd stammered.

"It's my fault. I wasn't supposed to be on this route. You weren't expecting me. I'm sure we can explain," the man said. He sounded nervous.

Zayd looked him over. He was young—about his own age—and wearing a uniform almost identical to Zayd's. Just another transportation worker passing through, and just like him, he wasn't on the schedule. *Stick to the story and nobody gets in trouble,* he reminded himself.

"What are the odds of two unscheduled transports going by on the same day? I'm supposed to make it to 18N by early morning with a med run. Name's Baba." Zayd clasped his hands behind his back and nodded his head at the other man by way of formal greeting.

"Simons." The other man mimicked his greeting, barely suppressing a wry smile. "18N? Where the road splits about three hours out?"

Zayd's eyes bulged with surprise at Simons' reference to the rendezvous location. "That's… right. Three hours if you drive 80…"

Simons beamed with recognition. "You can relax. I'm your contact."

Zayd's eyes were as wide as saucers. "Simons. That's right. Johnson said you were a real big guy."

Simons chuckled. "That's one way of putting it. Let's see how the other guy is doing."

Zayd slammed a hand into his forehead. "Oh, man. I forgot, I was going to make sure I hadn't killed him."

He rushed to the back of the vehicle, cursing and scrambling for the scanner as he went. Simons followed.

"They put a bunch of padding in those transport crates. I'm sure he's fine."

Zayd ignored him, still struggling to get the scanner to release the lock. Finally, it beeped, and the door rolled open, revealing the wreck of crates in the back.

"I don't even know which one it is anymore," Zayd moaned, starting with the one in front.

"Give them a shake. The one with a person inside is probably heaviest," Simons suggested, hopping into the back with him and shaking the crate by the door. The med-chips rattled inside.

Zayd complied, shaking the crate stacked precariously on the back bench. It rattled unenthusiastically. He shoved it aside and began working on the next one, which barely budged.

"I think it's this one."

Simons joined him as he battled with the scanner.

"Maybe we should just move him over to my transport," Simons suggested.

"What if he's dead?" Zayd asked.

"Don't know how to make him un-dead, do you?"

Zayd shook his head, frustrated and flustered as Simons pushed at the top of the crate.

"If he's hurt or something, we can help him. Then we'll seal him back up, and you can finish the job," Zayd said.

The scanner beeped, but the lid didn't budge.

"What are you going to do?" Simons asked, pushing hard on the lid as the scanner beeped again.

"I don't know. I wasn't supposed to crash the transport," Zayd admitted.

"Sure. I didn't think that was in the job description," Simons said.

The scanner beeped a third time, and under Simons' considerable force, the lid shifted.

"Do it again," he said, bracing himself against the transport's walls for a better angle.

Zayd nodded.

"I could call the accident in to Johnson and have him send someone to pick me up," he suggested.

"How will you explain the missing crate?" Simons asked.

"No clue, but I don't know what else to do," Zayd grumbled, struggling with the scanner.

"How 'bout I run you back to the border agent? You can report the accident. You can tell them the back lock came undone in the accident. They can't prove someone didn't come along and steal it—maybe even some fringe Resistee from the outside? We wouldn't know anything about that, would we?" Simons winked.

The scanner beeped, and Simons gave the lid such an aggressive shove that it flew from the crate. Zayd stepped aside quickly enough that the lid flew by his face, hitting the crate over his shoulder. The man inside yelped as the lid clattered to the ground.

"He's alright," Simons proclaimed, just as the unstable crate crashed down onto Zayd.

MORA ROSSI, CAPITOL CITY STATE

MORA WONDERED if she should worry. Would someone spy her lurking around the old factory across from the main markets? She was, after all, out in the open where anyone could see her, and it was evident she didn't belong anywhere near the industrial production area. Most of the other folks who frequented the black market were adults and could justify their presence there in any number of ways, but Mora was still a student. Her bright red uniform shirt stood out against the drab background like a bad infection.

But Mora shook off the notion of being seen as easily as it had come. No one ever noticed her. They would have to look up and pay attention to something other than their own lives and business to notice someone out of place. That wasn't how people behaved unless someone was acting strange, and Mora never acted strange. She always moved with the confidence of someone who knew they could get away with what they were doing. It was her camouflage—her superpower. That was how she managed to obtain goods and services that allowed her to work on her other, more important secret project.

Mora tucked the tiny chip into her front jacket pocket. It had cost eighty-five credits and a precious twenty minutes of her life to get it, but it would be worth the expense once she got it to her next destination. If everything went well, she'd have those credits back in her account, plus her finder's fee. While those credits were essential for her work, they weren't the primary reason she risked the black market located in old Resistee territory. Mora was on a mission to uncover the past.

Glancing back at Main Street, where the capitol split the city in two —west and east, old and new, theirs and ours—Mora ducked back out onto the road, nearly colliding with a tall, red-shirted teen clutching a brown market bag against her chest.

Mora dipped her shoulder, dashing out of the way at the last second.

"Excuse me," she breathed, offering the minimum deference required to disappear from the situation.

"Endgal alive, I didn't see you!" the girl said, shifting the bag out of her line of vision and propping it against her left hip. Mora recognized her immediately. Naomi Love, one of her classmates. She was tall, confident and beautiful, with piercing hazel eyes and a brilliant grin that Mora had never once seen directed her way.

"I was walking with my head down," Mora said, shifting her backpack over her shoulder, not wanting Naomi to realize she'd just come around the corner from the Hole.

Most of the students in her class didn't believe the black market known as the Hole actually existed, but she'd heard Naomi reference it on more than one occasion. All the students liked to romanticize the black market, but Mora visited the Hole frequently enough to know that none of them, including Naomi, were ever patrons.

"Mora?" Naomi asked, doing a double take.

"Yeah, I had to stay back and talk to Professor Meyers about my quiz scores," Mora offered, scolding herself internally for volunteering too much information. She knew better than to talk too much, but she had a bad habit of putting her foot in her mouth (a disgusting old-world phrase) when it came to girls like Naomi.

"Oh. I didn't know—I mean, of course I didn't know, but you know what I mean, I maybe just figured you were doing market errands too," Naomi said, shifting the bag, which looked heavy, again.

Spending time at the legitimate market would have been an acceptable excuse for being out after class, too, but Mora had already chosen academic insufficiency. *It's the most believable excuse I've got*, she consoled herself. It was the one people like Naomi questioned the least, anyway.

"I might have been planning on a little bit of market time before heading home," Mora said, wondering as the words left her mouth why she would add to the lie. She was already running out of time to make her delivery and make it up to the roof to check for Omen before curfew, and with her luck, her mother would be home on time to catch her breaking rules.

"Yeah. I swear the market is the *only* thing worth doing around here, and it's barely even open on school days. I convinced my parents to let me do our regular shopping just to have an excuse not to go straight home after school." Naomi rolled her eyes, making Mora smirk.

"Looks like you've got quite a haul," she observed.

Naomi glanced at the bag. "It's just a loaf of bread and a bunch of canned goods. Mom said not to bother with chicken until the price comes down again."

"I hate the taste of chicken anyway." Mora shrugged, hoping she didn't sound too agreeable. Was it agreeable if it was true?

"Seriously. I was going to check out the aesthetics booths, but now that I bought all this stuff, it's too heavy to lug around the market anymore. I should've gone first. Shows you what kind of a transportation dummy I am." Naomi laughed at her own joke, then cut the sound short, realizing too late who she was joking with.

Mora had some of the lowest scores in their class. Even with her mom's connections in the DDC, there was a good chance she'd be headed straight to transportation after graduation. None of the skilled labor or medic training courses would want to take her on.

She let out what she hoped was an amiable chuckle. "Seriously. But I heard they don't have anything new in aesthetics since they brought out those new nail colors."

Naomi looked away, and her smile, which had previously lit her face with the same brilliance as the force field-filtered sunset, no longer reached her eyes. "Mom doesn't let me paint my nails. She says anything that negates the scans is dangerous."

Mora bit the inside of her cheek, hoping her burning face wasn't visibly flushed. "Yeah. Mine, too," she lied. Morgan Rossi-Stern wasn't around enough to enforce such ordinances, but it felt like a truth. Mora was certain that if her mother were present enough, she wouldn't let her paint her nails. She was also certain that if her mom were around enough to care, Mora would paint her nails just to spite her.

Naomi brought the bag back to her middle, clasping it with both hands. "I better get going before I spill this stuff everywhere."

Mora nodded. "Yeah. It's getting late anyway. It takes forever to get across town."

"Oh," Naomi said, her discomfort becoming increasingly apparent. "I'm taking the tram."

Of course Naomi was taking the tram. No kid in their right mind would hike across town with a bag of groceries two hours before curfew.

"Of course," Mora agreed, wishing she didn't feel so stupid trying to have a regular conversation with a peer. "It's just that my mom doesn't like me being in such close quarters with other people."

"Of course," Naomi echoed. "That's why we do the monthly screening. We've got the family clinic plan."

"That's smart." The conversation was officially painful.

"Well, I better get to the tram if I don't want to wait around forever. It was nice running into you, Mora."

"You, too." Mora shoved her hands deep into her jacket pockets, trying to ignore the rivulets of sweat running down her sides under all her layers. The layers helped with the gusts of wind on the rooftop, but they didn't do much for awkward encounters with classmates.

Naomi had the decency not to run toward the tram stop. Mora watched her go, her gaze lingering longer than it should on her retreating frame.

Naomi craned her head over her shoulder suddenly, making Mora feel as if she'd been caught doing something she shouldn't have.

"Tell James I said hi and congratulations on the Institute."

Mora caught the way Naomi's grin made it to her eyes at the

mention of James and the Institute. "If I see him before fitness tomorrow," she said.

Naomi waved a hand over her shoulder without looking back again. The tram was pulling up to the curb. Mora tried to look busy lingering at a stand that offered a variety of baked goods. The little rounds of golden crust with citrus-y glaze smelled incredible, and Mora realized she was getting hungry. Unfortunately, between the purchase of the chip and the power source upgrade for her clandestine old-world tablet, she was fresh out of credits.

She looked away when the vendor gave her a scathing once-over, feeling exposed after her encounter with Naomi. Moments before, she'd felt invincible. Now, it seemed even the people who didn't know her could sense her low test scores and illicit activities.

Maybe the Hole had a smell that lingered on her clothes long after she departed. Mora didn't think so, but it had been a long time since she first ventured into the world of clandestine goods and Resistee lore.

Mora waited another minute while tram riders found their seats and the door closed. It departed without sound, and the second it did, Mora turned away from the bakery vendor and the legitimate market, taking a shortcut down one of the side alleyways that no one else dared enter. They were too dark and grimy, and even Mora had to admit she felt a thrill of apprehension when she thought about the outbreak videos while she passed through.

Fifteen minutes later, she was standing at the entryway of an old residence building that looked a lot like her own. It was closer to Main Street, though, and that meant it was only a matter of time before the renovations made their way to it and transformed it like the buildings on the Eastside—erasing the vestiges of the old world and its people from the city's surface.

Mora didn't linger too long on the dark thought before pressing the button for apartment 252 and waiting.

After about five seconds, the intercom crinkled, and an old voice cracked through the speaker. "No deliveries after 1600."

Mora wondered if Mr. Bower ever responded to the buzzer with anything else. "It's Mora, Mr. Bower," she said into the intercom. "We've got business."

"Hush your mouth, girl!" The speaker garbled at the edges of his command. "Pound twenty-three at the entrance and you can bypass the scan."

Adjusting the pack on her shoulder, Mora walked toward the door. Most of the buildings had updated systems that required a scan in for entrance and exit. It made contact tracing a lot easier. Mora wasn't sure if Mr. Bower's building didn't have one installed or if he'd just found a way to game the system. She didn't much care either way, but she did appreciate that she never had to leave evidence of her visits the way she did for a few of her other clients.

She entered the code on the keypad, and the door buzzed for entry. Mora pulled her hood over her hair and kept her head low so she'd be difficult to identify on surveillance. Once inside, she went past the elevators and into the stairwell to the second floor. Apartment 252 was on the far side of the building, but she was between shifts and prob-ably wouldn't run into anyone besides a few stragglers making their way home from school or market.

She reached the apartment just as the sun dipped behind the neigh-boring high-rise residence, causing the automatic hall lights to switch on. More than likely, Mr. Bower was watching her through the door camera, but Mora lifted her hand to knock anyway.

The door opened before she could, and a hawk-eyed older man with a ring of grey hair around a balding, golden-brown scalp glared at her. "Don't draw attention to yourself," he scolded.

Mora rolled her eyes, suppressing a smirk. "I wouldn't dream of it."

He ushered her inside, glancing furtively around the hall to ensure no one was watching.

She kicked off her shoes at the doorway before stepping into the small but tidy kitchen as Mr. Bower locked the door behind her. The apartment smelled of dried cooking spices and the fresh herbs growing on the windowsill.

"Did you get it?" Mr. Bower asked, coming up behind her.

Mora reached into her pocket to produce the little chip. Mr. Bower's eyes shone upon seeing it.

"It was a bit more than we talked about," she said, placing it in his hand. Experience had taught her things went better when she acted with trust.

Mr. Bower held the chip up against the kitchen light as though he could read the contents etched within the fine network of coded data. "How much?"

"Eighty-five," she said, helping herself to a seat at the kitchen table. "Plus my fee."

"I suppose we should expect a little bit of robbery in these situations," Mr. Bower mused, gathering his tablet. He joined her at the table, which was littered with little pots half filled with tiny green plants and a partially spilled bag of rich, umber soil.

Mora brushed the dirt away from the space in front of her before setting her bag on the table. She reached under her school-issued tablet to bring out her true prized possession—an absolute brick of ancient technology with two terabytes of old-world media.

"That ought to show up right away," Mr. Bower said as his hands danced above his tablet, replenishing Mora's account, making her twenty-five credits richer.

"Thanks," she said, cuing up the writing program she used for notes.

Mr. Bower tucked the chip into an old-world reader and waited for the data to convert. He glanced at Mora, noting her tablet. "What did that thing run you?"

"Three fifty and half of my soul," she said, making him snort.

"A bargain."

Mora agreed. "Considering how much old-world media it has on it, I happen to agree."

Mr. Bower was one of the few people in the city who understood Mora and her obsession with old-world literature. She supposed it made sense, considering his own obsession with the old history files. Mr. Bower collected wartime communication reports. Mora thought that maybe she ought to have more of an interest in that sort of thing, but she found it difficult to dedicate her mental energy to anything except for the books and other people's stories.

Now that she was situated and the exchange was done, it was time for another story.

"So, Miss Rossi," Mr. Bower said, settling in as the data transfer started, "what can I tell you today?"

"Your family were outskirt refugee survivors of the second outbreak, right?" she asked.

"Indeed we were," Mr. Bower agreed.

Mora had been working backward from Mr. Bower's accounts of the Resistee protests and subsequent outbreak. It was in telling these stories that he revealed he wasn't a lifetime resident of the Capitol City State. She considered the potential of everything he could reveal, trying to decide where to start. "Can you tell me about what it was like before the outbreak?"

CHAPTER
Three

ANIKA BABA, SCREENING CLINIC

"MS. FITZPATRICK?" Anika called from behind the counter, absently fiddling the order form with fingers clad in blue nitrile gloves.

"Present and ready!" the old woman called out to her, struggling to raise herself from the green vinyl seat.

No one offered to help her to her feet, which Anika hated, no matter how much she understood. People were still afraid to touch each other since the last outbreak scare. She tucked the clipboard under her arm and stepped around the barrier separating the laboratory from the waiting area as Ms. Fitzpatrick shuffled forward.

"How are you doing today, Abigail?" Anika asked, ushering the old woman forward with a warm smile.

"Fine as frog's hair—that's what my granddad would always say." She smiled in return before her face went slack with thought. "Though I don't suppose I've ever seen hair on a frog. Not even in the historical footage…"

Anika let out a small laugh. "I think that's the point, don't you? That if a frog had hair, you certainly wouldn't be able to see it?"

"Well, at least you know what a frog is," Ms. Fitzpatrick said.

"I remember my fourth-year natural history lessons." Anika beamed, extending her arm down the hall. "Med Room 2, please."

Abigail Fitzpatrick nodded and sighed. "You don't hear many people using the old phrases anymore, do you?"

Anika followed the old woman into the room, helping her ease back into the chair. Once she was situated and Anika was certain she wouldn't topple forward, she grabbed the clipboard to review the orders once more.

"Just the regular draw today?"

Abigail's face wrinkled into a proud smile. "That's right. I'm healthier than you could imagine—thanks to you and this premium plan."

Anika gathered the necessary supplies, fingers moving quickly to adhere the correct tags to each vial. "Oh, I'm certain it has nothing to do with me."

She was also certain that Abigail Fitzpatrick's health had nothing to do with the *premium plan*, but she wasn't about to say it. The large number of plan visitors made certain that she was never short on credits.

"Of course it does, dear Ms. Baba," she exclaimed. "Do you think I'd want to come back week after week if you weren't such a delight? It's not like I enjoy getting pricked, you know."

Abigail's eyes flashed wide and furtive. Anika tried to keep her expression placid, but she couldn't help the affection that flowed through her every time Abigail Fitzpatrick came in for draws. There weren't many citizens left like her—still attached to the old ways and willing to have some fun. She was a part of a fading generation that blended old with new, and even Abigail was too young to remember what it was like before. She only had stories.

Anika wrapped the rubber tourniquet above the old woman's elbow, then moved quickly to pierce the vein and complete the draw before her skin could bruise.

"You are the highlight of my week," she said as the first vial filled.

Abigail placed her free hand on the cuff of Anika's lab coat. "That's sweet, Ms. Baba, but… I don't know why you flatter me so… I'm not allowed to leave a tip!"

Anika switched vials and removed the tourniquet. "I don't need a tip."

"Oh? Mr. Baba is doing alright then?" Abigail winked.

"We both are," Anika agreed. Vial full, she pulled the needle, deftly replacing it with an organic swab and some medical tape. "Change the wrapping after one hour and absolutely no outside contacts to that tissue for forty-eight hours."

"Same as always," Abigail nodded, bending her arm as if she needed to work it to get the blood flowing again.

"You know the routine," Anika agreed, sealing the vials into a transport box and placing them through the hole in the wall. Three beeps, and the compartment's airlock engaged. A small whoosh promised that the vials were on their way to the analysis center.

Test done, Anika proceeded to remove her gloves, placing them in the biohazard waste bin as Abigail labored to uproot herself from the seat.

"Indeed, I do. I've only been at it for thirty-eight years now," Abigail said, still bending her arm in the manual-blood-pump motion.

"Our most loyal customer." Anika smiled, running her hand under the sanitizer pump to catch the foamed disinfectant. She rubbed her hands together, absently noting the passage of time.

"That's a nice color," Abigail said, lingering at the exit.

"Excuse me?" Anika asked, looking up.

"Your nails. You've done them up. I like that dark red on you. It complements your tone," Abigail clarified.

"Oh. Thank you. Yes, I got them done for tonight—it's our anniversary," Anika explained, shaking her hands out as the foam evaporated. She glanced down, proud, but self-conscious of her embellishment.

"Anniversary, you say? Well, that's a nice celebration. Which year?" Abigail asked, stepping toward her and reaching to embrace her hand.

The connection of her frail, wrinkled palm with Anika's slightly damp one made Anika all the more aware of the direct contact. "Seven years." She smiled, masking her discomfort.

"Seven! That's a lucky number!" Abigail proclaimed.

The other lab tech on shift burst through the entryway, pounding lightly against the side of the wall to draw attention. "Anika, Zayd's here," she said with a knowing, mischievous smile.

"Zayd?" Anika asked, pulling her hand back in bewilderment. Absently, she added, "He's early."

"Don't worry about that! I'm guessing he's got a surprise for your anniversary!" The tall woman, who also happened to be Anika's best friend, winked, tucking long braids behind her shoulder.

"My shift—" Anika started.

"Don't worry about your shift! I'll finish for you. Go!" She put her arm around Anika's shoulder and ushered her through the door.

"Oh…" Anika blushed.

"I got you, hon! And I put him in Med Room 4—you know, the one with the door latch?" She beamed at Anika.

"Thank you, Sophia…" Anika called back, positively abashed.

But Sophia had already turned to the lab to usher Ms. Fitzpatrick out for her.

Anika shrugged off the self-conscious feeling and focused her attention on the matter at hand—Zayd was waiting for her in Med Room 4. She lifted her chin and made her way over, trying to remember what she had on under her lab coat. He was supposed to call before he headed over so she'd have time to change into the blue dress…

The door was left ajar. She put her hand against the smooth surface and pushed, a wry smile lifting her lips as she said, "When I said I liked surprises, you know, this isn't exactly what I meant."

The door clicked shut behind her as she locked eyes with the slender, well-muscled man leaning back against the wall on the exam table. He lifted his shaggy, dark head, licking his lips. "Ani. Aren't you a sight for sore eyes."

"Who did you expect? Your mistress lab technician?" Anika questioned as she approached. Her hips swayed involuntarily as she moved toward him.

"You aren't supposed to know about that," Zayd protested, slinking off the table as Anika folded her body into him.

"And you were supposed to call so I had time to change," she scolded, hot breath against his waiting lips.

They kissed, two warm bodies surrounded by medical equipment and sterile surfaces.

"Happy anniversary, Ani," Zayd said. His words, along with the gentle pressure of his body against hers, made Anika's head swim, but something about his tone was off.

"What's wrong, Z?" she asked, pulling away from his embrace to study him the way only a wife could.

"Don't worry, it's nothing, but—"

"Don't tell me it's nothing. I know you, and that look does not mean *nothing*," she corrected him.

Zayd let out a heavy sigh, relenting to her scrutiny. "Alright, you're right. It's not nothing—but it's also not that bad. I just… need your help."

He shrugged off his thick canvas jacket. It took extra effort to remove the material from his left arm. His work shirt was torn from the elbow down. The shredded material was knotted around his bicep, just above the beginnings of the thick white bandages, already soaked through with blood.

Anika's eyes widened as she took in the state of Zayd's arm. She felt the pull of tension in her neck and lower jaw as she fought to contain the distress and anxiety at seeing her husband in such a state.

"Oh, Z," she breathed.

"It looks worse than it is, I promise. I just need you to give me a couple of stitches," he implored.

Anika was already situating a fresh pair of gloves over her blood-red manicure. The necessary supplies were already in the room. Zayd started undoing the flimsy tape that held the bandage in place.

"Don't do that," Anika corrected, pulling a needle and tissue adhesive from the second drawer.

"Why not?" Zayd asked, still tugging at the tape and wincing from the way the gauze rubbed against the wound.

"Because it's stemming the blood flow, and I don't have clearance to administer a transfusion if you pass out on my table," she said.

"It's not *that* bad," Zayd whined as the bandage fell away.

Dark blood oozed from the jagged tear that ran from his elbow down to nearly his wrist. It was clear to Anika that the wound was already several hours old. Old blood was dried rusty brown against the dark, matted hair on his arm. This was going to take more than *a couple of stitches.*

"You are unbelievable," she scolded, getting to work with the saline wash and disinfectant.

Zayd gasped as pink liquid ran darker into the waste trough.

"Unbelievably handsome? Unbelievably charming and irresistible?" He managed a smile through the grimace.

"You are not winning any points right now," Anika said.

Finally, the wash ran clear, and Anika sighed with relief. "It's not as bad as I thought. I think I can fix this."

"See, I told you! A couple of stitches, and you can get changed in time for dinner," Zayd boasted.

"Why did you wait? Why didn't you report this?" she asked as she worked, using large sutures to hold the adhesive where the tear was particularly nasty.

"Awe, Ani, you know how the factory gets with reportables. I'd be off work for more than a week of investigation," he moaned.

"And we would be just fine," she pressed.

Zayd grabbed her shoulder with his good hand, stopping her work and forcing her to look up at him.

"I don't want to be *just fine.* I want better for us. We've worked so hard. We *deserve* better."

Anika looked into his warm, imploring eyes. She would relent. She always did. His heart was too good, and she loved him too much for anything else. "I know, love. I just worry about you."

He pulled her into an embrace, kissing the top of her head through her dark, thick braid. "I love you so much."

A sweet smile pressed her lips thin as he released her from the embrace. She picked up her tools.

"Plus, I knew you could fix it," he added, giving her a swift smack on the butt.

Anika tried to force the smile away, but it was useless. "Quit messing around and let me get this finished," she scolded.

AMY PARK COULD HARDLY KEEP her eyes open after the double shift in the patient center. It had been like this since she washed from the Northern Laboratories intern program, and she didn't suspect that it was going to get any easier.

At least Reed's still in it, she thought, cranking the water to hot and willing herself to remain still under the scalding downpour so the heat could burn away the day and the still-festering disappointment. Reminding herself that even though her attempt was cut short, Reed still had a chance of becoming a prestigious scientist and going to the Northern Laboratories helped. They had dreamed of doing it together, making their city and their parents proud, but if either of them got through—well, they still beat the odds.

Institute medic was a better position than energy management for a program washout. If she did well in her residency, she might have a chance to rise up to instructor. That was a worthy mid-term goal, at least, considering her Northern Laboratories dream was gone.

She shuddered under the relentless heat but forced herself to remain until she felt clean. It didn't matter that she'd been in protective wear all day—that she'd gone through the decontamination rooms dozens of times—it always felt like she was covered in the nightmare infection. It invaded her senses as the unending barrage of the medical wing forced its way in via the echo of inhuman screams, wounds seeping grey pus as skin peeled clean of muscle and bone. The stench of death as patient after patient succumbed to the disease, fulfilling the promise of *donation*.

She was meant to be immune to it all. She *was* immune to some of it. She could tend to a sobbing patient as their appendages rotted off their body, cauterizing the wounds after taking dozens of samples and leaving them in the care of an onlooking volunteer, who was left to wonder who else might suffer such treatment under the guise of care. It was easy to think of the patients by their number—to forget they had names. Medical study—academic treatment—was just a daily aspect of her position at the Institute. One she had been conditioned to tolerate since her first day as an intern and was only more recently beginning to question.

Why was this grotesque dehumanization of the patients so necessary to the function of the institution? It made sense for the donation patients—the ones doomed to succumb—but what about the others? The ones who would be sent to cryo and transported to the Northern Laboratories rather than die under their watch for the purpose of scientific progress?

Park's growing unease went beyond the disease the patients were dying of. Why did they have to die without their dignity? Why were there so many donations?

She didn't know.

She needed more time to wrap her mind around patient treatment, and there was never enough time. Since her first day, she'd been inundated with too much information to memorize, but not enough to make any sense of anything. Her mixed-up feelings about the program —about patients and the volunteers and the shocking lack of autonomy—probably had a lot to do with her washing from the intern program, but she'd never be able to prove it.

Park cut the water when it didn't feel hot anymore. Wrapped in her towel, she stepped out of her tiny shower stall and into the steamy cubicle that made up her private bathroom. It should have felt like a luxury after the intern dormitories, but all she could think of was how much she missed the proximity of her peers. Most of all, she missed being able to look across any room and see Reed.

Since becoming an Institute medic, she had to wait until curfew hours to sneak out, hoping no one spotted her on the surveillance cameras. It was a risk she was willing to take. She needed to see him— needed to feel him against her and know he was okay. She'd risk losing her position and worse to know he'd made it another day.

Skipping the top drawer, where her resident uniforms remained folded and tucked neatly, she wiggled the bottom drawer of her dresser open and pulled the scientist intern suit out from where it hid behind the plain white shirt and brown pants meant for sleeping. If she were ever caught with it…

Honestly, she didn't know what would happen. She'd heard stories of people disappearing—of sudden infections and terrible and inexplicable accidents—but she didn't know if any of it was true or if it was all just meant to keep interns from bending the rules.

After dressing, Park grabbed the towel and ran it across her hairline a final time. A layer of beaded sweat had built up again, mostly from the heat of the shower, but also because of the angst that always grew as she readied herself to sneak out. Luckily, she knew the crisp outside air between the medical building and intern housing would cure it.

She looked in the mirror a final time, trying to imagine which parts of her Reed would see and what he would think of them. Her coarse black hair was maybe two inches long now. She was due for a trim. Maybe she'd buzz her hair all the way down like the other new medics so she could go more than a couple weeks without having to manage it.

It wouldn't be so bad. Reed was used to her with short hair by now. She was more worried about the red patches of skin where her medical garb rubbed against her neck. Her cheeks were still flushed from the water, and her hands were chapped and raw from so much washing and the hours spent in layer after layer of gloves.

She grabbed the medicated lotion and squeezed out a dollop of the white goop. It didn't really help the condition of her skin, but it made her hands feel better. She was ready to travel the empty halls and sneak across the campus grounds.

Dark carpet turned to slick tile as she made her way from the resident quarters into the medical facility. Benji was working tonight. He'd open the doors to the patient wing so she wouldn't have to register her identification card at the exit. Park had learned a couple years ago—long before she washed from the intern program—that it paid to make friends with the volunteers on site, no matter what the instructors suggested.

Fifty feet down the hall, a door opened, and the agonized wails of a patient wafted into the medical wing.

"You can't do this to me! I have rights!"

A volunteer garbed from head to toe in a thick, yellow protective suit exited. When he saw Park in the hall, he turned and put his blue-gloved hands into two chest-level openings in the wall. When he pulled them out, the elbow-length gloves were gone.

"Right on time as always," Benji greeted her.

"I don't want to keep you guessing." She smiled warmly at the curly-haired volunteer.

He returned the expression, joining her to walk down the long hall. "I think you're just afraid of what would happen if I fell behind on my duties because I was waiting for you," he said.

"It's hard work to find a reliable accomplice." She shrugged, offering him a wink.

"Yeah. Nobody wants to help the resident that sent a volunteer to cryo duty," he agreed.

Benji flashed his identification card, and the exit doors swung out before them. "It's split shift tonight, so Vang will be here when you get back."

"Oh," she said, sticking her foot out to stop the doors from shutting automatically.

"Is that a problem?" Benji asked, raising an eyebrow.

"No," she said, chewing her lower lip. "It's just that Vang was on my first shift. That means he didn't get a full recovery."

Benji shook his head. It was a resigned sort of motion. The kind people made when they recognized an injustice but were powerless to do anything. Eventually, all the volunteers adopted those sorts of mannerisms.

"We're shorthanded again after last month's cycle. And it doesn't look like things are getting better anytime soon, either. Word is, most of the volunteers in training are headed to the Northern Laboratories."

"I'm sorry, Benji…"

"Hey. Don't you go apologizing. It's not your fault, and it's not like you can do anything about it, either. It's your ass on the line as much as ours." Benji ran a calloused hand over his tight curls.

"That's not completely true," Park protested.

"Don't go thinking you're above authority around here. Even scientists disappear when they get too loud. You better get, or you'll run out of time," he said, nearly pushing her out the door.

"Thanks, Benji," she said, stepping the rest of the way out.

"Every time," Benji said, winking again as the doors swung back into their secured position.

Park turned away and ducked into the shadow of the medical building to creep toward the pinwheel of sidewalks that would lead her to the intern quarters. Though she'd been making this trip for a couple of months now, it never stopped the anxiety from filling her and tempting her to rush back to the safety of her dormitory. Benji was right—this sort of action could have real consequences for her. Worse still, it could hurt Reed, too. Park hated the idea of being the thing standing between Reed and the Northern Laboratories. The only thing she hated more was giving up the opportunity to be with him while he was still here.

Outside the austere concrete walls of the intern quarters, a cypress tree cast bulky shadows on the concrete pathway. Hidden within the misshaped umbra of branches, a lone figure waited. She rushed toward the darkness and was soon enveloped in Reed's urgent embrace.

"I was getting worried," he whispered, his lips close enough to her face that she could feel their movement.

"I'm sorry, I stopped to talk to Benji on my way," Park apologized.

"A volunteer?" he asked, pulling away to study her.

"They're all volunteers, Reed!"

"And you shouldn't trust them. They'll sell you out in a heartbeat to improve their positions. They're—"

"Whatever you're going to say, just don't. I don't want to hear it!" Park snapped.

"Why?" Reed asked, defensiveness creeping across his formerly relaxed, warm expression.

"Because it's not really you!"

Reed let out a heavy sigh, then tried to pull Park back into him. She resisted the open warmth of his form.

Holding her ground, she tried to read his face in the low light. Was it really possible he could change so much in just the few short months since she was dropped from the intern program? What was she missing?

"I'm sorry," Reed said. This time, Park let him pull her into him, relishing the scent of his freshly washed body. She tilted her head up as he brought his down, meeting him for the kiss she craved—the comfort only he could provide.

"Come on, let's get out of here," Reed urged, pulling her toward the side of the building.

She followed him to the door hidden behind thick shrubs. He moved the branches aside so they could both pass, then stepped up to the keypad, entering the unlock sequence manually. After seven keystrokes and a brief pause, the keypad beeped, and the lock clicked open.

"You haven't forgotten, have you?" Park asked as he gently tugged her arm toward the dark space inside.

"Forgotten what?" he asked, letting the door shut out the sliver of night light from the outside.

They dropped down into the nest of blankets and pillows they'd pilfered away over time, relishing the solitude. Her hands found him in the darkness, making her heart quicken.

"How we found this place?" she asked, melting into him.

"Right, right," he agreed, not really listening.

"Then say it," she pressed, fighting to keep her focus from the heady warmth of his proximity.

"Hmm?" he asked, nearly completely lost as he buried his face in the side of her neck while his hands moved upward under her shirt.

"Who gave us the code to this room?"

He sighed, pulling away from her so he could think. "I don't remember her name."

"But what was she?" Park pressed.

"A volunteer?" Reed asked.

"Exactly!" Park exclaimed triumphantly. "Try not to forget that."

"Why is it so important to you?" Reed moaned, reaching into the darkness for her.

"Because I don't want you to forget yourself. No matter how badly I want you to make it to the Northern Laboratories, I don't want you to forget who you are—who you were before... before they changed you."

Reed was quiet. His hands rested on the warm skin of Park's midsection. Though she couldn't see him, she could feel that he was struggling with something.

"Reed?"

"Yeah," he agreed, his voice wavering. "I won't forget. I'm sorry. It's been a tough week. I'm not myself right now."

He pulled her onto him, and she melted as things turned right in the world.

"Good. Because that's the Chase I fell in love with."

"I love you, too," he breathed, not acknowledging his first name.

She thought maybe she should let it go, but she just couldn't. It was too important. Before she was lost completely to the heat of the moment and the movement of his hands, she whispered, "He's the one I'm rooting for."

Five

MOE SIMONS, ENERGY MANAGEMENT REFUGE

THE ENERGY MANAGEMENT stations for the fusion power facilities were all perfect copies of one another, likely produced in the same prefabrication factory and installed around the same time. The climate changed between the locations, and the surrounding landscapes varied, but the little cabins attached to the fusion generators, along with their furnishings and the supplies delivered, never changed from one place to the other.

Originally, the homes were made for families, and fusion operation was marketed as a means to total independence, but that was before the first outbreak—and long before the DDC took over education and recruitment in the wake of the second outbreak. These days, energy management was a solo job. The scientists assigned to energy management came exclusively from the Institute, and while the job was assigned as an honor, it was more of a life sentence. After graduation, energy management personnel received their assignments and were transported to their stations, where they lived their lives in total isolation, save for occasional deliveries, equipment upgrades, and the very rare DDC visit for operations check.

It was the loneliest job in the world, which made it the perfect position for a dissenter and an ideal safe haven for dissenters moving around outside the cities to seek shelter in or disappear in for a while.

In Simons' sector of work, there were two dissenter-run energy management facilities—one on the outskirts of the southmost City State and one outside the Institute. He frequented both when he needed to hide or required supplies, but he preferred the Institute's facility. There was nothing wrong with Thomas Granger—he was a genial and hospitable old scientist with a knack for clandestine communication. Simons just happened to prefer the company of Ternice Williams, who took over the energy management facility outside the Institute about two years ago.

Strongly prefer.

Luckily for him, the preference was mutual, and though he was only able to visit every couple of months, he and Ternice had grown very close. It was their closeness, and the fact that they were entering one of their longest times apart, that compelled Simons to excuse himself to an early bed. While he was happy to dine with Granger after dropping his illicit cargo at the meeting point just north of the Deadlands, he couldn't wait any longer to make use of the secured communication line.

Well-fed and freshly showered, Simons let out a heavy sigh as he lowered himself onto the firm mattress with the spartan brown cover. He propped his tablet against the bedside table lamp and entered the code for the encrypted communication line, hoping against hope it was early enough still that Terni hadn't gone out to do her final system checks before turning in for the evening.

When he'd left her last, she hadn't been feeling well and had gotten into the habit of going to bed earlier than usual. Medical care was hard to come by at energy management facilities. They were well stocked with the basics of care, but it seemed like nothing she tried worked to ease her constant fatigue. He knew if things got much worse, she would be forced to request care, which was easier for her than for some of the management facilities farther out from civilization, but he also knew she would try just about anything before requesting additional DDC presence at her facility. Getting dissenters established in energy management was no easy feat, and neither of them wanted to compromise a burgeoning system so early on. They needed the facilities to run so smoothly that authorities forgot they required supervision.

It all sounded great, and Simons wouldn't be as clean, comfortable and connected as he was if it weren't for the dissenters' efforts, but the notion of Terni suffering on her own while he had no means to check in on her had been driving him crazy enough that he'd considered driving another full day just to see her in the flesh. If there hadn't been an Institute delivery scheduled to be on the road at the same time, he might have considered it, but in the end, he wouldn't dare risk unveiling dissenter activity.

The signal light in the top corner of his tablet turned green as the encryption finished and the connection was established. There was a brief second where his screen flashed from black to green to a blurry rainbow before Terni's face filled the space, her broad smile masking the dark shadows below her tired eyes.

"I can't tell you how happy I am that you aren't Granger popping in on my evening business," she said by way of greeting. The picture jolted as she settled her tablet on the table. She was in the kitchen, her back facing the stove, which was meticulously clean save for one pot she'd likely used for dinner.

"Has he been bothering you?" Simons asked, a critical eyebrow lifting as he brought his hands together over his lap.

"Don't you get jealous on me, Moe Simons. We don't work that way. Granger has just been checking in on me," she scolded. Her voice was light, though he knew she was telling the truth. They didn't work if they couldn't handle the long stretches of time apart, and she needed someone who could do more than check in sporadically between assignments. Granger had the advantage of always being around.

"I know it. I'm thankful you've got him. Have things gotten any better?" he asked.

A cool light shifted the bright amber of Terni's eyes as she nodded. "Most of what was bothering me has passed. I didn't have to request a medic."

Simons brought his chin down onto his fingers, relaxing into his lap. "That's good to hear. I've been worried."

Terni's lips quirked in a half smile. Simons loved the way the expression hinted at the depths of her brilliant mind. He loved everything about her except for the distance their roles put between them. "You've got more important things to do than worry about me," she said, reaching for a steaming mug Simons was certain contained freshly brewed coffee despite the late hour. "Like keeping your head up and not getting yourself or anyone else killed out there."

"I'm careful. There's a reason they have me doing what I'm doing," he promised.

He waited as she took a long sip, imagining he could smell the rich roast and caramel-sweet of her favorite sweetener, missing her more now than any number of lonely nights on the road.

"Have you heard about the recruitment program set up in the city? They're bringing healthy people without sick kin in for volunteer positions to fill the gaps at the Institute. Supposedly we've got people on the inside handling that," Terni said. She cupped the mug in front of her on the table, running long fingers along the smooth ceramic of the handle.

"That's good. There's a lot of work to be done, and we're only growing stronger if we're growing." Simons shifted, struggling to find a comfortable position for his large frame on the low bed as he stooped to keep his face in the frame.

Terni glanced down, running a hand along the edge of her close-cropped coils in a thoughtful gesture. "I don't know if it's good. Everything is moving so fast right now," she said.

Simons licked his bottom lip, considering her assessment. "I'm sure it's not faster than they're ready for. We're just two pieces of a much bigger picture. Dissenters have been working on this resistance for a long time, making careful moves."

She nodded, but he could tell her heart wasn't in it. He noticed again how tired she looked.

"I'm just worried we're getting too bold, you know? Moving so many people around, bringing in volunteers from the city to do who-knows-what. It doesn't matter how long this has been growing. When you bring in so many people, there's bound to be breaches in the system. What if we get folks in with Resistee attitude? That's all I'm saying." She ran her hand back up and over her curls before returning it to the mug, which had to be empty on account of her not picking it up for another nervous drink.

"We've got to trust that everyone's doing their job. I've been doing this for four years now, and things have only gotten more organized," Simons said.

"It's true," Terni agreed, and Simons could see the hints of her inner workings as she calculated the best way to communicate what she was thinking. "But there are growing pains in this sort of organization, and I haven't seen much of those pains lately, which makes me worry."

"Pains like the lapses in our communication network?" Simons asked, not really wanting to argue but frustrated with the distance that crept in whenever they spent so much time apart. "Or maybe pains like putting our most vital people in total isolation and making it near impossible for them to get help?"

He could see the heat as it deepened the rich brown of her cheeks, just below one of his favorite places to kiss her…

"I made a choice," Terni said, more harshly than he'd heard her speak to him before. "I could have asked for a medic, but I didn't. I've got supplies and a database, and I've had Granger to bounce ideas off of."

"But what if something had been seriously wrong? You still don't look all the way back to your regular self," Simons pointed out, crossing one leg over the other. He realized too late he'd put a dirty sock into the frame and brought both feet back to the ground. He reclasped his hands, resting his chin on his thumbs.

"I took a calculated risk. I'm alright. The problem has shifted, and I know what I'm doing here," Terni insisted.

Simons noted that she'd said shifted as opposed to resolved. He nodded along to her explanation, making sure not to minimize her perspective. She was smart, and Simons knew she was perfectly capable of handling a lot more than most people.

"It's not that I don't believe you. I know what you're willing to sacrifice to make things work for the dissenters."

She scoffed, and he raced to fill the space before she got too mad at him.

"We're all making sacrifices. I just want to make sure those sacrifices keep making sense."

"Moe…" She stopped herself. There was a hint of something hungry and desperate at the edge of her voice—an absence of restraint he rarely sensed in her.

"What is it?" he asked, seeing her fleeting vulnerability before she trapped it behind the steel doors of her will.

"Nothing," she said, her hand dropping to her side below the table. "We can talk about procedure stuff later."

"I can talk to you about procedure stuff whenever you like." Simons winked.

Terni exhaled a stiff laugh before letting her face fall back into a stern mask. "Look, all I want is for you to be careful. Take it extra safe. Think twice about who you trust with what information. Keep an eye out over your shoulder. This thing is getting really big, and someone, somewhere is bound to screw up. The DDC is run by a bunch of arrogant idiots taking over everything with pure hubris, but they can't be so blind all the time."

"You'd be surprised," Simons mused, knowing she didn't have a fraction of the interactions he did with DDC personnel.

"I know." Her smile was genuine this time. "I need you to keep yourself safe is all. I need you to get back to me in one piece."

"I need that, too," he agreed.

Terni nodded, fingering the edge of her ceramic mug. She glanced at the time in the corner of her tablet. "I need to go do my end-of-night checks."

Simons suppressed a yawn, not wanting her to see how worn he'd become. "Call you tomorrow if I'm not back on assignment?"

Terni shifted forward. More of her face filled the screen. "You think they're going to have you out my way anytime soon?"

"If they don't, I'll find a reason on my own," Simons promised.

"Just don't do anything stupid out there," Terni said. "I need you."

The words struck Simons straight in the heart, making him feel warm all over. He knew she meant for his role with the dissenters, but he also knew it was more than that. They'd become much more to one another than a like-minded coupling of convenience over the last year. It was obvious to both of them, and while it was exhilarating to feel so strongly, it was also terrifying.

"I promise I'll be so careful," he said before the communication ended.

Simons knew that if he had a choice, he'd be out there on his very next assignment.

CHAPTER
Six

MORA

MORA MULLED over the words filling the screen of her old-world tablet. It wasn't typical English. In fact, it didn't even seem like English at all, though she knew it was.

It's just different, she reminded herself. Art had to be considered—interpreted. That's what she liked so much about it. There was subtext. Nuance. It excited her.

This passage had taken her a few reads to make sense of. The first one was always just to get it in. She couldn't ever figure out what was going on the first time through—not unless it was really straightforward, anyway, and this one definitely wasn't. She was now on day three of reading it. Not that she minded—it was one of her favorite things about reading the old works. They revealed themselves to her one layer at a time. By the time she was ready to move on to the next one, it seemed like the whole story was different from the one she'd started reading. She got to uncover hidden meanings and subtle messages.

It made her wonder if the real world was that way too—subterranean. She had to figure that all the nuance in the old works came from subtlety in the world in which they were written. Mora wondered with excitement whether some of this subtlety could still exist today…

Maybe it just wasn't obvious because no one was making art anymore? There was no one to put interpretations and opinions out there for anyone to ponder.

Probably that was by design.

It didn't escape her that so many of the remaining scrawls of the Resistee movement read a lot like poetry. Even the text, furious paint against crumbling brick, spoke more truth than the most detailed educational content. Those messages were being erased, and with them went the lingering history of the people who dared to disagree with the *safety policies* enacted by the DDC in order to prevent unnecessary gathering and spread of a disease that was already well-contained.

As she considered the text, a message appeared across the top of her old-world tablet.

> where are you Mora???

Three question marks. She knew without a doubt that it was Jim. She double-tapped the message to confirm. The sender signature read *James Dunn.*

It took a few extra steps to reply on the relic. Jim would probably wait. In fact, he had likely already guessed exactly where she was and what she was doing. If she left him waiting long enough, he'd probably put his guess out before she could open the keyboard and press each individual key to generate her response.

Sure enough, just as she sent her message, another one came through.

> I'm on the roof.

> Are you on the roof again???

She smiled. Predicable Jim.

Another second passed as he processed her response.

> Is Omen keeping you company???

> No. Haven't seen him in a bit.

Mora chewed her lip as she sent the message. It had been more than a week now since she'd seen the bird, which was fairly unusual. Then again, Omen's visits had been spreading out over the last year. According to the nature book on her tablet, that might not be completely atypical. A raven, after all, might find a mate and set a territory in its third or fourth year of life. And wasn't Omen just a little over three now?

Three years ago, she'd found him—just a scruffy little hatchling lost from his nest. Granted, he was only about four feet away—what was the saying?—*as the crow flies*. She liked it in this context. He'd fallen out and wandered along the roof awhile, trying to find his bearings.

Mora had waited. She watched him as he cheeped and struggled but was too afraid to touch him and ruin his chances of reuniting with his parent—something the text suggested could possibly happen if she interfered. But after three hours, she didn't have the heart to wait any longer. The little chick was exhausted and probably terrified out of its mind. She scooped him up and placed him as gently as possible back into the nest.

Omen had shown absolutely no fear at her touch. In fact, he almost seemed affectionate. After further research, she'd discovered that he was a raven and that ravens were incredibly intelligent, discerning and able to form relationships with people. All of this was fascinating to her, as was the very concept that he was actually a raven!

Ravens were supposed to be extinct, along with many other, larger predatory birds. Yet here he was. Cross-referencing the text on her old-world tablet with her school tablet, she was able to confirm that there was no different bird he could possibly be. Her first instinct was to immediately tell someone. Luckily, she'd thought better of it. Jim was the only other person that knew about Omen, and she'd trust him with anything.

James Dunn was a nerdy and completely brilliant boy in her year at school. They were barely compatible, yet somehow, they had managed to stick together. He was diligent, hardworking and, thanks to recent Test results, on the Institute track. Mora was clever, sure, but there was something about her that kept her from being a model student. Maybe it was because she'd rather spend hours poring over old-world literature than piecing together code or solving differential equations... or maybe she just didn't want to be Institute track. (Not that she'd dare say that to anyone but Jim. Admitting you weren't interested in the Institute was practically treason.)

Omen's parent bird never returned. Mora snuck back up later that night with a small handful of cereal for the little bird, who the text said would eat just about anything. She returned every night with more food—grains, fruits, a bottle of fresh water and a baby-bird-sized dish. After a week, she started carrying a small glass jar in her pocket just in case she ran across a bug of some sort while she was out. She could tell that Omen preferred them to the cereals.

Despite the odds, Omen grew. He shed his scruffy down for silky black feathers. Though it was late by the text, he learned to fly. In those early days, when she was nursing the little creature, she was likewise poring through the works of Edgar Allen Poe. That's what made her decide Omen was a good name. It sounded dark and moody, but not quite like she was stealing it from another time.

Is he okay? Did something happen?

Jim's message drew her attention.

I don't know for sure. How can I know? I don't know where he goes.

The first time Omen flew off the roof, Mora had stressed for hours. He came back, of course. She was his parent bird now. He brought her a dead mouse. Though it disgusted her, she watched him tear it open with black talons that stained red with the creature's blood, relishing the fresh meat revealed at the crack of tiny bones. It was the sort of mouse she'd seen caught in traps in the apartments. Everyone knew they were a problem in the city. Supposedly, they'd been around since before the force fields went up.

Supposedly, nothing could get past the force fields. No mice, no birds, no people—Nothing.

Mora knew better now. A raven hadn't just existed inside the city without anybody knowing before the force fields went up. That was sixty-something years ago. And if it were true, that would have been the last raven—or there would be a lot more of them around now. Either way, they wouldn't be listed as an extinct species if that were the case.

Omen's mother must have flown in over the force fields. Maybe she came for the mice—or maybe something on the outside had driven her inside, to the safety of this rooftop.

But Mora didn't know how safe the rooftop really was, since she never came back to her egg.

> I told you that you weren't ready to be a parent! This is aging you prematurely.

Mora smiled at Jim's message. He had a sense of humor when he wanted to—not that he'd dare show it to anyone but her. It was their secret, just like Omen. But Jim definitely stressed about it more than her. According to Jim, she had no business on top of the roof. No business hiding an extinct bird, and absolutely no business with an old-world tablet full of forbidden data.

Just like Omen, Mora had considered not telling Jim about the tablet, but in both cases, she'd needed him. Jim had rigged up the charging port for her treasure. Mora knew she might have been able to figure it out on her own, but she didn't have the patience for it. She didn't want to dive into the contents in a week; she wanted to do it right now. And Jim was the logical answer.

> Maybe he's moving on. Maybe he found a mate. Maybe he has a territory outside the city now. He's going to grow up at some point!

Mora flexed her fingers. Though she regularly messaged Jim on the old tablet, it was clunky and awkward. She wouldn't dare send a message to anyone else using the old thing, for fear they might question how long it took.

> Maybe he can't get back through the force field.

Jim's working theory. That there was a glitch somewhere in the force field that the first raven managed to fly through. Then one day, she flew into the woods and couldn't get back to her nest. He was suggesting Omen may have suffered the same fate.

Mora didn't think so, though. His trips had been longer lately. Plus, she knew he'd been going out of the city for over a year now. He had started bringing back a different type of rodent—a *vole*. Another extinct species. He'd brought a lot from the outside. Lizards, mice, a squirrel once—although it was pretty badly mangled. Mora figured it was probably the spoils of some other creature's kill.

Over time, Omen had brought so many different critters to the rooftop that weren't supposed to exist that Mora was giving more and more thought to the idea that the force field was less about keeping people safe from the outside and more about keeping people in the cities contained. Keeping things hidden. It was a huge part of the basis for her supposition about why art and literature didn't exist anymore. What did the DDC label it? Subversive literature?

A threat to safety.

She'd told Jim about her theories before. He'd practically shuddered when she voiced her thoughts, but he still listened. He was a good friend like that. He never judged her for thinking something different from him.

A dark spot skittered across the sky just above the horizon. The shape grew in the orange light of sunset until she could make out the arc of Omen's wings. Mora let out a breath she hadn't known she'd been holding, sending a message to Jim.

> He's here. Guess they need to keep working on the force field.

She set the tablet on the brown canvas stretched across the old metal frame of the chair and moved to the ledge. Holding out her arm in greeting, Mora waited for Omen to catch the draft and glide down. He moved with such uncanny grace. Against the quiet backdrop of a city that had mostly gone indoors, she could hear the subtle rustle of his wings as he lit on her elbow.

Omen had surprising weight for a bird. Mora forgot each time between visits.

The onyx bird greeted her with a familiar clucking sound and an almost-whispered word: "*Mora.*" Ruffling his pointed tail feathers, Omen shuffled upward until he was perched on her shoulder.

"I missed you, friend," Mora said, stroking the tuft of feathers on Omen's breast.

"Hey," Omen cawed, then gently pecked at her knuckle.

"What's that? Nothing new for me? Was hunting bad out there in the great big world?" she teased.

They moved together toward the old nest. Mora pushed the tablet aside and squatted down on the chair, facing the concrete slab that made the nest's surface. Omen hopped off her shoulder and onto the rise, cocking his head back and forth as if to consider her jest.

"Or have you just missed the taste of milled grain?" She reached into her pocket to pull out the wrapped cereal she always brought.

Omen clucked again, an uncanny knocking sound a bird shouldn't be able to make, lifting first one leg, then the other. Mora watched him, unraveling the cereal. As he shimmied back and forth, she suddenly noticed the difference—something was wrapped around his left leg.

Mora forgot about the cereal, reaching down to study the bird. Omen cawed in protest, leaning forward to peck at her outstretched hand.

"Ow! Okay, fine. I'll trade you—cereal for your leg," Mora said, snatching her hand back and shaking away the sting.

Omen lifted and tilted his head, clucking in tentative agreement. Mora finished unwrapping the grain and dumped it onto the concrete slab. As Omen dipped his head and pecked contentedly at the little pellets, she brought her chin down to rest against the surface, studying the strange addition to her bird.

A thick piece of paper, dirtied by time and the elements, was folded around the scaly skin just below the feather line. It was held fast by a thin piece of twine. Someone had obviously placed it there on purpose.

Taking great care to not disrupt Omen's feast, Mora began to unwind the twine that held the paper. After three turns, the whole package came loose. Omen lifted his leg against the freedom, as though he'd just realized something had been encumbering him. Mora reached up and stroked the bird's head and neck.

"I've got it. Thanks for being patient."

Another cluck. "Jerk," he said, sounding quite content.

Mora's hands trembled as she grasped the paper, making it hard to catch the edge and unfold it. She played with the bent twine absently as her eyes fell upon the black markings hidden within the folds. The ink bled in places where the paper was discolored, but the handwritten message was clear enough to read.

Hello from the outside.

Mora stared at the note in disbelief. Someone—*from the outside*—had attached this note to Omen with the specific intent of reaching her. She blinked, as if she could clear her eyes and see what it actually was. As if it were an illusion, or a spell. But this wasn't a fantasy novel, and the note remained. The message scribbled onto it never changed.

This is unbelievable!

With the grains finished, Omen clucked, then chirped for Mora's attention. She petted him, reaching for her tablet. She needed someone else to see the message and tell her she wasn't imagining things.

It took an agonizingly long time to type the message.

> Are your parents home yet?

Jim replied instantly.

> Yes. It's getting late.

After another painful passage of seconds, she sent her message in reply.

I'm coming over anyway.

CHAPTER

Seven

ANIKA AND ZAYD

"I'VE NEVER HAD a nail polish stain like this before!" Anika moaned toward the other room.

"It'll come off. Just give it time," Zayd called back from the kitchen.

She let out a frustrated sigh, glaring at the discoloration that stained her nails.

"You're going to be late!" Zayd called again.

He appeared in the entryway, carrying a small brown package and a stainless steel mug. He offered them to her with a big grin.

"If I'm late, it won't be because of my nails," Anika said, rolling her eyes and accepting his offering.

"You're welcome for that too," Zayd said with a wink.

She gave him a peck on the cheek, then shook her head, amused. "I'll call at break to let you know my shifts this week."

"We can talk about it tonight," he protested.

Anika stopped at the door, holding it open with one foot while turning to face her husband with pleading eyes. "You know how fast appointment space fills up. I don't want to chance it."

Zayd stopped in the threshold, bending forward to place his forehead against hers. "Ani, it's the first of the month. They won't fill up that fast."

She glanced down, suppressing the tremble in her lower lip. He caught her chin with his hand and tilted it back up so her eyes met his. He ran his fingers up the smooth curve of her jaw and cupped her cheek. "But I know how important this is. So I promise I'll pick up, and we'll get it set."

"I love you," Anika whispered, both relieved and grateful. She kissed him, letting the brown sack slide until it nearly tumbled to the ground.

Zayd caught it just before it went over the edge of her folder. "Careful, I worked hard on those leftovers."

"My domestic hero." Anika grinned. She secured her grip on the package and turned to push the front door open again.

"Now go! I'm not getting blamed if you get docked credits for being late!" Zayd gave her a quick smack on the rear before rushing her out the door.

He waited until she'd rounded the corner toward the elevator before stepping back into the entryway and letting the door click shut. In the silence of his solitude, he let the grin slip from his face, his hand traveling up his arm to the fresh bandage that covered Anika's stitches on the gnarly wound. Even now, it throbbed under the multiple layers of protection. Part of him wanted so badly to give her the rest of the details of the incident, but he was worried she would never forgive him—even after everything they'd been through. The conflict of guilt and gratitude gnawed at him with the same throbbing persistence as the pain.

"We'll get through this, too, Ani," he sighed before heading toward the bedroom to get ready for his own shift.

<hr>

The commute was kind. Anika was able to catch the first transport to the city center, which saved her precious minutes and allowed her to drop her things off in her locker before clocking in exactly fifty-three seconds before her shift started.

Gloves on and lab coat buttoned, Anika took her seat at the large data screen in front of the patient waiting area. There were only three patients waiting—a slow start to the month compared to usual traffic. A quick glance at the log informed her that Cora Kennedy and Sophia Fields were also on shift. While Sophia was her best friend, Anika didn't care for Cora. She was rude, nosy and condescending toward the other technicians and customers. Rumor was that Cora landed the job thanks to some connections with a city DDC official—an uncle or something like that. And the rumors didn't stop there, either. Anika had heard before that Cora was transferred to the cities from the Institute program. If that were true, then her connection was no ordinary DDC worker. It would take someone in a pretty powerful position with a lot of pull and influence to land her such a cozy job after failing out of the Institute.

"Anika?" Cora popped her head around the corner, her blond, meticulously curled hair pulled back in a stylish ponytail.

"Yes?" Anika asked, glancing over between data entries.

"Could you switch gears and take over patients for me for a bit? I've got some things to take care of in accounting, and I don't want to get backed up." Though her tone was kind, it was clear Cora intended obedience. Asking wasn't in her repertoire.

Anika glanced at the waiting room again. Three people. With Sophia on shift, it definitely wouldn't require both techs working draws to stay on top of client flow.

Anika suppressed a sigh and pushed away from the data port. "Of course, Cora. Anything to help out."

"Thanks, Ani. You're the best!" Cora offered a false, cheery smile before clicking her tongue and disappearing back toward the archive room.

Only Zayd called her Ani. No one else—not even her own parents —called her Ani. Except Cora. Anika hated the way she used the name against her. There wasn't exactly proof that she was doing it, but that's what it felt like. Anika grabbed the electronic client folder and skimmed the check-in log. Sophia was in Med Room 2 with Hercules Abbot, 52, doing routine samples and an infusion. Unless half a dozen new clients walked through the door at once, they'd both be doing data entry within an hour to pass the time.

"Ms. Katrina Jones?" Anika called into the waiting room with a clear, authoritative voice.

A tidy woman in her mid-thirties stood from the pale green chair. Anika offered her a warm smile.

"Please follow me to Med Room 1. I'll be taking care of you today," she said, ushering the woman forward with a directive arm.

Ms. Jones glanced down at her watch, shaking her head. "You medics are on it today, aren't you?" she marveled.

"We don't like to keep our clients waiting long if we can help it," Anika agreed, following the woman down the hall toward Med Room 1.

The day remained slow. Another ten clients came through for various tests. There were a higher number of infusions than normal, given it was the first of the month, but even that couldn't keep Anika and Sophia busy through the end of shift. Two hours after the midday break, they were both perched at the data ports, knocking out data entry for the clinic's monthly metrics report. The waiting room was empty for the moment.

"Slow day for the first of the month, eh?" Sophia mused as she ran her finger across another line on the spreadsheet.

"Yeah, pretty slow," Anika agreed absentmindedly, running her teeth across her bottom lip as she reviewed her entry before submitting it.

"I mean, last month was a madhouse, don't you remember? We all got ten percent overtime credits to finish before the fifteenth," Sophia said, pausing her work to look over at Anika.

"What?" Anika asked, looking over as if she were only now listening.

"Last month we were slammed," Sophia repeated. "We had to work overtime to get everyone processed, and Cora made us stay late to get the metrics done. Don't you remember?"

Anika did remember, but it was just now coming back to her, as if it were a much older memory. She reflected on it, lost for a moment in a way that wasn't normally in her character. "That is strange, isn't it? Most of our clients have packages that cycle at least monthly."

"It's probably just the calm before the storm or something." Sophia shrugged.

"Maybe..." Anika said, pulling up the client cycle list. She ran her finger down the left side of the screen, tracing each name without reading it. She then pulled up the cycle dates for each customer and split her screen so she could compare the first of last month to the day's activity.

"Soph, did you finish logging your client entries for the day?" she asked.

"Yeah, a while ago. Why?"

"Abigail Fitzpatrick didn't come in for a draw today."

Sophia pursed her lips together and made a *hmm* sound. She rolled her chair over to look at Anika's screen.

"Maybe she was busy today."

"No." Anika shook her head. "That woman is like clockwork. Every time—the first and the fifteenth. I think it might be her only outing."

Anika highlighted Ms. Fitzpatrick's name to pull up her records, which confirmed her statement. The data went back years in a repeating pattern of ones and fifteens.

"Talk about dependable..." Sophia mused as Anika scrolled the screen back to the last entry. As the data refreshed, Sophia gasped.

"Anika!" She reached over her shoulder to press her finger against the appointment comments. Another window popped open over the list, detailing the routine draws. Below all the within-range notations, next to the final test—the only one that mattered—was a one-word entry.

Positive.

"No," Anika whispered.

"I don't believe it," Sophia agreed.

Anika pushed away from the monitor as though looking at it were causing her physical pain. "It can't be possible. Ms. Fitzpatrick doesn't have contact with any high-risk individuals. She's the least likely person to get infected!"

"Don't I know it," Sophia said, then, her eyes growing into wide, golden-rimmed saucers, she asked, "You don't think there's an outbreak, do you?"

"An outbreak?" Anika asked, trying to not let the bolt of shock the suggestion sent shooting down her arms affect her. "You see one positive result, and your automatic conclusion is an outbreak?"

Anika let out a burst of laughter. The sound, along with the feeling of her shoulders shaking as she expelled the air, offered a small sense of relief.

Sophia's expression remained stern. "Think about it, Anika…"

"I am, Soph!"

Anika offered up an incredulous smile, but it faded as she studied her friend's face. Sophia crinkled her brow, deep in contemplation.

"It makes more sense than Abigail Fitzpatrick contracting an infection any other way, doesn't it? I mean… a woman like that—the only way she's getting the virus is community spread."

A chill spread through Anika's chest. Sophia was right. A little old woman who lived alone in the center of the city was very low risk. Abigail Fitzpatrick was a woman of extreme caution. She followed all the community rules and lived her life as though danger were hiding around every corner. There was basically zero chance that she might have contracted the virus through some form of negligence.

Cora appeared suddenly from the back room, her long absence barely noticed by the two other women.

"What on earth are you two still doing here?" she exclaimed with cheerful authority.

"Hello, Cora. Long time no see!" Sophia greeted her with false enthusiasm.

"We were just getting ahead on data entry at end of shift," Anika explained. She was never one to stir up trouble with authority, even if it was barely earned.

"Data entry? On the first?" Cora let a bright laugh ring through the empty space.

"We got so behind last month," Anika explained.

"Oh, we're just fine. You girls should get out of here!" Cora pressed, stepping forward and shooing them away from the monitors.

Anika stood and pushed her chair back toward the counter, but

Sophia remained, pressing her hand against the entry pad to keep the screen active.

"Were there any major changes to the plan cycles that we missed?" Sophia asked.

"Not that I know of, why?" Cora asked.

"We had a thirty percent reduction in clients today," Sophia explained, citing the list that Anika had pulled up only moments before discovering Abigail Fitzpatrick's fate.

"Well, it's only the first. We can't accurately compare metrics for a month with one day. Why would you even try?"

Though her voice was strong and certain, there was a nervousness to her demeanor. She raised her right hand to rub her earlobe in a telling gesture that neither of the ladies missed.

"That's true, but there's a big difference between the statistics for the first of this month and the last three. That's notable even if the data levels out this week," Sophia replied.

Anika glanced at her friend nervously. Though she didn't disagree with her, she was uncomfortable playing a role in any level of dissent.

"I'll take a look at it first thing. We can always submit a report," Cora said dismissively. Her tone was now as icy as her meticulously coiffed hair.

"Did you know Abigail Fitzpatrick tested positive?" Sophia asked. She wasn't even trying to hide the accusation in her voice.

"Who is Abigail Fitzpatrick?" Cora scoffed.

"She's an older woman—one of our oldest clients. She's come in on the first and fifteenth of every month for the last thirty-eight years. We found her positive when we were looking into the client anomaly." Anika rushed to explain before Sophia could inject more attitude into the situation.

"Oh, I think I know who you're talking about—the real handsy one!" Cora scoffed again, shaking her head with disapproval. "I suppose that's not a surprise… the way she touches everyone…"

Anika forced her face slack. Cora didn't need to know how wrong she was about Ms. Fitzpatrick.

But Sophia wasn't so forgiving. She never liked to let something like that go if she could help it.

"Abigail Fitzpatrick is a paranoid old woman who lives alone and afraid. She couldn't have gotten it incidentally. It would have to have been community spread."

Cora pulled her lips into a stern line. Anika couldn't be certain, but she thought that perhaps the woman looked paler than usual, as if some of the certainty had drained out of her.

"That's ridiculous. If there were an outbreak of any sort, we'd be the first to know! Abigail Fitzpatrick was a foolish old woman who probably did something without thought and paid the price."

The words pierced Anika's heart. She knew they were as untrue as they were cruel.

"Enough of this paranoia. Clock out and enjoy your evening. Things will only get busier this month."

This time, neither woman objected. Cora watched them retreat to the break room before turning brusquely back toward the archive room.

CHAPTER
Eight
ANIKA

"THAT WOMAN IS COMPLETELY INSUFFERABLE!" Sophia moaned.

Anika shook her head, glancing back at Sophia before opening her locker.

"I mean, what's the point of even saying that about poor Ms. Fitz-patrick?" Sophia asked, banging her own locker door so that it popped open with a dutiful clink.

"I don't think she must have liked her very much," Anika mused.

"Handsy? Where does she even get that?"

Anika was methodically pulling off her lab coat and overpants.

"I don't know. I mean, Ms. Fitzpatrick has grasped my hand before. I'm sure she's grasped yours, too. She's very old-world in that way, even though she's paranoid."

"That's true, but hand grasping is one thing—it's not *handsy!*"

Sophia flung her lab coat into the soiled linens bin, then repeated the action with her sweater. Anika mimicked her actions, but with much more purpose and caution.

Side by side, the ladies washed their hands in contemplative silence before returning to redress in clean clothes from their lockers.

"Soph…" Anika started. Her voice was tentative. "You don't really think there's an outbreak, do you?"

Sophia pulled her head through her clean shirt, a soft coral that complemented the warm brown of her skin, then paused to consider the question.

"I suppose not, really," she said, then added reluctantly, "and Cora's probably right. We'd be the first to know."

"Yeah, you're right," Anika conceded, uncertain why she wasn't more eager to agree with her friend.

They continued to dress in silence. Sophia turned to her locker mirror to pull her braids into a high ponytail and apply a bright red gloss to her lips.

Anika sighed, then continued the conversation she was having inside her head. "But how on earth did she get it?"

"I don't know, Anika, but… how well do we really know Abigail Fitzpatrick? Sure, we've seen her twice a month for years. We talk, exchange pleasantries and know the minor details of each other's lives, but… maybe we read too much into it," Sophia suggested.

"What did we read into it? That she only pretended to be careful? That the top-tier package was for show? Does she have a secret family?"

"Or lover." Sophia winked.

Anika stopped fussing with her belt. "I hadn't considered that."

"Exactly. That's my point. We had a false sense of security." Sophia nodded her head with self-assured certainty.

"You realize what you're doing, right?"

"What am I doing?" Sophia asked, a mischievous grin stretching across her face.

"You're agreeing with Cora," Anika said.

Sophia gasped. "How dare you! I thought we were friends!"

"You were as wrong about me as you were about Abigail Fitzpatrick," Anika teased.

"I'm getting you tested, then!" Sophia jabbed.

They both laughed, delighted and completely recovered from the shock of Ms. Fitzpatrick's diagnosis.

"I don't know how I would survive here without you, Anika. You're one in a million."

Anika blushed, pulling the remaining personal items from her locker. The folder slipped out from under the brown package.

She'd forgotten about it. How was that even possible? Nothing was more important to her right now!

But she had. The entire day had come and gone, and she hadn't given it a second thought—hadn't called Zayd on her break.

"What's wrong, Anika?" Sophia approached, noting the change in her friend. When she saw the folder, she squealed, making Anika spin on her heels to face her.

"You're doing it? You're actually doing it? When?"

Anika opened her mouth to speak. "I—we—"

"I'm so happy I could hug you! You guys are going to be perfect parents!" Sophia gushed.

Anika flushed under Sophia's adoration. "Thanks... I'm excited, too."

"What's the matter?" Sophia asked. "Are you having second thoughts? Are you nervous?"

"What? No. I want this more than anything," she affirmed.

"Then what?"

"It's just... I was supposed to call Zayd on my break today, but I didn't..."

"Have you been taking the pills?" Sophia asked.

"Yes, of course," Anika said.

"That's all it is then: you forgot. The pills do that."

"They do?"

"That's what Eedie said when she did it. She said she was a full-on mess by the time things were established."

"Oh..." Anika paused to consider Sophia's proclamation. She ran her index finger along the smooth edge of the folder before allowing herself, only momentarily, to split it enough to touch the precious contents—approval.

"You've got some nerves, that's all. Nerves and hormones. Why don't you get the call done before you get out of here? That way you can enjoy your ride home and have—ahem—another great night with Zayd."

Sophia winked in the same way that always made Anika blush. She had a point though, about taking care of the appointment before going home. Zayd would be agreeable…

"Alright, sweetie. I'm going to get out of here and leave you to it. You can tell me all about it tomorrow," Sophia said, pulling her jacket on.

"Alright. Yes, I'm going to do it," Anika said, pulling her shoulders back.

"That's right, you are! Bye!"

With those final words, Sophia blew her a kiss and disappeared through the door, leaving Anika to contemplate her folder and phone call in silence.

After a long moment, Anika opened the folder, relishing the feel of establishing the crease line as the fibers crunched and bent together, breaking the seal. The folder contained two documents—one a thick, cream-colored certificate of qualification with a dark scan code for registration, the other a regular sheet that enumerated the details of the qualification along with instructions.

Looking at the contents made everything more real, more immediate. They were going to be parents. She was going to be a mother.

All she had to do was scan the certificate into her profile, then check with Zayd on his schedule and—

There was a loud bang. Anika jumped to her feet, startled. Adrenaline rushed toward her fingertips, making her already jumpy hands go numb.

What on earth?

Then she remembered that Cora was working in archives. Nightmarish visions of her body being crushed by overstuffed and poorly balanced file cabinets flashed into Anika's mind. She shook her head, forcing the graphic image away. It was an unlikely scenario.

Besides, it was much more likely that Cora was working on the archive database computer. The file cabinets were just an antiquated backup system to satisfy some ancient paranoia.

Still, she felt compelled to make certain Cora was alright. Unpleasant or not, no one deserved to be left in peril.

Anika closed the folder and tucked it back into her locker with her tablet. She exited the break room quietly, listening for some indication of where Cora might be working. There hadn't been a repeat of the initial bang. Things were eerily quiet for so early in the evening.

The faint click-clack of nails on a keyboard wafted down the hall. It had to be the archive room—all other entry pads in the building were virtual. Anika followed the sound, all the while wondering if Cora left the door open out of paranoia—maybe the empty building made her uneasy, too.

As she approached, she could make out Cora's sing-song voice. She was talking to someone.

"No, there haven't been any issues with the changeover."

Anika stilled, waiting to hear the response, but it never came.

Cora spoke again. "That's right, fifteen percent."

She was speaking to someone remotely. Anika considered calling out, for fear of being caught eavesdropping. But instinct stayed her tongue.

"I think it went off beautifully. Without a hitch."

Changeover? The conversation was vague. All the same, Anika couldn't help but wonder if there had been some sort of change to the company's employment policy. *Would it affect her hours? Would it affect her qualification?*

"Nothing to be terribly concerned about, though employees did note a drop in patients compared to previous months."

Cora had a strange habit of calling the clients patients—something Sophia suggested had to do with her time at the Institute. So maybe this was about a change in testing packages?

"Only one." More clacking, followed by silence. Anika imagined an inhale of breath.

"Abigail Fitzpatrick. Uh-huh. Pesky older woman who lives alone that a couple of employees have a soft spot for."

That confirmed it, then. This was about the clients—with the mention of Ms. Fitzpatrick, it also had to be about infection.

"No, no others," Cora confirmed.

Anika's heart raced. What could any of this possibly mean? What was Cora doing in the archive room, and who was she reporting to?

Chair wheels slid across bare tile as Cora stood. "Of course. I'm shutting down here right now. I'll send their search report straight over before locking up."

If Anika didn't want to be caught listening in on Cora's conversation, she had to move now. There was a pause between her brain's plea for action and her body's compliance. Finally, she whirled around in the hallway and moved silently back toward the break room. Five quick steps later, she pushed the door open and plunged her whole body forward, forcing herself to let the door ease soundlessly back into position.

Why was she so scared? She hadn't heard anything, really. And the chances of Cora being upset that Anika was moving to check on her after whatever the bang was were low.

But she couldn't shake the feeling that something was off.

Could Sophia be right about an outbreak? Was there a cover-up? Could Cora be involved?

The notion was ludicrous. Anika forced herself forward to gather her things. The call could definitely wait until she got home. She didn't want to be here a moment longer than necessary.

Anika listened as Cora turned the locks to the archive room. Her sturdy heels clicked on the tiled hall floor, stopping just outside the break room.

"Ani… are you still here?" Cora called through the door.

Anika's heart jumped out of her chest. She forced it back into place, clearing her throat to respond in as normal a tone as possible, "Yeah, I was just finishing a couple phone calls before heading home."

"Well, it's time to get going. I'm locking up, okay?"

Cora's voice was light and airy. There wasn't a hint of suspicion within it. But that only went so far to calm Anika's frayed nerves. She smoothed her jacket before stepping to the door. She pulled her shoulders back with a quick inhale and tuned the handle.

"Of course. I was just getting my things."

Cora smiled. A small strand of hair fell from its perfect placement, drifting down before she darted her hand up to tuck it back. "If I didn't know better, I'd think you liked staying late."

Anika offered a meek smile in return. "No, I just don't like taking anything home if it isn't necessary."

Cora shifted her weight from one foot to the other. "Well, why don't you just take yourself home?"

"Right. I'm just out now," Anika agreed, stepping past Cora into the hall and walking toward the exit.

"Goodnight, Ani," Cora called after her, continuing her journey to the front data station to recover the search reports.

Her hand resting on the door, Anika paused to call back, "Good night."

When she turned to exit, she caught a glimpse of her discolored fingernails.

CHAPTER
Nine

PARK

PARK DIDN'T KNOW if she could explain what was happening at the Institute. At least not in a way that Reed would understand. Transitioning from the intern program to being an Institute medic was like pulling back the curtain on a performance she hadn't realized was happening, and it was becoming increasingly difficult to convey to him what she was seeing. Communicating with him in general was becoming more difficult, which was disconcerting. They used to be so close. Unlike the other intern couples at the Institute, Park and Reed had been together before they arrived. They had studied for the Test together, dreamed together about life as scientists in the Northern Laboratories. Their relationship wasn't a fling of convenience. They were in love. They understood each other… usually.

Park knew it was difficult for Reed to continue in the intern program without her. To have watched her Northern Laboratories dreams snatched away from her by a margin of only a few percent. It made her feel like she was somehow less, but Reed never put it like that. He only struggled to see her perspective lately. She knew it was the strain of it all because she still felt that same strain. But she needed him to hear her like he used to. If he couldn't, then what was the point of being together anymore?

It was all or nothing at this point. They would lose each other soon, and Park didn't want to suffer that loss unless it was with her whole heart. She wasn't willing to lose it in pieces like the intern program demanded they lose everything else about themselves.

Reed greeted her under the old tree, and their bodies enveloped each other like they always did. It felt better when they were like that. Warmth in the cold night.

Park pulled away and looked earnestly into Reed's shadowed eyes. "I need to tell you something."

They retreated into the darkness of their secret haven, and Reed listened.

"I'm not sure I can explain it because it doesn't make any sense at all, but I have to try. Something is going on with the patients."

"Okay, Park, I can believe that. They said that there's some sort of upcoming shift in our program—something that's going to change our testing or something. Maybe it's related."

Park lifted at his response. At least they would be starting from a point of convergence this time.

"Normally, when we do intake samples for a new patient, any positive test gets marked for transport north, but lately we've been drawing follow-ups for almost every single patient."

"Are they getting more sophisticated? Maybe there are clinical trials going on up north?"

"That's the thing—after the follow-up, some of the strains aren't getting tagged for transport to the Northern Laboratories."

"They're staying at the Institute?"

"No—they're getting marked for something else." Park finally landed on the strangest part.

"Oh… that's surprising."

"Where else could they be going?"

"I have no idea." Reed shifted his body into Park, sending a mixture of thrill and warmth from every point of contact, making her want more. So much more. Park suppressed the desire, forcing herself to focus on the conversation until she saw its end. Until he saw her.

"You have no idea? They haven't said anything?"

"Only what I said—that there's a shift in the program."

Park chewed her lip, thinking it over. "You have no idea what the shift is?"

"Not yet, anyway, but I bet it's related," Reed said excitedly.

Park nodded into the darkness. "Maybe they're getting too crowded in the Northern Laboratories."

"Maybe," Reed agreed, his hands trailing down her body, her back, her hips, stirring a deep pang of longing. His hands came to a rest at the hem of her waistband. She could feel the heat of his bare skin tucked up under her shirt against her own bare, hungry flesh. Pausing, he asked, "Was that it?"

Park hesitated. What came next would inarguably cause unwelcome tension.

"Amy?" The sound of her name on his lips after so long nearly brought her to tears.

His hands danced gently across her back, making her ache for when things between them were simple. When they both believed in making positive changes—when *she* believed.

"Not all the tests are coming back positive," she blurted out.

"Well, that's good, isn't it?" Reed asked, his voice lightening.

"It should be…"

"*Should be?* What does that even mean? No infection is great! It means the patients can go home," Reed said, dropping his hand from her body. She nearly choked on the coldness left by its absence.

"But they're not going home," Park whispered.

"No?"

"We move them to the L-wing, and someone from the DDC comes to run a bunch of tests."

"That's a good thing, isn't it?" Reed asked. It was clear he was getting annoyed with the noncommittal twists of the conversation.

"It should be, only… only none of them make it out of the L-wing. The ones that leave go into cryo after about a week—from no infection to cryo. And none of them are getting sent north."

"Something's wrong with the initial testing, then," Reed concluded with ease.

"For every single patient?!" Park countered. "And why would none of them go north?"

"I don't know, but there has to be an explanation! It's not like someone is shipping them off to die. Come on, Park! What are you even trying to say?"

There it was—the break she'd been expecting. Reed was loyal to the cause through and through. Every day he spent in the intern program drove him a little further along, and at the same time somehow chipped away at the critical brilliance of his implacable mind.

"What reason is there to keep it under wraps? Why is the DDC heading a medical wing? I mean, think about it. Why would any part of the Institute want to hide a problem with initial screening? That's about the most dangerous thing that could happen on this campus."

"I'm sure it's getting sorted. It's only a matter of time before there's some sort of formal report and a change in policy and procedure," Reed exclaimed.

"Why are they all getting shut away? Where are they getting sent?" Park repeated the problem to his unquestioning faith.

"I don't know! How do you even know where they're going?" Reed snapped.

She had to tell him. It would be the end of their connection, but she had to.

Her heart seized at the knowledge of what this would do to them—what the Institute had done to them. She wished she could melt into him one final time before it was done—she craved the feeling of their union, but there was nothing to be done.

"The volunteers."

The room filled with nothing. Darkness swallowed all the sounds so that they sat together, alone in silence.

Park waited, hopeful despite herself. Maybe there was some part of Reed left that could believe her. Some part that could overcome whatever was happening to him and bring him back to her. But to be a scientist meant to separate from all others—to rise above insignificant things like compassion and human connection. This was where she had failed and he had not.

The physical attraction that still existed between them had masked their disconnect for too long. Now, her body shuddered at the absence of his.

Could she have kept these concerns from him for the chance of one more night? She knew she couldn't. It would have been too much of a betrayal of herself. The closeness would be a lie.

"Park, this is getting ridiculous."

"It is! You just can't see which parts are ridiculous anymore," she agreed.

"What's that supposed to mean?" Reed asked.

"You've changed, Reed! You aren't thinking right anymore. The volunteers are people like you and me! If you can't see them as anything more than props for your own accomplishments, then who are you anymore? They're doing something to you in the program!"

"Do you really believe that?" he asked. His feet scuffed on the ground as he stood. The darkness felt colder with the absence of his body.

He didn't pace, for fear that he'd knock something over, but she could feel the angry energy radiating through the room.

"The volunteers are turning you against the scientists. They're blinded by their connection to the patients." The conclusive tone in his voice wasn't meant for her. It was clearly a statement meant to explain the situation to himself—to exert his superiority. As a scientist, he was separate from the Institute's underclass—the volunteers who provided the labor to keep the whole operation going, often at the cost of their lives.

"Reed… listen to what you're saying—that doesn't make any sense. The volunteers depend on the scientists more than anyone else. They're on our side."

"You're not making sense!" he snapped.

"Reed…" her voice faltered as she lost all hope. This was the end, and it was going very badly. She found her voice again and pleaded, "You know me."

Reed breathed out a long exhale before dropping back down. Immediately, the space filled with his warmth. An arm reached out and wrapped around Park's shoulder.

"I'm sorry. I'm being harsh, aren't I?" His voice was so soft.

Park leaned into his shoulder, wishing the contact didn't have to end—wishing it meant more than it did.

"I hate that you've changed," she said.

"Me, too," he agreed.

They sat in silence for a while, enveloped by darkness.

"Don't you see how strange things are lately?" she asked, needing him to give her at least this.

"I think you need to give it time," Reed said. Her body tensed against his, so he added, "But I do see that it's... weird."

It was something. Park decided to hold onto that, even though the hope was likely false. She turned her head so that her face lay flush against his chest. He lifted his hand to run across the line of short hair that danced just above her ear. The sensation sent a thrill down her spine.

"I missed you last night. How many hours are you working lately?" he asked. His voice vibrated into her, mingling with the *thud thud* of his heartbeat.

"Two double shifts with an eight in between. I couldn't break," she said.

"You must be so tired." His lips danced across the tip of her ear, moving down to her neck, leaving a trail of sensation and making the room suddenly too hot.

"You, too—I know how long you're studying," she countered, trying not to pant.

"It's true—but it's not with *them.*"

She didn't know if he meant the patients or the volunteers. She wasn't sure he distinguished between them any longer, and she didn't want to know. This was his peace offering, and she wanted desperately to accept it.

"I feel like something's wrong," she said.

"Then something probably is wrong," he conceded.

She wanted so badly for it to mean that he was coming around to understanding that she might be right, but she knew chances were low. Still, it was *Reed.*

His hands found her in the dark, and she melted into them, forcing every other thought away from her mind except how good he felt. She'd done it—she'd told him what was bothering her. He'd listened. It hadn't ended them. Wasn't that the victory she'd craved? They were still together.

In the wake of their passion she lay, her head pressed against his rising and falling chest, listening to his heartbeat. He was asleep, as he often was by this time in their meeting. She didn't know how she managed to stay awake when exhaustion pressed against her temples with such persistence, but she did.

But tonight was different. There was no peace. Something niggled at her insides as she rose and fell with Reed's steady breaths. It wasn't just their conversation. It was the way Reed could separate himself so completely from her concerns, how easily he could dehumanize the volunteers. She worried if she could do such a thing with the patients, and he could do it with the volunteers, that it might not be such a big stretch for him to do it to her as he approached his departure to the Northern Laboratories. To make matters worse, she sensed a problem growing within the Institute walls and wasn't certain she could manage to steer clear of it. Worst of all, she wasn't sure Reed would be there for her when it all came about.

CHAPTER

Ten

MORA

MORA POUNDED down the hallway to apartment 346 without heed for the peace of the other residents. She pounded on the door with the brass numbers, knocking with a dogged persistence. She didn't pause to listen for the approaching footsteps that might grant her entry.

They would know it was her.

The door opened with a sharp certainty. Her last knock didn't make contact, and her hand fell through empty air, colliding with her thigh.

"Mora." A tight-faced woman greeted her with absolutely no enthusiasm.

"Good evening, Ms. Dunn. I'm here to see Jim," Mora responded with a very false polite smile.

"It's nearly dinner hour. It's not appropriate for you to barge in—"

"Doreen, is that Mora Rossi?" Richard Dunn called from the sitting area.

"You know very well it is," Doreen Dunn responded without glancing back at him. She kept her thin fingers rigid against the side rail.

"Let that girl in right now!" he snapped.

Doreen paled at his demand but relented, removing her hand from the doorway and stepping back to allow entry. Mora kept her smile sickly sweet as she passed.

"Thank you, Ms. Dunn. I promise I won't stay long," Mora oozed at her. She turned to Richard with the same grin, only slightly less false. "Good evening, Mr. Dunn. How are things at the poultry factory?"

"Oh, just fine, Mora. We're well on track to produce quota this quarter," he responded with genuine pride.

"That's fantastic. I'll make sure to mention the good news tomorrow when Mom has dinner with me."

Richard blushed, as she'd expected him to. "Well, you don't have to, but that's very generous of you."

Mora pointed herself toward the room at the end of the hall, eager to move past the gauntlet of parents.

"Make certain to wash, dear!" Doreen called after her.

Mora turned her body a sharp ninety degrees and said, "Of course. I wouldn't dream of forgetting," before darting into the bathroom and shutting the door.

She ran hot water over her hands until they stung, then reached for the soap.

People were so paranoid—especially people like Richard and Doreen Dunn. She'd been on a roof, not in a crowded transport. She wasn't carrying any risk of infection into their apartment.

She thought of the strange piece of paper tucked into her back pocket. *Then again…* A little extra hand washing hadn't ever hurt anyone.

Forty seconds later, she was running her hands under the ultraviolet dryer and listening for Jim to emerge from his room. She knew he was expecting her.

But she didn't hear him. All she heard was Doreen and Richard's hushed conversation.

"—Don't think it's appropriate for him to be spending time with someone so willfully obstinate," Doreen lamented in a tone that wasn't even quiet.

"Now, Dor, you know who her mother is. Kids like to be antagonistic, and with a mother like that, she's bound to push the boundaries," Richard scolded her.

"Of course I do! But what about the risk? What if someone thought James—"

"According to James, she's very bright. It's not like she's off to transportation or anything," Richard said.

"She's not getting any honors, either. I think she's a bad influe—"

Mora opened the bathroom door with a loud clank that she knew would set both of them on edge. It was stupid that they'd have such a conversation in her presence—even if she'd closed the door. Obviously she'd heard them. She stomped ungracefully down the hall to remind them she hadn't taken her shoes off at the door.

At the end of the hall, she stopped and tapped twice on the plain white door. As she waited, she kicked off her shoes, making sure to leave them in the middle of the hallway.

The door opened inward to reveal a scrawny, seventeen-year-old boy with dirty blond hair and thin glasses perched atop a freckle-covered nose.

"You got here fast," James Dunn said, stepping aside to grant her entry.

"I told you I was coming," Mora snapped.

He closed the door after glancing down the hall to where his parents stood in motionless shame and terror at the moody creature they believed to have too much power.

Mora wasn't even the one with all the power—it was her mom. She was a Department of Disease Containment liaison for one of the newer branches of personnel oversight. Her main function, as Mora barely understood it, was in personnel disbursement, but even that barely made sense. Supposedly, she balanced populations and the job placements between the City States, but Mora didn't understand why those population flows always seemed to be out of the city and never in. Besides all of that, she wasn't even a higher-up in the DDC. The people she worked for were way more powerful.

That's who James' parents were afraid of, not Mora.

She collapsed onto Jim's bed, falling into his blue comforter with a heavy sigh. "They hate me, you know."

"What? No—no they don't," James stammered, settling back into the swivel chair at his desk, which he dubbed his *workstation*.

Behind him, the desk was covered with projects—an open circuit board and soldering kit, a virtual dissection model, a half-eaten piece of toast with congealed spread. Amidst it all, his data tablet was perched, message port open to their conversation.

She gave him just enough side-eye for him to see her disapproval. "See? Even you can't pretend. I'm a pariah."

James blushed self-consciously. "It's just the way you act. Like the rules don't apply to you. They think you're asking for infection."

"And it has nothing to do with how my scores practically guarantee I'm not getting anything more than a clinical position in the city, if even that," Mora said, rolling her eyes.

"You could make it to the Institute if you wanted," James whispered, allowing his chair to swivel so he was sitting half-facing the bed and half-facing the workstation. He picked up a tiny screwdriver and fumbled with it idly.

"Yeah, right. If wishes were fishes," Mora scoffed. It wasn't even her wish.

"Is that from one of your books?" James asked, turning back toward her.

"Yes and no. It's something people used to say when something was impossible, but the original limerick was actually *if wishes were horses...*"

"What's the difference?"

Mora sighed again, bringing her fist up to her forehead. "Well, for one, a horse is a pasture-grazing beast of burden, while a fish is an aquatic-dwelling—"

"I know that!" James snapped.

"It's literary, okay?" Mora sighed.

"Did you come here to have another literary discussion?" James asked, fingering the tip of the screwdriver. He twisted it as though he were driving a tiny screw into the tip of his finger.

At that, Mora popped up, life returning to her golden-brown eyes.

"No. Omen brought me something," she said, reaching into her back pocket.

"Another new mouse species?" James asked in a mixture of curiosity and disgust.

"No—and I'm not sure I can even say he brought it. Someone gave it to him—attached it to him, that is—to bring to me!"

That got his attention. He scooted the chair all the way to the edge of the bed, so close that his leg nearly brushed against hers. Almost.

Mora pulled the tattered slip of paper out of her pocket and smoothed it out on the bed so he could see it, still half-convinced he would look at it and say he didn't see anything. That it was all in her head like a hallucination she'd conjured to fulfill her most ardent wishes.

The folds and crinkles of the paper were different now after the journey in her pocket, but the message was still the same. *Hello from the outside.*

He studied it for a long, silent moment, enraptured. Mora could feel her heart beating against her chest as she waited for him to react. When she decided that she'd waited long enough, she finally spoke.

"Where do you think it came from?"

"It's a joke," he said, still staring at the water-stained note.

"A joke?" She forced his eyes away from the message with a gentle squeeze of his wrist. He had to know how important this was to her.

"Do you think it's actually a message from outside the city?" he challenged.

"Do *you* think someone else in the city bribed Omen, fabricated a message and is somehow stalking us to watch our reaction?"

"It can't be from outside! Who?"

James shook his head, turning away from the message. A flash of fear darted across his face.

Mora eased herself to the edge of the bed, chasing his retreat. "Jim… think about it. It *has* to be from outside. We need to find out why. We need to know who sent it. What do they want?"

"Do you hear yourself, Mora?"

"We can't ignore it, Jim. This could be the most important thing that's happened in a long time. Contact. We could be the only people capable of learning what's really out there."

She held fast to his wrist, ignoring the rapid flutter of his racing pulse as she pleaded with him.

"It's too dangerous," he whispered.

"It's dangerous not to do it!" she insisted. "It's dangerous to sit here and accept everything we're taught. We already know there's more on the outside than they're telling us. It's not just the voles and the crickets and the—*blackvine weevil.* It's everything, and you know it! There could be people out there! He could still be out there!"

"I don't know any of that," he objected weakly.

"You do too, and you have to help me. You promised!"

"I was twelve!" he squeaked.

"So was I, but I remember, and once upon a time, you believed me. You can't deny everything like everyone else."

James fidgeted with the edge of his shirt, worrying a loose string until the seam came undone. Mora scooted closer to him, grabbing the message and bringing it into the shared space between their legs.

"Help me."

She watched him with large, pleading brown eyes, her dark, messy curls sticking out from her partially fallen hood to halo wind-chapped cheeks. He would relent. He *always* relented.

"If the message is real—"

"It has to be real!"

He let out a sigh, blowing the air straight up so it displaced the short hairs that hung over his forehead before starting again. "*If* it's real—then we have to have a plan. Let's start with confirmation."

"How do we confirm it?" Mora asked, both giddy and apprehensive. All this time searching. All of the interviews and stories led her to this moment—if Jim would just help her.

"I have a plan."

He set to work, clearing the non-essential contents from his desk and making room for Mora to join him.

CHAPTER

Eleven

ANIKA

THE COLOR HASN'T FADED. The thought screamed inside of Anika's head as she sat at the edge of the examination bench with the flimsy paper sheet draped across her unsettled legs.

"Try to relax, Ani," Zayd encouraged from his designated partner chair. He reached forward and patted her hand.

She pulled it away instinctively, as if afraid he'd notice, or that it might transfer into him somehow. She hadn't mentioned her discolored nails since taking the polish off, but the thought of it nagged at her daily, mixing with all the other conveniently inconvenient hints.

The stain looks worse, not better.

Ms. Fitzpatrick is gone. Transported six days after her last draw.

Twenty other no-shows.

Outbreak...

Zayd reached again and snagged her hand, giving it a firm, reassuring squeeze. "It's going to be fine. Everything's looking great."

If only he knew what she was really worried about... But she hadn't told him. The prospect of saying it out loud was too terrifying.

Still, she wanted to tell him—to reach out and have him meet her in the dark spaces of her mind. No one could comfort her like he could.

He would understand. He would banish her fears and carry her back into the light.

Unless…

The door opened, and a slim woman in a white lab coat with pulled-back hair entered, holding their chart and smiling. "Ms. Baba?"

"Y—yes. That's me," Anika squeaked, clearing her throat.

The doctor chuckled, moving to the stool in front of the exam table and lowering herself to it.

"It's normal to feel a little nervous during these preliminary appointments. Happens all the time." She glanced at the chart again before adding, "But I don't think you have anything to worry about. You've ticked every single box so far!"

Zayd beamed at the statement, looking over Anika with pride. "That's my Ani. She's a bit of a perfectionist. Never leaving anything to chance."

The doctor nodded, setting the chart aside before reaching for a fresh pair of gloves.

"All that's left is the physical examination, and then we'll set your appointment. It's usually smooth sailing from there," the doctor said as the second blue glove snapped into place.

She placed two feet on the floor and scooted herself forward, all the while pulling up the spindly silver stirrups for Anika to mount herself upon. She did so awkwardly, still grasping the pale blue sheet that kept her decent.

This was it. The last step in a long line of qualifications before they were officially to become parents. She might even enjoy this monumental though not quite comfortable moment if it weren't for the nagging thoughts.

I've always worn my gloves, she reassured herself as the doctor went to work. The pressure was an uncomfortable distraction.

Zayd scooted his chair closer to the exam table, making far too much noise. Anika watched the top of the doctor's forehead crinkle in response and wondered if Zayd noticed.

If he did, he didn't care. He squared his body with Anika's and leaned forward so his head was level with hers and his cheek crinkled on the flimsy paper cover.

"Hey," he said, reaching up and brushing the side of her face. "We did it, okay? This is it."

She nodded, splitting her attention between his affection and the doctor's actions, searching for an indication that things were going the way they were supposed to.

The doctor continued her checks, mostly ignoring whatever was going on above the blue paper sheet. There was some pressure and prodding, but nothing too terrible. Her sister had really exaggerated the physical exam. But she'd done it alone. Anika had Zayd.

The doctor sat up.

"That's it," she said, rolling back from Anika's legs.

"It's over? Is everything..." Anika scrunched her face, trying to discern the doctor's expression.

The doctor stood, removing the exam gloves and turning toward the biohazard waste. "Everything looks perfect!"

Relief washed over Anika, making her body tremble as though she'd just broken out of a high fever. She hadn't even realized how tense she'd been. Maybe that's all any of it was—anxiety over the appointment, the last step.

I've been making problems in my own mind.

"See? Look at that! Flying colors as usual." Zayd beamed. He leaned forward and planted an overly affectionate kiss on Anika's cheek.

Anika flushed, gingerly pulling her legs out of the stirrups, taking great care to keep the sheet in place. The doctor chuckled at Zayd's antics, moving to the sink to do her follow-up wash.

"You may be sore in the next day or so. Removal of the device can do that. So just know that's normal," she said, her back turned as Anika replaced the sheet with her bottoms.

When everything was situated, the doctor turned back to end the transaction. Zayd helped Anika to her feet, putting a reassuring arm around her shoulders. Anika was startled to realize how much she needed him standing there, holding her up. *So much anxiety!*

"Has anyone told you there might be a chance you'll succeed before the appointment?" the doctor asked.

"How common is that?" she asked.

"It's rarer these days, but… maybe up to twenty percent of our patients manage it without assistance," the doctor said.

It struck her then. She was one of their patients now—a prospective mother. The thought made her even weaker than she already felt.

"Well, doctor, I'm guessing you should give them a heads up because I've got a feeling about me and Ani." Zayd winked and dipped his head down to touch hers.

The doctor laughed again, but where the other chuckle was genuine, this one was polite. Anika swooned. She nearly felt sick. Likely a side effect of the removal and the hormones she'd been taking.

"Alright then, you can head out the exit and down the hall to your left. The nurse at the station will confirm your next appointment," the doctor said, ready to be through.

Zayd saluted her, squeezing Anika to his side and reaching for the door. The doctor's eyes followed his movement, landing on the white gauze taped to his bare forearm as he turned the handle.

"What's that from?" she asked, causing Anika's heart to nearly burst.

"This?" Zayd looked at the bandage as though he'd completely forgotten about it. "I got myself on the corner of our counter at home. It's had a chipped tile for the longest time, and I keep meaning to fix it. I guess that'll be a lesson to me, right?"

The wound was healing nicely. The scab was firm and supple. He would only have minor scarring from the incident. Even Anika tended to forget about the patch job he'd suckered her into doing for him.

The patch job she'd given him right after his shift ended. At the *factory*, not home. She didn't know why he'd lie about it.

The doctor picked up her tablet and reopened their file, scanning through the information as they waited. Zayd kept one hand on the handle, squeezing Anika's shoulder as though she might not remain standing without him—and she might not. She felt woozy, as though the world were going to spin out from underneath her. Her temples pulsed, making her want to close her eyes and shut out the world.

"I don't see it in your file," the doctor mused, glancing up as if to verify the wound was still there.

"Eh," Zayd shrugged. "It just happened. And you know Anika is a tech. She patched it straight away."

The doctor drew her lips into a line, considering the discrepancy between the file and Zayd's fresh wound. Anika watched, her heart pounding and a distant scream growing in her head. Why did it feel so… *wrong?*

Anika watched as the doctor ran a finger across her tablet screen, closing the file. She turned the device and tucked it under her arm. Her face was back to neutral. Anika couldn't read any of it.

"These things happen, don't they?" she said, seeming to shrug off the explanation.

"Yeah. If only you could disaster-proof me," Zayd laughed.

"Isn't that the goal? I'll mark you both down for a retest on your way out. That way, we'll have an updated clearance for you both between the incident and your appointment. Easy as that." The doctor smiled at them.

Zayd nodded his head, still pleasant, and opened the door so they could exit.

Anika still felt weak. She felt like everything had just gone wrong.

CHAPTER

Twelve

PARK

PARK PITCHED FORWARD over the wastebasket and vomited again. This was the third time in two days. Something was definitely wrong.

The auto-screener should've picked it up by now…

She leaned back, relieved but miserable. Maybe the malady had already been detected. Maybe she should open up her own file and get the diagnosis so she could start treatment.

No sooner had the thought occurred to her than there was a ping on her tablet, indicating she'd just received a message from a superior authority.

Park groaned, in no mood to deal with bureaucracy. Reluctantly, she stood, reaching across her workstation to grab her tablet. She fell back onto her bed, resting her head against the wall as she cued the message.

It was from medical.

She was right. Something was wrong. At least she wouldn't have to sleuth it out herself. The sooner she dealt with it, the sooner she'd feel better. The message loaded onto her screen.

A medical anomaly has been detected. Please report to clinic at 0730 for full examination and diagnosis.

Important: Do not report to the main desk. Proceed straight to the diagnostics room and sign in. You will be greeted immediately.

—Medical Officer 0231

Since joining the Institute, Park had been ill exactly twice. Both times, she'd received the automatic notification to report to clinic, but neither message was like this. This one had further instructions—strange instructions. Her curiosity was immediately piqued. Another unusual development to interpret. Maybe getting sick wouldn't be a total disaster.

The first time she got sick was with a standard flu virus. It was in the first month, and more than half of her cohort ended up infected—supposedly typical when interns from different communities took up residence with one another. Though inter-city vaccination was nearly universal, they couldn't account for every viral mutation.

Both the illness and the explanation served as an important reminder of exactly why the Institute was so important—the disease they fought was undergoing constant mutations that made it virtually impossible to defeat. Like a cancer, there were so many variations and permutations that it would take a herculean effort to crack. The scientists destined for the Northern Laboratories were the world's only hope.

She'd been destined to be a scientist... once upon a time. Had it really been less than a year since she was bumped from the program? Everything had changed so much since then. Working in the medical facility had opened her eyes—she saw things she had overlooked in the single-minded business of being an intern. *Like Reed,* she thought.

Nothing was as straightforward as she had once believed. Although Zoribiatus still plagued society, the Institute seemed geared toward something else—something new. Whatever it was, only the volunteers seemed to have a complete picture of it, and that didn't do anyone any good because they were constantly dismissed, dehumanized and often killed in the line of duty before word could get around. It all seemed like part of some plan.

Park glanced at the clock. Fifteen minutes to get to medical.

She didn't want to wait. Instead, she finished dressing and ran a wet cloth over the top of her short hair. The cool felt good, making her realize exactly how miserable she was. She grabbed her ID card and headed out the door.

Though classes were starting for the interns, the halls were quiet. Shift changed on the hour, meaning that most everyone on site—save for the officials and administration—was either hard at work or doing their best to catch a few precious moments of rest before work began. She padded silently across the dark carpet toward the clinic. Where carpet turned to brilliant white tile, she turned right, away from the main medical wing.

This early, there wasn't anyone waiting at intake, which made bypassing check-in that much easier. She slipped past the entrance desk, toward the main hall. At the third door, she lifted her badge. A quiet beep indicated that her information had been scanned. A moment later, the latch on the door released.

Park put her hand against the door and gave it a gentle, cautious push. She listened for an indication that it was okay to enter.

"Hurry up, please," a gruff voice called.

She jumped at the command, moving quickly to comply. Once in the room, she pressed the door closed until the latch caught. An older medic stood inside next to the examination bench. His bald head shone in the bright lights as he took her in through glasses that reflected so dramatically in the bright light that she couldn't see his eyes behind them.

"The, uh, message said to come straight back," she stammered.

"It did indeed. Come have a seat," he said, offering her a chair instead of the examination table.

She lowered herself into it, fighting the wave of nausea that threatened to upend her.

The old medic watched her with a critical eyebrow raised over his thick glasses. His face seemed stuck in a permanent grimace, his forehead scrunched into a half dozen lines that looked as though they never faded. But behind his unpleasant countenance and the thick glasses, Park thought she caught a glimpse of concern.

Before she could interpret him further, the medic pulled a small packet from his lab coat and offered it to her.

"Take these, and take one right now. You'll feel better," he said, holding the foil between his thumb and index finger.

She stared at it for a moment, bewildered, before following instructions. A tiny white pill popped out of the foil with a little pressure from her thumb. She swallowed it without water, hoping that whatever relief it promised would be instantaneous.

"Do you know who I am?" the medic asked her.

She did—or at least she was pretty sure she did. He was the top medic for the Institute. Though she only knew him by rumor, she had to assume that's who she was speaking with. The likeness was too uncanny.

"You're Chadwick Garth."

He nodded, his expression unchanging. It was such an unpleasant expression. The moment she thought it, a wave of relief overtook her. The nausea lifted, and her head felt inexplicably clearer.

"Feel better?" he asked knowingly.

"Yes."

"Chadwick, you know your stuff," Garth chuckled. Still, his face somehow managed to stay unpleasant, as though laughing caused him some sort of physical discomfort.

Park reveled in the relief and, for the first time in a while, realized that she was hungry.

Garth continued his interrogation—or whatever this was—without allowing further interruption.

"I'm glad you're aware of who I am and what my position here is. That will save us some time. I'm your director, in a roundabout sort of way. Obviously, under normal circumstances, I'd leave low-level Institute medics to my subordinates, but there's something I want from you."

Garth spoke in a slow, even clip. He was confident but nonchalant. He looked at her but never made direct eye contact.

"You need something from me?" Park asked, blinking through her incredulity.

"I have a job I want you to do, Miss Park. Something I think you'd be particularly well suited for."

Park tried to keep her face neutral. The notion of the head medic at the Institute recruiting a lowly first-year medic—a washout from the intern program—was laughable. He shouldn't even know she existed. But here she was. And here he was offering her a position. Park swallowed, knowing there was no way to process the situation and react. She had to go with her gut.

"What's the position?" Her mouth was so dry that the words felt like cotton balls scratching against the back of her throat—or maybe that was a side effect of the medicine.

Garth kept his eyes on her, scrutinizing as though he could read right through her and hated everything he saw.

"I want to move you to the L-wing. On paper, you'll report to Maddoux, but in reality, you'll be reporting directly to me."

"What does that mean?" Park asked.

Garth let out a sigh, seemingly put out by her density. "This change in position will transfer you to the jurisdiction of the DDC. I've been asked to select a medic that I find to be appropriate for the switch, and I've chosen you. While I'm complying with the request, I'm making my own request—to you—to ensure that I am informed as to the situation in the L-wing."

The L-wing. It had been the subject of her own angst and curiosity only a few weeks ago. The reason for the fracture between her and Reed, and the cause of her growing unease. Garth was giving her an open invitation to investigate. She could discover for herself what was really going on, why not all patients tested positive and why every single one of them still ended up infected.

"I'm going to need your agreement posthaste, I'm afraid," Garth interrupted her train of thought.

"Why me?" Park blurted. The way the tendon tightened on the side of Garth's neck and the way he managed to shrink her with his piercing gaze made her immediately want to take it back. Instead, she tried to explain. "I mean, surely there are more qualified medics on campus to do the job, so why would you pick a dropout like me?"

Garth pressed his fingers to his chin, dipping his head down in quick acknowledgment of her statement. He sat back in his chair with an expression of smug triumph. "Because, Park, the reasons you assume you're wrong for the job happen to be the reasons I believe you're exactly right. You're green. That means you haven't learned your ways around here. The DDC will perceive you as easy to mold. You're a recent *transfer* from the intern program, meaning that you're educated in the desired policies in addition to your training and skill level. Plus, you'll be beholden to me, so I can rely on you for accurate information."

Park raised a curious eye to the old medic. "What makes you so sure you can rely on me?" she asked.

A smile broke across his unfathomably unpleasant face as he answered. "Because you're pregnant, and you're going to need my help."

CHAPTER
Thirteen

MORA

"HOW DO you know when Omen will be back?" James puffed as he followed Mora up the rickety fire escape stairs to the final high-rise apartment.

Mora had balked when he'd said he would be coming with her, but the excitement of executing his plan was too much, and he'd told her exactly that. He wanted to witness history in the making just as badly as she did, even if his reasons were slightly different. He wanted it badly enough to break a few rules (poorly enforced rules, as Mora had repeatedly proved) to be there.

"He hasn't left for days. I think he's waiting for my reply," Mora said, swinging her body up to the last rise.

"That's a smart bird," James said, joining her. He looked up at the overhead ledge. "Where do we go from here?"

Mora gave him a mischievous smile. "You're not going to like it, but follow me. I won't let you fall."

James paled as he watched Mora launch herself onto the first set of grooves and handholds carved out of the apartment building's dilapidated brick. Time had begun the erosion, and Mora's deliberate construction had sped up the process. She scooted sideways a couple of steps before stretching her hand backward. She looked down at

James expectantly, a broad, crooked smile stretching her face in the golden glow of twilight.

"I can't do that…" James protested, feeling woozy just looking at Mora's heels hanging out over nothing. The toe box of her shoes rested on the gravely surface of weathered bricks, and her hands rested on the roof's ledge. It looked entirely unsafe.

"Sure you can. It's just like the obstacle box," she insisted.

"The obstacle box is four meters off the ground and surrounded by impact-absorbent flooring," James objected, eyes fixed at the point where Mora's shoe shifted, loosening tiny grains of brick and sand that skittered down the building and caught in the breeze.

Mora rolled her eyes. "That doesn't change the technique. Reach up and I'll walk you through it. Here, give me your hand."

James watched in horror as Mora leaned even further from the building, bending her knees and urging him on with her outstretched hand.

"Careful! I think I'll die if you fall," James gasped, pushing his hands out and stepping back as if he could will her hand back into place.

Mora laughed, her dark eyes lighting up with mischievous golden flecks. "I'm not going to fall, Jim. Don't be so dramatic! I'm going to help you onto this dang roof so that *you* don't fall."

James flinched as she leaned out further to reach for him, then relented so she wouldn't overbalance. Her small, warm hand wrapped around his clammy palm. Gently, she urged him forward until he was standing flush with the wall.

"See that brick about a foot up from the rail? That's your first step. You can put one hand on the sill, and I'll keep you secure over here. It's two little steps before you can hold the roof ledge," she coaxed.

James swallowed hard but allowed her to pull on his hand as his foot found the designated step. He forced out the repeating image of plummeting to the alley below as he shifted his weight and grasped at the windowsill. He was up. One step down.

"See? It's not so bad."

With his eyes firmly on the wall right in front of him, he couldn't see her, but he was certain Mora was beaming—glowing with an ear-to-ear grin.

Mora eased him up two more steps until he could grasp the roof ledge. After making sure he had a good grip, she flung her body over the ledge. James had to close his eyes and hold his breath at the whoosh of air her movement caused, but before he could settle into panic, her hands were there again, urging him upward.

When the whole ordeal was done and his feet were planted firmly on the rooftop, he dared to look around. It was like a different world. He could immediately see why Mora loved it up here. Stretched out in the dusky light of the setting sun, the city looked far away and insignificant. All around the horizon, he could detect the wavering shimmer of the force field surrounding them, but beyond that, he could sense the *more* she always went on about. He watched her move to her corner where a refurbished lounge chair leaned against a row of planter boxes with fragrant, dainty green plants poking out.

"Pretty great, right?" Mora said, still incandescent with happiness.

"It sure is something," he agreed, his eyes lighting upon the empty nest. "Where's Omen? I thought you said he's been waiting for you?"

Mora eased herself into the lounge chair, setting her backpack against it. "He has been. He'll be here. A bird's gotta feed himself more than a few handfuls of grain each day, you know? He's probably out mousing or something."

James nodded, scanning the horizon for a sign of the black shadow crossing the vast sky, struggling to remember what had possessed him to come up here.

"He'll be here, alright? Sit down, relax and take in the view for a while," Mora coaxed, gesturing toward the fabric stretched across the frame immediately next to her body.

James eyed it critically.

"It'll hold us both," Mora snapped, rolling her eyes and scooting as if to give him more space. The action did little to make room.

"I'm bigger than you," James pointed out.

"Duh!"

He relented, self-consciously easing onto the seat, trying hard not to sit too close to Mora. The brown cloth gave a little under his weight but held fast. Seated far too close for comfort, he held his breath. He had no idea what to do with himself and zero clue what he was doing sitting on a roof. Alone. With Mora.

"What gives, Jim?" Mora asked, leaning toward him until her shoulder bumped his.

James let all his breath out at once in a noisy groan. "I can't stop thinking about how dead I am if I get caught up here!"

"You worry too much. I'm up here all the time, and I never get caught!" Mora said.

"Yeah, but that's you. You've got this way about you that makes it seem so easy. I think you could get away with murder. But not me. I'm doomed to be caught."

"Is that why you're such a rule follower? Because you're scared of getting caught?" Mora asked, leaning against him. Whatever amount of comfortable James wasn't, Mora clearly was.

He considered the question, weighing his answer against what Mora believed… and what she wanted from him. He watched for her reaction as he chose each word.

"Sure, I don't want to get in trouble, but… I believe in the rules. I believe in what we're trying to do as a society—the DDC, the government, the cities… the Institute…"

Mora's face wrinkled for a moment, then she shook her head, her wild curls swishing out around her shoulders. "Yeah, well, I think there's more to it than the stupid disease safety, and this is going to prove it. We're going to find out who's *really* left outside the force fields!"

"You mean besides near-dead?" James asked.

"Maybe there aren't any more," Mora suggested.

James considered her suggestion, knowing what she was hoping for and not wanting to spoil it. He wanted to remind her of the footage, the lessons, and the fact that just three weeks ago, Mr. Andrews had left for the clinic and never returned. But contradicting her would mean there was no hope for the father she lost before she and her mother escaped into the city. And he knew Mora well enough to know that her father's survival on the outside was her dearest hope. Instead, he just sighed. This wasn't going to be easy. He wasn't sure why he'd thought coming up here with her would make it so, but it was too late now. There was no taking back the thirty-six floors they'd scaled. He wouldn't dare undo the tracking code he'd embedded into the fine weave of the paper on which they'd written their carefully worded response. And now his alibi depended on an uncomfortable dinner with Mora's mother!

Mora watched James' consternation, her expression softening as he fought to contain his runaway thoughts. "Hey Jim, it's not like I don't get what you see."

He blinked and forced what was supposed to be an easy smile. It felt unnatural on his face. "No, it's okay. It's not like you have to believe the same things as me, it's just that—if you could see it like I did, then maybe we could do this together."

"Do what?"

James flustered. He hadn't meant for it to happen right now, but it was.

"You know... go to the Institute, become scientists and find a cure?"

"Oh, Jim! You know I could never make it to the Institute! I'm not smart enough!" Mora laughed.

"You are too," he protested.

"Tell that to my annual score report—tell it to my mom!"

Everything James tried to do seemed to fall to pieces in Mora's presence. "Sure, your scores aren't great, but that's because you never *try*. If you cared enough, you'd do as well as anybody else out there."

"That's just wishful thinking, Jim. I can't do what you do! I can't hide a tracking device in a piece of paper. I can't virtually dissect a human body by memory! Those are *your* gifts."

He blushed. "You have your things, too, Mora."

"Yeah, well, my things aren't exactly allowed in this world. I belong in the time before, and you know it." She kicked at the gritty surface of the apartment roof.

"You belong here, now," he said.

"I never have." Her eyes caught something in the distance. James followed her gaze until he saw the black silhouette growing against the dusk sky. Omen was on his way to greet his mistress. Mora pulled her backpack onto her lap to retrieve their message.

"Have you ever even tried to do well on the Test?" James asked, sensing he was running out of time. This conversation always happened in slow motion in his head. He always had time to untangle and sort his thoughts so he could say the perfect thing.

Mora flustered. It was strange to see her in such a state. "It's not that I don't try; it's that there isn't an amount of trying that will make a difference! And it doesn't matter anyway! The last Test is done. It's over."

"You could petition?" James suggested tentatively.

"Why would I petition? Why would I—" He watched as realization struck her like a ton of bricks, jolting through her nervous system like lightning.

"So you could come with me," James mumbled, shoving his hands in his pockets and turning his bright red, too-hot face away from her searching gaze.

Her mouth moved as she searched for the right words to console him. "Oh, Jim…"

"You don't have to say anything," he said, still trying and still failing to not look at her face.

"But I do. I need you to know—"

"You don't owe me anything!" James protested as she bobbed back into his field of vision.

Mora grabbed his shoulder, forcing him to face her. "I do, Jim. I do! We're friends. I care about you. I owe you the truth," she said.

"I already know. I know you don't feel the same about me," he said, forcing himself to look up from his shoes into her beautiful, searching eyes.

She blinked, suddenly struggling to meet his gaze, as if the intensity were too much for her to bear. "I feel a lot of things for you, James Dunn. I feel all the things I could possibly feel for someone like you. Respect, admiration, love—the friendship sort of love, you know…"

He broke her gaze at that, trying to not let her see the pain lancing through his heart. "Those are good things, I know. I'm grateful you feel that way—about me, I mean," he whispered.

"You're so good, Jim." Mora reached for his hand, forcing her fingers between his and grasping.

"But not good enough?" he ventured.

She squeezed hard. "You are good enough, Jim!"

He searched her face, mind reeling, wanting to know why, if he was so good, she couldn't feel for him what he felt for her. He wanted to ask, but the words wouldn't form.

She must have been able to read it on his face, though, because as Omen's dark form approached, she told him. "I don't like boys, Jim."

Her grasping hand burned a hole through him that went from his sweating palm all the way up through his aching heart.

CHAPTER

Fourteen

ANIKA

"SO YOU DID the draw at the outpatient lab and not here?" Sophia asked, eyeing Anika incredulously.

"It doesn't feel right to mix business and personal matters," Anika explained, using her gloved hand to smooth the label onto the last vial. "Besides, it was convenient to get it done on our way out of the appointment."

"It's convenient to have it done at a top-of-the-line, state-of-the-art laboratory," Sophia argued, taking the tray of vials and queuing it into the delivery slot.

"Are you suggesting that the mother lab isn't suitable?" Anika asked, removing her gloves and moving over to the wash station.

"You know I'm not. I'm just saying we would've taken care of you and Zayd—and you wouldn't have had to dip into your credits," Sophia tutted, tossing her gloves into the biohazard bin and waiting for her turn at the sink.

"Spending the credits wasn't a hardship," Anika said, moving away from the sink.

"That's not the point. Why didn't you wait?"

Anika sighed, still feeling weak, though not as poorly as she'd felt the previous day at the appointment. Maybe Zayd was onto something when he suggested that her body was priming itself for the pregnancy. He wanted her to reduce her hours and get more rest. She had argued that her job wasn't taxing—and was the more lucrative—but he'd dismissed her. He was on deck for a status change and had been taking extra responsibility for some time. It was the reason he didn't want to report the injury. But it didn't explain why he'd lied about it to the doctor. He said it was because he was afraid she might submit something official that would get back to his work file, but that seemed unlikely to Anika unless—

Unless something about the injury carried a contamination risk.

"Where did you go?" Sophia asked, waving a damp hand in front of Anika's face.

"I'm sorry?" she asked, blinking.

"You zoned on me something fierce!" Sophia laughed.

"I'm sorry, I haven't been myself," Anika apologized.

Sophia wrapped her arm around Anika's shoulder and gave her a quick squeeze. "I know. It's the hormones. Eedie was the same."

"That's what Zayd said," Anika shrugged Sophia's arm off her shoulders. Contact still made her jumpy. She'd finally told Zayd about her fingernails—showed him the greyish-purple discoloration that stood out on her index and middle fingers. He shrugged it off, kissing each finger in turn and insisting she was overreacting to a stubborn stain from a new brand of polish. It was just the stress of the qualification process. She knew how she got about these sorts of things. *Performance anxiety*, he called it.

"That man knows you better than anyone else, and I'm still bitter about it," Sophia concluded as they made their way down the hall toward the break room.

"Would you rather I registered as a partner with you?" Anika laughed. It felt good to laugh. She hadn't been doing nearly enough of it lately.

"Don't think I haven't considered it," Sophia said, reaching out for the handle. "And I wouldn't hesitate to stop you from making poor decisions like testing out of lab."

"Testing out of lab?" Cora's high-pitched voice caused both of them to turn their heads. Her head was tilted to the side so that her luxurious blond hair hung off-center. Behind her innocuously quizzical expression, her eyes held them like steel traps.

Sophia pushed on the door handle, fully intending to dismiss Cora. Anika envied her boldness. She could never shrug off an authority figure like that, and Cora specifically set her on edge. "It's nothing, Cora; I was just complaining that Anika spent credits having a draw done at the mother lab instead of waiting to get a draw here."

"The mother lab?" Cora asked, raising a thin, manicured eyebrow and stepping away from the doorway to the archives. She'd been in there all week, only emerging to check the status of patient flow at the front or review the reports before Sophia and Anika sent them off. Anika thought of the strange conversation she'd overheard the night she'd stayed to make her appointment. Wasn't that part of the reason she'd been so unsettled this whole time?

"Yeah, Anika's officially one of their patients." Sophia gave her a proud nudge. Anika swayed under the gentle force of it.

"Ani," Cora gasped. "That's huge! Why didn't you say anything to me?"

"Why would she?" Sophia scoffed.

"Soph, don't be rude," Anika hissed under her breath.

"We're all friends here," Cora smiled, baring her perfectly straight, white teeth.

"Of course. I just hadn't thought to. I'm sorry to exclude you," Anika said. Cora's expression made her think of an image from a textbook—something animalistic and not at all friendly.

"Well, we've righted that now, haven't we? Now, what was this about doing your draw?" Cora closed her mouth so that her pink lips pursed together and paled at the edges despite the stain of makeup.

"It was nothing really—just a matter of convenience. Zayd had a little scratch that they didn't have on file since the original draw—the one we did here. So the doctor ordered a retest before our next appointment," Anika rushed to explain.

"A scratch?" Cora asked.

"From our countertop," Anika confirmed. Sophia gave her a curious look that made her feel even more flustered. Why was she downplaying his injury to Cora?

"Zayd did?"

Was that relief Anika detected in her voice?

"That's right," she said.

Cora chewed her lower lip for a moment before she realized they were both watching her with curiosity. Her face immediately brightened into its normal artificial expression. "Well, it is a shame you spent any credits on that at all! I wish you'd just done it here."

"Noted for the future," Anika said, feeling sheepish to be the subject of such attention. She turned to follow Sophia into the break room.

"Why don't we do it here anyway?" Cora said.

Anika's stomach lurched. Sophia stopped so abruptly in front of her that they collided.

"Why?" Sophia blurted.

"Because our processing is faster. Why should she wait longer? The sample results will register as completed in her file as soon as they're processed, and then it will be done," Cora said without missing a beat.

"My next appointment is two weeks from now," Anika said. Her mouth felt dry.

"You don't want to wait that long. Let's do it here. Right now," Cora pressed.

"It's really okay—" Anika protested.

"I insist," Cora said, her lips pressing into a pink line again. She reached for Anika's arm and practically pulled her away from the break room.

Anika tried to tell herself that she was overreacting. Cora was just being nice, but as she followed her back down the hall to the draw rooms, she fought the same nagging dread she'd been fighting for weeks.

The stain... Ms. Fitzpatrick... more no-shows... outbreak...

No matter how many times she told herself it was impractical to harbor such negative thoughts, they managed to creep in and take residence. She suddenly realized Cora was talking.

"... Sophia is so right, you know. Those clinics really can't compare to ours, and you have the privilege of getting a free draw."

"I suppose it was the nerves that kept me from thinking straight," Anika offered.

"Of course—Such a big step!" Cora said as they walked into Med Room 1. She turned, brandishing a big, artificial smile that didn't reach her eyes. The expression turned Anika's already gravely stomach to ice.

"Why not just use the lab station?" Anika asked as Cora shut the door.

"I'd like to do a full physical since we're at it," Cora said, pulling fresh gloves from the wall.

Anika swallowed. *Her nails.*

She took a slow breath, forcing calm. There was no need to worry. Of course she wanted to get a check on her nails. It was foolish not to. Cora could put all her worries to rest and tell her she was stressed over nothing.

"Sounds good, Cora."

Anika pulled off her lab coat and took a seat on the exam bench, noting the bizarre déjà vu of it. Cora pulled two sample vials and a butterfly needle from the supply drawers before pulling the visual examination kit from its compartment. Anika watched her in silence.

"What's the big archive project?" she asked as Cora checked the focus on the lighted lens.

There was a long pause while Cora synced the system with her tablet. Anika squirmed. Finally, a green light flashed indicating a successful sync, and Cora turned to Anika.

"Oh, it's part of a systems audit. Apparently, there's some big change in testing coming straight from the Institute, and we're first in line to get the beta system if we pass muster," Cora said cheerfully.

"That seems… big," Anika mused, at a loss of what else to say. She tried to remember the details of Cora's strange conversation… fifteen percent, changeover and Ms. Fitzpatrick. Not a lot to go on.

Cora brought the light scanner up to Anika's face. She looked past the bright glare like she was trained to and waited for the scan to complete so that she could blink away the sting.

"All clear," Cora said as the machine beeped. "You have such lovely eyes."

"Thank you," Anika said as Cora moved the scanner down.

The scanner beeped again after clearing facial pigmentation.

"Won't you be glad when we can ditch this antiquated technology and rely on remote scanning?" Cora asked as she moved the scanner down Anika's neck and arms.

"It's not too terrible. At least it's quick," Anika suggested of the pigment and discoloration scanner they used to detect tissue changes related to infection.

Cora made a *hmm* sound as she passed the scanner across Anika's forearms. "It's the proximity I don't like. Being so near patients without confirmation of health."

"So many of our clients are regulars doing preemptive testing. It doesn't bother me," Anika said.

"You're braver than me." She moved the scanner over Anika's hand, pausing when she glimpsed the fingernails.

"New nail polish," Anika blurted.

Cora ran her gloved fingers across the discoloration. "Have you stained before?"

"Only with black," Anika said, then added, "This one was a dark red."

Cora didn't respond. She pulled the scanner over the nails and waited for the beep. The scanner flashed red. *Error*. She pressed the rescan button and waited again.

Error.

"It's not scanning?" Anika asked, trying to sound calm. Of course nail discoloration would register as an error with the pigment scanner.

"I keep getting the error E5 message," Cora confirmed, referencing atypical, but non-diagnostic out-of-range results. She moved the scanner over Anika's hands, which had already passed, and cycled it. The scanner beeped clear, but when she returned it to the fingernails, the lights flashed red immediately.

"What does it mean?" Anika asked, knowing full well it didn't mean anything other than the scanner couldn't read the pigment in her fingernails beyond the stain.

"I'm not sure. I'm going to note it on your samples, though," Cora said, not even attempting a smile.

There were no other errors. She placed the spent scanner into the decontamination compartment before dawning a second set of gloves for the sample draw. Anika had never seen Cora double glove before. It gave her a sinking feeling. Cora wasn't the best at drawing. She often missed the vein on her first shot, which Anika usually chalked up to carelessness. But today she wondered if it was carelessness or apprehension.

She filled both vials in silence, then offered Anika the clean gauze and let her remove the needle. Anika watched Cora pull labels for the vials as she wrapped her arm.

"Wait here a minute; I'm going to check on something real quick," Cora said.

Instead of inserting the vials into the delivery slot, she tucked them into the palm of her hand and, using her shoulder, pushed through the door, leaving Anika to stew in her own dread.

This was beyond unconventional. The vials shouldn't have left the room. Anika listened to Cora retreat down the hallway—toward the archive room by the sound of it. She strained as if she might be able to discern Cora's intent by listening, closing her eyes and focusing.

"What's with Cora?"

Sophia's question burst through Anika's mind like thunder. She gasped, staring wide-eyed into Sophia's quizzical expression. "You scared me!"

Sophia leaned against the open door and scrunched her eyebrows. "What's going on?"

Anika lifted a trembling hand to her face to stifle the building sob. "I think something's wrong. My nails are—and Cora's involved in—in —I don't know!"

Sophia dropped her tough act and moved to comfort Anika, but before she could make it even halfway across the room, Cora's firm, cold voice commanded, "Don't go near her. She needs to go to quarantine."

Fifteen

ZAYD

"I WASN'T sure if I was going to see you out here again," Simons said by way of greeting when Zayd pulled into the rendezvous area.

"What are you talking about? I've got a perfect track record!" Zayd said, jumping down from the driver's seat.

It was nearly dusk, but beneath the trees, it may as well have already been nightfall. A thick fog was rolling in from the west, giving the space where the road met the trees an other-worldly feel. This would be Zayd's first multi-day run, which proved he'd earned some amount of respect from Johnson and whomever else he worked for by pulling off the first run—no matter how disastrously he thought it had gone.

"Is that what they're calling wrecked vehicles and lost goods these days?" Simons asked, clasping his arms behind his back.

On impulse, Zayd decided to throw caution to the wind and clasp the large man's forearm. Simons watched the gesture for a moment before breaking into a wide grin. He unclasped his hand and brought it forward to embrace Zayd's. An old-world handshake. It felt right.

"Johnson said the accident made the whole thing look even more believable than what they had planned. Said the DDC will be looking for trouble from the outside instead of missing people on the inside," Zayd explained, moving to the back of the transport, scanner in hand.

"That's smart," Simons agreed.

The door slid open on the first try.

"Yeah. And DDC border monitoring gets to go on thinking I'm a huge idiot that can't drive straight down an empty road."

Simons laughed as Zayd jumped into the back of the transport. This one was loaded front to back with heavy crates—*mixed goods*—that Zayd would ensure arrived at their final destination. Nestled between the crates, against the hollow spot between the cargo area and driver's compartment, was their passenger.

A tall, black-suited man with bronzed skin and swept-back wavy hair stepped around one of the towering stacks of crates as the men approached, holding a dimming orb of light. Simons paused at the sight of him, eyes fixed on the slim black DDC suit.

"This is Ajay Kumar, DDC systems analyst," Zayd said with a proud smile.

Simons licked his lips, clearly unnerved by the other man's uniform.

"They said I should travel in uniform. In case there was an issue, I could claim to be on official business, at least for a moment," Ajay explained.

"Johnson says this guy is real important to the cause. He's paying me triple what he did last time to pull this off," Zayd added, excitement gleaming in his eyes.

"Kumar, do you know where you're headed from here?" Simons asked, ignoring Zayd's additional information.

Ajay straightened his shoulders. "To the Institute, where I will spend the next five to ten years learning about their key security systems along with two other officers and reporting critical information. If I'm suspected or caught, I'll have to spend a great deal of time in hiding, likely in isolation, until the DDC ceases hunting for me or presumes I'm dead."

Zayd wondered if he wanted to know so much information about what Mr. Kumar was up to. By the look on Simons' face, he thought he was wondering the same thing. But he'd asked, probably to measure if Kumar was a spy or an actual dissenter refugee.

"Why aren't they just sending you through inter-city transportation?" Simons asked.

It was a valid question that Zayd was embarrassed not to have thought of on his own. Suddenly, Zayd realized the long pole Simons was carrying had a blade at the end of it.

"It's a dissenter placement. It's not a formal transfer," Ajay said, keeping his eyes on the blade at the end of Simons' pole like he knew it'd been there the whole time.

"What's the deal, man?" Zayd asked, turning to Simons.

"We don't transport DDC folks," Simons said, not taking his eyes off Kumar.

"I'm not DDC, I'm dissenter," Ajay insisted. His hands were up now, and he was backing away from Zayd and Simons. "The DDC position is how we're going to get the inside information we need."

Simons didn't move. His forearm flexed as he gripped the pole.

"There are more of us," Ajay said, speaking faster now. "On the inside. We're making our way in so we don't have to guess at what's going on anymore. So we can start acting instead of reacting. There are people in the capitol, at the Institute, and soon, we'll be in the Northern Laboratories, too."

"You hear that, Simons? It sounds like this thing is really growing," Zayd said, putting a hand up against the man's rock-hard exterior.

The blade on the pole retracted.

"I need to make some calls," Simons said.

Ajay slumped with relief. Zayd let out a nervous chuckle.

"I guess I should have expected I'd be earning my credits on this one."

"Do you mind putting your hands out?" Simons asked. It was a question, but Zayd didn't think there was much room to decline.

"My hands?" Ajay asked.

"I'd like to search you before I make those calls. Out of an abundance of caution, let's say," Simons explained.

"You may search me," Ajay conceded.

"Good. Good," Simons said, pointing the pole at Kumar. "Your hands?"

Ajay raised them toward Simons, struggling to suppress the slight tremor. Simons moved the pole over the man's hands with a swirling motion, and the thin wires sticking out from the top suddenly glowed with electricity, wrapping around them, binding them.

"Is this necessary?" Zayd asked.

"We don't stay a secret group if we trust the wrong people," Simons said, leading them all out the back of the vehicle.

Simons left Zayd holding the pole, which he called a lashing pole, while he stepped into his own vehicle to make a call. Zayd fidgeted, keeping his finger far away from the engage button as he sat across from their refugee/DDC prisoner on the damp forest floor.

"Do you have any family?" Zayd asked, unable to stand the silence.

"I have parents, of course," Ajay said, giving Zayd a nervous glance.

"No, I mean a partner, kids—the whole happy family?" Zayd corrected with a laugh.

"Oh," Ajay said, understanding the question. "No. People in positions like mine don't have families."

"People in the DDC don't have families?"

"Dissenters don't have families," Ajay clarified, lifting his hands and shifting his legs in an attempt to get comfortable.

Zayd pushed the pole forward to give the man enough slack to reposition himself. He didn't think Kumar was much of a threat and was just waiting for Simons to make his call so he could come back and apologize. "Why not have a family?"

Ajay pulled a knee up, finally resting his bound hands against it and looking Zayd in the eye. "What we do is risky enough. There's no need to bring more people into that risk."

"They don't need to know what you do," Zayd protested, rejecting the notion that what he was doing could be dangerous to Anika. It was his neck on the line, not hers. And even then, it's not like he was doing anything serious like infiltrating the Institute's information systems. He was just driving a transport vehicle!

"It's not only about what they don't know. It's dangerous in more ways than saying the wrong thing to the wrong person. It's about the risks we take out here, too," Ajay said.

"You mean like infection?" Zayd asked. It was the one thing he hadn't been worried about, but maybe he'd been wrong.

"Infection. Attack. This space out here between City States is the DDC's war zone. They are conquering it," Ajay said.

"It's all barren, abandoned space. What's left to conquer?" Zayd fidgeted, not tending to the pole sitting in his lap.

"Do you really think every last member of the communities living outside the force fields fled to safety during the last outbreak?"

Zayd hadn't thought about it. As usual, he felt like a fool for not considering the world as deeply as everyone else. He'd just taken it for granted right up until the Resistee movement started getting blamed for every new ordinance.

Simons' door slammed shut as the two men spoke. They watched his approach, and Zayd could tell by the big man's expression that all was well, which was good because his insides were suddenly in turmoil. His hands fell to the pole in his lap, and he fumbled it back into his grasp. He would not be the reckless fool in yet another critical situation. "We good?"

"We're good," Simons confirmed, stooping over to take the lashing pole. He pressed the button to release the electric current, and the bindings around Ajay's hands came undone. "But we can never be careful enough when it comes to this sort of thing. It's more than your life or mine. There's a whole lot of folks whose lives are on the line."

"That's what I was telling Mr. Baba. To be a dissenter is to put your life in the hands of the cause," Ajay said, standing to brush himself off.

"To finding the truth?" Zayd asked, head spinning.

"To taking back control," Simons corrected.

"You mean from fear of the disease?" Zayd asked, trying to get back on solid ground again. He knew about the fear and manipulation —how the authorities and the DDC kept people scared to keep them from wanting to know more and do more. He lived through the impact of the city clear-outs.

"From the disease itself," Ajay said.

Zayd stared hard.

"If there's no disease, what is there left to fear?" Simons asked.

"And that's why dissenters don't have families. There is too much at stake. A dissenter with a family might risk the wrong thing—the family for the cause, or the cause for their family," Ajay concluded.

"I've got a family," Zayd said, overwhelmed by the wash of emotions, both hot and cold, that flooded through him. He shoved his hands into his pockets. Maybe he'd made a terrible mistake to get involved, even if he agreed with what they were doing. He wasn't even sure he'd done it for the right reasons. Sure, he wanted the truth. He wanted to understand who was benefiting the most from keeping people locked up and afraid. But mostly he wanted the credits. He didn't want Ani to have to work so much once the baby was here. He'd been telling her he was due for a big promotion.

"You've got kids?" Simons asked, sounding genuinely curious.

"Not yet… or, not that we know of yet," Zayd said. The hot and cold feeling solidified into a sick churning in his gut.

Simons raised his eyebrows. "That close, eh?"

"That close," Zayd agreed.

"That's a good thing," Ajay said, seeming to contradict what he'd said only moments before.

"You just said dissenters couldn't have a family…" Zayd puzzled.

"Not for a job on the inside, but a transport guy like you? Having a family makes you look like a paid idiot. Someone who was doing favors with no questions for a few extra credits and a cozy life for some kiddies," Ajay said.

The cold-hot sick feeling shot electric pulses down Zayd's arms as he realized how everyone else must see him—how Johnson told him he should appear, and how he'd gotten out of the accident on his first run. He really was a credit-hungry idiot who couldn't take care of his burgeoning family without the extra work.

Simons interrupted his train of thought with a gentle hand on his shoulder. "None of us here think that. Dissenters recognize each other for what we are. We're the ones who are trying to make a difference."

"Do you have a family?" Zayd asked.

"I've got a someone," Simons said, eyes sparkling with affection.

"Kids?" Zayd asked, as if Simons having a family could change the implications of his.

"No kids," he said easily. "She's out Institute-way, and they do something to them that keeps it from happening."

"Where do we go from here?" Zayd asked, not wanting to let the conversation go any further into territory that made him question what he was doing or why he was doing it.

Simons put a hand on Ajay's shoulder. "I'll be driving Mr. Kumar to just outside the Institute, where a contact will meet us and collect him. I'll then be taking some goods to the next city for the next contact, and so on and so forth. You'll drive the rest of these goods to their destination and return home without incident this time, and you and I won't see much of each other until the next guy makes his way onto Johnson's roster. But I don't imagine that will happen for some time if we're making a man of Kumar's rank disappear this time."

It sounded so simple. Like when Johnson explained what the dissenters did and how they did it. Zayd didn't think he'd ever think of it like that again after this assignment.

He swallowed hard, trying to grasp for a way to be useful. "I made some plates before I left. Let's all have a bite before we take off."

CHAPTER
Sixteen

PARK

DAY ONE IN THE L-WING, and already Park was in over her head. There hadn't been time to process Garth's news—not the details of her assignment nor the shock of learning her condition.

How could she be pregnant? Didn't all interns have the sterilization procedure? The one that was supposed to prevent it?

Garth said there were errors sometimes because the human body is tricky and resilient. He guessed that she and Reed had just gotten lucky.

Lucky? Park wasn't sure that was the right word for it. An unlikely statistical outcome, maybe. If only she could figure out what it meant for her—for her position at the Institute, for her safety, for the... *life* growing inside of her, unbidden and, until these last few days, completely unknown.

"Are you listening?" Maddoux asked, crossing her arms so the top of her lab coat revealed the trim black suit underneath.

"Yes, of course. I apologize; I didn't sleep well last night," Park said, snapping her eyes up to focus on the severe woman. It was true that she hadn't slept well. She was up half the night vomiting despite Garth's little white pills. At least she felt fine now.

"Is something troubling you?" Maddoux asked.

"Troubling? No… only perhaps that I'm eager to do well. I'm excited for the position and don't want to mess anything up," Park said, rubbing her hand across her freshly trimmed hair. She thought this would fit well. Garth had said they'd like her coming in green from the intern program.

Maddoux nodded slowly, taking her in. Park hoped she wasn't focused on the red rims around her eyes or the way her heart beat rapidly inside her chest like she was a trapped rabbit. *Does it have a heartbeat yet?* She wondered before forcing the thought out of her mind. It wasn't time for that line of speculation. Garth would want a full report of what she was about to experience, and Park had a feeling the quality of her care might depend on how well she performed—both as a new L-wing medic and as a double agent.

"I only said I'd be changing out your key card so you'll have access without an escort," Maddoux repeated, still watching her.

"Oh, that will be fine. I didn't realize you wanted a response," Park said. She *had* heard after all.

"You'll report to the medic-in-charge at the start of each of your shifts. They will give you your assignment list for the day. You are to follow it explicitly—no impromptu treatments. Things run a little differently in the L-wing than the rest of the medical facility," Maddoux said, guiding Park down the hall.

"I understand. I still need approval for impromptu treatments in the general medical facility, anyway," Park said before correcting herself. "Needed, that is."

Maddoux glanced back at her and offered a curt nod. "The transition should be easy then. The biggest difference is of course the added precaution and testing. We're dealing with a new development in here."

At the mention of the purpose of the L-wing, Park perked up, though she tried to do so without being obvious. "Is it a new strain?" she ventured.

"For now, you're on a need-to-know basis. The purpose of the L-wing is currently classified to the highest level of security. You'll be versed in the additional safety precautions so you may conduct yourself correctly, but that will be all until you've trained through and received proper clearance," Maddoux said before scanning her ID at a doorway. The light blinked green, and the lock clicked. Maddoux pushed her way through the door and urged Park to follow. She did so without hesitation, knowing it was expected of her.

A medic with jet-black, close-cropped hair and rounded cheeks stood upon their entry. "Maddoux," he greeted formally before turning his head to take Park in. "Is this our new addition?"

"Handpicked by Garth," Maddoux said with an edge of pride in her voice. Clearly Garth was well regarded by at least one DDC official. Park wondered if anyone had even the slightest idea that he was spying on their clandestine operation.

"Wonderful." The medic smiled, turning his attention to Park. "I'm Dr. Wong. I'm in charge of morning shift on a four-day cycle. Luckily, you're starting on day two, so I'll be able to give you a little consistency before the switch."

There was that word again—as if any of this had anything to do with *luck*. She gave him a polite nod. "Park."

Dr. Wong's face brightened with a sheepish half-grin that erased at least ten years. He addressed Maddoux. "She's awful young?"

"A transfer from the intern program. We're quite pleased with the selection. She has excellent scores and several months now in the general medical sector. We feel the transfer should go smoothly," Maddoux affirmed.

"Very good then," Dr. Wong said.

"She's level four clearance, so nothing on the trials. Start her with simple clinical, and we'll go from there," Maddoux said, stepping back toward the door as though she were suddenly very eager to end the meeting.

"Got it. I'll make certain. Thanks for the delivery. We sure could use the staffing," Dr. Wong oozed. Park noted that Wong's cheerful disposition managed to almost turn Maddoux friendly. Almost.

The DDC official excused herself, leaving Park to the instruction of Dr. Wong. She couldn't help but feel grateful. Though Wong was yet another superior, his easy friendliness didn't put her on edge the way the DDC official had. If she'd be working with people like him, maybe the position wouldn't be so bad after all.

The door shut, and the lock clicked back into place. Park tore her eyes away from it and tried to force herself to focus on Dr. Wong.

"You're looking a little green," he said, gathering some things from the desk.

"Am I?" Park asked, swallowing back a random churn of bile. "I guess I'm nervous—or excited." *If only he knew.*

Dr. Wong laughed. "I suppose that's to be expected. Not every day an intern gets such a sudden promotion." He looked over at her and winked. "If you could call it that. Come on, I'll introduce you to our patients."

Park followed him out the door and back into the white-tiled hallway. She had a feeling she'd be doing a lot of following in the days to come.

"The patients in the L-wing are a bit different from the main medical facility," Dr. Wong said.

"How so?" Park asked. She had to quicken her step to keep up with him.

"Most of them don't seem very sick. That's part of the problem—and part of what makes it so dangerous."

He stopped at a marked door. Park recognized the digital numbering that denoted what patient resided within. Dr. Wong put his hands into the holes in the wall to don the thick, blue, elbow-length gloves. Park followed suit before he slid his ID card and opened the door.

Park was used to the screams. In the main medical wing, they all wailed. It was a mixture of the physical pain and the mental agony of knowing what was happening to them. But this room was quiet save for the soft music wafting from somewhere near the bed.

"Good morning, David," Dr. Wong greeted, ushering Park through the doorway.

An older man sat at the base of the bed, his bare feet pale against the white tile. His hair was thin but well brushed. He looked up at them with bright blue eyes, his face covered in a few days' worth of grey stubble. "Dr. Wong!" he greeted. "Good to see you again."

Park didn't know what to think. In the main medical area, all the patients were bedridden. They knew they were sick, and no one referred to them by their names. This man was sitting on his bed as though he'd just returned from a morning stroll, bright and cheerful… and he might be dangerous.

"We're just here to do the routine checks, as usual. This is Park. She's our newest," Dr. Wong said. He turned to unlock a cabinet filled with supplies. Park watched David with morbid fascination. He seemed so normal. Dr. Wong seemed so at ease with him. She couldn't believe he'd turn his back.

David studied Park while Dr. Wong pulled swabs from the cabinet. Park was completely divided between the curiously well-seeming but probably dangerous man sitting on the bed and Dr. Wong's growing stack of materials.

"Dr. Park—" David began.

"No, it's just Park," she said, then blushed. She didn't know what made the difference in a medic's status between basic medic and doctor at the Institute.

"Alright then, Park, tell me about yourself," David said, crossing one leg over the other. That's when Park noticed the ankle braces. They confined him to the bed area. She suspected they might give him leave to use the restroom in the opposite corner, but that was it. Now she understood why Dr. Wong was so at ease.

"What do you want to know?" Park asked, still feeling foolishly out of sorts. The words *I'm pregnant* danced on the tip of her tongue because they kept screaming over and over in her mind. She wouldn't be saying *that*.

"Do you like music?" David asked.

Park blinked. "Music? I suppose I do."

Dr. Wong turned with his arms full of equipment. "David here is a music aficionado. He collects it from the old world and new."

"What you're hearing now? That's a song from twentieth-century America," David said enthusiastically.

"He's not supposed to have access to restricted materials, but in the L-wing, we bend the rules for our best patients," Dr. Wong said, winking at Park again.

Park noted that Dr. Wong was a winker. She decided to store that information in case it became useful, then realized that she hadn't responded. She swallowed hard, not knowing what to do with herself.

"David, if you would? You know the routine," Dr. Wong said.

"Oh, right. For you, Dr. Wong, I won't complain." David sighed before scooting back on the bed and placing his hands against two metallic cuffs.

The cuffs closed automatically around his wrists with synchronous electronic clicks. Dr. Wong placed the equipment on the tray by the bed and began sorting it, urging Park over to his side.

"Thanks, David. Now, Park—we're going to do a series of swabs, a draw, and a physical scan. David knows the routine, and he's pretty good about it. That's why I picked him as our first patient for the day," Dr. Wong explained, picking up the nasal swab suspended on a long, thin wire.

"You picked me first? I'm honored!" David chuckled.

Dr. Wong pulled down his face shield, and Park did the same. He tipped back David's head and pointed the swab up. "Never do this without the face shield—you don't want to get what they've got."

"Is he infected?" Park asked.

"Most assuredly!" Dr. Wong said.

"He shows no symptoms—no manifestation," she objected.

"That's the crux of the issue," Dr. Wong said, plunging the swab up David's nose. The patient flinched against the assault. "He's got positive blood markers with no progressive manifestation. It's our job to track him until we know why."

Park wondered if that was level four clearance sort of information. She didn't dare ask the question though, in case it wasn't. Either way, she was happy to have at least one thing to report to Garth after this.

Dr. Wong retracted the swab. David wiggled his nose. His eyes watered, and he looked like he wished he could rub his face. "Man, that stings," he said.

"Sorry, David. Worst is over." He plunged the swab into a holding liquid and broke off the wire tip. The vial had an automatic sealing cap and a digital ID number. Dr. Wong inverted the liquid over the swab, then placed it in the outgoing pile.

"Now, let's get some blood," he said, pulling the butterfly needle from the stack.

Seventeen

MORA AND JAMES

"I'M SO proud of you, James. Qualifying for the Institute is such an honor!" Mora's mother, Morgan Rossi-Stern, gushed as the three of them sat down at the dinner table. She turned to Mora, who was barely paying attention, her mind still reeling from what had happened on the roof before Omen landed. "Aren't you proud of him, dear? Isn't it an honor to befriend someone so… accomplished?"

Mora turned her head so her mother couldn't see her roll her eyes. "It really is great for Jim."

"And his family!" Morgan added.

Yeah, I get it, Mom. I'm letting you down as an insufficient offspring, Mora thought as she reached for the bowl of lightly dressed mixed greens. She couldn't look either of them in the eye.

"Thanks, Ms. Rossi, but I'm sure Mora could pass, too, if she wanted to petition for a Retest," James said. His cheeks were crimson, which made his whole sweet, round face look flushed.

Morgan beamed at the statement, jerking her head over to Mora and gasping, "Are you going to petition?"

Mora flinched. *Way to go, Jim. I'm never living this down.* "I wasn't planning on it. I think Jim overestimates my potential."

Suddenly, she was able to look her best friend in his traitorous eyes again, so she gave him a stare that was meant to be icy and hateful, but he just smiled.

"Well, I don't think there's any harm in giving it one more shot. Maybe James is right, honey. You don't know unless you try," Morgan ventured, looking pleadingly at her daughter.

"Yeah. All you have to do is *try*," James parroted. Mora knew he thought she was throwing the Tests by not caring. Hadn't he heard that was supposed to be impossible?

"I just don't think it's in the cards for me," Mora said. All the while, she was thinking, *I'm more the write-covert-messages-on-encoded-paper-and-send-them-out-of-the-city-with-my-illegal-pet-raven type of girl. You know? The type who owns illegal contraband that would make Mom's DDC heart stop? That's more me. I'm not Institute.* But there was no way to actually say it. Sure, she could say it to James, but not to her mom. She studied the woman, who was still wearing her DDC suit at the dinner table despite having time to change. Daughter or no, her mother would immediately report her. That's the kind of person she was.

"Well, I think James is right, and you have my full support if you decide to petition," Morgan said, meaning to conclude the matter.

"I'll take that under advisement," Mora mumbled. She gave James another sour look that only made him smile back at her hopefully.

"When is graduation this year, anyway?" Morgan asked, changing the subject. She should know, Mora thought. Everyone else's mom knew when their seventeen-year-old children were going to graduate, but not Morgan Rossi-Stern. She was far too important to keep a date like that in mind. She was far too important to realize how miserable her daughter was.

"September 12," James offered.

Mora wanted to strangle him, even if he was her best and only friend.

"That doesn't give you a lot of time before you're off to the Institute!" Morgan proclaimed.

Mora thought it was fitting that she reacted to Jame's future without even considering what September 12 meant for her.

"No, it doesn't. But I'm sure I'll be prepared by the time it comes around."

She half expected him to add, *especially if Mora goes with me*, and if he had, she might have decided to murder him with her fork right then and there. Lucky for him, he didn't, so she didn't have to kill her best friend in front of her mom after all.

"What a mature attitude," Morgan oozed. Mora wanted to gag at her mom's fake voice and the way she seemed to suck up to James. As far as she could tell, it was the same Jim who had been over last month for dinner—the one her mom hadn't given a second thought to. But not anymore. Not now that he was an *Institute man*. She plunged her fork into one of the nondescript squares of over-baked chicken, wondering if this one had been processed personally by Mr. Richard Dunn himself.

The dinner table was quiet for a few moments except for the *tink* of silverware against plates and the occasional clunk of a glass returning to the table. Mora preferred it to the awkward conversation. She never had to talk to her mom when they didn't have company. And what was she supposed to say to Jim now? She'd told him! She'd told him after all this time, and then Omen showed up and there was the message that wouldn't tie right onto his leg, and they had to rush back into the apartment before her mom got home demanding to know why they were on the fire escape and *who pried out those screws?* Then the little bits of freedom that made Mora's existence worthwhile would be dashed away.

"Oh, sweetie, I'm going to be out on assignment again this week-end," Morgan said, interrupting Mora's spiraling thoughts.

Okay, we also talk when she has to tell me she's going, Mora corrected her earlier assessment.

"How long this time?" Mora asked after swallowing the dry pulp that was supposed to be meat. Maybe chicken had always tasted this way and her mom was a terrible cook, but she didn't think so. She thought it had to do with the fact that chickens shouldn't grow up in factory buildings. Maybe she should ask Mr. Dunn what they did to the poor chickens to make them turn out this way.

"Four days, according to the schedule."

Mora nodded.

"Where are you going this time, Ms. Rossi?" James piped in.

Mora wondered if his parents put him up to this level of polite chatter. Sure, James was polite, but it always seemed so over the top when it came to her mom.

"We're doing an off-site population survey and reporting it directly to the president," Morgan replied.

It was meant to sound nonchalant, but Mora knew that tone all too well. She was bragging. Her mom liked to flaunt the power her position gave her. Mora hated that about her. It made her seem cold and evil.

Or maybe Morgan really was cold and evil. It was, perhaps, the thing Mora was most afraid of—that her mom was more of a shell of a person than an actual person. That she really was incapable of love and compassion.

Mora stood suddenly from the table, unable to tolerate the company or the activity a second longer. Her chair made more noise than she meant for it to, causing James and Morgan to look up abruptly.

"I'm done. My, um, my stomach has been bothering me," she mumbled, excusing herself.

Morgan watched her take her full plate into the kitchen and dump the contents into the trash. She opened her mouth as if she were about to say something, but nothing came out.

James glanced from Morgan to Mora and back again before popping up out of his own seat. "I think I'm done, too. Thanks so much for dinner, Ms. Rossi, but Mora and I have a few assignments we need to work on."

Before James could excuse himself, Mora slammed the door to her room. Morgan reached out and squeezed his forearm. "James. So responsible. I'm so proud of you."

James swallowed and waited for Mora's mom to release his arm, but she didn't. He tried not to squirm. He knew his parents would be mortified if he did anything to mess this up right now. He cleared his throat. "Umm, Ms. Rossi?"

She squeezed his forearm again, as if she hadn't heard him, and continued, "Would you like for me to put in a good word for you with the Institute branch?"

Inside his head, his parents' voices urged him to agree and thank her for the incredible offer. But it felt wrong. And he knew what Mora would think—what she would say to him if he let her mom get involved in his future. A future suddenly devoid of Mora.

I don't like boys.

"I really appreciate the offer, Ms. Rossi, but I don't think that's appropriate. I'll go into the Institute like everyone else."

Her face shifted into stone, and her hand dropped away from his arm. "Of course. So responsible," she said again with an icy voice.

"Thank you," he said, grabbing his plate and moving into the kitchen. He imagined Mora standing on the other side of her door, listening to them and hating him for the way her mother poured affection on him that she should have reserved for Mora. It was wrong, the way Ms. Rossi treated her. Even if she was a little strange, a little—defiant—she was still her daughter. She was still incredible!

He deposited his plate into the kitchen sink before turning to Mora's closed door. As he went, Morgan called out to him, "Your parents must be very pleased with you."

James turned, trapped between obligation and desire. "They absolutely are," he agreed.

Morgan nodded. "I know I would be."

James could practically feel Mora listening from the other room. The walls in the apartment were paper thin, the doors were practically hollow, and everyone knew you could hear right through them. Ms. Rossi knew Mora could hear her. "Did you see our papers from the history assignment? Mora's paper on the pre-closed-city communities was incredible. She should have gotten the top score. I'm sure you're very proud of her."

Her lips pressed into a fine line. "Mora is stubborn and unprofessional, and with her attitude and penchant for fantasy, she has no future."

James felt a flash of rage that Morgan would talk about her own daughter that way. He suppressed it and said, "She just feels lost sometimes. She doesn't feel like she belongs—"

"She thinks I don't know," Morgan said, her voice so low he might have misheard her.

James' heart skipped a beat. "What?"

"She thinks I don't know what she does—on the roof," Morgan clarified.

Immediately, James's mind flashed to the image of Omen retreating from the rooftop with the slip of paper tied to his foot. Where was he taking the message? How did Morgan know about it? Had she planted him there to entrap her own daughter? His tongue turned to sandpaper in his mouth.

Morgan laughed. "Don't look so surprised! I know you knew about it."

"I don't—I didn't—" James stammered, not certain what he was planning to say.

"And you're worried I'm going to turn you in right along with her," Mora whispered in a sing-song voice.

James froze. He hadn't considered the possibility. What would it do to his parents if she reported him? What would it do to his future? His qualification for the Institute?

Morgan gripped his arm with an icy hand, pulling him toward her so their eyes were level. "Do you think I would report my own daughter?" she demanded.

He did.

"I know you love her very much," he said.

"What sort of a reflection would that be on me?" Morgan said. James could feel the puffs of her breath against his cheek. That Morgan wouldn't report Mora should be a relief, but something warned him not to dare. He was right.

"I'll keep her and your little rooftop secret so long as you promise me one little thing," she said.

"What is it?" he asked, his voice revealing his terror.

"I need Mora to attend the Institute."

James felt a sick rush of dismay. "She needs to pass the Test," he protested.

"I know that. But in order to pass the Test, she first needs to petition. I can't convince her to do that, but you, dear boy—we both know how she feels about you. I always turn a blind eye when her door shuts behind you, don't I? You convince her." Morgan kept her face so close to his that it felt damp from the deluge of exhaled moisture. It was uncomfortable and so, so unsanitary.

"Even if she petitions and they let her take it again... she has to pass it," James said.

Morgan pressed her cheek against James' face, her lips actually touching the side of his ear. James stared straight past her into the hallway, where yellow light glowed under Mora's closed door. "You can take care of that, too, can't you?"

"QUARANTINE? Why would she need to go to quarantine?" Sophia scoffed, shooting an unmasked derisive look at Cora.

She stepped into the med room, ignoring Cora's warning, and wrapped a still-gloved hand around Anika's shoulders.

"You shouldn't be touching her. She could be infected! I'm going to have to test you now, too," Cora moaned.

Anika's head swam with woozy panic. Her face was pale, her hands clammy as she struggled to make sense of what Cora was saying.

Quarantine. She might be infected.

"Anika, you need to sit down. You look like you're going to pass out," Sophia said, urging her onto the exam table.

Anika complied, her knees buckling out from under her as she struggled to suck in enough air through the bars constricting her chest.

"I'm going to be sick!" she panted.

Sophia handed her the emesis bag without breaking her hold—a practiced clinician tending to a squeamish first-time client. "I've got you. It's just the pills. Those pills do a number on just about everything about you. That's what Eedie says. That and Cora probably freaked you out," she said, ignoring the fact that Cora was standing right behind her.

Anika vomited into the bag, once, twice, then a third wave that made her gasp for breath as the foul taste lingered at the back of her mouth. Her throat burned, and her head throbbed with the pressure of it. She panted shallow breaths, begging it to be over.

"Vomit is a biological fluid, still considered contagious despite its acidic nature," Cora warned.

"It's fine. I'm still wearing my gloves, Cora. This is what we do. Anika isn't the first client to puke on the exam table," Sophia said, taking the bag from Anika and sealing it into the secondary container before waving her hand over the bio-waste sensor and pitching it through the opening that appeared before her.

Anika wobbled as Sophia's hold loosened. Everything felt unreal. Like it was happening around her instead of to her. A bad dream where she couldn't run or scream or even move at all.

"Did she tell you about her nails?" Cora demanded, still standing back from them, looking on with a combination of fear and derision.

"Her nails?" Sophia asked, confusion breaking through her implacable expression.

"You can see them from here," Cora said. Her voice was colder, the fear that had laced it only moments earlier now slipping beneath her Institute-polished surface.

Anika's gut clenched again as Sophia glanced down at the greyish tint of her nails. Their eyes met in a wordless exchange. Question, concern, trust.

"It's just a stain. That always happens when she paints her nails," Sophia said.

Only when I paint them black, and it's always gone by now, Anika thought. Sophia knew it. Until recently, they always did their nails together. But Sophia wasn't scared. Anika had seen it in her expression —the confidence that this was just Cora freaking out, not her worst nightmare come to life.

"The scanner reported an error. It coded it as out of healthy range," Cora pressed.

"When is the last time you read the SOP for the scanners? Clients wearing polish are disqualified from physical examination until nails are cleaned and treated," Sophia countered.

"Why do you even wear it? Altering the body's natural pigmentation is an unsafe practice," Cora demanded.

Anika was feeling a little better. Maybe it was the nausea passing, or the undying trust and support of Sophia standing with her in the room.

"Temporary body alterations such as nail polish and makeup are allowed when community risk is below yellow. We've been in a phase of low-to-minimal risk for six years now. You can buy polish at the primary market these days. We're in the green!" Sophia thrust her bright pink nails at Cora as if to prove her point.

Anika was watching Cora's face now, and she was seeing what Sophia refused to see—what Zayd insisted wasn't going to happen again—not now or ever, the way things went these days.

"We aren't in the green anymore, are we?" she asked, seeing the truth before Cora answered.

It was obvious, given the reports from the last month, the reduced clients, Ms. Fitzpatrick. Sophia could see the truth, too, now that she was looking.

"What is it? Yellow? Caution and quarantine for high-risk workers?" Sophia asked.

It was worse than that, Anika knew. It had to be to produce the numbers their clinic was seeing.

"Red," Cora said.

The word fell on a silent room, too terrible to fathom.

Community spread. Imminent lockdown. In-city outbreak.

"No," Sophia whispered.

"How?" Anika breathed.

"It's classified for now," Cora said.

"You can't classify an outbreak!" Sophia whirled on Cora. Standing a full head taller and with her braids pulled into an impossibly high ponytail, Sophia loomed, imposing. But it was just an image—a mask for her fear.

"This is different. This is something else," Cora scrambled to explain.

"You mean it's not Zoribiatus?" Anika asked, hope daring to rise above her churning fear.

"It is," Cora said, dashing out the glimmer of hope.

"You aren't making sense. I'm going to call the DDC Office of Infection!" Sophia snapped, trying to brush past Cora and out of the room.

"It's a new strain," Cora said, putting her hands up to stop Sophia from leaving. "A new strain of Zoribiatus that isn't acting like the other ones. They're trying to track it down and catch it quietly."

"But people could die if the disease progresses," Anika objected.

"That's the thing. This one isn't progressing—to a point."

The women were listening now, sobered by Cora's earnest expression and the damning implications of what she was suggesting.

"We're trying to catch it early and trace it through community contact until we've got things under control. We don't want a panic. We can't have a panic. That's why I've been in the records. We're working on the list of community contact, and Anika—you're on the list." Cora gave her what was supposed to be a sympathetic expression, but the look stopped at the crinkle of her eyes. Within those folds, her eyes remained as dark and cold as the boundless nights.

"How could this happen?" she whispered, reaching for Sophia's gloved hand for support.

Sophia had moved to clasp her hands behind her back, and Anika wondered if the act was subconscious.

"I'm not at liberty to share that with you. But Anika, I can't let you leave here until we've got results." Cora nodded toward Sophia as she stepped away from the exam table.

Anika's heart sank. She knew what this meant for her—for all of them.

"Okay. Alright. That's fine. I just wonder if... Sophia?"

"Yes?" Sophia asked, quick to respond and ease the guilt she felt for abandoning her friend, for stepping away even if it was done in self-preservation.

"Could you ring the factory for Zayd?" Anika asked.

Cora would let her do that. The second Zayd knew what was happening, he'd come. His shift leader would let him. They were close, and he knew what the couple had been working toward. And when

Zayd got here, Cora would let him come to her—she'd have to because if she was at risk then so was he. Zayd would need to be tested, and then they'd know.

But at least they'd know together.

"I'll call right now," Sophia said, looking relieved to leave the room.

"I'll get Med Room 2 set up for your draw," Cora said, following Sophia out of the room. She stopped long enough to shut the door. The lock clicked in place, leaving Anika alone.

She looked around the room, trying to orient herself—to ground herself in something that would help things make sense. She had been exposed. To a new strain of Zoribiatus. *By whom?*

It had been more than a hundred years since Zoribiatus began ravaging societies. With decades of research, there were facts Anika knew to be reliably true: community spread was rare and most often happened when people were working closely with someone they didn't know to be infected—through fluids, like when dressing a wound without personal protection, through sexual transmission with a person with progressed infection, or through contaminated equipment. Infection without community contact was rare, but possible through contaminated water sources—community pools or showers. During early outbreaks, there had been a large number of medical infections—organ donation, blood transfusions, tissue grafting. She shuddered at the thought of how devastating the spread must have been before people knew what they were dealing with.

Once the disease had spread widely enough, things were so much worse—families caring for their sick, not realizing what would happen once the disease reached the brain and began its sinister work. Even for those the disease had not touched, there was the terror of not knowing if it was safe to leave the house. The danger of open spaces and of not knowing if you could trust the people living under the same roof. So much devastation. So much death.

They'd learned a lot since then—developed informed societies with customs formed around the evidence-based principles of safety. Community spread was supposed to be a thing of the past. Everyone knew how to be safe. Even the people who could still remember stories of the old world understood why things must be the way they were now. Because through all the iterations of disease—through the first outbreak that nearly destroyed the world, to the second, which threatened people's burgeoning trust in one another and the emerging society, there was one thing that never changed, no matter what scientists learned about the disease. Despite the leadership's best efforts—the scientific intern program at the Institute, the DDC and the work in the Northern Laboratories—the disease was always fatal, and there was no cure. Zoribiatus remained, always a threat. That was fundamental to life now.

Anika knew the next steps if she was infected. It was fundamental to the education she'd undergone to become a level-two medic at the clinic. If she was infected, Sophia would step into the room garbed in level four personal protection.

She would explain to Anika that a medical transport vehicle was on its way, and she would be required to board it and head to the Institute for medical treatment. She had seen the video the newly diagnosed patients watched, explaining necessary treatment and medical research, along with the inevitable subjection to cryogenic treatment and transportation to the Northern Laboratories to participate in and benefit from cure research.

Or would Cora do it in her place?

Anika felt the familiar tendrils of panic as she thought about who would come through the door next. She felt trapped. She *was* trapped. Though any clinic worker could code in to the exam room, once it had been locked by a clinician, not even a medical ID could open the door from the inside.

"This might still be a mistake," Anika told herself. Her voice sounded hollow and flat to her own ears in the empty room. It should have echoed against the tile floors, but it was dampened, perhaps by the fog of fear that thickened the air.

Her nails could be stained from a bad batch of polish, but if there truly was community spread, that was unlikely. Even though Anika hadn't had any illicit contact with anyone since her last test, she had undergone a number of intimate procedures.

And then there was Zayd…

There was a gentle tap on the door before Sophia stuck her head through. She still looked mostly like herself, but Anika saw the mask of apprehension stretched across her smooth brown skin.

"How are you doing?" Sophia asked in a soothing voice.

"Terrible," Anika confessed.

"Of course. But I have some bad news, and I hate to put it to you like that." Sophia hesitated at the admission.

"What is it?" Anika pressed, a sick feeling cementing her to the exam table.

Sophia paused, and the seconds of silence stretching between them made Anika feel as if she were spiraling away from reality and everything she knew. Finally, Sophia said, "I couldn't get hold of Zayd."

CHAPTER

Nineteen

PARK

"JUST TO BE CLEAR," Garth said, pacing back and forth in front of the swivel chair Park was planted in.

The exam room was empty except for the two of them. It was early morning again, before the first shift of workers took their stations. Park had just given Garth a report of her first week in the L-wing and was waiting for him to make the sense out of it that she could not.

"They are all infected, but none of them are ill?" he asked, as if repeating her statement might unravel the mystery.

"That's what Dr. Wong said, and it's written in their charts," Park confirmed, doing her best not to fidget with the buttons on her over-sized lab coat.

"Positive blood tests, visible manifestation—"

"Not all of them have visible manifestation of the disease," Park corrected, fingering the smooth edge of the button resting just below her abdomen and thinking about what grew beneath the multitude of layers.

"How is infection detected, then?" Garth asked, rubbing the uneven stubble left on his chin from a bad, two-day-old shave job.

"It's different for each of the patients I've seen. A positive test from a city screening clinic or a follow-up from a workplace injury… There's one woman who ended up here just because they couldn't diagnose her persistent wound—some sort of psoriasis—and the city doctors finally decided they ought to have the Institute take a look. She came in just last week," Park explained.

"How many from intake screening at the Institute?" Garth asked, referring to the prospective volunteers who arrived on site for rapid testing.

"I haven't met every patient yet, but none that I have met came from Institute testing," Park said.

Garth shook his head as if he could rid it of some troublesome thought. His glasses shifted down the bridge of his nose as he did, but no sooner did they slide than Garth had them back in their place. A fine sheen of sweat made the bald top of his head shine as he labored over the conundrum of the L-wing.

"None of them infected at the Institute? That seems unlikely to me, how about you?"

Park fussed on the button, wondering if she could worry it off the lab coat. He didn't really want her opinion. He was just using her presence as an excuse to process ideas. But when he didn't say anything further, Park scrambled to formulate a coherent facsimile of her own thoughts.

"Instances of infection have been down overall for the last few months," she said.

"I asked you if you thought it was likely for none of the L-wing patients to have come from Institute programs," Garth said, giving her a stern look that made her want to wither into oblivion.

"Institute infection rates are typically high—about four for every one city infection if we include the rapid screening patients..." She caught the widening of his eyes behind thick glasses and rushed to clarify her thoughts. "But I agree with you. If there's a new strain going around, we should see it at the Institute first. Even if it started in the cities—which should be unlikely—the spread should be centered around the Institute."

Garth nodded, finally ceasing his incessant pacing to drop down onto the stool across from where Park was seated. He was quiet, lost in thought, doing a thousand calculations at once in order to plot his next move. Park waited for him, stomach gurgling and unsettled despite having just taken another of the little white pills.

"Have you eaten anything today?" Garth asked.

"Ugh," Park said, the thick sound getting stuck in her throat as she scrunched her face at the notion of putting food onto the sick unrest that made her stomach dance.

"The nausea will improve if you quit letting yourself get so hungry," he admonished, sliding his stool back against a file cabinet. He opened the second drawer, pulling out a package of chocolate-covered graham cookies. Park recognized them as the same ones she used to save credits for back in the cities. Garth tore one end of the package open, taking one before handing them her way. She accepted after only a moment's hesitation, deciding it was worth the risk if a chocolate-dipped treat might make her feel less sick.

Her fingers began to melt the chocolate the instant they made contact. The cookie slipped in her grip as she took the first bite. It was instantly sweet and crumbly with just a whisper of bitter, dark flavors beneath. She thought these cookies must be different from the ones she used to buy because those had never tasted quite this good.

The cookie was gone in two bites, and Park was reaching for another when Garth asked, "Have you decided what you want to do yet?"

The question made her heart leap against her chest. She glanced at the door as if she might be contemplating a hasty departure. Once she articulated her decision, there would be no going back. But there was nothing to go back to. There was no escaping this, even if she evaded Garth's question. She couldn't escape the inevitability of her situation —the thing growing and changing inside of her.

She swallowed the gummy, too-big mouthful of cookie, trying to clear the lump that formed in her throat.

"Not yet," she said, making sure her words were clear despite the dryness of the cookies. She used to eat these cookies by the half dozen, washing them down with a flavored beverage as she walked home with Reed after school. When the roads were clear, they would link fingers. It was an almost imperceptible breach in safety protocol—one they'd gotten away with a hundred or more times before their academic test results came in and they loaded into a transport for this new life.

Suddenly, and not for the first time, Park ached to be near Reed again. She wanted to feel his arms wrap around her as she pressed bare skin against his naked chest. She didn't care that it was what had gotten her into this mess in the first place. She couldn't do this without him. She couldn't make this decision alone.

"You want to talk to the fellow who helped you get here," Garth said, not needing her to voice her line of thinking.

"He deserves to know," she said.

"He can't do anything about it."

She turned away from this truth, incapable of handling Garth's unapologetic bluntness. The chocolate coating turned to mush against the wrapper coating as she gripped the cookie package too hard.

"He can't help you. He won't be around the Institute long enough to see it born, even if something like that were possible. Perhaps keeping it from him is a kindness."

"He didn't ask for this!" Park snapped. She locked in on Garth's unfeeling expression, hating the way he could speak so callously about her and Reed and this thing they now shared but couldn't share.

"Neither did you," Garth said, unfazed by her sudden anger.

"This wasn't supposed to happen," Park said, tears slipping down her rounded cheeks and mingling with the chocolate still staining her lips.

"I've been looking into that," Garth said, piquing her curiosity.

"Looking into what?" she asked, wiping a white sleeve across her leaking eyes.

"The procedure," Garth said, reaching for the crushed package of melted-chocolate cookies Park held in a death grip. She relinquished them, and Garth extracted a piece from one of the still mostly solid cookies. "I don't think the failure was an accident."

Park dropped her hand back to her lap to stare at the aging doctor. "What do you mean?"

"Look, I'm only telling you this because you need my help no matter what you decide. Now that you're in the L-wing under direct scrutiny from the DDC branch of the Institute, your life depends on keeping quiet. But there's more to it than that. What I'm about to divulge could not only ruin something we've been working on for a long time, it could get people killed—a *lot* of people."

Garth regarded her as if she were the least trustworthy person he'd ever encountered. He looked as though he were about to change his mind and send her back out to the L-wing without any information at all.

"I won't say a thing." She thought about mentioning Benji and the other volunteers—the way she kept their secrets—but decided better. They weren't fodder for her own negotiations, even if those negotiations were for her own life.

Garth read this in her silence, as if he could see the locked boxes she kept her secrets in, and approved. His expression never wavered from one of sour distrust, but when he spoke, she could hear the dismantling of his defenses. She was somehow on the inside of his trust circle now.

"Not everyone who works here is government through and through—even old government before the DDC takeover. Some of us are here because we don't have a choice, but that doesn't change what we believe. And as our numbers grow, some of us are starting to be here on purpose. We're climbing the ranks and making decisions behind shut curtains. Like a virus, we're infiltrating the DDC's systems and infrastructure to serve our own purposes and stay abreast of things."

He was still speaking around the truth, as if saying things plainly might somehow compromise the very existence of dissent within the Institute, but Park wasn't surprised by it. Since arriving at the Institute almost three years ago, she'd come to understand that everything here was dangerous.

"You're fighting back," she whispered.

"Shut up!" he demanded. "Doing something like this requires careful planning. It requires sacrifices."

Park got the sinking feeling she was beginning to understand what he was saying. *Sacrifices like me.* "Who was supposed to get pregnant?" she asked.

"We usually have a good idea of who is doing what in the intern program. We have eyes inside the dormitories, remote health monitoring… We catch things early when we want to, but you aren't in the dormitories, are you?"

Park swallowed back the feeling of the graham cookie trying to make its way back out. It wasn't the persistent nausea that plagued her every waking moment. This was emotional. It was the outcome of understanding washing over her.

"You're washing other interns—or maybe you already have. But you didn't account for me and Reed," she said.

"It was only supposed to be one, but we suspected there would be others. We thought there was only one other who we took care of. But since you're here, we were wrong," Garth confirmed.

Park understood. It was a clever plan, leaning heavily on the right-to-choose measure. Most people, given the environment of the Institute and the prestige of the scientist position, would choose to stay in the intern program. Anyone who washed would seem like just that—a wash from the program. Unqualified.

Park even thought she might know who it was. Emery. She could picture her—tall, reddish hair and intelligent smile, hung out with the outspoken intern—Mason. Always in trouble, always getting called into Professor Amos' office…

"Where did she go?" Park asked.

"You mean where did *they* go?"

Park's mouth dropped open, unbidden. She couldn't fathom the work that went into moving multiple interns without scrutiny.

"Emery and the Mason boy were sent to energy management. They'll be manning the fusion station outside the capitol with an exorbitant amount of scrutiny—at least for now," Garth said.

"They've gone already?" Park asked, stunned that something so big could happen and she didn't even know. It reminded her how removed she was from the other interns now. It also meant Reed hadn't thought to tell her. The realization stung.

"We sent all energy management out early to keep things quiet," Garth said.

Park nodded, understanding how profoundly she'd been left behind—what a problem she was for Garth and the others now that she remained, a beacon for whatever they'd done in secret and thought they'd gotten away with.

"I need to talk to him," Park insisted.

Garth made a sour face. "We need to keep this quiet!"

"You moved Emery and Mason together. You gave them the choice!" Park snatched the package of cookies from the doctor's hands, deciding that she was hungry now and he was keeping sustenance from her for nefarious purposes.

"They knew before this started. It was a calculated move. We thought we had the collateral under control," Garth said, as if he could justify their actions.

She crammed a whole cookie into her mouth, mashing it against her teeth with a thrust of her tongue and making Garth wait for her to chew and swallow. She was angry, so angry. It didn't matter what they were trying to accomplish within the Institute. It didn't matter what ills the DDC was executing behind closed doors. No plan should risk an entire intern cohort getting pregnant to move one couple. Nothing could possibly justify using people like this.

Park swallowed the dry mash of cookie, wishing she had something to wash it down. She was a part of this mess now, through and through. It wasn't just the fetus growing inside her. It was the L-wing. It was the strange people free to roam in the pens created by their cuffed hands and feet. It was the secrets held within Maddoux's tablet and the scribbles Dr. Wong put into each patient's charts. She was a part of that now, too. There was no easy way out.

But, Park realized as an idea occurred to her so clearly she marveled that it was only just forming, there might be a way out, albeit not an easy one. That didn't matter, though. She could unpack the hard parts as she went.

"I want to keep it," she said, throat clogged by the remnants of cookie.

"Do you?" Garth asked.

"It's my right," Park pressed, hoping he wouldn't make her spell out the complexity of the decision for him on the spot. She didn't think she could. She was only just coming to terms with the fact that this truly was what she wanted.

"It is," he agreed, tarrying as if he could wait her decision out.

"You want someone inside the L-wing. You want to know what the DDC is up to and how the new variant is spreading. I'm your man for as long as you can keep this thing hidden," Park said. She really was feeling better now. Probably it was the sugar and carbohydrates from the cookies hitting her bloodstream and giving her brain a chemical jolt.

"An offer with an expiration date," Garth noted, impressed.

"That's right. I play your games and join your team. And when the time comes—as payment for what I've done for you—you get me out."

MORA'S THOUGHTS delved darkly as she waited at the intersection of Main Street and Endgal Avenue—the crossroads at the heart of the city. Two trams passed one another, filled with stone-faced workers commuting to their shifts. The northbound tram was headed toward the manufacturing and distribution factories where workers produced and sifted through goods before they sent them off to the depositories or onto transportation vehicles bound for other force-field-protected cities. The southbound workers were headed toward the agriculture sector—to the greenhouse factories and meat processing—to deal with the raw and perishable goods that would go straight to market.

Main Street, with the capitol building at its center, was the major artery of the city—carrying the most vital people and systems. It also served as the dividing line between the old and the new—for now, anyway. Already, workers and equipment spread out on the Westside, working earnestly to cover the bones of a world whose existence people would rather deny. A world Mora yearned to hold on to.

Mora crossed the road after the tram departed, ducking past the scaffolding set against the Main Street Depository, stepping around the group of teens whose hands clutched bags of goods and possibly a few treats. The depositories on this side of the street weren't as fancy as those on the Eastside. Even on Main Street, the division was clear. The bakeries here sold breads and cereals. On the Eastside, you could get a cake or, if you had enough credits, some of those cream-filled pastries that always adorned the tables in the capitol building when the graduating classes celebrated the Institute-bound students.

Mora's mouth watered at the thought of the delicate, flakey crust surrounding fluffy, sweetened cream. She got to eat two of those pastries last year when her mother brought her to the graduation ceremony. Mora knew it was because her mother wanted her to see the Institute-qualifying students and be impressed. She had already been frustrated that Mora wasn't scoring anywhere close to qualifying on the Test and wanted her to get serious about studying. Mora knew how her mother felt, and maybe she felt a little guilty about not caring, but she hadn't cared. She didn't want to go to the Institute. Mora wanted to leave the city, but only to see for herself what was on the other side of the force fields and glimpse what was left of the larger world. The Institute wouldn't give her that, and besides, she didn't want to live a life of rules, regulations and restrictions. She wanted to exist on her own terms.

That was true until she'd heard what her mother had said to Jim. She heard every word, and while Jim hadn't spoken directly to her about it, she knew she would have to do something to keep him from being punished.

When Jim had finally come to her room, she'd opened the door before he could even knock. One look at the scarlet tint of his cheeks and ears, and she knew she couldn't make him ask her to petition. They sat side by side at the edge of her bed, bodies touching at the shoulder, elbow, and thigh, silently watching as the little red blip made its way slowly across the satellite map on her secret old-world tablet. They watched until Omen settled for the night and the red dot came to a rest in an area that looked like empty space.

"The program can't process the resolution of the signal," James said, finally breaking the silence.

"It's too much of a risk to put the tracking program on the other tablet," Mora said.

James stared hard at the fuzzy red dot sitting at the boundary of a too-straight line between beige and green on the map, thinking. Mora could always tell when James was thinking hard about something. She knew he was formulating a solution. "Could you get a blank processing card from the Hole? I could probably write a program to upgrade the image."

"I could," Mora agreed, thinking about the lengths James was willing to go to help her.

"It will never be as clear as the real-time maps, but I think I could get it a lot clearer. Then we could track Omen's trip more accurately."

His offering was clear—something for her. Always, he was willing to do something for her. He had never asked for anything in return until earlier, on the roof.

He had asked her to petition for a Retest before her mother threatened him. He had asked her to want to be with him.

For James, the notion had been romantic. She could tell, suddenly, even though she couldn't say how she knew. So she'd told him how she felt—to spare him, yes. She loved him and didn't want to hurt him. But it was more than that. She wanted him to see her—to understand her in a way no one else did.

She couldn't change how James felt any more than she could change herself, and in the dim hours of the early morning, long after he'd left and she lay restless in indecision, she realized she didn't want to change it. If she wanted Jim to see her completely, then she needed to see him, too.

He hadn't asked her to petition for a Retest after Morgan had cornered him, and he hadn't asked her to reconsider her feelings for him. So how could she ask him to reconsider his feelings for her? Or his pride in qualifying for the Institute?

Truth was, she couldn't do either. Instead of worrying about what any of it meant or how things might turn out (something she was prone to do), Mora made her decision. She dressed in the grey light of early morning, gathered her school things into her bag and slipped soundlessly out of her bedroom. She found her mother's tablet and scrawled a quick message on her locked screen. She was leaving early to talk to the administration department. She would miss her the rest of the week but didn't want to wake her. She was sorry for storming out on dinner.

Morgan would think James had spent those extra hours behind Mora's closed door convincing her. James could use that assumption to his advantage so he and his family could remain safe and in good standing until they were off Morgan Rossi-Stern's radar. All Mora had to do was petition for a Retest.

She would also have to study hard enough to make her efforts look valiant. And that would make James look good, too. They would study day and night. Every opportunity they had to be seen by a parent or professor, Mora vowed to be seen studying. That's how she would buy enough time to plan.

James needed her to get a high score on the Test. Mora needed to plot her escape.

She had secured her Retest date before the start of her morning class, and she had survived the rest of the day with only minimal agony because now she had a plan. Plus, a trip to the Hole always brightened her spirits.

Mora had been a regular at the black market since she'd turned twelve and finally overcome the fear of everything her classmates said about it. *Vendors kept near-dead in cages. Everyone who went came out infected. If you were caught, DDC agents sent you straight to patient treatment at the Institute.*

But Mora had sought the Hole out anyway. It didn't matter what old wives' tales suggested. She sought it like she did the pre-outbreak history and anything else that connected her life in the City States to the world outside. She groped desperately, feeling as if some strange force were trying to sever that connection.

She wouldn't let that happen if she could help it. If the connection were lost, she would be lost with it. She would never know if her father was still out there. She just had to be more careful about it now that Jim's future was on the line. She'd have to scale back on some of her more clandestine behaviors, like hiding on the roof and going to the Hole. But before she did, she needed a few final things.

Along with being a black market, the Hole was a testament to people's insatiable desire to connect to the past. So long as people worked, salvaged and researched outside the force fields, they would find those connections, and because it was human nature, they would take advantage of the treasures they obtained. People who worked on the outside, walking through the abandoned and untouched cities of old, could bring the outside in. Through the salvaged technology and refurbished goods, they could turn pieces of history back to life for people like her, people who were willing to hear and remember their stories.

Mora didn't come from a family who told stories or kept track of their history; thus, she was driven to understand by any means. Morgan Rossi-Stern's denial of their own past outside the City States and the erasure of her own earliest memories made her daughter crave the old world even more. Mora treasured her old-world tablet more than any piece of information or technology the City States could provide. If she could walk through the force field and into the outside world, she would do it.

She knew she was in the minority, wanting to hang on to the vestiges of the old world, but she didn't care. Where other people saw crumbling brick and moldering siding, Mora saw character and a history that was being erased right before her eyes. Aesthetically, she liked the way the buildings on the Westside all looked different from each other. She could tell they were all built at different times by different people with different ideas about what the world might become. She liked feeling connected to her roots. Though her mother never spoke about the world from before, and children weren't taught about it at school—they never learned anything before the events leading to the formation of the City States and their saving systems—Mora still felt that she belonged to the world that existed before. And pieces of it were still out there. She could feel the connection in her bones.

A short woman with fiery amber eyes stood guard at the entrance to the Hole. Mora looked a moment too long at the way she leaned against the wall, scanner pointed nonchalantly toward where Mora might hide a government ID card.

"Shannon here today?" Mora asked, identifying herself as a regular patron.

"I'm not sure. I haven't been through the stalls," the woman replied, pulling a lock of hair back behind her shoulder and readjusting her cap with a crooked grin.

Again, Mora got the sense her look lingered too long and that the woman might notice.

"I guess I'll find out," she said, ducking her head as she slipped through the unlocked doors.

The Hole was quieter than usual. Many of the vendors were either not set up for the day or had packed up early. As she walked through the sparsely populated stalls where voices blended together, Mora wondered if the location of the Hole would change once the workers and scaffolding made it this far out.

Snippets rose above the din and caught her ears.

"Any news?"

"Dehydrated or canned?"

"Can you help me send this?"

"Looking for some mouse traps…"

Someone was always looking for mouse traps. Mice were a downright nuisance in the older buildings, and the regular markets never carried traps. She thought it was because doing so would mean having to admit there were mice, and admitting there were mice meant having to admit that a whole lot of other things might exist, too.

Like ravens.

"One hundred credits for a replacement screen?" someone shrieked.

Or a world where people could live outside of force fields.

"Well, hello there, little friend," a familiar voice called out.

Mora turned at the sound and found Shannon rising unevenly from their perch on a partially caved-in crate. "There you are," she said, approaching the booth.

"Not in my normal spot today," Shannon conceded, limping up to their table's edge.

"I can see that," Mora said, thinking Shannon's limp looked worse than usual.

"Any good lessons lately?" Shannon asked, trying to guess at what Mora was seeking.

"I actually have had a hard time seeing my lessons lately," she said.

There wasn't much need for code. They knew each other, and the Hole was quiet. Mora could come straight out and ask for what she wanted, but she liked that Shannon preferred to keep up the ruse even when the building was empty.

"Are you having a hard time keeping up or are your screens blurry?" Shannon asked, thoroughly stumping Mora.

She was no good with electronics. The only reason she was passing her tech class at all was because James was basically doing her work for her. It was one of the many deficits she'd have to rectify before her Retest.

"I need a blank processing card," Mora admitted, not finding the energy to keep the game going.

"What size?" Shannon asked.

Mora glanced to the side, biting her lower lip. "I... I don't know. Something for the satellite image program."

Understanding lit up the vendor's face. "Hold on," Shannon said, lifting their index finger toward her. They turned to the cabinets on a rolling cart, opening and closing several drawers before finally returning with a little black-and-silver thing. "This will do the trick."

"How much?" Mora asked.

Shannon's face glowed with mischief. "Three hundred."

"No way. I'll stare at fuzzy trees!" Mora protested.

"Aren't you going to offer me a counter price?" Shannon asked, wiggling the processing card in front of her.

"Why should I bother? You're just going to rob me anyway," Mora said.

"You hurt me with these lies!" Shannon whined.

"What's a fair number?" Mora asked, feeling worn and impatient.

"Thirteen is a lucky number in roulette," Shannon quipped.

Mora had no idea what they were referencing. She waited, refusing to show her hand.

"Seventy-five if you promise not to tell anyone where you got it," they said.

"Fifty and I promise not to turn you in," Mora threatened.

"And send an old friend to quarantine?" Shannon asked, placing a hand over their heart.

"Is seventy-five fair?" Mora asked.

Shannon placed the processing card on the table, pushing it toward Mora's waiting hands before adjusting the settings on their scanner. Mora tipped her school tablet in their direction. There was a beep, and the transaction was done, leaving Mora seventy-five credits poorer and the proud new owner of a sub-par old-world processing card.

"Always a pleasure doing business with you, kid," Shannon said, offering her a toothy grin.

"You're just saying that because you make out like a criminal," Mora said, shoving the card into the outside pocket of her canvas jacket.

"Anything else for you today?" Shannon asked, being polite, though it was clear they expected their business to be done.

"Yeah," Mora said, surprising them. "Do you know what a bug-out bag is?"

ZAYD WAS RUNNING by the time he passed the capitol building, so he didn't see the sandy-haired teen stepping off the capitol steps onto the newly redone sidewalk. They collided with so much force that the boy fell backward, his backpack breaking his fall against the steps.

"Geez, kid! I'm sorry. Are you alright?" he asked, rubbing his smarting arm as he scrambled to help the boy up.

"I'm… I'm fine. I think," the kid gasped, trying to right himself.

Zayd grabbed the boy's forearm over his jacket like he was taught to, helping him upright. "You're alright?" he asked again, fighting the urge to run.

"Yeah," the boy said, wincing as he pulled his pack off his shoulder.

Zayd didn't have time for this. He should go. Anika needed him. He was about to say as much when the boy pulled out his broken tablet.

"Oh… no…" he moaned. His despair wrapped around Zayd's already constricted chest, and he knew he needed to make it right.

"I can pay for it," Zayd said, drawing the boy's attention from the bent and crushed screen. Zayd licked his lips, heart thundering like a trapped animal's. "I can do a transfer—right now," he pressed.

"It's school issued," the boy said, obviously confused about the proper procedure for fixing the situation.

"Do you have your account number?" Zayd asked, impatient to get this done so he could go to Ani's clinic. How long had she been waiting already? Hours? Days? What had Johnson told her about where he was? And above the other thoughts was the one banging against his panicked mind: *Was she okay?*

"I can get a replacement. I've never broken one before," the boy protested.

"Do you know your account number?" Zayd snapped.

"You don't have to pay, sir," the boy said. He sounded uneasy, maybe a little scared.

"I want to, okay? Can you just give me your account number?" Zayd was practically begging now.

"It's 46623," the boy mumbled.

"I'll cover the replacement and a little extra just in case. You're not hurt, are you?" Zayd asked, his fingers flying through the air to make the transfer.

"No," the boy said, putting the broken tablet into his bag so he could stand.

"I'm putting a little extra in for that too—just in case." The tablet beeped to signify the transfer had gone through.

"I said I wasn't—"

"If anything else comes up, you can track me down by my account number," Zayd said, shoving his tablet into his back pocket. He extended his arm as he moved away, joining the impatient flow of pedestrian traffic moving north past the capitol building. "Again, I'm really sorry, kid."

The boy watched, dumbfounded, as Zayd rushed away at a fast clip—not quite a run, but picking up speed with every stride.

Zayd was trying not to run, but he couldn't help himself. He told Anika he was doing a work-through shift for the weekend, which meant that he should have been in the factory when she called and should have been home already. He didn't know what Johnson had said to her. He didn't know what this was about, but he knew it must be serious because she hadn't picked up when he'd called. Clinic hours were over, and according to Anika, they were up to date on charting and reports, so there was no reason for her to still be at work.

Of course, there were reasons... She could be sick or injured. She was taking those pills, and there were so many side effects!

The multitude of reasons raced through his head as he turned east off of Main Street, covering the final three blocks to the clinic. He allowed himself to consider every absurd possibility except for one until he saw the transport vehicle parked in the rear lot meant for loading and unloading equipment.

Zayd stopped at the front door, sweat coating every part of his body, running down his neck and making his shirt stick to his skin underneath his canvas jacket. He used the back of his sleeve to wipe his forehead before running his hands through his hair to force it back into place.

His eyes darted to the front door, where the *Closed* sign was lit up above the touchless entry pad. His heart hammered hard in his chest, and his pulse whooshed beneath his rigid breaths. He could barely contain this wild panic inside his body.

Briefly, he considered pounding on the front door until someone—ideally Anika—came to open it for him. But if Anika could answer the front door, she would have answered his calls. And there was a transport vehicle out back, engine humming as it idled.

The unwelcome thought clawed to the front of his mind and, though he knew better than to let it all get to him, he cried out.

"Ani!"

The streets were empty. All the pedestrian traffic had moved on to the markets and residential areas. Working shifts were underway. There was no one here to hear him, so he yelled again.

"Ani!"

He started toward the alleyway, his sweat turning sickeningly cold against his overheated skin as the sun sank below the towering brown and grey buildings. His footsteps echoed nearly as loudly as his pulse. Behind the humming vehicle, Zayd noticed a message graffitied on the clinic's back wall—something about *the root of evil*. The rest was obscured behind the hulking transport. The clinic was refinished years ago, so the message had to be fresh, perhaps painted by the lingering ghosts of the old Resistee movement. It was hard to exorcise ghosts from such an ancient city.

As he approached, he could see the driver behind the protective, shatter-resistant glass. They were wearing a respirator and long blue gloves, with hair cropped so close to their scalp that Zayd couldn't detect its color. The passenger door was open.

"Ani!" he yelled, certain his voice carried over the sound of the engine at this distance.

"Stay back!" a loud voice commanded as he came around the side of the vehicle.

A slender woman stood in yellow protective garb and elbow-length blue gloves, a perfect ponytail sticking out the back of a respirator mask. Her hand was facing out toward him, but she was looking through the clinic's open door.

Zayd was fairly certain the woman was Cora. He knew enough about her from Anika's complaints to recognize her despite the personal protection outfit.

"I'm looking for my wife," he said, stepping forward to stand between the loading door and the outside wall of the clinic.

"This area isn't safe for pedestrians," Cora said, as if she didn't recognize him and couldn't guess who he was.

"Her name is Anika Baba. My name is Zayd. She's my wife. She called me, and I'm here," Zayd said, putting his hands out ahead of him as though he were soothing a wild dog.

"You shouldn't be here, Mr. Baba. We're dealing with a contamination risk," Cora said, still watching the clinic doors.

From this angle, it was difficult for Zayd to see inside the clinic, but he had a good enough imagination to combine with the context clues. He wasn't surprised when Anika emerged into the alleyway.

"Ani," he called, taking another step forward.

"Zayd!" Anika sobbed at seeing him. His heart constricted with a mixture of grief and relief at seeing her. She was fine. She was distraught but in one piece and standing. He could unpack the meaning of this situation later, knowing she wasn't in mortal danger.

"Mr. Baba, I'm going to need you to step back!" Cora commanded as Anika moved into the alley. That's when Zayd saw the restraints.

He didn't know how he'd missed them before. Probably because he was panicked and distraught. Her hands were bound in front of her, and there were a series of metal wires around her neck and chest. It wasn't until he saw the pole follow her out the door that he realized what it was—someone had Anika bound by lashing pole.

Ignoring Cora's warnings, Zayd burst forward, closing the distance between them in two swift strides. "Ani, what are they doing to you?"

"Mr. Baba, I must insist—"

"You can't insist on a damn thing! If you're sending her to the Institute, then I'm volunteering," Zayd said, cutting off Cora's unwelcome command.

There. Let her sit on that, he thought, wrapping his arms around Anika's trembling shoulders. He could feel the electric buzz and heat of the lashing pole's bindings. He looked past her to see the figure in full biohazard suit wielding the pole.

He placed a hand on either side of Anika's face, lifting it so she would meet his gaze. "I'm so sorry I didn't get here sooner."

"Zayd… don't touch me," she gasped, her body shuddering with anguish.

"You're infected?" he asked, not needing her to answer. If she was about to get on the transport, and if Cora and this other person were garbed up like they were, it was pretty clear, but he wanted her to tell him what happened. "Was it an accident in the clinic?"

"No," she whispered. Her lips trembled as she fought for words. "I mean, I don't know. There was an exposure, and Cora did the exam. My nails… the scanner…"

Zayd dropped his hands to her bound hands, grasping them gently and turning them to look at her nails. "Did you tell her how they always stain?"

"The blood test came back positive," she said.

His heart sank. He didn't believe it. This type of infection didn't happen… not in the cities where no one was ever sick. Not where the disease was more of a fear tactic than a reality.

"Then it's wrong," he insisted, bringing Anika's hands to his lips. He pressed a chaste kiss against her greyish fingernails. "We'll go to the Institute, and they'll run more tests. You'll see. It's a false positive. We'll go to the Institute so they can confirm, then we'll go home."

Fat tears flooded Anika's deep brown eyes before running down her cheeks in perfect streaks.

"There's no such thing as a false positive," Cora said, intruding on the couple's private moment.

Zayd wheeled on her. "There's no chance Anika did something to get infected. Strange things happen every day, so I'd appreciate it if you butted out of it!"

Cora's mask stretched as she opened her mouth in shock and indignation. Zayd felt a surge of satisfaction at having made her feel those things. He stepped toward her before she could retort, lifting his bare hands in defense—the same hands that had just touched his supposedly infected wife.

"I'm going to need you to move back," came a muffled voice from the biohazard suit holding the lashing pole.

"Release the hold on that thing, and I'll do whatever you want," Zayd commanded, keeping one hand up and reaching toward Cora's paling, wide-eyed face.

"I'm not supposed to let the patient loose until she's on the transport," the wielder said.

"You're a volunteer?" Zayd asked, glancing their way.

The person nodded, the fabric of their suit crinkling.

"I guess as of right now, I am, too, so how about we drop the act and all get on that transport? We can sort everything else out once we're moving," Zayd said.

The volunteer hesitated. Cora made a slight squeaking noise when they released the wires from Anika's neck and chest but didn't protest any further.

Zayd gave them an appreciative nod before entwining his hand between Anika's bound hands. He gave them a squeeze before leading her up the transport's steps. The volunteer followed them into the transport, where Zayd helped Anika onto one of the bench seats in the back.

The transport vehicle door shut as Zayd took his seat next to Anika. Nobody tried to stop him from sitting so close to her. He kept his hand wrapped firmly around hers as the transport pulled away from the clinic. Anika rested her tear-streaked cheek against his shoulder, and he kissed the top of her head alongside her thick braid. He caught a final glimpse of Cora watching them as they pulled away from the clinic, gloves pulled up to her elbows, mask still firmly in place. Even from here, he could see the fear written across her over-garbed, over-protected body. He refused to allow himself to be afraid of the woman he loved.

Wrapping his wife's trembling body in his firm embrace, Zayd turned away from the clinic to face forward, watching the roads as the transport traced the same path he'd taken earlier.

CHAPTER

Twenty-Two

PARK

THE HALL of the main medical facility was quiet when Park entered through the double doors she had no business passing through anymore. She blinked at the permanent brightness that drenched everything. Workers and patients alike were prone to losing track of time in the medical branch of the Institute. It was the reason volunteers switched shifts more often when they worked on the medical side. They were required to rotate out at least six hours for every fourteen on a shift. Medics and doctors rotated more frequently, too, but they were guaranteed an eight of rest between shifts that never extended beyond twelve hours.

Park was extra jumpy as she made her way down the main hall. Having been out of the rotation since switching to the L-wing, she didn't know who was on shift tonight. She didn't know the status of the patients, or if any of the required medically trained personnel were on shift. She didn't know if Benji or Vang were working, or if both had been cycled out of the medical circuit. Maybe someone was put on a transport bound for the Northern Laboratories. Word was they were even more shorthanded in the labs up there. The risk of being exposed while sneaking out was high, but she had to see Reed.

A door in the side hall opened, admitting an uncaged wail into the eerie silence.

"If you won't help me, then kill me! Just kill me already and be done with it!"

Park's stomach turned at the desperation in the patient's voice. Those weren't the cries of someone unhappy with their level of care. They were the sounds of donation.

The door shut, cutting off the terrible cries. She stopped, knowing that whoever had just exited needed to see her behaving typically if she were going to make it to her destination. The worker was tall, garbed in the thick yellow of the volunteer's protective suit. Their back was turned to her, but Park knew it was Benji.

"A donation?" she asked, making the worker whirl.

"Endgal alive, you scared me!" Benji breathed, pushing his face shield onto his head so his dark, humor-filled eyes peered out at her over a wide grin and close-clipped beard.

"So did you. I'm not supposed to be here anymore," Park said, tucking her bare hands into her lab coat pockets. She wore her lab coat almost constantly these days, afraid someone might notice a change in her figure if she didn't. It was still early, but these things happened suddenly sometimes, and without definitive patterns.

"I heard you were moved to L-wing," Benji said. Clearly, the volunteer chain of communication was alive and well within the Institute.

"Two weeks ago," Park confirmed. "I'm on my way to becoming a resident doctor."

"DDC certified and all?" Benji asked, feigning being impressed.

"If I make it that long," Park said. The volunteers never needed more than a hint to understand there was more going on than meets the eye. They knew things weren't right at the Institute. They were aware of the dangers and devastations and always seemed to know when something was happening long before anyone else.

Another door opened further down the hall, letting loose the gentle sound of a patient sobbing. Park turned toward the sound.

"New kid. Gemini, I think. You'd like her," Benji rushed the words out to assure her.

"Any medics or residents on shift tonight?" Park asked.

"No. We've got an on-call for Mr. Donation in there, just in case he decides to turn early, but otherwise don't have any criticals."

The new volunteer approached them while pulling on a new pair of gloves. Underneath the thick strap of her face shield, her thick brown hair was braided into a tight twist and tucked into the collar of her suit—a style that was becoming more popular with the volunteers. "I didn't think we had a resident on shift tonight. Did the screamer turn early?" she asked, repeating Benji's assertion.

Benji ushered the other volunteer into their circle with the quick motion of a gloved hand. "No. This is Park. She's not a resident yet. She's a friendly. Fresh from the intern program."

"Not so fresh anymore," Park corrected.

"How come I haven't seen her on shift?" the girl asked.

"Because you're too green to know everyone yet," Benji admonished.

"I'm no greenie—been here three weeks from the city program. Name's Jemani," she said, glaring at Benji.

"I work the L-wing now," Park said, attempting to squash their argument before it could get out of hand. "It's nice to meet you, Jemani." She took great care to pronounce the name correctly.

Park had her hand tucked behind her back before she had a chance to think about it. The new volunteer looked her up and down.

"L-wing? Doesn't that make you DDC?" Jemani asked. Park swore the girl's eyes lingered where her lab coat pulled against her stomach. It wasn't much, but Park was hyper-aware of it. In her mind, her barely swelling abdomen stuck out in a three-foot radius around her.

"The DDC is running the L-wing, yes," Park conceded, unclasping her hands and shoving them back into her lab coat pockets. Jemani was clearly not a DDC sympathizer. More and more often, the volunteers weren't. Especially not the ones coming in from the city recruitment program, showing up without someone's life on the line. Park wondered why so many were critical. Theoretically, a volunteer should be an enthusiastic supporter of the Institute and the DDC, but the opposite was happening. She knew that was why Reed and the rest of the interns were all so distrustful of them. The thought reminded her of the purpose of her clandestine passage through the medical wing.

"I should get going. Are you on shift through the night?" she asked Benji, trying to ignore Jemani's scrutinizing gaze.

"I'm off at 400."

"I won't be long," Park said, knowing that unlike so many times before, she was telling the truth. There would be no losing track of time. There was too much at stake to linger, even if Reed was more himself tonight.

"I'll keep my ear out for you, then," Benji said, looking down the hall—likely at the doors making up his duties for the evening. They were all currently falling behind schedule. "I'll teach Gemini what to listen for."

"How come she gets my name right on the first try and you can't be bothered?" Jemani asked, crinkling her nose at Benji.

"Thanks," Park said, slipping away from the two volunteers before she was embroiled in whatever squabble they were having. Knowing Benji, the name thing was meant to be a bit of hazing. The volunteers had their own systems and hierarchies within the Institute, but Jemani didn't seem like the sort to wade through systems and wait her turn. She gave the impression of someone who was already at the top of her own hierarchy.

Park made her exit just as one of them opened the door to another patient, filling the hall with the sounds of agony once more. She let the door shut behind her, hurrying away from those sounds and into the foggy chill of the night.

It was strange, she knew, how quickly she'd forgotten the distress of the medical branch. After months of working with patients and volunteers, she'd thought the screams were embedded in her psyche, but it had only taken two weeks—fewer than fourteen days—to begin to forget the agony of the patient experience within the Institute.

The L-wing was different. The patients there were calm. None of them suffered from the agonizing progression of the disease. The fear that plagued the typical patient experience was completely absent from the entire L-wing medical setup. But it wasn't just that... There was something else about the L-wing that made it different from general medical. She just couldn't put her finger on it.

She thought she saw Reed's dark form waiting in the shadows of the old tree, but she was wrong. He wasn't waiting for her in their usual space.

It's because I haven't come in so long, she told herself. She didn't want to think it was because he'd washed out of the Northern Laboratories intern program without her knowing. Somehow it was worse to think he'd vanished without her knowing than to think he'd just quit waiting for her.

He wasn't hidden in the shadows of the tree or lurking on the dark side of the intern housing. Park was about to give up looking when he appeared at the entrance, doors shutting silently behind him.

"I almost didn't believe it when I saw you walk past!" Reed said, taking her into his arms as she greeted him.

"I'm sorry. So much has happened," she breathed into the side of his neck. He was freshly showered. The scruff on his neck meant he'd gotten a haircut in the last day or so. He smelled like soap mingling with the permanent exhaustion of too much pressed into a small space.

"I know. I have so much to tell you," Reed said. He placed his hands on her shoulders and used them to move her gently away from him. In the darkness, she could feel him searching her.

"What's wrong?" he asked.

She needed to tell him. She was terrified of his reaction.

"I'm training to be a resident," she said. "I've got DDC clearance while I finish my work."

This was an easier starting point. It was safe. She knew he'd be proud, and from there, they could make their way to the more important things together.

"Park… That's fantastic!" he oozed, like she knew he would.

"I know, right? It's almost a dream come true." *Almost as good as going to the Northern Laboratories with you*, she meant. He would understand her meaning.

"Did you hear about the big upheaval?" Reed asked.

Park's stomach did a flip that felt like tiny feet running a mile a minute across her insides.

Too soon for that, she thought, but she dismissed the distraction. She had no idea if it was too soon or right on time for that sort of a thing. Her specialty was infection. Her education didn't cover the technical aspects of pregnancy, and there wouldn't be a lot of opportunities for her to rectify that reality until Garth got her out of here.

She realized she hadn't responded to Reed's question. He was waiting for her, gripping too tightly at the fabric of her lab coat in anticipation of her response. Park couldn't believe he knew about the others—that Garth and whoever else's secret had come out so quickly. But Reed was smart and observant, so it wasn't unbelievable that he'd figured it out.

"I know about Emery," she said, giving him the opportunity to fill in the rest with what he knew.

"Emery? They failed out months ago. I thought you knew. Emery, Mason, and Lasso all failed out. Rumor is Mason might've actually gotten infected, but that's just rumor. Most folks say they just got moved to different programs," Reed said.

Months ago? Park guessed that the timeline fit but couldn't believe Reed hadn't mentioned it to her. But if he hadn't mentioned it, maybe he didn't know *why* Emery and Mason had been moved.

"Did she say anything before she left?" Park felt suddenly bashful about sharing the news.

"Nothing. We didn't even see them again after the assessment." Reed shrugged.

Park squirmed a hand up between them to fidget with the button over her stomach, thinking. "So if you weren't going to tell me about Emery, then what were you going to say?"

"The ranking system changed! The DDC has come in with a whole new assessment, and everyone's rankings changed all at once. It happened during class. Sima went from top ranked to third from last. It was wild, Amy; she totally lost it," Reed gushed.

"Did it force her to drop?" Park asked, shocked that Sima, who had always done very well, could drop so rapidly.

"She's still around, but after they talked to her, she hasn't been the same," Reed said.

"What do you mean? Who talked to her?" Park asked.

"I can't say. It's all classified." Reed gave her arm a noncommittal squeeze, and Park felt their distance even more acutely than the last time they were together.

"That's okay," she said, even though it was anything but. "I've got a bunch of classified stuff going on, too. That's just how it is in the L-wing."

She dropped the news about the L-wing on purpose, hoping it would catch his interest. She could tell him she was working there now even though she wasn't supposed to say anything about what it was like on the inside.

"L-wing?" Reed asked, his interest piqued.

"That's right. My new assignment." She gripped at his hands, her own fingers getting icy and stiff in the chilly night air.

"So you know about the new project?"

Park thought about lying. The *yes* was on the tip of her tongue, begging her to give it life so he would tell her its relevance. But something stopped her. Maybe it was nerves, but maybe it was a gut feeling. Reed was different.

"I don't. I'm still figuring things out," she admitted.

Reed looked disappointed.

"Do you still talk to the volunteers?" he asked.

"Who do you think's going to let me back in when we're done here?" They'd been over this so many times that she couldn't take his derision seriously.

His hands came away from hers, leaving a cold rush of dewy air where their warmth once was. She felt the chill all the way down to her spine.

"You can't seriously be on about them still!" Park protested, groping for his hands in the dark space between them.

"Trusting the volunteers is a stupid move, Park. You'll get yourself in trouble," he admonished.

"How else am I supposed to see you?" She knew he understood what it took for them to be together. At least, she thought he knew.

"Maybe we shouldn't meet like this anymore," he said, voicing her worst nightmare.

"You can't mean that," she breathed.

"I can," he said, his voice dark with conviction. "I can if it means you don't screw up my chances."

She stepped back from him as if he'd just slapped her.

"I'm top ranked now," he said, not following her into the darkness. "I'm not going to let you mess that up."

"Reed…" she begged.

"I mean it, Park! We can't keep acting like children! I'm an intern now. I'm going to be a scientist."

He ran a hand over the short stubble on his scalp.

"What we have isn't childish!" she snapped, thinking about how incredibly adult it was, right down to the very adult consequence growing inside of her. She'd meant to come out here to tell him about the pregnancy—about his impending child—but things were going sideways.

"It is, Park, and I think it's time for us to stop," Reed said.

When she didn't respond, his voice softened, but he didn't reach out for her.

"I love you. You know that, but it's best to accept that all we really have is memories. You're staying here, and I'm going—" He stopped, as if he'd just thought better of telling her where he was going. He let out a deep breath and started again. "Park, I don't want you to come out here again."

She stared at him, her mouth making a perfect O-shape as she processed her disbelief.

"I'm pregnant," she blurted.

Just then, a light flashed on at the side of the building. Reed whirled away from it, and before she could stop him, he retreated back into the intern quarters, leaving her alone and exposed, unsure if he'd even heard her.

Twenty~Three

JAMES

JAMES RACED down the cracked alleyway between the two dilapidated buildings, for the first time not worried about who might see him scale the creaky old ladder up onto the fire escape. He had news for Mora.

Broken glass and synthetic diode conductors tinkled against one another as he pulled himself onto the first landing of the fire escape and his pack bumped against his shoulders. He would have to tell her about the encounter with the wild man outside the capitol building, too, but there was an order of priority to things. Mora was expecting him later this evening, around the time Morgan would be calling to check in from her assignment. Mora would answer, and Morgan would see the two of them at the dinner table, eating bland quiche and poring over virtual models of the metabolic systems, all promises kept.

Jim couldn't wait until then. Even now, he would likely not have time to say everything he had to say before they had to make their way back into the apartment building, but he had to try. Mora had to know what he'd done.

The first three landings weren't hard. He knew what he was doing, but by the time he passed the fourth and began up the fifth, the laddered system began to shake and waver with his movement.

Looking down to where his feet flaked off iron dust that the building's bricks seemed to absorb in both strength and color made James woozy. How could something so old remain so steadfast against the ravages of time? He did his best to ignore the thought, and for the rest of the climb, he didn't look at anything beyond where his body connected with the ancient structure.

He replaced thoughts of imminent doom—of dormant infection, terminal falls, discovery and quarantine—by imagining Mora's reaction to his appearance on the roof. Would she be surprised he'd made the climb on his own? She would expect him to message if he had something to report to her. He knew he was predictable. Of course Mora would be surprised to see him on her roof. The more important question was: Would she be happy to see him?

The problem with doing something thoughtlessly was that eventually he would encounter trouble he didn't see coming. That was the whole reason for thinking something through before doing it. If he was careful about planning, he could anticipate any hazards along the way. If there were too many hazards, he would know well in advance that the mission should be aborted.

This was, of course, one way in which Mora was very different from him. Mora was different from everyone in this way. She never thought things through. She didn't need to. When Mora wanted to do something, no matter the reason, no matter the risk, no matter the dangers associated with that thing… she did it anyway. She could just close her eyes and jump.

The word *jump* made James' stomach do a flip as he reached the top landing of the fire escape. The rail on this level was rusted out. Nothing stood between him and the cold air that would offer little friction in his plummet to the hard asphalt below. The haphazard handholds Mora had chipped out of the building to reach the roof filled him with the same sinking anxiety. He was trying hard not to think of the empty space surrounding him, but it was consuming his every thought, forcing him to think, of all things, of physics.

To others, there was the physical form of the building's gritty surface, and then there was the asphalt below. This in and of itself was terrifying. But he knew there were approximately seven septillion particles composing the atmosphere between him and imminent demise because he'd already done the calculation in his head. The abundance of matter between him and the bottom didn't make him feel any better, though, because even with drag, a fall from this height would be as frightening as it was deadly.

When Mora jumped, she sprouted wings to sail through the air, allowing the currents of possibility to carry her to new horizons. When James jumped, he thought about the molecular makeup of biological systems, which he had memorized. He could calculate the impact force per square centimeter based on the surface area of the average human body. This was not an advantage. Mora had the ability to do the same but refused. That was part of what made her so incredible.

James knew that her mother, his parents and many of the teachers thought of her as reckless, unreliable, even unwise. But they were wrong. If it weren't for Mora, he wouldn't be suspended 110 meters in the air, one hand gripping the roof, holding on for dear life as the wind whipped through hair that needed a serious trim. If it weren't for Mora…

He let out a sound that was monstrous inside his head, but in reality was barely a grunting exhale, as he hoisted himself onto the ledge. The wind roared across him in a vengeful gust, as if dismayed at not managing to tear him from the building. James pressed his face into the gritty surface of the ledge, relishing its solid-ness.

"I wouldn't stay there if I were you. That ledge is going to go any day now."

James froze, feeling the cold sweat that clung to every surface of his overwrought body for the first time since he'd started the climb.

"What happened to your face?" Mora asked. There she was, standing right next to him. Of course she hadn't been waiting next to the ledge the whole time, which meant he'd been laying there practically kissing the rooftop in the gusting wind long enough for her to notice him and walk over, completely undetected.

James turned his head and was greeted by the black fabric of Mora's favorite sweatshirt. She said it was ideal for the rooftop because the wind always blew her jacket open. She liked that she could pull the strings tight on the hood and not bother to pull her hair back the way she had to at school.

When he tried to sit up, he felt the ledge shift under him and panicked, sure it was going to give, just like Mora had warned. His arms flailed, and he teetered for a moment before pitching forward and directly onto her. She wasn't expecting it and collapsed on impact. Their bodies fell together in a tangle of fabric and skin, James screaming and apologizing the whole way down, eyes shut tight as they collided with the spongy, decaying surface of the old track.

"Jim?" Mora wheezed, so close to his ear that her lips were practically touching it. "I can't breathe."

His eyes flew open, and he scrambled to get up. "I'm sorry, Mora! Did I hurt you?"

Instead of getting up, he fell backward, landing hard on his rear for the second time that day. He could feel the bruise blooming there.

"I'm fine," Mora said, brushing herself off and sitting up. "I'm just trying to figure out what under Endgal's microscope you're doing up here!"

"I wanted to tell you something," he said, feeling suddenly foolish for thinking this couldn't wait. What had been so important that it required a near-death experience to be said?

"What did you do, talk to the president?" Mora mused, reaching over to tousle his already wind-whipped hair.

"No. I talked to the headmaster," James said, the import of his message making its way back to the forefront of his thoughts.

Mora's forehead creased as she scowled at the scuff marks on the toe box of her boots. "About graduation?" she asked. Her expression darkened. "About the Institute?"

"About the Test," James said, catching Mora's attention. Her head came up, a wisp of hair blowing across her face as her brown eyes searched his. He adjusted his glasses self-consciously and noticed for the first time since his earlier collision that the frames were bent. He took them off to study the damage.

"What about the Test?" Mora asked. He could feel her quizzical gaze as he tried to bend the frames back into shape.

"You don't have to take it, Mora. It's not fair that she's trying to make you," James said, thankful he had the glasses to focus on instead of staring into Mora's impossibly deep, impossibly beautiful eyes. "I asked him to reject your petition."

"Why did you do that?" Mora demanded. She sounded angry.

James seated the glasses back onto the bridge of his nose. They were better now, but the fit still wasn't right. That task done, he had no choice but to look at Mora, who was, in fact, very angry.

"Because she shouldn't force you to go to the Institute if you don't want to," he said.

"I thought you wanted me to go to the Institute, Jim? You said you wanted me to go with you!" She was practically wailing.

"I did," he admitted. This time, it was James who reached out. He grabbed her hand, forcing himself not to think about how warm her skin felt pressed against his—so smooth. "But I was wrong. I was being selfish. If you went to the Institute, it would be for all the wrong reasons. It would be for everyone except for yourself."

Her lips trembled as she listened to his explanation. His fingers wrapped around hers, intertwining and holding her as if he could prop her up with nothing more than this embrace.

"I don't want that for you. I want you to be happy," he said.

A single tear made its way down Mora's wind-chapped cheek, getting lost in the hairs that clung to her face. She reached up and pulled the hairs away with her free hand.

"It's too late, Jim," she said, trying to pull her hand free of his grasp. He didn't let her loose until she pulled more definitively.

"She can't send my family away if she thinks I tried," James said.

"She can. She'd do it just to punish you for my bad decisions," Mora spat, bitter words turning her lips down.

"I'll do my part. I'll beg openly in front of her for you to petition. She'll see that there was nothing I could do to make it happen. You'll petition, and Hartman will reject it. He'll see your biology scores, and he won't hesitate. I told him you cheated on the last assessment," James explained.

"He can't reject my petition," Mora said.

"He'll have to. Academic integrity is a precedent for petitions," James argued.

"He can't reject it because it's already been approved," Mora said.

"When?" James asked, a sick, sinking feeling rushing through him that had nothing to do with the height of the building or the gusting winds.

"This morning. I went straight to the Department of Testing offices," Mora explained, folding her hands over her propped knee.

"Oh," James said, mimicking the action. It was just like Mora to bypass the middleman.

"Yeah," Mora confirmed.

"So you're going to the Institute after all?" James asked, a glimmer of that recently dead hope igniting in his chest again. *Maybe,* he thought, *just maybe, we'll make the best of it.* The interns spent their first couple years together, and while Mora didn't have a chance of going full scientist, she'd probably make an awesome energy management tech—or a medic.

But Mora had other ideas. She could see the hope plastered across James' rosy cheeks and written in the bright light of his sky-blue eyes. For a second, she thought of giving him the whole *only if you tutor me like your life depends on it* speech. But it was better to dash that hope before it had a chance to grow wings and soar. Like she'd done before.

I don't like boys, Jim. I don't like boys, and I won't spend my life at the Institute becoming my mother.

It would be cruel to leave Jim hoping for something she could never give him. And she knew it was for the best. She owed him the same love he selflessly gave to her.

She thought again of her trip to the Hole. Her purchase.

"I'm going to run away," she said.

Twenty~Four

OMEN

AS THE SUN rose over the tops of the dense forest growth, burning away the dewy mist that was prolific outside the city's force field boundary, a lone black raven emerged from the undergrowth. The bird was large for his age and far better traveled than any of his surviving counterparts. He stretched his wings to catch a current of air just above the trees, riding it to a suitable altitude. From here, he could take in the whole city. The city meant home, a large meal, and the comfort of a familiar face.

The woods outside the shimmering city barrier called to him, and though he followed that call more boldly each passing month, he longed unabashedly for the simple comfort of easy feasts on city rodents and the way his nest came with a handful of cereal. Inside the shimmer, he was more invisible than he was out here. He blended with the shadows cast by the tall buildings. People never looked to the sky the way the creatures on the outside did. The raven knew the woods should be his home, but so long as his person remained inside that shimmer, so would he.

He rose higher, caught a gust of air headed toward the city, and began moving in that direction. It wouldn't be long now. The bird kept his burdened foot tucked tightly against his body as he flew, eyes sharp on the lookout for other avian travelers. Further out, the scents of upturned earth and heavy machinery tainted the wild air. Without understanding completely, he tasted the change they brought. In the west, the direction he'd come from, he caught the scent of death. This sort of death had existed his whole life, but the raven knew it was an unnatural smell.

Decaying things shouldn't rise up from the earth. The oldest parts of his intensely bright mind understood that dead and dying things were meant to return to the earth. They were intended for the vultures and four-legged beasts to feast on as insects and larvae helped return the rot to the land. Dead and dying things weren't supposed to reach into the sky and prey upon the living.

It was this innate understanding that had led him to the encampment of people in the clearing between shimmering cities. They understood the wrongness of the decaying things, too. They were like his Mora.

That was why, when the woman had opened her hand and offered the fresh slices of apple, he'd reacted. It was where the foundation of trust began, and it was how he ended up now, for the third time, allowing the strange attachment to be placed on his leg as he traveled between two spaces that felt almost equally like home.

The bird was thinking about this duality of home when he passed over a vehicle taking a turn away from the city, noticing it but not assigning any real value to its presence on his route. Like other person things, vehicles existed both inside and outside the city's force fields, but he never had to mind them because they never saw his graceful form cut through the sky. He knew the vehicle was an inanimate thing and it was the person inside—a lone man, in this instance, driving south on what the outside people called the Institute Road—that controlled it. He knew that if the vehicle was headed south, it was to the other shimmering city because there was nothing else south to travel to.

The world beyond the southernmost City State was a dead land, filled with scorched earth and dead things that rose up to die again. The raven didn't understand how the dead things could be born from a dead land again and again, but he accepted it was so and avoided the area. If his Mora ever joined him in this outside world, he would teach her to avoid the dead land and its dead people. He wanted his person to join him in the woods, but he couldn't teach her to fly. He hoped the note might teach her for him, so they could be free wild things together.

Twenty~Five

MORGAN ROSSI-STERN

MORGAN ROSSI-STERN SHOULD HAVE BEEN tired. She'd been to four City States in only three days, plus a quick stop at the Institute, but she wasn't tired at all. She felt invigorated.

Scratch that—she felt like she was on top of the world, which, in both a literal and metaphorical manner of speaking, she was.

She was traveling by hovercraft, which meant she'd spent many hours at altitudes far above the rest of the City State population. Morgan liked traveling by hovercraft. It was fast, efficient, luxurious, and exclusive. She might not be a top-ranking DDC official, but Morgan considered herself an invaluable cog in the working middle of the department. She wasn't the mind making the decisions (yet), but she was the hand that carried out those decisions. The right tools, as Morgan saw it, were as necessary as the skilled workers who wielded them.

There were benefits to DDC middle management. The biggest of them was knowledge. Morgan operated on the cusp of informational clearance. In her position, she knew much of the same information as her superiors, while employees even one rank below her knew almost nothing.

Morgan knew about the outbreak emerging within the cities. She knew it was concentrated among the oldest generation—the last of the city residents surviving from the world before. She knew this outbreak disproportionately affected the working class—a detriment to production and distribution, but it was essential to the changes that would support the DDC's most ambitious goals.

Morgan knew how many families the outbreak would devastate, and she knew about the resources the DDC was putting in place to accommodate the generation of children about to grow up without parents and grandparents. She knew how devastating this would be to the youth emerging from the education program, and she knew how scared this upcoming generation would be. Scared and dependent.

So much would be lost from a world that had already lost so much. The schools no longer taught colloquial history. Arts and literature took a back seat to mechanics, mathematics and biology. Young people learned that critical thinking was only valuable to the fundamentals of scientific deduction. Even the most educated citizens would form their hypotheses based on a curated and ever-narrowing flow of data pre-approved by DDC systems for analysis.

Even so, too much information existed to make control a simple and efficient matter. There were still too many avenues of communication. It wasn't enough to control the education systems. The sources of information also needed to be controlled. That's what drove the DDC's focus on removing old-world text and media from society. And they had their ways. The universal database of information, asking people to submit what information they had—media, texts, stories, images—to a centralized location to be catalogued into a single resource.

It was so much easier to control information when you knew where it was coming from. The DDC, by way of government overreach, had come to control much of the old-world data and could allow or restrict access based on their own goals.

But even this wasn't enough.

Certain pervasive avenues of information remained—black markets of human resilience like the Hole. This new outbreak would deal with them much like the last had handled the Resistees, and in doing so, the people would have their newest threat.

But even more important than the black market was the pesky existence of that indomitable flow of information:

Oral history.

You can't squash a society's entire existence by taking its data. The human mind was its own database of information that was widely transmissible. Take a book and no one can read it again, but those who have already read it still remember and can tell the stories. Take the readers, though—that was how an entire world could be erased.

This was an essential part of governing. Critical for next steps. It came at a great cost, Morgan knew. And this was why her position was so important—why it came with so much privilege. She was one of the few who both carried out the tasks and knew their purpose.

It meant she could maneuver in the world in a way that few others could. She could position herself and her family to flourish in a dying world. It meant she could keep Mora safe, even if the stupid girl didn't know what was good for her.

Morgan knew about the old-world tablet, of course. She knew the girl was dabbling in information that should guarantee her status as a statistic in the upcoming outbreak, but Morgan had every intention of circumventing the consequences. The erasure was meant for people who refused to adapt. Mora might not know what was good for her, but Morgan, thankfully, knew what was coming and had every intention of controlling the outcome meant for lesser people.

Mora would go to the Institute. She'd managed to guarantee it. Between the Dunn boy and Mora's own over-inflated sense of justice, she'd managed the right balance of cruel and cunning to make it seem as though Mora had made the choice on her own. It was the sort of manipulation that had taken her from such humble beginnings to such a stellar position in the DDC, and it had worked, hadn't it?

Mora had called, just as Morgan knew she would. The Dunn boy was with her as Morgan had known he would be, and they were studying. Mora had already secured her Retest. She'd done so to spare the Dunn kid and his family from Morgan's vengeful intentions.

In truth, Morgan wasn't capable of doing much to the Dunn family beyond reporting that they might have some data marked for elimination. While that might result in internal movement, it was just as likely to result in a whole lot of nothing. But neither Mora nor the Dunn boy knew this, so things had worked out exactly as Morgan had intended.

Mora was safe, well on her way to the Institute, away from the outbreak.

In the meantime, Morgan had finished her four-city investigation and identified a pattern of misappropriated credits related to the technology sector. Three shipments in the last six months had failed to reach their destinations. One of them appeared to be the result of a transport accident along the main road, but even that incident required thorough scrutiny. Five of the six crates of transportable goods were recovered, and the involvement of outside forces was questionable at best.

All the data pointed to activity from the inside. *Resistee activity*, her superior officer had suggested, but Morgan didn't think so. The Resistee movement was a cause—a belief that swept people into a dangerous frenzy and made them demand a return to freedom of movement, freedom of choice. They were demanding freedom to get themselves infected in the next big outbreak, if you asked Morgan. This recent activity was something different, though. Whoever was behind the shipments and lost goods might be aiming for the same thing as the Resistees, but they were being a lot more subtle.

Luckily, Morgan had managed to trace two of the three shipments —including the accidental collision—to the same individual with an inexplicable bump in credits. She was now landing back in her home city, just outside the capitol, in time to file her report and set up an encounter with said worker before he was sent out on a third emergency delivery.

She would set things up so he wouldn't see her coming. She intended to follow him outside the force field where she was fairly certain he might be meeting someone else—a third party who was making portions of the goods, and possibly more, disappear.

Morgan smiled as she disembarked from the hovercraft, her short hair tucked under the short-brimmed cap of an inter-city DDC official. She was very good at what she did, and soon she would unearth exactly what Mr. Baba was transporting in his misappropriated vehicle to earn himself such a substantial increase in credits.

THE INSTITUTE SPLIT the canopy of treetops, conjuring visions of white bone bursting through dark skin and forcing Zayd to remind himself it was nothing more than stark concrete in dim forest light. Their journey to this point had been painted in Sitka spruce, Douglass fir, western hemlock and red cedar, giving the impression they'd been moving further from civilization rather than directly into the supposed pinnacle of medical care. Zayd had only known the names of the spruce and fir, and even then, only as a general sort of tree, but Anika had been able to fill him in on the rest.

"The western hemlock are those big ones there," Anika said, lifting her head off his shoulder to peer out the window at the passing greenery.

The space where her head had been felt cold and empty, like maybe she was running a fever. He felt her absence as though every moment of connection between them grew more vital the closer they came to the Institute. The fear he forced back kept creeping forward, trying to whisper to him. *You won't be able to keep her close. You can't save her. This might be your fault —*

"The ones covered in moss?" he asked, forcing the whispering voice back. He ran his hand up her arm, fingers gently grazing the soft fabric of her work shirt the way he knew she liked.

"The whole forest is covered in moss, or can you not see?" she replied, giving him a critical look that meant she'd managed to relax a little.

"It's just more obvious on those massive trunks. The moss is like a big blanket," Zayd said. He wanted to kiss her. He wanted to pretend like nothing was wrong and they were only taking the type of quick little trip they used to fantasize about before the cities had closed to recreational travel. But his shoulder was cold, and the volunteer in the yellow protective suit was sitting two rows behind them, watching.

"*Attention to detail* never showed up on a single one of your academic reviews, did it?" Anika teased. Zayd hoped it meant she'd forgotten about the volunteer.

"And you paid too much attention," Zayd retorted, sneaking a kiss to the top of her head. *Warm.*

"My great-grandfather worked for the parks system, preserving them. When the disease came to his town, he took my great-grandmother and Nani into the forest. They lived there for almost three years and probably survived the worst of it thanks to his knowledge." Anika's voice was soft, almost a whisper, as if she didn't want anyone else on the transport to hear this precious family story.

"Have I ever mentioned that I love your great-grandfather for doing that?" Zayd always used this line when Anika shared their story, and it never failed to please her.

She reached across her body to place a hand over his. The grey color beneath her nails was undeniable, but Zayd still refused to accept that it meant anything. "I feel the same about your ancestors and their ingenuity in a crumbling world."

There were fifteen people on the transport vehicle, not including the driver and the yellow-clad volunteer. Zayd and Anika were one of three couples. The nine other passengers appeared to be traveling solo, their faces sullen, their eyes sunken deep into sockets that had long run dry of tears. Aside from the couples aboard the transport, no one seemed to know each other; thus the ride had been mostly quiet. The couples whispered to one another, grasping for privacy under the roar of the massive engine as the behemoth vehicle crawled across the asphalt strip parting the overgrown land.

When they finally stopped at the concrete wall surrounding the Institute, what little conversation there had been died away as a massive gate rolled open, offering them entry. The vehicle rolled under an archway that read *Institute of Scientific Education and Disease Treatment* and into a circular courtyard surrounded by towering grey buildings.

The vehicle pulled to a stop at a yellow line, and the entire world was swallowed by silence as the driver cut the engine. Passengers looked from the windows to one another in anxious anticipation. Zayd grabbed Anika's hand and squeezed as if he were expecting someone to try and rip her from his side. He forced back the voice whispering that someone would soon do exactly that.

The vehicle's double doors slid open with a pneumatic hiss, and a yellow-clad person stepped inside.

"Exit the vehicle in an orderly fashion. One person at a time. Wait at the exit to be received. You will be searched, then a volunteer will escort you to screening. Upon screening, all infected individuals will be brought into the treatment facility. Uninfected individuals will be brought into the volunteer orientation facility," the greeting person droned. Their voice was only slightly muffled by the yellow suit, as though their respirator had been modified specifically to allow them to give instructions.

"What if we already have our infection files?" one of the vehicle passengers—an older man with thick white hair and a too-many-days unshaven face—asked.

"Everyone on this transport will go through screening. We will intake your files and distribute patients accordingly," the greeter instructed.

"Will we be given treatment?"

"Can we opt to go straight into cryogenics?"

"Can I please call my son?"

The formerly silent passengers spoke over one another, each new question louder than the one before.

When Zayd was seven, he'd been disenrolled from class for two weeks on account of a viral infection. It wasn't anything serious—just a fever and a sore throat that burned and swelled like he'd swallowed a hornet's nest. After three days of medicine, the fever and the pain had let up, but he had to make it seven days without a fever before he could be cleared to return to classes. His mom had gone back to work, and he was bored with classwork and historical footage of outbreaks, so his dad had decided it wouldn't hurt anything to take him to work. His dad drove one of the in-city maintenance vehicles and did electrical grid work in the residence buildings. Zayd got to follow him from job to job, watching him measure the current signal at each building, replace pieces and wires on aging receivers, and record it all on his scanner.

After a few stops, Zayd became fascinated with the flash of greenish-blue light that appeared each time his dad pressed the test button on a grid plate. He knew the light was a product of the grid, meant to visualize where the energy was concentrated so there would be an accurate measurement, but he'd misjudged how strong that surge was. A sign on each plate warned workers to keep their bodies clear of the test area when measuring grid signal strength, but Zayd hadn't bothered to read it.

When his dad had gone back to the truck to get a replacement piece, Zayd had pressed the test button, curious to see the light up close. His thumb had been sitting inside the test space—just his thumb. But when he'd pushed the button, the shock he'd received was unlike anything he'd ever experienced. Pain, panic, shock…

That's what hearing the passengers shout and beg their questions felt like.

"We will answer all your questions in due time. Please form an exit line," the greeter instructed, their voice artificially raised to ring out above the din of terror.

The tide of noise receded, slowly at first as passengers hung on to the possibility of having their questions addressed, then all at once as they realized that it was futile.

They exited the vehicle one at a time into the waiting sea of yellow-clad volunteers. Out the window, Zayd could see them get searched. Volunteers collected personal materials before the newcomers were escorted in a growing line toward the automatic doors of the nearest grey building.

"I think here is where we will part, my love," Anika whispered, her breath soft against Zayd's ear.

"Not until we have to," Zayd insisted.

Anika squeezed his hand as they approached the exit together. In front of them, a middle-aged woman with slightly greying hair relinquished her ancient-looking wristwatch to a waiting volunteer.

"Next," the greeter commanded.

Anika tried to step forward, but Zayd held fast to her, reaching to pull her into a firm embrace. She turned then, placing a barely trembling hand against the side of his face. Her thumb brushed his dry cheek. He looked into her glistening eyes with just-contained panic.

"Please don't make this harder than it has to be for us," she begged, trying to exude strength for the both of them.

"I can't let you go," he said.

"You will be right behind me."

He knew it was true but still couldn't let go. The spot on his shoulder was cold without her head pressed there. The whole world was too cold, even with her hand still pressed against his face. He willed it to remain, to burn a hole in him with a fire that could never be extinguished.

"I can't—"

She pressed her thumb over his lips, cutting off his words.

"We can," she said, slipping her hand out of his and stepping off the transport into the waiting volunteers.

He watched them search her as she waited, hands up. They scanned her file before relieving her of it, then ushered her forward. She glanced back over her shoulder as they left, and the greeter called for Zayd to step into the next set of waiting volunteers.

"Do you have a file?" one of the volunteers asked as Zayd stood, numb, with his hands outstretched before him. He caught one last glimpse of Anika before the automatic doors slid shut. Her dark hair had mostly come undone from her long braid and was cascading down her back, shimmering in the gold of the evening's fading light.

"Do you have a file?" the volunteer repeated, dragging Zayd back to the present.

"No. I'm a volunteer," he said as the other one patted him down.

"This way, please," the volunteer said, ushering him forward.

Zayd followed eagerly, hoping to catch up with Anika inside the screening building. He had no idea how long the process lasted, only that it was "accelerated" compared to testing in the cities. Results took as long as a week to process within the cities, so that didn't mean much. He wondered if they had a lounge inside the screening building, if he might turn a corner and be reunited with Ani after only the briefest of separations.

The doors opened to a blinding white entryway. A woman wearing a white lab coat sat behind a white desk, her hair clipped short.

"This one have a file?" she asked the volunteers.

"Volunteer," his escort said.

"Screening to the left," she instructed, pressing a button Zayd couldn't see so the doors on the left swung open.

He moved with his escorts down a narrow hall lined with a curious number of doors to a room filled with brown chairs. One of the women, who had been traveling with an elderly man, already sat in one of the chairs. Her back was unnaturally straight, her jaw clenched tight. *Rigid*, Zayd thought absently.

"Wait here. Someone will take you back to screening," Zayd's volunteer companion instructed, turning to leave.

"Will I see Ani again?" Zayd asked, panic blinding him to the fact that neither of the volunteers would know who he was talking about.

"If you pass screening, you will be taken to volunteer orientation," one of them said.

"What about Ani?" Zayd said again.

The volunteer nearest the door scanned a badge to unlock the door to exit. Neither of them turned.

Zayd scrambled internally to say the right thing—the thing that would get a response. "The... uh, patients. Will I be able to see a patient after screening?"

"No."

The door shut before Zayd could process the definitiveness of the response.

CHAPTER

Twenty-Seven

PARK

THE L-WING BUZZED with nervous energy as Park made her way to the central station to check in and find Dr. Wong. She'd heard about the transport. Twelve new patients from the capitol was notable even to the volunteers, many of whom had arrived on transports just like this one with infected family or friends. But never this many at once.

Vang said they only got four new patients in the main medical wing.

Park made her way past an L-wing medic with a supply cart traveling too fast in the other direction. She twisted her body to the side and pressed up against the wall to let them pass. She had a headache, her pants were too tight, and she wasn't in the mood for her extended shift this evening, but none of that managed to stem her curiosity. It wasn't just the way the patients in the L-wing were treated or their extended stays. She couldn't explain it to Garth yet, but there was something peculiar about the L-wing patients that escaped description.

"Park! There you are," Dr. Wong called over the counter of the central station where a masked medic tapped away at a built-in screen as he waited.

"I only just got the shift notification," Park said, hoping to brush over the extra time she spent having a snack and using the bathroom (twice) before garbing up and heading over.

"Of course. We weren't expecting such a sudden need," he said, clearly not registering any serious delay on her part.

"Rooms four, six, eighteen, and twenty-three," the masked medic said as their fingers danced over the expanded map of the L-wing layout. "Files are uploading now."

Park's tablet beeped at the same time as Dr. Wong's as she scurried to his side, trying not to sound breathless and out of sorts.

Four rooms for four patients, she thought. Between these four, the four that went to main medical, and one sent straight to cryo, they were still missing a few patients from the transport. *Or Vang's numbers were wrong.* Park doubted that. There were too many mysteries surrounding the Institute these days.

"It's a big day today, Park. Are you ready to do some work on your own?" Dr. Wong asked, raising an eyebrow over his glowing tablet to meet her curious gaze.

Park blustered at the notion. "I'm not supposed to have clearance for solo work—"

"Oh, I know, protocols and such. But this is the DDC. We're allowed certain privileges. Exceptions to the rules, you might say. The ones who would check up on you are the ones granting you those exceptions."

Dr. Wong was gushing. There was a twinkle in his eye that Park found profoundly disquieting.

He's actually excited about the new patients, she thought, a new level of terror settling in.

"Of course, Dr. Wong. If you believe I'm ready, I'm honored," she said, going with her gut to find the right response. She was supposed to be an eager new medic, fresh from the intern program and half-brainwashed with whatever propaganda had turned Reed against her.

Thinking of Reed sent a painful jolt through her body. She'd been trying to *not* think of him. It was bad enough that she was uncomfortable, nauseous, grumpy, and confused all the time. She didn't want to add betrayed and heartsick into the mix.

I don't want you to come out here again.

His final words were on a repeating track in her mind—a precursor to the silence of his abandonment. She wasn't even certain he'd heard her declaration before retreating into the safety of the intern dormitories. And for what? To evade the over-tired set of volunteers making their way to a dreamless sleep from their shift in the screening and cryo building?

"…think I'll have you visit David again—he's an easy patient—before taking over one of the new patient intakes. What do you think?" Dr. Wong was saying.

Park realized she hadn't been paying attention and scrambled to fill in the missing pieces with the most likely scenario.

"I like David. I agree he's a good first solo for me."

Dr. Wong smirked at that, swiping his finger above the surface of his tablet to send the file her way. "I'm fairly certain he likes you, too. Do you think you can handle the intake in twenty-three? The volunteers will do patient restraints and setup."

Park had done patient intake in the main medical wing before. There was nothing terribly difficult about it—the volunteers handled the patients. All she'd have to do was the intake blood work and scans.

"I think I can handle that. Anything I need to know about L-wing intake?"

"The patients here are different, so be nice. Many of them stay with us for some time. Their cooperation and compliance are invaluable," Dr. Wong said, scrolling through the new patient files on his tablet.

"Be nice. Got it," Park said. Strange how his instructions were so contrary to the training she'd received in the intern program and on the main medical floor.

There was a flash of something incoming on Dr. Wong's tablet.

"I'm going to give you the patient in twenty-three. I think it's a good match. A younger woman—not much older than you. Perhaps she'll see a friendly face. You do have a friendly face."

A file appeared on Park's roster. Dr. Wong was rambling now, and Park wondered what was drawing his attention.

"Should I report back to you when I'm finished?" she asked, hoping to end this meeting and get on with her shift.

"Yes," he said, fully immersed in whatever had come through.

"Alright," Park said, wondering if she needed to offer a formal goodbye before taking her leave.

Dr. Wong didn't look up, so after taking a few backward steps, Park turned and headed for her first assignment of the evening—patient 00Z52 or, as he was known by Dr. Wong and the people he'd left behind in the cities, David.

As usual, David had old-world music playing through the speakers mounted by his bed. He sat up, skinny legs sticking out from beneath a terrycloth green robe, gnarled feet buried in a pair of fuzzy green slippers. His thin grey hair was matted in the back, sticking out in wild tufts around large ears. Park suspected David didn't mind his appearance much more than he seemed to mind his indefinite residence, confined to a narrow radius around his bed in the L-wing.

He barely moved when she entered the room, eyes closed as the music swelled to a powerful crescendo that even managed to stir something inside of Park, who had never cared for music—neither the old-world nor the new-world variety. The song, an old instrumental recording—she wasn't sure what instrument—filled her with a strange sense of longing. That almost indescribable feeling seemed to match whatever the old man on the bed was feeling because as the ache inside of her became nearly tangible, she noticed a pair of tears gather at the corners of his shut eyes before trailing down his cheeks, following an unpredictable path along deep age lines.

She waited, almost breathless, as the music rose, fell, rose again and then, both suddenly and finally, concluded, leaving an aftereffect in the room that buzzed like a physical presence.

"Incredible, isn't it?" David asked, wiping his eyes as he noticed her standing against the door.

"Yes," she answered with a soft smile, following Dr. Wong's decree to *be nice*. It was easy to do despite knowing the viral danger that lurked within the man. Then, not knowing she was going to do it, she asked, "What is it?"

"Music, Dr. Park." David smiled, crumpling the tissue awkwardly in an arthritic fist.

"Just Park. I'm a training medic, remember?" she said, forcing herself to move into the room with purpose.

"A training medic set loose to do solo draws in the government's most top-secret medical wing?" David said, stunning her. He pulled his feet onto the bed and placed his braced hands and feet against the magnetic binders to secure himself.

Park didn't know if the cameras in the rooms had audio feeds and didn't care to find out through this or any other questionable conversation with a patient, so she asked, "That song you were listening to just now—what was it?"

David was fully restrained now, the lights on his bindings flickering green and blue with a positive connection. Park gloved up in the medic's section of the room before approaching his bedside, pushing the tray of equipment into the space where his unfinished lunch had been.

"Suite No. 1 in G Major. For cello," David said with dreamy grey eyes that stared more through her than at her.

David's favorite songs always had strange names that only made sense in a world long gone. That he both knew those names and seemed to understand their meaning amazed her. She opened the sterile pack of sanitizing wipes to clean the nearly transparent skin of his forearm. His blue veins looked as though they might burst straight through his paper-thin skin, making him seem suddenly more monstrous as he lay there, head pointed in her direction, watching and not watching.

"Why was it so... sad? Full? Why was it the way it was?" she asked, trying to dispel the temporary rush of discomfort she'd felt when picturing him as one of the monsters—one of the fully transformed donations.

"Ah," he said, a knowing look lighting up his face. "That was the cello."

"You said it was *for cello*," Park agreed, lining up the needle with the thickest of the veins.

Pulsing, bulging, gushing disease.

"That's the instrument—if you could call it that," David explained. He didn't wince when the needle went in. His blood splashed a rich, dark red inside the rapidly filling vial.

"Is cello not an instrument?" Park asked, switching one vial for the next with an expert hand.

"A cello is torment, frustration, and most important of all, a thing of immense sadness," David said.

Park switched to the third and final vial, releasing the tourniquet band and preparing the treated bandage. "That sounds terrible."

"If you could hear it in person… it's the most beautiful thing you'll ever experience." He continued to look up as she pulled the needle and placed the bandage.

"You've heard it?" she asked, then rushed to clarify. "In person, not just recordings?"

"I played a bit when I was younger—before the force fields went up. Mostly the viola. Some clarinet, chords on a piano."

Park recognized *piano* and knew it was the instrument the tones of the city announcement were designed after. She understood music and its historical role, but clearly she didn't *know* music like David did.

"Of course, my grandfather was the real musician," David continued. "How do you get to Carnegie Hall? Practice!"

Park scanned him for a temperature, thinking he was ranting. Ranting was a sign of disease progression, which, according to Dr. Wong, very few of the patients in the L-wing experienced.

There was no temperature, though. David was merely speaking of a thing Park didn't understand.

"Practice the instruments?" she asked, trying to engage.

Be nice.

"Of course. That's where the torment and sadness come from," he said. His voice was bright and clear, confirming that this wasn't a fevered rant.

"Full scan today, David. Is that alright?" Park asked, setting up the scanning program on her tablet.

"You're the doctor," David said, then corrected himself. "Medic."

"That's right. I'm the boss." David smiled when she winked at him.

They were quiet for a long time while Park traced the scanner over every surface of David's disrobed body, comparing the results with the week before.

"I thought the sadness was the music," she said finally.

"The cello is a tool for human emotion. It's the range of the instrument that does it—like the human voice. It can evoke a powerful response," David explained as Park finished the task. She covered him before stepping back from his bed, pulling the medical tray with her.

"Do you mean that the music sounds sad because the cello sounds like a human voice?" She placed her hands into two holes at shoulder height in the wall at the back of the room. When she removed her arms, the over-layer of gloves had been removed. She re-gloved, rolled the med table into the sterilization box, then sent the samples to be processed.

"No. It doesn't sound human," David said. The restraints beeped, releasing their hold on him. He sat up, pulling his robe more securely around his middle before absently rubbing at the cuffs. "There's just something in our brain that makes us feel that way about it—*almost* human. And it hurts."

His explanation sent chills down her spine. David flipped through a small device until the beginning notes of a new song wafted through the room. He let out a sigh as if those notes were soothing a terrible pain.

"Thank you for your cooperation, David," Park said, swiping her ID card over the lock pad. The door clicked open.

"Thank you for your humanity, Dr. Park."

The door closed. As she made her way to room twenty-three, Park couldn't stop thinking about cellos.

Twenty-Eight

ANIKA

ANIKA WAS STILL TREMBLING when they brought her in. She couldn't help it after what she'd seen—what they'd done! And the worst of it all was that she couldn't see Zayd.

They put him in that room, too, she thought as the yellow-clad volunteers ushered her through a third set of doors that opened automatically at the swipe of a badge. She didn't know where she was going because no one would speak to her, but she wasn't going to the same place as the other infected people from the transport, and she knew it had to do with the room with the monster in it.

She could still feel the creature's stink clinging to her skin. There was no amount of washing, no sterilization, no inoculation that would ever make her clean again. It didn't matter that it hadn't come close. It didn't matter that there had been a force field separating her from it for a majority of the time. Never in her life would she have believed she would wind up so close to one of the diseased.

It looked right at me!

There had been a moment, as she stood alone and the air vents cycled, when she had stared through the semi-transparency of a force field up close and the creature seemed to meet her terrified gaze. Its sunken, cloudy eyes stilled as it peered at her—no, through her—and she thought she might recognize some form of human emotion on its shriveled, grey face.

There was an electric *clunk*, and the air changed. The smell of diseased, decaying flesh filled the room, and she gagged. The sound drew the creature's attention, and it pulled against heavy restraints. Anika screamed as the creature sniffed the air with a hungry growl. It was as if it were blind and trying to locate its next meal by means of other sensory input. While it sniffed and twitched and screamed and strained against its restraints, another concussive sound vibrated through the room, and the shimmer reappeared as the force field engaged. The creature continued its rampage.

It all happened in an instant—a matter of seconds—but to Anika, it felt like an eternity. The stench remained when the force field returned and hung in the air along with her terrified screams. A voice came through on a speaker then, informing her the air in the room would be cycled and she would have to endure the whole thing all over again.

The force field came down a second and a third time, each time making the creature more frantic—more desperate to reach her. It pulled hard against the restraints, wailing and gnashing, one of its arms bent at an unnatural angle. On the third cycle, it lunged forward with such ferocity that the oddly angled arm dislocated with a resounding *pop*. The creature jerked again, and its flesh began to tear as it wrenched itself free of the broken and bound appendage, reaching toward Anika with an arm that wasn't there anymore. When the force field re-engaged, someone in a dark suit and knee-length lab coat came to tell her she would have to wait a moment while they made a call. It was only then that she was ushered into the hall and her hands were bound together by two thick metal cuffs placed on her wrists. The cuffs hummed with energy like the wires of the lashing pole and held fast to one another as she waited.

After a time, the door opened, and another one of the transport passengers emerged, ushered by a different lab-coat-wearing, black-suited worker and a yellow-clad volunteer.

"It was going to attack me!" the old man blubbered, chest heaving.

"That is what we call a non-response," the woman in the lab coat said.

"Its arm. Its arm was off!" the old man continued, still reeling with panic. "Didn't you see its arm was off? It was going to attack me."

The suited coat handed the file to the volunteer before returning to the dark vestibule where another passenger would be received.

"Please come this way," the volunteer urged the man.

"Where are you taking me?" the old man pleaded. Anika could see the tears streaking his face.

"This is the way to cryogenics," the volunteer said.

"Right now? Isn't there treatment?" the man asked, his feet planted as if he could resist the power of the much larger volunteer.

"You don't have any injuries. No need for stabilization." The volunteer brought their lashing pole forward, pressing the button and wrapping the man's torso with the magnetic bindings.

"Samples. The Institute needs samples for investigative purposes!" The man sounded as if he'd just read the brochure for treatment at the Institute.

"All information from your file has been considered, and the Institute has declared you a candidate for immediate cryogenic slumber." The volunteer's voice was dispassionate. He whipped the pole forward, and the old man had no choice but to walk forward or fall and be dragged.

They moved down the hall faster than Anika thought someone in that configuration would be able to go, the old man crying and begging the whole way. His last plea before the double doors leading toward cryogenics closed was, "My son! I have to tell my son. Let me call him!"

The man who told Anika to wait returned with two volunteers. He wore a slim smile that didn't touch his eyes. "I'd like you to follow these volunteers to your quarters," he said in a cordial voice that contradicted his expression.

Anika followed them, not wanting to cause a scene lest they revoke her polite reception and decide to drag her out like the man. The volunteers led her in the opposite direction, through another set of doors and down into a tunnel that emerged into what she suspected was one of the other buildings. They walked through white-tiled halls with bright light reflecting off every surface. The air smelled clean and sterile like the exam rooms in her clinic.

They walked past door after door, from which no one emerged. There was a central desk ahead of them with a high surface, meant for standing. A man with a stethoscope hurried past the desk in the opposite direction, tablet in hand, clearly distracted. The procession stopped at a door with the number twenty-three printed above the entry pad. The nearest volunteer swiped their card, and the door swung wide, revealing a small room with a bed, a table, one of those portable bathrooms for the very old and infirm, and an empty, white counter.

Anika was instructed to sit on the bed. She did so without complaint, still thinking of the monster in the room and the crying man. The volunteers worked together, one unbinding her wrists as the other fastened the same sort of restraint rings around her ankles, laying her back and adjusting her limbs until the restraints caught against the current from plates attached to the bed, locking her in place.

"Lashing secured," one of them said, giving her right arm a shake to ensure it held fast.

"Confirmed," the other responded, shaking the rings attached to her feet, which were now spread about two feet apart in a highly indecent position.

The volunteers turned to leave, filling her with the same frantic panic she'd accused the old man of when he was taken to cryogenics. She forced herself to breathe, preparing a calm inquisition. *Will someone be here shortly?* But the door shut before she was composed, leaving her alone with the terror of her own racing thoughts.

Thankfully, someone did arrive shortly after she was abandoned—a young woman with short, black hair and smooth, medium-toned golden skin.

"Hello. My name is Park. I'm a medic-in-training, and I'm here to do your intake," the woman said, pushing a cart into the room.

"Park," Anika repeated through numb lips. Her whole body tingled with nervous anticipation.

Park moved into the room, pushing her cart right up to the bedside.

Anika recognized much of what it contained. They were the tools of her profession.

Former profession.

"How are you doing, Ms. Baba?" she asked as she set to work organizing what she would need. Her voice was kind. The young medic was nervous but displayed none of the fear Anika had seen etched onto Sophia's face. There was a clinical coolness to Park that reminded her of Cora, but not completely.

"I'm a little overwhelmed," Anika said, thinking that this offering of partial honesty would be a fine way to test the waters of this situation.

"I can imagine," Park said. She left her tray of medical equipment to thrust her hands into a hole in the wall. They disappeared up to her elbows, and when they emerged again, she was wearing a second layer of blue-gloved protection.

"Is the infection definitive?" Anika asked, noting the extra precaution.

"You wouldn't be here if it weren't," Park said, tearing open one of the sanitizing wipes on her tray. She ran it over the inside of Anika's exposed forearm, leaving a trail of cool, over-sensitized skin in its wake. "There are too many fail-safes in place between your clinic results and this room for a false positive to make it through."

"Why didn't I go straight to cryogenics?" She didn't know if she wanted an answer, but she was too anxious not to ask. She didn't need medical treatment, so there must be some need for additional testing. The Institute was a research- and education-based medical facility.

Park placed the needle expertly. Anika didn't even have time to look away before the job was done and the first vial began to fill with her blood. The tourniquet didn't even hurt. Park had applied the exact right amount of pressure.

She's very good.

"I don't know," Park said. They were already on the second vial.

Anika let that sink in, trying to decide if Park was being completely honest. Park removed the tourniquet as the third vial filled. Anika moved her fingers to speed the process along even though it wasn't necessary. This was a fast and easy blood draw.

"The creature tried to attack me," she said, watching a single drop of blood bloom on the medical adhesive Park used to cover the draw site.

The young medic paused at this, nearly fumbling the vials and confirming what Anika had suspected since the old man stumbled from the screening room claiming the monster had attacked—the creature's reaction to her was atypical for an infected person.

Park sent the vials through the slot to whatever testing facility the Institute had set up. Her face was pinched in consternation. As she set up the scanner for the next phase of intake, she spoke, choosing her words carefully.

"That's probably why you're here."

"The Institute?" Anika asked, trying not to flinch as Park gently cut her clothing away. The cool air bombarded her senses, triggering severe horripilation. The creep of the medical scissors as the fabric came away from her sleeve only worsened the sick chill.

"The L-wing," Park said, finishing the job, rendering Anika completely naked and fully exposed. "This isn't the regular medical facility. This area is for patients with a… strange presentation." The scanner beeped as Park began the first input.

"What do you mean, strange?" Anika demanded, trying hard to ignore the horror of such vulnerability.

Park's lips thinned as she considered the best answer. She ran the scanner down Anika's middle, waiting between each quadrant scan for the baseline data to record—the exact pigmentation and variation of Anika's skin, likely measured against an entire database of patients.

"Patients in the L-wing don't seem to get any sicker than they were when they first came in," she said.

It was Anika's turn to be quiet now. Park was at her hands, taking time to rotate her palms up and down under the scanner.

"The disease doesn't progress? For how long?"

Park finished the job, setting the scanner aside. "For as long as they're here, at least," she said, pushing the tray outside of the blue line on the white-tiled floor. "There's a robe at the foot of the bed for you."

Park stepped outside of the blue line, and the restraints binding

Anika to the bed released. Her appendages clunked suddenly against the mattress, and she scrambled upright, reaching for the robe. Anika considered this news and the reliability of the young woman sharing it. Her gut said the medic was trustworthy—for now. There was something about her. The way she held herself, maybe.

Park kept her back turned until Anika was covered. "Is there anything I can get you to make your stay more comfortable?" she asked once Anika was seated at the edge of her bed, fuzzy green robe tied at the waist, legs crossed underneath her.

"I would like to speak with my husband," Anika said, deciding she might as well give it a shot.

Nice job on the tracking paper. Our communications specialist missed it. Thankfully, one of our techs is familiar with the organic electric diode slips you used to track your message. It almost felt like real paper—almost.

Since you know where we are, I'll let you in on a little secret: by the time this message reaches you, we will know not only your location (which we are fairly confident we're already aware of, thanks to your little friend), but also the remaining details we couldn't get from your official government file.

You're in a bit of a bind. Things aren't looking good on the inside, so consider this your formal invitation to join us out here. Additional encryption inside. Looking forward to your response, Mora.

MORA READ THE MESSAGE—ONCE, twice, half a dozen times, reeling. A fine line of sweat ran down the back of her neck, and her hands trembled as she fingered the encrypted slip woven into the paper. Who were they? Where did they come from?

"How do they know your name?" James asked, reading the note over her shoulder. He reached for it, but Mora turned her body to block him. She couldn't let it go—not yet—not without understanding. Could she let herself hope that the writer knowing about her meant something? She read it again, trying to discern the answer as Omen shifted his attention from his favorite bits of the cereal to Mora's shoulder.

"How do they know your name, Mora?" James demanded, louder than before.

"Mora," Omen repeated. The sound was a near-perfect replication of James' voice. He said it again, gently nibbling at the side of Mora's face, soliciting affection as James looked on in horror.

Mora reached up and scratched absently at the side of the bird's neck, still holding the note with her unoccupied hand. Still reading.

…your official government file…

You're in a bit of a bind.

What could they possibly know that she didn't? She was certain it was a *they* sort of situation. The communications specialist and techs the letter mentioned probably weren't fabrications. James was a special sort of clever, which was why he was going to the Institute. Mora doubted the person who first touched her communication was also gifted enough to uncover James' encoding and add to it. Like the letter writer said, it was a team. *A team of people living outside the City States who knows more about me and the goings-on of the City States than I do…*

"You didn't say Omen could talk!" James accused. Mora finally looked up from the letter to find James staring at Omen, his eyes wide with a mixture of terror and wonder.

"He's a raven, Jim. Ravens are one of the smartest birds," she said. It wasn't time to be freaked out by natural mimicry.

"He told them your name!" James said. He was speaking significantly louder than usual, a sure sign of his discomfort.

She thought about correcting him—telling him they couldn't prove Omen had revealed her identity—but they'd been certain in their correspondence to not give any other identification. Instead, she said, "I can't be the only Mora."

"Does Omen know your last name?" James looked at her through narrowed eyes, his brow scrunched as though he expected her to say the bird did.

"No, he doesn't!" she said, leaning over to check his shoulder.

They both went quiet again, Mora still scratching at Omen's neck and chest feathers. When James reached for the note, she didn't stop him. After a few minutes of tinkering, he scanned the back of the paper with his tablet—his *new* tablet, freshly distributed through the school's replacement program without investigation since he'd never damaged or broken a school tablet before.

"Are they actually a community on the outside, or is this some sort of DDC trap?" Mora asked while he worked. A while back, one of her clients had told her a story about the DDC infiltrating Resistee communication to identify and eliminate organizers. Now she couldn't stop thinking about it.

"It's a valid question. We should be careful, but..." he trailed off, lost in thought as he attempted to make sense of the encryption.

"They have my government file," Mora said, filling the void of his incomplete thought.

"They *say* they have your file," James corrected. He switched programs to read through an instruction manual. Mora waited until he found what he needed and returned to the task. "They might be bluffing. Hand me your tablet—the old one."

"They know my name," Mora said, placing the brick-like old contraption next to his state-of-the-art system.

"Your bird knows your name," James said, attaching a networking device to Mora's tablet so it could receive the signal from his. He almost smiled when he worked like this, and Mora couldn't help but think he was going to be happy at the Institute—if not because of their mission, then because he would be able to do the incredible things he was born to do.

"How would they know I'm in trouble?" Mora asked.

"Lucky guess," James said, moving back and forth between the two devices to make sure things were working. "You're a smart kid with an illegal pet in a city that doesn't allow that sort of thing."

Mora considered this as James finished his task. It made sense on the surface. The sort of kid who would reply to a message pinned to a raven's leg was probably the kind with trouble.

"They would have to know what the cities are like. They'd have to guess that ravens are supposed to be extinct. There's no way for them to know I'm a kid…"

Unless someone on the outside knew who she was. She didn't dare voice the thought out loud.

"They didn't say you were a kid. They said things weren't looking good for you on the inside. That could be true of an adult, too. I've almost got this—it's a communication program!" James said, awe supplanting his former trepidation.

A thought suddenly occurred to her. "What if it isn't about me at all? What if things aren't looking good for anyone in the cities?" Her mind was racing, certain she was onto something.

"They said it was an outbreak—that the protests and gatherings spread the disease faster than they'd seen since the beginning," the old woman had explained with a quivering voice, placing her hand on Mora's as she recounted the story. "But there never was an outbreak. They just made the problem disappear, then blamed the real problems on the Resistees. Do you know what a scapegoat is?"

Mora had looked up the term and read of its use throughout history and fiction. The next time she had checked on the old woman, there had been no answer. There hadn't been since.

"What if the DDC is planning another outbreak?"

James was barely paying attention now, lost in his work in a way Mora found both infuriating and inspiring. "We'll be able to ask what they meant in a minute," he said.

"I could never do what you're doing," she said, taking in the way her tablet had transformed. The keyboard was still a rudimentary touchscreen, but the program was elegant.

"This one was tough, but you only have to do basic code identification to pass the Test," James said.

"I'm not going to pass the Test," Mora said. Her lips pursed together in a scowl that darkened her expression.

"I saw your last study set. You're a lot closer than you think," James said.

"I'm a lot farther away from a high score than you want to believe," Mora countered.

"If you're just planning to run away, why are you bothering to Retest at all?" James asked. The way the question spilled out of him made Mora believe it had been burning up inside of him for a while and he had only now found the courage to ask.

"Because running away takes time to do right. Petitioning to take the Test and studying to do well buys me that time. It makes me look like I'm planning to stick around," she said, then, by way of changing the subject, asked, "Is it ready yet?"

James looked at the indicator at the top right of the screen. "It's still trying to break through the network barrier."

"This would be easier if we just did it on your tablet," Mora said, standing suddenly. Omen spread his wings, taking to the air at her abrupt motion before settling again on the ledge to watch her pace in stiff, short bursts.

"It's way too risky to set up direct communication on a school tablet," James said, his eyes widening at the suggestion.

"You didn't have to get a school tablet," Mora said, sending a critical glare his way.

"It would've been a total waste to buy a personal tablet. You get three breaks without investigation, and this was my first."

"Braggart," Mora accused. Her tone was light.

"How many tablets have you broken since your first year?" he asked.

"Four," she confessed, cheeks heating at the admission.

"How?" James stared at her, eyes wide with incredulity.

"I'd love to tell you my secrets, but you've got too many goody-good rules to live my lifestyle," she teased.

Omen called to her, "Hey." And she relinquished the last of the cereal. He munched at the puffy squares, dark beak pecking eagerly at the sweetened crisps.

"Do you smash them against the building or throw them off the roof?" James asked.

"I stepped on one waking up in the middle of the night to go to the bathroom. And the other one, I don't know for sure. It was in my pack, and it just stopped working," she said.

"Were you at the Hole when it quit working?" James asked.

"Yes." Mora resented the question, but it was senseless to deny it.

"Someone probably had a wiper," James said. She knew he was right. He didn't ask about the other two, and she let the matter drop.

"What are you planning on using the credits for?"

"I don't know yet," he admitted.

"Do your parents know you have them?"

"I gave the guy a dummy account number. Nobody knows I have them until I spend them. In theory, I could use them without anyone ever knowing if I'm careful," James said.

"I didn't know you did mercenary accounting." Mora smirked.

"There's a lot you don't know about me." The tablet beeped, signifying a successful network breach.

"I'm starting to think you're a downright criminal," Mora said, springing toward the tablet.

"Criminal-adjacent," James corrected, leaning in beside her. "What are you going to say?"

Mora's fingers hovered over the keyboard as she considered, then typed. "The first thing my correspondent said to me."

> Mora: Hello from the inside.

They waited. There was no way of knowing how long a response would take. The screen shifted from white to red as the sun dipped below the next-highest building.

"When do you need to go?" Mora asked, closing her jacket against the cold. She didn't want him to leave but knew he would have to soon.

"I should have left a while ago," James said. She imagined the panic his parents would feel thinking about him walking home at dusk.

"Probably."

"Should we get downstairs before your mom gets home?" he asked.

Mora let out a huff of air through her nose. "She's not home tonight. On assignment again."

"Where?" James asked, probably just to keep the conversation moving.

"Who knows? She doesn't tell me anything unless it's about how much I disappoint her."

"Would it be safe to move this endeavor downstairs?" James asked. He was looking out to where the buildings cast long, dark shadows over empty city streets. Beyond them, the sunset bled into a mass of dark earth—blurry and obscured by the force field.

"Are you scared of the dark?" Mora asked, uncertain why she felt compelled to tease him.

"Maybe scared of climbing down that first bit in the dark," he admitted.

"Do you want to stay tonight?" she asked. It was a foregone conclusion. James never wanted to go home unless it was to work on one of his projects, and his current favorite project was right in front of him.

"My parents won't like it," he said.

"They don't have to know Mom's not home," Mora said.

"True," he agreed, packing up his own tablet and the network supplies. Mora's tablet was good to run on its own now. Mora picked it up, staring at the blank space where eventually the response would appear.

"We're already breaking a bunch of other rules and boundaries. What's one little sleepover?" she asked.

"Harmless criminal-adjacent shenanigans," James mused, using one of his favorite words she'd taught him.

Mora put the tablet in her pack, stroking the top of Omen's head one more time before grabbing James' hand. "Let's drive some parents crazy."

James squeezed back, swallowing hard at the prospect of descent. "Yeah. I'm running out of opportunities to break a bunch of rules."

"That must be a relief," Mora said, leading the way to the ledge.

"Yes, but that's probably ignorance on my part. I'm sure I'll get to the Institute and immediately miss my criminal past."

"Doubtful," Mora laughed.

She led him down, impressed at his growing confidence as he descended to the top of the fire escape. Though he was getting better about it, he still didn't breathe until they were about three floors down. Then he glanced back at her with ruddy cheeks and an unabashed smile. She let him lead the way back to her apartment window. By the time they made it back inside and replaced the screws in the window frame, Mora's message had a reply.

Thirty

SIMONS

WHILE MORA EXCHANGED messages with a woman named Georgia who was most certainly not government or DDC personnel and who absolutely had her government file *and* knew things about the cities that neither of the teens knew, Simons drove an empty transport vehicle down the main road toward the energy management facility outside the Institute. His new contact had missed his rendezvous.

The man might have hit another tree, but Simons dismissed the idea as unlikely. Baba was green, but he was competent. He wouldn't hold a single panicked action against the man when he'd otherwise done a stellar job. Baba hadn't even flinched when the DDC employee had walked out of the back of the transport. With Ternice's warning echoing in his mind, Simons knew he wasn't wrong to do a check on Kumar's story and supposed position, but he hadn't kept his cool while doing it. That Kumar hadn't gotten knocked into a concussion was Baba's doing, and Simons wasn't proud of that. He strove to be more levelheaded.

For all of his apparent blunders, Zayd was the sort of even-keeled fellow Simons aspired to be. He liked the guy. Zayd was a family man, or would be before long. In this world, it took a lot of guts to start a family. *Or faith*, he thought, harkening back to a concept so many had left behind with the old world. His mother had a lot to say about faith, but never in the presence of others. Growing up, faith was a concept for a tight-knit group of people who only showed their alliances behind closed doors. It was the thing that fueled the commotion in the streets as his people fought for their humanity. Their faith held them up individually and held them together as a community in a hard world, and now it was likely the foundation for Simons' own desire to become one of the dissenting few in the wake of the Resistee dissolution.

Disagreeing with the rules and regulations adopted in the name of keeping people safe took faith. Especially when the rules kept growing, and most especially when he didn't disagree with all of it. He'd seen the ravages of Zoribiatus with his own eyes and knew the risk would always be there. He'd witnessed the disease's progression and its final outcome. In his travels as a dissenter, he'd seen the near-dead as they wandered the open wilderness, hungry and lost. He knew about their transformation from docile to deadly when they sensed uninfected flesh, and he knew the disease wasn't done taking its toll on people, either inside or outside the cities.

But Simons didn't believe that the Department of Disease Containment, after taking over the entire government and remaking the new City States, was truly making decisions in the best interest of the citizens. It was no coincidence that things from the old world were disappearing at the same rate as the new infrastructure appeared. It wasn't just to keep people safe. It couldn't be, because what harm could vestiges of an old world cause? They weren't contaminated.

History is the voice of a people, he could hear his mother saying. *You can't destroy a society without erasing their history.*

When he was young, he'd dismissed it. What did a few books have to do with people's lives? What could stories from a world that didn't exist anymore have to do with now? The people from before didn't know about the war, the disease, the collapse. They didn't know what it was like to be afraid of a soulless creature bearing down on them, wearing the face of a friend. They didn't know about a ruling class that would throttle the voice of the people. He knew better now.

Losing his parents—his steadfast father, his unrelentingly faithful mother—along with the devastating dissolution of the rest of their community during the Resistee riots and outbreaks, had taught him how important that history was. The world might be different now in some ways, but in many others, it was more of the same. The methods of manipulation changed, but the bottom line would always be control.

When he was a child, his mother's insistence that he understand the past of a long-gone world seemed useless. Now, he understood that the DDC's greatest weapon was denial of information. There was less substance to a society of people who were taught math, science and weaponry while neglecting art and history. The differences of the decade following the outbreaks were so stark that Simons had become afraid to let the piece of his family's history that he carried inside himself show through. Until the dissenters recruited him, rekindling his faith, he'd learned to keep himself hidden, appearing as an empty vessel with an aptitude for combat and heavy labor.

Belonging to a network of people who wanted to understand the past and the present, to use humanity's collective history to make a difference, made him believe the old world wasn't completely lost. There were others who remembered like he'd been taught to remember. Together, they made sure the old world, the lost people, and his own family and faith hadn't been entirely erased like he'd thought. He'd found hope in the wake of loss.

But it seemed history was repeating itself, as his mother had promised it would. Baba didn't show. On its own, that wasn't terribly concerning. Any number of things might have happened—a delay in departure, a call-off due to an internal breach, unfit cargo. But when Simons called his contact—a nameless member of the organization (because nameless people can't be implicated if things go sideways)— they instructed him to go into hiding until further notice.

He didn't like it. He'd had to go into hiding before, but never on such short notice and with so little information. He was already hours into his journey when the notice came through that the energy management contacts had been updated.

According to the new list, the station nearest the capitol was officially under dissenter control. He'd known a dissenter placement had been in the works for a while now but hadn't expected it to be official so soon. In times past, there were usually several months of uncertainty while the new placement got settled, and Institute oversight made travel difficult.

It might have been nice to know about a closer safe haven half a day ago, but by the time the message came through, Simons was closer to the Institute management station. If he were completely honest with himself, knowing about a closer refuge wouldn't have changed his course anyway. It had been far too long since he'd had an in-person visit with Ternice.

By the time Simons pulled off the main road, circumventing a dense copse that blocked the view of the old road, its surface broken down and overgrown, the full moon was high in the sky. He caught a glimpse of it before descending into the darkness of the forest. He was used to it by now. He was getting good at navigating dark, untamed places.

Twenty minutes later, he eased the vehicle between a pair of giant hemlocks and cut the engine. Simons preferred the spot on the other side of the river, but he'd used it the last two times he'd visited. He needed to mix things up. A transport vehicle was a difficult thing to hide, and it was a bad idea to get too predictable. In this world, unless you were DDC, predictable was dangerous.

He grabbed his pack and began collecting what he thought he might want in the event of an extended stay at the energy management facility. There wasn't much. He grabbed his canteen, a roughly drawn map, his tablet, a handful of meal kits, and the only physical book he had on hand—a story about old-world monsters hidden by human forms. The last thing he did before opening the door was grab the lashing pole he always kept on the passenger seat. It was a long walk to the force field boundary, and Simons had every intention of getting there before dawn.

Thirty-One

MORGAN

MORGAN ROSSI-STERN DIDN'T LIKE BEING wrong. In fact, she was so averse to being wrong that she never made decisions, filed reports or took action until she was certain not only that she wasn't wrong and wouldn't be wrong but that she could be praised by higher-ups for how right she was.

By the time she typed the message that lit up Mora's school tablet to inform her she would be out of the capitol on business, Morgan was so certain of her right-ness that she'd already set her trap for the impending arrest and interrogation. The possibility of her being wrong about Zayd Baba was statistically insignificant. So when the hour of capture was upon her and there was no one to capture, she was understandably upset.

Morgan had been tracking the disappearance of factory goods and personnel for months. Her supervising officer was certain the disappearances were related to unregistered personnel outside the City States. It was a good enough theory, but Morgan knew better. There was nothing left outside the City States. Anyone remaining on the outside was doing well just to survive. She had firsthand knowledge of the communities that used to exist out there. *Used to.*

Morgan suspected the disappearances were more closely related to the construction of unmonitored black-market communication devices, and she aimed to prove it by capturing the criminals behind the disappearing goods.

She had a name, a point of distribution, and a history of illicit credit accumulation. It was the credit accumulation that had led to her certain conclusion. Nailing Zayd Baba was supposed to expose the illegal movement of technological goods and give the DDC the final clue that would reveal the nature and extent of illegal communication.

This bust should have been the biggest crackdown on non-sanctioned communication since the Resistee sweeps. Baba's arrest should have meant shutting down this new uprising before it took off, and Morgan would be single-handedly responsible for keeping this resistance under wraps. She'd been certain!

There was no discernible reason for Baba not to make his scheduled transportation run from the factory. She tracked the credit transfer twenty-four hours before departure, as it had been done for his previous jobs. Her inside source informed her the transport was loaded at the factory. All she had to do was intercept Baba's route to whomever he was meeting. It was that simple.

But Baba didn't show.

Because he didn't show, Morgan hadn't been able to track down his outside contact. Now she was significantly further from breaking down the network of criminal activity outside the City States than she'd predicted, and her review was coming up.

No Baba meant no outside arrests. No Baba meant no proof of connections to the unsanctioned distribution of goods from the technological pieces factory and no way of knowing what those goods were being used for. No Baba meant no promotion. It meant she was wrong.

Morgan sat glowering in her sleek, oversized, government-issued transport vehicle, waiting for Baba to show—possibly late, possibly having encountered trouble at the DDC checkpoint. Even though getting caught at the DDC checkpoint would be a success, Morgan preferred the version of events where she made the capture. She chewed the nail on her left thumb. It was a disgusting habit, she knew, but she needed something to channel the nervous energy as her carefully calculated capture was rendered into a false promise.

Baba had made a liar out of her. The very thought of it filled her with an indescribable rage.

She'd waited all through the day shift and well into the swing shift before daring to call the trap a bust. During the whole time she'd been waiting, not a single other transport vehicle had made its way through.

The transport she'd meant to catch doing the exchange with Baba was long gone by the time she'd thought to drive up and down the road in search of it.

She had no way of knowing that around the time she took a call from Mora, who was clearly hiding something—*again*—the driver of that vehicle had pulled off the road, having been alerted to her presence. By the time she realized things had gone wrong and thought to head out in search of Baba's contact, the vehicle was long gone.

All that remained was to call in a sweep.

"I want near-dead around all outskirts," she said to the DDC technician who took the call.

"That's going to take a lot of manpower. Is all outskirts really necessary?" the tech asked.

She took her time setting him straight. A person in his position had no right to question her judgment. He didn't have the same information she did. He didn't know how far a determined fugitive could run.

The approval for the sweep came through at the same time as another, unexpected message.

"Baba didn't show up at work today," her informant from distribution headquarters reported. Baba had apparently departed from the city with no clear indication of why, and for some inexplicable reason, his floor shift manager hadn't reported his absence until end of shift today.

By the time the sweep was set, she had learned the full story of Zayd Baba's unbelievable disappearance. He didn't just fail to report to factory duty—he'd departed for the Institute. His wife was sick.

"Cross contamination?" she asked.

"Volunteer," the DDC contact corrected.

Morgan practically rolled her eyes out of her skull.

"What a waste."

She remained in place, waiting for news as the sweeps went out depositing near-dead around the outskirts of every City State. With so many near-dead on the loose, anyone traveling through the territory would be exposed—or consumed.

CHAPTER

Thirty~Two

SIMONS

SIMONS LEANED up against the deep, grooved bark of a giant Douglas fir by the shallow bank where the river widened. This was the long way to the energy management station, and after more than thirty hours of driving, waiting, worrying, and more driving, he was feeling tired enough to wish he'd thrown caution to the wind and stashed the transport on the side of the river that gave him a shorter walk.

He set the lashing pole against the tree and tipped the canteen to his lips, relishing the feel of the cool water as it filled his mouth and poured down his throat. The nights were chilly but not cold enough to dissipate the heat of his exertion. He didn't dare take off his jacket. The thick canvas was an important safeguard against the snagging branches and tearing fingers of thick underbrush. He couldn't exactly walk through the City States unnoticed if he were covered from wrist to bicep in barely healing scratches.

He checked the time on the old-world wristwatch he only wore when he was out on a mission. 23:48. It was the dead of night. At this point, he'd be lucky if he managed to sleep before the sun came up. He'd always been lousy about sleeping in daylight.

Simons screwed the cap back onto his canteen before replacing it into his pack and zipping it. The growl of the zipper sent a chill up his spine, highlighting the fine sheen of sweat that had broken out over most of his body. There was something about the sound that made him pause. *Uncanny valley,* his dad would say.

He dropped the pack, instinct taking over as he groped for the lashing pole that should've been propped against the tree at his side. It wasn't there. He wanted to look but didn't dare tear his eyes away from his surroundings. It was dark, yes, but he was certain he could see something moving on the other side of the bank. Above the constant rush of water, he heard the sound again—not the growl of a zipper but the deep, guttural sound of brutal, unmasked hunger.

Braced against the tree, he lowered himself until he could feel for the lashing pole on the ground. There were more noises now. The creature's approach no longer blended with the ambient sounds of night. He could see the thing clearly as it emerged from shadow and brush, tall and lean with a hawklike nose standing out against otherwise shadowed features. The creature's hair stood out light against the night, darkening into a dirty, stringy mess at the shoulders. The near-dead monster searched for him, turning its head as if its hawkish nose might work like a homing beacon. If given enough time, Simons knew it would.

Moving slowly, careful to not make a sound, Simons groped for the lashing pole, hand dipping again and again into damp fern, fuzzy moss, and moist ground. From here, the near-dead creature looked like a man. It wore the fitted shirt and dark trousers of someone who might have once cared about their appearance. The trousers were a little short, and white socks peeked out above red-and-black sneakers with untied shoelaces. The thing's head swiveled back and forth as if he were merely out for a midnight stroll, taking in unfamiliar surroundings. The only thing revealing the creature to be inhuman was the terrible moaning growl that emanated from its torn throat and chest.

The near-dead creature stumbled out onto the bank, toes splashing at the shallow edges of the river. It walked like a man, but only just. The movements were jerky and uncoordinated, as if some parts of his body were moving faster than others and he didn't have the logistic control to coordinate it all. The front of his shirt was stained dark with dried blood from his injuries. The tear in his throat looked like a deep gash in a coagulated mound of murky gelatin.

Simons' hand finally made contact with the smooth metal of the lashing pole handle. He wrapped his hands around it, still cautious to keep his movements subtle but eager to transform the pole into a functional weapon.

As far as weapons went, Simons had always thought the lashing pole was a poor example. It was too lightweight to do much serious damage, and the blade only stayed out when the handle was twisted. The magnetic twine was great for restraining, but how much use could it be if he were fighting for his life?

He was about to find out.

His weight shifted as he lifted the pole inch by inch into a fighting stance. The shift wasn't enough to knock him off his feet even though his legs were spread wide around the brush and roots surrounding the old fir, but it was enough that he staggered, and his stagger wasn't silent.

The creature's terrible noise transformed from a sickening, growling moan to a predatory snarl. The head wasn't on a swivel anymore. The creature was looking right at him with a stare so intent Simons had to physically suppress a scream. It began to move, those slow and fast movements blending together to create much smoother locomotion than before. It was gaining fast.

Simons stood, abandoning his effort to move slowly and remain silent. He held the lashing pole in front of him, debating the merits of turning the blade out versus trying to engage the magnetic bindings, unable to decide on the best course of action. He could make out the milky white of the creature's eyes now and regretted not pocketing the pulsar gun when he parked the car for the night. If he had his range weapon, he wouldn't have to worry about the nuance of wielding the damn lashing pole with his life on the line.

But that wasn't entirely true. He might be able to shoot the near-dead monster, but at this close range and with the creature moving so quickly, he was just as likely to miss and suddenly have it right on top of him. He'd be left without any defense.

There's a reason people use the lashing pole, he reminded himself as the creature erased the final few feet between them.

Simons' first hit was instinctual. He pulled the pole over his head and slammed it down on the creature's shoulder, temporarily halting its progress. The impact vibrated up his forearms. There was a cracking sound as the thing's collarbone broke and the pole sunk in with the sickening sound of yielding flesh. At only twenty-six years old, Simons was an exceptionally large man with a fair amount of strength and force to support his girth. The blow he'd landed would've floored any ordinary man or beast, but the near-dead weren't ordinary.

That's unnatural, he thought as the creature peeled itself away from the lashing pole with a frustrated wail. It didn't even seem to register the devastating injury to its shoulder. It only seemed upset that its progress toward its next meal had been temporarily slowed.

Simons used the pole to push at it again, this time with more measured force, trying to gauge the creature's strength and response. It wailed again but kept coming, not even trying to knock the pole away. The thing barely seemed to register that the pole was in the way. It only appeared to comprehend that Simons was the prize and something was in the way.

Simons used the tip of the pole to nudge the creature away again. He was curious. He knew it was dangerous—probably more dangerous than anything he'd ever encountered before. Like everyone else, he'd grown up with the videos, studying the information files and taking tests about the safest and most efficient ways to evade near-dead attacks. He'd seen them, driven past areas decimated by their presence, watched as others handled the reality of infection, but none of that had felt real like this. He was still scared, but not as scared as he had been when he first realized he was about to initiate hand-to-hand combat with a near-dead.

One bite, one scratch, and his life would be over. The disease would take over, and he'd be in a race against time to enter a cryogenic slumber before his mind was lost and he, too, was part of a near-dead army. The dissenters were close to having their own cryogenics facilities, but their operations were small and their capacity smaller, so Simons knew that if he wound up infected and needing cryogenic sleep, he'd have to submit himself to the Institute and join their archives. He would prefer to avoid that ultimatum.

He pushed harder as the butt of the pole jammed the creature right in the diaphragm. This time, it lost its footing, falling backward and landing hard on its ass. It wailed in abject frustration, and Simons decided it was time to end what remained of the thing's miserable life.

He turned one hand over the other, revealing the fine blade at the end of the lashing pole. When the creature fell, it moved out of striking range. Simons waited for it to come forward again, this time certain he needed to dispatch the walking, breathing disease-bomb in front of him. When it stood, Simons met it with the blade end of the pole, shoving it into the soft flesh between ribs. To his utter horror and astonishment, the creature pushed back against the blade, causing it to tear further into vital organs.

Simons gaped. The weapon had to have punctured at least one lung, if not both. The near-dead monster shouldn't be able to stand—or breathe, for that matter. But it did exactly that. It stood and wailed, jerking its body forward and backward on the blood-slick blade.

How long are near-dead supposed to be able to live without breathing? Simons wondered as he struggled to force the creature away from him once more.

It screamed again—a wet, gurgling sound as a pinkish fluid began to froth at the wound site.

The creature would die of this injury, but Simons knew it wouldn't be anytime soon unless he could do better.

It's not human, he thought, retracting the blade to pull it away from the creature's body.

He struck again, this time with the wire bindings instead of the blade, and this time, he aimed for the head. The magnetic lashings wrapped around the creature's face and neck. It wailed, throwing its hands toward the sky but catching them on the lashing pole. The force of it nearly pulled Simons from his feet, but he had more than fifty pounds over the scrawny thing.

When the creature wailed, he wailed back at it, channeling the horror of the coagulated blood and pink, frothing chest. Every time it lifted a hand to fight the restraints, Simons shifted his grip. He was analyzing the position, trying to find the right angle—the right move to end this encounter.

Finally, he saw it. He waited for the creature to shift and try again, then took it. The near-dead snapped its jaws at him, and he dipped the pole down, angling the top upward and twisting one hand over the other so the blade punched up into the brain.

Motion stopped immediately, and he knew the creature was dead. He pulled the lashing pole backward, and as it came free, the creature slid almost silently to the forest floor.

Simons stood over it, sweat-drenched and breathing hard. He stabbed the blade into the creature's head two more times before kicking its shoe. The creature didn't respond. He stepped back from it, screaming in victorious relief.

"That's right! You tried!" he yelled into the darkness.

Nothing responded. He stood over the dead thing a few minutes longer, trying to decide if there was something more he needed to do. When nothing came to him, he retracted the blade at the end of his lashing pole, bent down to pick up his pack, and went on his way.

The sun would certainly be up by the time he tried to get some sleep now.

CHAPTER
Thirty-Three

ANIKA

ANIKA WENT through the list on her restricted-access tablet again, the flexible synthetic metal of the cuffs clinking against the screen. She still wasn't used to them, but in the grand scheme of inconveniences, the cuffs around her ankles and wrists were nothing. They were much better than having no freedom at all. They prevented her from approaching the door or the facility and housekeeping cabinets lining the far wall, but unless there was a medical team in her room, she could otherwise move as she wanted. She had her own little restroom, a cabinet where she could put things she requested, and of course, the bed. It was a tidy prison.

At first, she had refused to take advantage of any of the accommodations the medics offered to her, certain there had to be a catch to the luxuries. "You can't miss something you haven't been given," Ms. Fitzpatrick would have said. But as the weeks of isolation and boredom dragged on, she started to understand what she was being offered and why.

"I will never leave here," she said, adding *literature* to her list along with historical accounts of the twenty-first century and an interesting video documentary called *The First Patient of the War*.

She had access to things she'd never dreamed of—stories, videos, accounts of historical events, music… She could also request carpets, curtains, trinkets, and activities. If it was on the list, it could be hers in a matter of days. Anika suspected these offerings were meant to buy compliance—or maybe complacency. These seemingly clandestine allowances were an attempt at keeping the patients within the L-wing from wanting for anything as long as the illness didn't progress.

She hadn't had to figure all of this out for herself. Park had been incredibly informative, and even Dr. Wong was forthcoming about the extent of her stay and her role in the Institute's research. When she'd first refused any of the accommodations Dr. Wong had presented, Park had explained those accommodations were meant for her comfort. Anika had been stubbornly adamant that the only thing that would make her comfortable was to see Zayd again, but Park was up-front about that impossibility.

Anika had access to all the information her father had ever craved. She could read the stories Ms. Fitzpatrick had talked about during her innumerable clinic appointments and listen to the top hits from every generation, but she would never be able to share it with another soul.

Zayd was here at the Institute with her, but he might as well have been worlds away. She would never hear his laugh again as she recounted the highlights of her day, never feel the warmth of his embrace or the softness of his touch. Against the reality of this realization, she ached for any little piece of him she'd once taken for granted. She wanted to eat one of Zayd's terribly dry sandwiches, cry about losing the position at the premier Eastside clinic, or fight about their credit balance—anything but this reality that felt more like a nightmare.

"What will happen to him?" she asked.

"He'll either be transported to the Northern Laboratories or take on a more permanent position at the Institute," Park said.

"Will he be safe?" She didn't need Park to answer after the long hesitation. Between the constant look of fatigue, the careful way she checked the cameras, and how she only spoke freely when Dr. Wong wasn't in the room, Anika knew there was no safe place within the Institute.

"Can he go?" Anika asked.

"What do you mean?" Park asked.

"I mean, can he leave the Institute? Can he go back home and return to the life we had before?" she pressed.

"Volunteering is a permanent choice," Park said.

Anika knew it was, but it was difficult to hear. She didn't try to stop the tears as they fell. There was no point hiding her grief from the young woman, who was clearly going through her own distress. "How can I live with myself, knowing I've done this to him?"

Park put a gloved hand on Anika's arm. She got the impression this wasn't a sanctioned level of closeness, even in the L-wing. "You didn't do this to him," she said.

"You don't understand! I thought that maybe the infection came from him! I thought he was hiding something from me. I thought that if I was infected, then he must be, too. If I had thought for even a moment that it had just been me, I never would have allowed him to come," Anika said, tears turning to sobs as the permanence of the situation overtook her.

Park sat silently with her as she wept, waiting for a respite from the grief. Anika took her time recovering, letting the grief fill her, overwhelm her until there was nothing else. In the quiet that followed, Park took her wrist and placed it gently against the bed frame so the magnetic lock engaged. Park's body was crossed over her, back facing the door and the camera with its endlessly blinking blue light.

"I might be able to help him." Her voice was so quiet, Anika was pretty sure no recording device could hear her.

"You can help?" Anika chose her words so carefully it hurt.

"We'll see what I can do." Park smiled. "Now, would you mind putting the rest of your restraints in place?"

Restraints in place, Park began her work. Anika did her best to relax as the draw began, but she couldn't. The medic said she could help. If that meant Zayd might not have to spend the rest of his life at the Institute, she would not rest until it was so.

The door to Anika's room cycled through the lock before opening, and Dr. Wong strode in. Anika noticed the way Park ducked behind the sampling tray upon his entry, likely trying to hide the way the middle two buttons of her lab coat strained against her expanding stomach.

"Good morning, Ms. Baba. How are you feeling?" Dr. Wong smiled with too-straight teeth as he scanned her file and read the data.

"I am not happy," she said, feeling more like being honest than accommodating.

"I'm sorry to hear that. Have you given any of the accommodations a look? I think they might help with your transition," Wong suggested, peering over Park's shoulder at the state of her work.

"I would rather talk to my husband than have any number of artificial comforts," Anika said. Park said she would try to help. Anika wouldn't give that secret up any more than she would give up the possibility that she could see Zayd one last time.

"I'm sorry, Ms. Baba, but there is too much of a contamination risk for me to let that happen," Dr. Wong said. He didn't look at her as he said it. He was still looking between the data and Park's samples, practically quivering with excitement.

Park's eyes widened as he indicated what he was looking at. She glanced at Anika. "Does she know?"

Neither of the medics were speaking to her. She may as well have not been in the room.

"I don't know. Has she said anything to you?" Wong said.

Anika wanted to scream at both of them but didn't dare. She was restrained. She was too vulnerable to stand, but somehow, looking between Dr. Wong's excitement and Park's abject terror, she knew.

"I want you to do samples again tomorrow and then in forty-eight hours to confirm. Even if we don't make it to completion, this is an astounding research opportunity," Wong was saying.

Anika understood, then, what she was to him. *An astounding research opportunity.* She wasn't a clinician or a wife or even a civilian. She was a patient.

Dr. Wong looked up from his tablet and gave Anika another ridiculous smile. "Ms. Baba, I understand how difficult this transition is. It is for all our patients in the L-wing. I'm so sorry we can't allow you to communicate with anyone outside. The situation here is delicate. But I can't encourage you enough to please, please consider some of the accommodations."

"There's nothing I want," Anika said, fighting the tears that threatened to begin again. It was one thing to cry in front of Park, who had been kind and compassionate and offered to help her and Zayd. She couldn't give such vulnerability to the doctor who looked at her like a medical breakthrough. Not when she knew that breakthrough wouldn't change her outcome.

"I understand. You need time. But the days here can be long, and we would like to offer you any little thing that might make those long days pass a little more easily," Dr. Wong said. He was straightening the collar on his lab coat, preparing to make his departure without so much as a second look at Anika.

That was fine by her—she didn't need the doctor scanning the pallor of her tear-streaked face or measuring the opacity of her sclera. Park would do those things for him.

"I will consider," she said, wanting to speed his exit along.

Wong brightened. "Wonderful. I'll be back in forty-eight hours."

To Park, he said, "Have tomorrow's samples expedited, and link processing to me for notification."

That done, he was gone. The lock cycled, clicking into place as the door's vacuum seal set.

Park continued to stand there as if she didn't know what to do next. Anika looked at the woman who had offered to help—who was, aside from the role reversal, in the same situation as her.

"How far along am I?" she asked, jarring the medic from her trance.

"You knew?" Park asked.

Anika shook her head. "No. I knew it was a possibility—we were trying. But I didn't think we'd succeeded. It has to be fairly new."

Park licked her lips, glancing down at the file. "All of the data is in micrograms per unit—there isn't a number correlated with time..."

"I know those numbers," Anika said. Then it suddenly occurred to her to ask, "Do you?"

Park shook her head, an expression of poorly forced neutrality exposing her angst as her hand traveled briefly to her middle. "No. There's a lot I don't know."

Anika nodded. "That's okay. I can help you." Her barely audible whisper echoed the words Park had spoken moments before.

"Thank you," Park said, submitting the samples before turning back to the bed to remove the magnetic hold. "Since I'll be back tomorrow, we can skip the full scan."

She pressed the release button, and Anika's hands fell to her sides. Park was still within the boundary of her range. Anika didn't know if that was purposeful or a sign of her inexperience, but she didn't care. She reached out and grasped the medic's hand, caressing the single layer of protective nitrile between them.

"He can't ever know."

Park's face tightened, battling between frustration and understanding.

"He can never know! If he knows, he won't leave," Anika insisted.

Park hesitated as if she wanted to argue but seemed to be warring in her own mind.

Who was she fighting for, Anika wondered, and what was her story?

She squeezed Anika's hand, seeming less concerned about the single-glove barrier than she'd been on previous visits. "Alright. Because it's your call."

Relief flooded Anika. "When will you do it?"

Park faltered. "I don't know if I can yet. I said I would try, and it might take some time."

Anika gave Park's belly a meaningful look. "It can't be that much time."

Park brought her hand up as though she meant to caress her stomach again but refrained. "I'll talk to him," she said.

"Good," Anika said, triumphant.

"If you go through the list," Park added, drawing a curious expression from the woman.

"Explain," Anika demanded.

"If we're going to do this—you for me and me for you—then it has to look like we're getting along. Like you aren't resisting being here. Dr. Wong is going to keep coming back—more than he already is. He wants the patients comfortable," she explained.

Anika suddenly understood. "Well, then. I will have my list for you tomorrow."

CHAPTER
Thirty-Four
SIMONS

BY THE TIME Simons made it through the force field barrier and onto the energy management property, the sun was up and warm. Despite the harrowing journey and the life-threatening encounter, he felt great. He was alive, young, healthy, and about to spend an indefinite amount of time laying low with the love of his life. He hummed one of his mother's old songs as he climbed the porch steps, not bothering to hide his approach. If Ternice was having a typical morning, he'd find her sitting at the kitchen table, finishing her third cup of coffee after doing morning system checks. If she was moving more slowly, he'd have breakfast cooking by the time she came back.

Instead of either of those things, she walked into the mudroom as he was removing his boots, her arms full of laundry, her stomach poking out from beneath a too-small undershirt, her sleep pants rolled down to sit beneath the swell. She froze, her sleep-smudged face transformed by the shocked "o" of her speechless mouth.

"Moe!" she gasped, thrusting the bulk of linens in front of her stomach.

He beamed, his sleep-deprived mind not yet registering what he was seeing. "Hey, baby. Surprise."

She gave him a weak smile in return, stammering over her words as she reached for a blanket that spilled forward from her pile. "I didn't know you were coming. I mean, I always hope you will, but it's been so long since…"

"I know," he said, leaving his supplies and crossing the space between them. "Months. I didn't know I could make it that long without the feel of your skin against mine first thing in the morning."

Keeping his hands tucked behind his back, he bent forward and kissed just below where her bonnet exposed the smooth brown skin of her forehead. "Maybe that laundry can wait? Because I really need to wash," he suggested, unable to help the amorous grin spreading across his lips.

Ternice studied him, shock quickly transforming to confusion, bewilderment, and a hint of anger. "Is that really all you've got to say?"

Simons blinked. Alertness forced its way to the surface as he struggled to respond. "I missed you. I've said it a dozen times."

She rolled her eyes, dropping the linens and stepping back so he would really have to look at her. "I told you we needed to talk."

Simons stared, this time seeing what he'd missed in his exhausted, happy haze.

"Terni? You're…"

"If you say 'fat,' I'm going to scream," she warned.

"I was going to say 'pregnant,'" he said, mind whirring. He started to reach out for her but stopped himself. He needed to wash. He didn't know if she wanted him to touch her.

"Yes. It turns out a lingering flu and a growing child have a lot in common," she said.

"I didn't know. How could I know?" he stammered.

"It's alright. I didn't tell you, so that's on me. For whatever reason, I didn't think you'd find out like this. I thought it'd be sooner. I thought I could make it easier," she explained.

"How far along?"

"Difficult to tell without a cycle, but six, maybe even seven months," she said.

Simons paused. He knew his brain wasn't working at full capacity.

He wanted to be careful about what he said. How he said it. Still, the best he could come up with was, "How did it happen?"

He knew *how* it happened, but it wasn't supposed to happen. Hadn't she had the procedure they did at the Institute to keep it from happening?

"My best guess is a statistical anomaly," Ternice said.

"The procedure?"

Simons knew he was being an idiot. He couldn't seem to stop himself. Some combination of shock and sleep deprivation had taken over, and he was nearly out of his mind with how badly he wanted to shower, but he couldn't walk away from this conversation. He couldn't walk away from realizing she'd been like this—carrying this burden, this secret, all on her own, waiting for him to come.

"I had it. Just like everyone else. That's why I didn't realize what this was when you were here last. It turns out you don't think of pregnancy when pregnancy isn't supposed to be an option." Terni let a very small, very derisive smirk lift the side of her mouth. "There's a disclaimer in our database. I don't think I ever read it. Probably the only people who ever read it are the ones who end up like me, and for all I know, I'm the only one, so maybe I'm the only one who's ever read it. It says in the very small likelihood that the procedure fails, to seek additional services. Very small likelihood isn't zero chance, and I guess that's all it took," she concluded.

"How long have you known?" he asked.

Ternice put a hand on her hip and leaned into the wall. "Like I said, it took a while. I didn't even consider it until I started to feel something. Not even when my clothes quit fitting. I explained that away by telling myself I eat too much when your hungry ass is here. But there was a point in time where I had to accept that pregnancy was the only possible explanation."

He nodded dumbly. He thought he understood. He had no idea what it felt like to grow a whole other life, so why should she? What did either of them know about it? In their life, in their line of business, it wasn't supposed to happen. And clearly, it had been the furthest thing from his mind, too, so why would he expect different from her?

"Why didn't you tell me?" he asked, hoping he didn't sound accusatory. He had no idea what he would've done in her position.

"Because this isn't the sort of news you drop on someone via encrypted connection. You deserved to hear it straight from me," she said, reaching up to stroke the dense shadow of hair on his jaw.

"I would have understood," he protested.

"Maybe. Probably," she agreed. "But what if something like this got out—even in our network? What if someone found out? What if the wrong person found out? This is dangerous, Moe."

Hearing the truth of it drove their situation home even more. Images of the frothing monster from the woods flashed into his mind. He shook his head, trying to erase them.

"You need rest," Terni said, taking in his exhaustion.

"You need me," he countered.

"No. We need each other. Right now, you need to take care of yourself. I know what your drive was like even if I don't know everything that happened in between. You're dead on your feet—"

Simons forced the near-dead monster away with a hard blink.

"Did you hear me, Moe?" she said.

He nodded. "Let me shower," he murmured, forcing his eyes to stay open.

"Go," she said. "I'll have the bed ready."

Simons leaned forward, trying to kiss her, but she brushed him away.

"Safety first. You shower. You sleep. We'll talk," she commanded.

Simons moved on numb feet.

"It's going to be alright, Terni. We're going to figure this out," he promised, not having a clue how they'd accomplish such a thing.

"That's right. Now get your stinky self into the shower before you pass out. I can't move you if you go down," she teased.

He left her to shower, and she fixed his bed before leaving to perform the essential tasks of energy management, pretending for a few more hours that things weren't about to change forever.

Thirty-Five

MORA

WE NEED YOUR HELP.

Those four words had played over and over in Mora's head since her last conversation with Georgia. She heard them in her dream-filled sleep. They stirred up in her an urgent desire for what Georgia and her Free People had to offer. Mora read these words instead of the message her mother had left to replace her actual presence—like so many mornings since Mora was old enough to dress herself and make it from the apartment to the tram in time for the day's first class.

We need your help.

Georgia wanted what Mora had to offer. She'd seen everything Mora was, typed into four different files: *aptitude, engagement, application,* and *potential.* She knew Mora's overall score—46 points, *low*—and that she wasn't headed for any glamorous career despite her new endeavors to score decently on the Test. Georgia knew all of this, knew about her corrections file, and still she wanted *her.*

Mora—
Urgent business. Local, so home tonight.
—Mom

Morgan never left detailed messages. She especially never included any professions of love or affection for Mora. Morgan Rossi-Stern worked for the DDC. She was above frivolous emotions like telling her daughter she loved her. She wouldn't dare be caught compromising her judgment like that. The closest she came to love was raising Mora out of duty and obligation. Mora knew Morgan's idea of duty was what made her resent Mora's lack of reciprocal obligation. Mora's existence at the bottom of the class, paired with her disinterest in everything Morgan did, was her greatest insult.

Mora was still thinking of Georgia's invitation when she was supposed to be studying the metabolic transfer of ATP within the Krebs Cycle, and she failed the exit quiz for the class despite Jim's pleading looks from across the room.

No one will believe your score is true if you can't do better, she admonished herself, moving from biology to physical systems. At least she sat next to Jim in physics. He'd keep her from making a devastating mistake on their perpetual motion project.

"What's with you today?" James asked, clipping the magnifying lenses over his glasses so he could see the fine coil of wires energizing their magnetic field.

Mora wasn't great at physics, but she was decent with electricity and magnetism, which she proved by getting a green screen as she correctly labeled the magnetic fields on their virtual diagram.

"Thinking about how much of a waste of space I am here," she said. If anyone overheard their conversation, they'd likely think it was about Mora's academic struggles. Her scores weren't exactly a secret.

James stilled, looking at Mora through the magnifying lenses, which made his pupils swim like blinking, swollen dots in a pale blue sea. The effect was comical and disturbing all at once, and Mora knew he understood what she was saying. She'd told him already that she planned on running away but doubted he'd believe her until she had somewhere specific to run to.

Before last night, her plans to run away from the city had been crude at best and foolhardy at worst. If she left the force field boundary of the City States, she'd be a target for any wandering near-dead or the wild dogs rumored to rule the spaces between civilization.

Although she wasn't exactly convinced that the outside world was packed full of wandering near-dead ready to tear any foolishly errant city dweller to shreds, the rumors about wild dogs were substantiated. Even if most of the ecosystems had collapsed, Mora knew there were mice out there, and if there were mice, then there should be predators. If Omen and his fellow birds could subsist on the prey, dogs could, too.

"Don't do anything unnecessarily dangerous," James said. When he noticed their teacher approaching, he pointed at the panel tuned to receive a small amount of energy from the grid.

"Everything I do is dangerous," Mora said, poking one of the fine tools into the space between the coils and the future mount for their magnetic rod. She felt the pulsing cycle of attraction and repulsion as the coil processed the alternating current. She looked up from their project to offer the professor a brilliant and obviously insincere smile. "Isn't that right, Mr. Myers?"

Professor Myers gave her a barely contained scowl as he assessed their progress on his tablet, then, noting James, said, "Good job on the field diagram, Dunn."

"Mora did the diagrams. I'm calibrating the power circuit," James said, swiveling his buggy, magnified eyes over to the professor.

Myers' scowl vanished, replaced by wide-eyed curiosity as he glanced between the two of them. "Well, then the kudos are yours, Ms. Rossi," he said, sounding unconvinced by his own words.

"Thank you. I'm going to take them and *run*." Mora smirked, waiting for Mr. Myers to move on to the next group of students, who were struggling with their direct-current model.

"Nobody here knows I'm smart," Mora whispered when Myers was out of earshot.

"That's more your fault than theirs," James countered, putting down his screwdriver and checking the circuit diagram on his brand-new, school-issued tablet, which was two models newer than his old one.

"It's not my fault stories about the consequences of absolute power resonate with me more than the impact of air resistance on the energy dampening of grid power." Mora's eyes rolled as she twirled the tool between forefinger and thumb.

"Which one is that?" James asked, setting the tool kit aside and grabbing the magnetic cylinder.

"*Animal Farm*," Mora said.

James lifted an eyebrow. "What does farming animals have to do with absolute power?"

Mora closed her eyes. Jim could be so dense sometimes, especially for a genius. "First of all, it's called *Animal Farm*, not farming animals. And second of all, it's an allegory, which means it's a story meant to tell about another meaning—in this case, about how corrupting it can be to have too much power."

"That's what the *Animal Farm* story is about? Too much power causing a problem?" James asked, only partially paying attention as he connected the signal from their miniature machine to his tablet. Mora slid her own tablet toward him, knowing he'd do both in half the time it would take her to secure the same connection.

"It's a lot like things here, don't you think?" she asked.

James pulled up the signal settings and flipped through options Mora hadn't even known were there. She made a mental note that she'd need him to teach her that before the Test, which was rapidly approaching.

"I just don't know about that," he said, returning her tablet.

The connection signal on the screen read *strong* next to the pared-down options for recording their class data.

"You're so dumb for such a smart guy, Jim. Of course the DDC has too much power. It runs everything—the cities, the Institute, the Northern Laboratories, the people, the government. We can't even vote!" Her voice rose higher than she'd meant. Realizing, she ducked her head down into her tablet as Professor Myers made his way back around to their workstation.

"What's the issue here?" he asked, hands folded behind his back.

Mora's heart was beating too hard and too loudly in her chest and ears. The tips of Jim's ears and the sides of his neck were flushed bright red.

"I said, we can't vote on who gets to place the magnetic cylinder and who gets to record because there's only two of us," Mora said, hoping she'd only yelled the last part and not the part about the DDC.

"I apologize, but we're short two students today," Mr. Myers said, the look on his face suggesting he didn't believe her explanation at all. Jim and Mora never fought in class and never preferred having more than the two of them for class projects.

"Tell that to Mr. Perfect over here." She thrust her thumb toward James' face as he stared too hard at their project diagram.

"I thought I heard you say something about power?" Mr. Myers said, ignoring her statement and fishing for more of their previous conversation.

"I did. I said too much power was going to corrupt our circuit because we have too much resistance," Mora raced to explain, thankful her last study session with Jim covered that exact topic. She hoped she had it right. Although if she didn't, Myers would probably take it as further evidence that she was nothing more than her Test scores.

"Power and resistance? Is that what you're arguing about?" Mr. Myers asked, a wry smile touching his lips but not his eyes.

"I've been studying," Mora stammered. Myers didn't usually pay her this much attention.

"Would you just shut up!" James blurted, causing both their heads to turn.

"I was trying to tell him about the resistance in the circuit—"

"Endgal save us! Mora, I told you it was just going to be one night. It was an experiment, and you're embarrassing both of us right now with all your complaining about *power dynamics* and *circuits*. Professor Myers has better things to do. I told you I still think you're very attractive, but I'm going to the Institute," James said.

Mora's jaw dropped.

Myers looked between the two of them, the smirk transforming into something that actually reached his eyes. "Enough personal business. I expect data by the end of class," he said, checking James' shoulder in an uncomfortable gesture as he moved away from them.

James was breathing too fast to look normal, and Mora couldn't stop staring at him. Neither of them said a thing to one another until class was over. They collected their data, submitted the energy loss of their model, and placed it in their laboratory cabinet. When they left,

James just ahead of Mora, Myers was still giving him the same peculiar look.

They burst out into the dull grey of an overcast sky against towering buildings before Mora called out.

"What was that?"

James stopped, reaching for Mora's wrist and pulling her close. "Did you see the way he was looking at you?" he growled.

"Of course I did. He thinks I'm an idiot. I'm pretty sure he hates me—"

"He heard what you said!" James snapped, keeping a firm grip on Mora's arm as they descended the school steps and joined the flow of human traffic on the walkways.

"I told him I was talking about the circuit," Mora argued, unable to pry her wrist free from his grip. His intensity was unsettling.

"Power and resistance, Mora? He's going to think you're one of *them*!" James said.

Mora froze, suddenly understanding what he was talking about. "A Resistee?"

Mora knew what most people believed about the Resistees. The legacy of the Resistee movement lingered in every whisper of malcontent—unfairly, according to her interviews. *Scapegoats*. Now, anytime an individual or group dared to question a new safety measure, like when that group tried to shut down the new Eastside clinics last month, people accused them of being new-wave Resistees and demanded they be handled before things escalated. It never mattered if the protest was peaceful. People were afraid of what had come before. Riots.

The Resistees were the ones who said fear of outbreak wasn't enough to shut down action and activity, and in the end, they were the ones who suffered the most losses. That was where her textbook actually agreed with the personal accounts.

"I'm not a Resistee," Mora said, finally wrenching her hand free from his.

"Sometimes you sound like one." James gave her one of his looks— the one that said he wasn't going to let her argue no matter how stubborn she was feeling.

She let out a long sigh. "I'm sorry, Jim. I'm not trying to ruin anything for you."

They walked past Main Street, headed the way Mora typically walked past the Hole.

"I'm not worried about me. I'm going to the Institute. Nobody's going to think I'm a Resistee. But you, Mora? You're halfway there, and even you don't realize it."

Mora felt hot despite the persistent chill of the changing seasons. Was it wrong if she were? She was about to pose the question when they turned the corner and came up against a large DDC barricade with two officials posted in front.

"You can't pass this way. You need to route around on Fourteenth," the nearest official said, placing a blue-gloved hand out to stop their approach.

Mora looked at the official. She knew exactly why the alley had been barricaded.

The Hole.

"What's going on?" Mora asked, trying to peer past the large barricade. She couldn't see much beyond the large transport vehicle.

"Classified, honey. Just containment business," another official said.

"It's not an outbreak, is it?" James asked. He sounded perfectly mortified, but Mora could tell by the look on his face that he was playing a game Mora had forgotten.

"Can't say, buddy, but we're doing our job to keep you safe," the first official said, probably aging Jim down by at least two years.

Mora widened her eyes, reaching for Jim's hand and holding it just in front of her—a forbidden gesture in public unless you were under-age. She schooled her voice and asked, "Is it okay if we go past? My mom doesn't like when I don't walk straight home. Please!"

"Hey, kiddo, Fourteenth is barely a detour," the first official said. His voice had also changed. He was talking to children now.

"I've still got a tracker on my tablet!" James whined, selling it about three times better than Mora.

"I'm fifteen credits from getting a new top," she added anyway.

The second official caved first, looking around the street-side behind the barricade. The two officials met one another's gazes.

"Move quickly. This area isn't secured yet," the first official said.

Mora flashed a huge smile in his direction. "Thanks, mister!"

She tugged Jim's hand as they skated around the barrier, pushing up close to see between the cracks of the wide blockade.

"We could have gone around," James started, letting himself be pulled.

"Don't you know where we are?" Mora demanded, peaking through the widest crack to see where a dozen officials were leading factory employees—*Hole vendors*—bound by wires at the end of long poles.

"Mora, we better get out of here," James said, realizing exactly where they were.

"In a second. I'm looking for someone," she said, straining to see if Shannon was among the captured vendors.

She leaned until the barrier piece moved, and one of the black-suited officials whirled at the sound. When Mora met the DDC official's eyes, she realized she was staring straight into her mother's stern face.

"Run!" she whisper-yelled, pulling Jim until they were both in motion.

Thirty-Six

MORGAN

THAT UNMISTAKABLE FACE had been staring right at her. She knew those brilliant brown eyes and unruly halo of raven-black curls better than she knew her own self. Then, in the time it took her to blink, it was gone.

Morgan Rossi-Stern wasn't prone to whimsical imaginings and thus knew she hadn't imagined Mora staring back at her through the DDC barricade, but she still struggled to believe how quickly the girl had disappeared once she'd been spotted.

"Rossi!"

Her head snapped back to the task at hand, meeting the curious gaze of the infiltration liaison with practiced restraint. "What?"

"I asked if we were onboarding all of the prisoners?" Chen asked. He was looking at Morgan like he was trying to sort a complicated data file. She had no intention of letting him resolve this particular dataset. She'd done too much work to keep Mora out of it.

"Standard protocol is to bring them all into processing. At the very least, they need due diligence testing before prosecution," she said.

"All of them are being prosecuted? What about the customers? Shouldn't they only get a fine?" Chen asked.

It was in Morgan's authority to make that call. Initially, when she'd been assigned the task of clearing out the black market, she'd only planned to process the vendors, but this escalation was exactly the sort of distraction she wanted to keep Chen, Sanchez, and Smith focused on the task rather than the little mouse snooping at the barrier.

"Association with commerce of uncleared materials from infected areas is grounds for prosecution." Association was a loose enough term to include perusing black-market old-world goods.

"That's a little harsh, isn't it?" Sanchez asked as Morgan brought the first of the bound vendors to the transport, handing the lashing pole his way.

"It's the public officer's job to prosecute. Finley may decide to let the shoppers off with a slap on the wrist and a hit to their credits. What he does isn't up to us. Our job is to infiltrate, investigate, and arrest."

She accepted another lashing pole from Smith, guiding the prisoners from the Hole raid, one after another, onto the transport for processing. The earlier moment, when she was all but certain someone would spot Mora looking in on them, seemed to pass without further attention. "Besides, everyone from that building needs to be tested. With all the illegal goods in there, who knows what contaminations we're dealing with? We could probably trace the current infection to this cesspool. I'd put a week of credits on it."

"Do you think we'll get names from this lot?" Sanchez asked.

"We may have the whole community in this one go," Chen said, bringing up the next set of prisoners. "This is the biggest clandestine operation we've busted to date."

"Twenty-three by my count, and eleven of them vendors," Smith agreed. "Our names will likely go out on the DDC network, and we'll wind up with a bonus before the end of the month!"

Morgan doubted that but wasn't planning to ruin anyone's mood before the job was done. This was an efficient team, and she got the benefit of being the lead. It was exactly the sort of task she needed following her failure to bring in the smugglers. The sweep she'd ordered had only turned up one dead patient. Given the animal activity in the forested area outside the Institute, it was likely that patient was the victim of *natural causes* rather than human activity. The raid on the Hole was the perfect diversion.

"Did you see those kids poking around the barrier a minute ago?" Sanchez asked, hauling the third from last of the prisoners onto the transport.

Morgan stiffened. She didn't keep any pictures of Mora at her station in City DDC, but she couldn't be sure. Most folks in City Affairs had access to the same data she did, which meant anyone who had looked her up had seen the file on Mora, complete with academic and security images. She shifted her grip on the lashing pole, trying to decide if it would be more distracting to disengage the lashings or twist the pole. Did this guy look like a runner?

"Couple of Westsiders taking the fastest route home, according to Big and Burly," Chen said, using the team's nicknames for their guards.

A couple of Westsiders. She'd only seen Mora but was certain the Dunn boy was with her. She waited, curious what else Chen might divulge. As the infiltration liaison, he had the most immediate access to relevant data. If anyone decided looking into the kids was worth it, Chen would be the one to identify Mora.

"They don't teach kids to stay clear of DDC quarantines anymore? What if we'd been taking down a small horde of near-dead?" Smith mused.

"Kids these days don't believe in the near-dead," Sanchez said, giving the lashing pole a hard push to move the prisoner down the transport's aisle.

"They sure do. I did one of those meetings last year—safety in the classroom? I volunteered because I got a second year, you now. Kid pissed his pants when we showed the video," Smith shot back.

Morgan relaxed as the conversation went sideways again but didn't let up on her grip. *This guy doesn't look like a runner,* she thought, noting the prisoner's sideways lean.

"I'll send a warning blast to the apartments on the Westside. We'll do a mandatory clinic report for all school-age residents by week's end. That'll get all the parents in line," Chen suggested.

"Mess with their credits. It's the only way to keep 'em in line. Some kids gonna have a sore spirit when the parents realize their weekend credits are going to unscheduled testing," Sanchez chuckled.

Morgan found herself agreeing, training back the bitter smile from thinned lips. But she was finally satisfied no one was going to follow up on the kid at the barricade. "We've been at this forever. Let's get this group over to processing so I can write my report," she barked, pushing the last prisoner onto the transport. It wasn't technically her job or her branch of the department, but whether they were infected or not, Morgan was certain every one of the prisoners on this transport would be en route to the Institute by the time parents were depleting their credits at the clinic this Friday.

Thirty-Seven

ZAYD

ZAYD SAT in one of the low, orange, upholstered chairs in the corner of the volunteer lounge, staring into nothing. He was too exhausted to think and too heartsick to want to think. It'd been far too long since he'd let go of Anika's hands and let her walk into the care of the Institute, away from him. She'd been certain they'd see each other again. She'd promised, so he'd let her go. He'd trusted her because he always trusted her. But the Institute had made her a liar and him the fool that hadn't thought it possible.

"Oh, you'll see her again," the volunteer escorting him to intake had said. "They'll let you watch when they put her in cryo, just to make sure you know they've got your whole heart in their cold box."

If he'd known it would be like this…

Zayd didn't know what he would have done because he hadn't believed it would come to this. The fact that Anika had been taken to the medical facility and he hadn't seen her since meant she was infected. There was nowhere else to take her. The two of them couldn't run.

When the Institute was first created, people had flocked to it by the dozens, then by the thousands as stories of Henry Endgal and the first mass-produced inoculation spread through the burgeoning City States. It was a miracle and a blessing, but then came the second outbreak.

Viruses evolve. Zoribiatus hid and changed, and when it re-emerged in the fringe communities, spreading out like tendrils through the main infrastructure, the Institute changed, too.

Before the second outbreak, anyone whose disease had not yet progressed to near-dead state received the inoculation. If there were only a fresh bite or scratch, a patient would stay for observation. If the disease didn't manifest or progress any further, they were released. If the disease did progress, or if the treatment didn't generate a response, the patient would go into cryogenics with the rest of the patients who had gone too far to be saved by existing technology. Some were early in their progression; others had transformed into the near-dead state or been collected in the first Great Cleanse organized by the DDC to make the world livable again. No one worried. The scientists had found the first cure—the inoculation. It would only be a matter of time until they could find a solution to help the patients whose disease had progressed but had not yet fully developed into the *near-dead* state.

After the second outbreak, things were different. Studies confirmed that the second outbreak began not from the near-dead missed in the first Great Cleanse, but in people who had been infected and then inoculated. The virus went dormant in their bodies. Individual cells either adapted or died, but as a colony, the Zoribiatus virus didn't die. Eventually, every patient who lived long enough for the virus to change and mature within their bodies experienced a sudden re-emergence and progression.

The failure of the Institute's first treatment planted enough mistrust to create a widespread disaster. Families hid their patients, hoping not to lose them to cryogenic slumber while they waited indefinitely for a cure.

When the cities began to crumble, people ran. They took the infection with them, giving rise to the problem that still existed outside the safety of the carefully constructed City States.

That's when everything changed. The Department of Disease Containment made testing mandatory. The force field barriers went up, and non-essential travel between communities was forbidden. The

Northern Laboratories dedicated half of its facilities to research and defense against the roaming groups of near-dead patients, more violent and insuppressible than before.

Thanks to these efforts, the second outbreak was resolved in just a few years, but society was never the same. Although patients reported to the Institute without issue once more, the hope the inoculation had provided was replaced with a grim acceptance that the Institute was the only option—submit to cryogenics or lose your humanity in the slow, mindless decay of near-death.

Zayd knew all of this, but like a fool, he'd still hoped. There was something inside of him determined to hope. It was the same part of him that had decided to join the dissenting group of smugglers. He'd hoped Anika was flagged for the Institute out of an abundance of caution. Her fingernails *always* stained from nail polish, and nobody inside the cities got infected anymore. Nobody carried the dormant Zoribiatus from the second outbreak. There was too much testing. Travel was too controlled. It was supposed to be a mistake.

Anika had told him about the outbreak on the way to the Institute, but still he hadn't believed. He'd kept denying there was anything wrong with her, right up to the moment he came out of the room with the wailing monster and she didn't. That was the moment he'd become a volunteer. Quickly, he learned that almost every other volunteer was here for the same reason. They came *with* someone.

Infection. Devastation. Heartbreak.

There were so many volunteers at the Institute, even after the last group loaded into a giant transport vehicle and headed north to the Laboratories alongside the cryogenic cylinders keeping their loved ones alive.

If you can call it that, Zayd thought. He tried hard not to think about what came next. *It will be Anika's turn soon.* The thought came anyway, keeping him awake at night. In the meantime, Zayd did everything he could to learn so he could survive long enough to see her again.

"You doing alright, man?"

Zayd looked up from the dark boots that had infiltrated his line of sight, past the brown-and-blue volunteer uniform and into the face of a handsome young man with a close-cropped beard.

"What sort of a question is that?" he asked, not bothering to meet the man's gaze.

The other volunteer set a mug on the table in front of Zayd before settling down into the chair on the opposite side, forcing himself into Zayd's field of vision unless he turned away.

"An earnest one. People talk. Lot of us are worried about you," the volunteer said, taking a slow sip from his own mug.

"What are they worried about?" Zayd asked, glancing at the other man's mug, then the one on the table.

"You don't eat. You don't drink. You can't keep up in training."

All true things, Zayd knew. But he'd been in denial, telling himself he'd eat when he knew Anika was okay. That his will to survive would strengthen when he knew she would survive, too. He'd told himself that training in a weaker state didn't matter because the danger lay ahead, not in his current tasks.

"I'm having a hard time with the transition," he said.

"You're worried about your girl," the volunteer said. He caught the flash of surprise on Zayd's drawn face and nodded. "Like I said, people around here talk."

"Her name is Anika," Zayd said, not certain he liked this other volunteer talking about *his girl*.

"I know that, too." The volunteer took another long drink, leaving only a little of what was in his mug before setting it on the table.

"How—"

"Look," the man said, cutting him off in a low voice. "A lot of volunteers show up in a state like yours. It's rough, and the only reason you're here at all is because of how much you love whoever you came here with. Believe me, I know."

Zayd settled, watching the other volunteer with more interest now.

"If you want to have a chance of making it around here, you've got to start taking care of yourself. Volunteers depend on each other. If you don't shape up, we won't make it to the thaw." The volunteer gave him a pointed look before dropping his eyes down to the mug.

Zayd picked it up, noting its contents were warm. "What's in it?" he asked.

"A little something to help with the hurt," the volunteer said.

Zayd gave the mug a sniff. The dark, steaming contents were laced with some sort of spirit. A strong one, by his guess.

"So the Hole has tunnels all the way out to the Institute," Zayd mused. He must've been smuggling more than people in those shipments. He took a long drink, relishing the way the elixir burned down his throat as the artificial warmth spread inside of him.

"Who said anything about tunnels?" the volunteer asked, a flash of concern crossing his face.

"Oh, nothing. I was just thinking out loud. You know, the Hole? Like if it were an actual hole, it might lead to—oh, never mind," Zayd said, taking another drink to shut himself up.

The volunteer watched him for a moment, retrieving his own mug. "Right," he agreed.

Zayd was halfway through his drink by the time the man spoke again.

"You must have some important friends, Baba, because I've been here awhile, and I haven't seen the sort of thing people here are doing for you," the volunteer said.

Zayd froze mid-drink, looking at the man sitting across from him, completely lost. "Do you mean this drink? What are you talking about? How do you know my name?"

"I've been here awhile. My man didn't make it, you see, so there was no reason to move up to the Northern Laboratories. And people talk. The sort of people talking about you are talking from the inside and the outside," the volunteer said.

Zayd couldn't make sense of it, and his concern for whatever this meeting was mounted. He put the mug down, shoving it away.

"Relax, I promise I'm friendly," the volunteer said. "It just happens that I know a lot of the folks who have been talking about you, Baba. Like I said, I've been around here for a while. Name's Benji."

Benji. Zayd had heard the name around, mostly from the newer city recruit—Jemani.

"What do you want with me?" Zayd asked. He should start taking things around here more seriously. He didn't want people talking about him. Volunteers weren't exactly high status at the Institute. If he'd attracted attention, it could only mean one thing: Anika was in trouble.

"I don't really want anything from you, Baba. I'm just the messenger," Benji said, crossing his arms across his lap.

So this was about Anika. Alarm bells went off inside Zayd. A sick, anxious feeling counteracted the warming relaxation the drink had deposited throughout his system.

"Well, why don't you deliver your *message* and be done with it?" he snapped.

Benji gave him a hard look. "Hey, man, I get it. Things aren't looking good for you. You're a volunteer at the Institute. I get being mad about it. But that's not my fault. Careful where you spread your wrath."

Zayd tried to contain the frustration welling just below his surface. Though in the heat of the moment, he didn't care much for Benji or his admonishment, he didn't have much of a choice but to remain contained. Hearing whatever Benji had to pass on about Anika, or the people who knew something about her, depended on Zayd's ability to navigate this situation. Besides, the man had brought him a nice drink.

"I'm sorry, friend. Like I said, it's been a difficult adjustment," Zayd said. Most of the anger stayed below the surface.

"Right, right. I know how that goes," Benji said, as if the whole thing were already water under the bridge.

He stood, and for a terrible second, Zayd thought he was going to walk off without delivering the message that had brought him.

"Why don't you follow me? There's someone I'd like you to meet," Benji said, reaching out a hand for Zayd to take.

Zayd balked at it, amazed that the man would offer his bare hand to a nearly complete stranger. He had almost forgotten what to do with a hand.

He took it at the last second and stood. When he turned to follow Benji across the room, he noticed the lounge was completely empty. The little lamp in their corner was the only light left. Benji flipped the switch behind them, creating a darkness that was nearly total, before expertly navigating the both of them across the room to the door. Benji opened it with careful silence, swinging it outward like the portal entrance to another dimension. He held it in place and waited. Zayd looked at him, curious.

"Only you, man. This is where we part—for now." Benji tilted his head toward the exit, indicating Zayd's path.

Zayd stepped out of the volunteer lounge into the shadowy darkness of the Institute grounds. Benji let the door shut behind him, and Zayd felt sudden terror.

This was a trick.

He only had a moment to consider the consequences of this situation before a young woman stepped out of the shadows, wearing a dark medic suit and a lab coat that was too tight around her midsection.

"Mr. Baba?" she asked, eyes wide with curious concern.

"Yes," he agreed. What else could he say?

"My name is Park," she said. "I've been caring for your wife."

CHAPTER

Thirty~Eight

PARK

PARK WAS USED to taking risks. She'd been taking risks as long as she'd been at the Institute because that's what it had taken to be with Reed. She told herself it had been worth it. It gave them three years they wouldn't have otherwise had, regardless of how things ended. And things only ended because of the Institute and its training program. It had nothing to do with Chase Reed.

Eventually, he'll understand, Park told herself. Maybe once he was in the Northern Laboratories, focusing on cure research instead of compliance.

She didn't know if she was lying to herself or if she really believed Reed would find himself again. But she was deluding herself to believe that what happened to Reed would matter to her. Obviously, it wouldn't. He was preparing to leave for the Northern Laboratories, and if Garth stayed true to his word, Park would be leaving the Institute for places unknown to raise their child. They would never see each other again. Reed wasn't part of her decision-making process anymore.

But now, even with Reed out of her life, Park was still taking risks. Increasingly bigger risks. Reporting classified L-wing information to

Garth, hiding a pregnancy she wasn't supposed to have, befriending a patient, and now…

At least working with volunteers to sneak around the Institute grounds didn't feel like a new level of risk.

Anika's husband stood dumbfounded. Park could have expected as much. He'd probably been told he wouldn't see or hear anything of his patient until the cryogenic slumber process. Still, seeing his reaction was different from imagining it. This was the sort of moment she would revisit again and again. There had been a thousand micro-moments like this since her shift away from the intern program. They kept surprising her.

Most of those moments were with the patients in the main medical wing as they navigated the devastating loss of their humanity. Moments of sadness and flickers of empathy would break through the barrier she'd built in her heart against the patients' constant screams of agony. But these moments had been different since she began working in the L-wing with Dr. Wong's explicit instructions to *be nice*.

Since when had Park needed someone to tell her to be nice to anyone? She'd been nice her whole life, so maybe the real question had become: when had she quit being nice? When had she quit seeing the patients as human? When had their screams gone from intolerable to the background noise of her daily reality?

Park knew the answer to this question was the key to everything that had gone wrong at the Institute. She saw it in the division this place had created between her and Reed, in the way the patients were seen in the main medical center and the L-wing, and in the cruel division between scientists and volunteers. Park's own humanity remained intact, re-blooming with each passing day while Reed's was wiped away in preparation for the Northern Laboratories. Until she made her exit, Park was committed to make use of it.

"Your wife asked me to find you," she said, looking for a reaction from the stunned man.

"Anika…" Zayd breathed. Park watched him struggle to get a hold of himself. "She's—is she alright?"

Park nodded, rushing to give him the reassurance he would need to trust her. "She's receiving treatment in a special branch of the medical center."

Zayd's face fell. "Before she goes into cryo."

Park had seen it before with other volunteers. They all experienced the phase where they actively mourned their patients. The ones whose patients went into cryogenics moved on quickly from the Institute to the Northern Laboratories. The ones Park knew best were those with friends and family that didn't make it. Zayd was the first she'd ever met who wasn't either of those things.

"She won't be going into cryo—at least not for a long time," she said, milling through all the things she should and shouldn't say. She was taking a risk, yes, but she wanted to keep them both as safe as possible.

"Is she not infected?" Zayd asked, his hands shoved deep in his pockets against the night's chill.

It was a reasonable question, and she hated to dash his hopes further. "No. She's infected."

Her words did exactly what she'd predicted they'd do. The man's grief and pain were tangible. What she said next would make all the difference. If Anika's husband didn't comply, they'd all be lost.

"He will listen to you. Tell him it was my choice!" Anika had insisted as they'd plotted together.

"Your wife has an emergent strain of the virus. It's very new, and what we know is limited as well as confidential. But so far, all the patients who present with this strain of Zoribiatus show no disease progression beyond initial presentation."

Zayd ran a shaking hand through close-cropped hair, eyes darting between Park and the empty space surrounding the volunteer quarters. "She won't get any sicker?"

"Not yet, at least," Park confirmed.

"For how long?"

She could see the hope blossoming across his face and knew they were headed in the wrong direction.

"For a while. But as long as she's infected, she will never leave this place," Park said, delivering what was meant to be the critical blow.

"If the disease won't progress… can you cure her?" Zayd asked.

Clearly, he wouldn't go down easy.

Park sighed, wishing she could undo the buttons on her pants and uncomfortably snug lab coat. She was expanding at an alarming rate, and if Garth didn't provide the modified wardrobe she needed, her condition wouldn't be secret for much longer.

"No."

A shadow darkened his face. "But if the disease isn't progressing, there's time for clinical—"

"It's not that simple!" Park said, cutting him off. His mouth shrunk to a fine line Park knew contained his mounting frustration. *More truth*, she decided. "The testing she's undergoing in the L-wing isn't meant to treat or cure her. It's meant to understand the strain of Zoribiatus. No one is working on treating the patients here."

"Then she should go to the Northern Laboratories," Zayd said. Park admired his tenacity.

"L-wing patients don't go to the Northern Laboratories," she snapped.

"I'm not going to give up on her!"

"I know. She said you wouldn't," Park agreed, catching him off guard. "She said you wouldn't want to leave her—that being with her was why you'd come here in the first place."

"What was I supposed to do? Let her get on that transport alone?"

Park didn't know what he was supposed to do. She would have gotten on the transport if it had been Reed. But that didn't change the situation they were in now.

"Of course not. But now you're both here. Anika can't leave, but you can. There's a transport leaving for the Northern Laboratories. I don't know when yet, but it's not going to make it to the Northern Laboratories. There are people here and on the outside. They're going to get whoever is on that transport out of this place," she said.

"No. I won't!" Zayd said.

"It's what she wants. It's her choice," Park argued.

"It's not. It's mine." Zayd's fists clenched at his sides.

"If you don't go, she will spend the rest of her life, however long that is, knowing you sacrificed yours."

"You would do that to her?" he growled.

Park met his rage with a determined stare. She'd made a promise to her patient. "You'll never see her again, you know. You'll end up infected. That's what happens to all the volunteers at the Institute—infected or worse. And she'll hear about it. She'll know you threw your life away for her. Is that what you want?"

This was what Anika wanted her to say to him. She wanted him out of here as badly as Park wanted to get herself out of this place.

Zayd stared at her, hands still clenched as if he might strike out, moist puffs condensing in the air between them, creating halos of reflection in the soft light.

Tears welled in her eyes, threatening to spill over as she considered how alike their positions were—how impossible the thing they both had to do was. "I know you think you can't live without her. I know because I'm leaving someone behind, too. She is asking you to do the most impossible thing."

Zayd glanced down to her middle, and everything about him softened. She blinked hard, not wanting him to see the pain it caused her, even if it could sway him. It wasn't a pain she could share.

"How far along are you?" he asked.

"I don't know," she admitted. "Maybe halfway there? Maybe a little more. This place isn't exactly set up with experts in that area."

"It's starting to show."

His words sent a hot flush down her neck in a mixture of terror and embarrassment. Of course she knew it was starting to show. None of her pants fit anymore, and the lab coat pulled away between each button. But without context, most people in the L-wing ignored it if they saw it at all. She was always hiding behind a medical tray or her tablet. She had none of those things now.

"It won't matter once we get out of here," Park insisted, crossing her arms self-consciously across her expanding middle and trying hard to ignore the steady thump-thumping that had started about a week before. That movement, the ever-present tap and thump of growth inside her, was a persistent reminder that everything mattered.

Zayd looked at her, clearly warring with himself. "Ani and I were trying before…"

"I know. She told me," Park said, uncomfortable with the turn of the conversation.

"She knows?"

Park laughed at the way his eyes flew to hers. "She figured it out faster than you, which really freaked me out."

"Of course she did. She'd spent the last six months with her nose in every article about the process. She was so excited—*we* were so excited."

The sadness in Zayd's voice made Park ache for what they were losing—not just each other, but the family they were supposed to have, the life they would never share. It was all too familiar and yet foreign at the same time. There had been a moment, after she'd realized she was pregnant, where she'd imagined herself and Reed together with a child. But that was all. Before she'd gotten sick and Garth had taken over her life, there had never been a possibility. There had only ever been her and Reed—at the Institute, hoping against hope they might continue together at the Northern Laboratories. But none of that shared hope had ever included a family. It was nothing like what Zayd and Anika were experiencing.

"I'm sorry," she said, meaning it more than she ever could have before the realization.

"I am, too, for whatever you're losing here," Zayd said.

"We don't have to lose everything—not if you agree to leave with me," Park implored.

Zayd let out a heavy sigh, losing whatever war he was waging internally.

"Anika said you would want to help me. Here… and once we're out there…"

These words weren't hers. She would never ask for something like that, but Anika had insisted this was what Zayd would need before he agreed to leave. Watching him now, Park knew Anika had been right about her husband.

"On one condition," Zayd said.

"What?" Park asked, hoping it was something she could actually agree to.

"Let me see her. I need to hear it from her."

Park's heart sank. She didn't know if she would be able to meet his condition, at least not without Garth's help, and she didn't know if she wanted to include him in this.

Thirty~Nine

SIMONS

SIMONS STOOD in the kitchen of the energy management facility outside of the Institute, trying not to look as lost and overwhelmed as he felt as Ternice brewed coffee.

"The baby will be here in two—maybe three months. Like I said, it's really hard to calculate without a cycle, but at least I have your visits to set the calendar by," she was saying.

Simons didn't know what to do with the information. It was too real, too present, too soon. "What are we supposed to do?"

"There's nothing to do, Moe. This baby is coming one way or the other," Terni said, offering him a steely look that personified everything he loved about her. It made him ache.

She poured hot water over the grounds, inhaling as they steeped before reaching across the counter to return the boiling pot. He caught her hand as it retracted and ran his thumb over its soft surface. "I know. I'm just trying to figure out what we're supposed to do about it. You can't be here alone with a baby," he said. It's all he'd been able to think about since realizing she was pregnant—had been pregnant and alone this whole time, keeping it to herself.

It wasn't safe. Even if she was right and the pregnancy was a result of an explainable margin of error in the procedure, it wasn't safe because Terni wasn't supposed to be pregnant, and that was a big problem. Energy management techs didn't get pregnant.

There wasn't supposed to be anyone else on energy management grounds. No one was supposed to be able to get in, and she wasn't supposed to be able to get out. Her pregnancy was undeniable proof that energy management facilities were not as impermeable as the government believed. It would spoil the convenient illusion. The dissenters had worked too hard to secure control of the management stations for it to be ruined by the existence of one pregnant management worker. Or, if they waited much longer before someone from the Institute checked, a baby.

"Maybe they won't check. That's why the dissenters decided on the fusion stations in the first place, isn't it?" Simons asked.

"Maybe not if this station were way on the outskirts or far up north. But I'm Institute adjacent," Ternice pointed out, filling two mugs with coffee and adding sugar.

"It's never been an issue for me to be here," Simons protested, reaching out for her.

She brushed him aside with a hard exhale, slamming a drawer and turning away from it to face him. "What would you call this? Because I'd call it an issue!"

Simons resisted the sting of her words. Ternice was only experiencing the same panic and pain consuming him. The situation felt hopeless.

"Can you get a message to our folks on the inside? If we can delay any activity on the facility until after the baby is born, maybe we can hide it—especially if we have notice before anyone shows up. Sort of like we do when I'm here?"

Terni grabbed the hand she'd refused moments before, giving it a firm shake and squeezing so hard Simons knew it was meant to hurt.

"This is a baby, Moe, not an *it*. We're talking about a full-blown human being—a child! I'm not going to be able to tuck this child in a back room and keep them from crying just because I say so. Babies cry. They need constant attention and care."

"I can—"

"You're not always going to be here, Moe!" she wailed before stopping herself. There was a silent moment while she contained herself. She swallowed what Simons was certain was her terror and hopelessness, and a striking serenity overtook her. When she spoke again, her voice was soft and controlled. "You will rarely be here. You have a job to do—*we* have jobs to do, and we're talking about a child who doesn't belong in any of this!"

He squeezed back, bringing his other hand to envelop hers. It was cool within the fiery warmth of his own. "I know that, baby, I know. But if I had to change the whole world to make this work, I'd do it. I'm not sacrificing you for this cause. You're too important to me, and this child is going to be the same—a bit of both of us."

"You can't throw away the dissenters on account of me. You can't throw away everything we've done," she protested.

"Then run away with me. Come with me, and we'll do it together," he said, deciding this was the best solution for all of them.

It wasn't the worst idea. They both knew the history of fusion station workers attempting suicide or going AWOL. It was a lonely, psychologically demanding job, and not everyone was up to the challenge. Hope swelled within him as he saw a way forward for the first time since understanding the depth of their predicament. He could almost see their future as it bloomed in his mind. They would run away. He would end his burgeoning career as a coyote for the dissenters, and they would start a new life with new identities somewhere quiet. They would raise a child, and maybe, once things were settled, they could figure out how to do something else for the cause— something new that wouldn't keep them apart.

"No," Terni said, destroying the image in Simons' mind before it could fully form. "It's too risky."

"Staying here is too risky!" Simons protested. He grasped for the thing he almost had, but it poured through his fingers like the water of a running river.

"If I leave here, the DDC will know something happened. They'll start investigating, and if they do that, they might find the other stations. They might find the people we're sheltering. The whole operation could be revealed."

Simons understood her logic but wanted to reject it. The DDC couldn't care that much about one person at one energy management facility. "It's not new. Others have abandoned—"

"After what? Years?" Terni demanded. "I've been here barely two years, and between the new equipment installation and the training, I've hardly been isolated! The weather is good; I've got tons of supplies. It's just not believable. Maybe if this had happened a few years down the road, but it's too soon. Leaving would make people look, and we can't handle what they might find."

"Anything worse than them finding you pregnant, or a screaming baby?" Simons demanded. It was his turn to let the anger and fear drive.

"I'll get them to hold off until the baby is born," Terni said, a mask of resolve settling over her.

"And then what?" Simons demanded. "You said it yourself: you can't hide a baby."

Terni leaned into him, her body and her considerable stomach pressing perfectly into the spaces they always fit. His arms went up automatically, enveloping her and not minding one bit that there was more of her between them than before. She reached up to cup the sides of his face, running her fingers across his freshly shaved jaw. Her hands were gentle as she turned his face toward her, fingers brushing the sensitive flesh below his lips just low enough that he couldn't kiss her.

"You're right," she said, looking pleadingly up into his searching eyes. "I can't hide a baby here. I can't raise a child in the middle of nowhere without human contact—just me and on rare occasions, if nothing bad happens, you."

He tried to speak, to complain that they were about to talk themselves in the same circle, but her thumb pressed into his lips, begging him for silence. She dropped her other hand down to his arm, using gentle pressure to pry it from around her. He let her do it, his hand caressing her side as she dragged it to rest on the rounded mass of her belly. "I can't keep this child, Moe, but you can."

He felt the rise and fall of her breaths through the thin fabric of her stretched shirt. The place where his hand rested was both her and more than her. Underneath, there was a gentle flutter as the life inside stirred, perhaps moved by the weight of him or maybe just ready for this to be done.

"I can't do that, Terni. I'm no father," Simons said, bringing his head down to rest against hers.

"And I'm no mother, but here we are," Terni countered, resting her hand on top of his so they both rose and fell with her breath.

"I only want to do this with you," he said.

She nodded, their bodies moving in sync. "I know. I want the same. But I've been thinking for a while now. There've been a lot of long nights for me to consider. This is what it's going to look like for you and me. For us, this is what doing this together is going to look like."

He thought for a long time as they breathed and rocked in the silence of the energy management kitchen. Simons brought Terni's face up to his, kissing her deeply as if drawing her breath away. She wrapped her arms around the back of his neck and lost herself in the embrace. When her stomach got in the way, Simons picked her up and shifted her to the side, tilting his head so there was even less space between them.

He kissed her like he might never have another opportunity and only broke away when Terni pulled back, saying, "I thought you were going to feed me."

He watched her, his eyes glittering with unshed tears.

"Do you still know how to make that rice dish? The one where you mix the vegetables and that awful meat together until it all tastes better?" she asked.

"Casserole," Simons said, smiling.

"That's right. Make me a casserole," Terni said, turning her body away from him to open the pantry door.

He accepted the bag of rice from her, moving over to the counter to gather the required dishes. "If I do it when I leave here, I should be able to get some false papers. Then when it's older, the baby can go to school in the city," he said, pulling out a strainer to rinse the rice.

Terni put two cans of carrots, peas and corn onto the counter. "Them, Moe. A baby isn't an it."

"That's what I meant," he said. "But they can go to school in the city. I'll find one of those boarding places for residency."

"Those are for orphans," Terni protested.

"I'm going to have to do something. Even if I can get a job inside the city, I'll be gone all the time," he said, hating how natural the conversation sounded.

"What do you mean, if?" Terni asked.

"I mean, I'm a maintenance worker. That's my technical title. I drive a repair vehicle around the cities and along the road to do maintenance. How am I supposed to find something that pays enough credits to survive in the city?" he asked, not meaning for it to sound so harsh.

"How can you keep working on the outside if you've got a child to raise?" she countered.

"How can I raise a child if I can't move around freely outside? How can I do it if we can't come see you?" he demanded.

They stood in the kitchen, backs toward one another, unable to turn. Simons knew that if he turned, he wouldn't be able to follow through with this agreement. He would reject it entirely and insist she run away with them. Playing make-believe about a life he might actually have to live and arguing about the details was easier, even if it broke his heart.

He dumped the rinsed rice into a pot and put it on the stove to cook before searching through the drawer for a can opener.

"I trust you," Terni said. He almost didn't hear it because of how much he was rattling around in the drawer of forks and spatulas.

"Trust me for what?" he asked.

Her hand went to his arm. It came nowhere near being able to wrap around his bicep, but she pulled as if she were strong enough to overpower him. He relented as if he were overcome.

"I trust you to do this," she said. He realized she was crying. "No matter what you decide to do—however you decide to do it, I need you to know that I believe in you to do it right. You're going to raise this baby right."

He wrapped his arms around her, and when her head was buried in his chest, he finally allowed himself to cry.

MAYBE RUNNING AWAY HAD ONLY BEEN a fantasy—a dream that made Mora feel like she would do something big with her life without actually having to leave. It might have been enough to believe that somewhere out there, someone wanted her. Not anymore.

If there were any part of her that didn't believe she could truly leave, it died when she saw the raid on the Hole. It was the only thing left in the stupid city that made existing worthwhile, and it was gone. Sure, there was Jim, and she did love him, but even he wouldn't be there much longer. What was the point of staying in a city whose heart was vanishing?

Mora wiped at the side of her face, which was dry thanks to the ripping wind on the rooftop. The gesture was automatic, as if she could erase the oppressive emotions welling up inside of her with the back of her sleeve. Nothing was that simple.

She handed Omen another slice of apple—his favorite of the offerings she would bring from school sometimes. While Mora found the slices mealy and flavorless, the raven seemed to savor them, closing his eyes as he tipped his head back to swallow the pieces.

"Better you than me," she said, watching him finish the last piece.

"Hey," Omen responded in a soft voice that was reminiscent of her own.

"Don't 'hey' me; you're the one that also eats mouse guts." She scratched the side of his neck before settling into the chair with her old-world tablet.

Omen had been sticking around a lot more lately, as if he were waiting for something. If he was, Mora didn't know what. Maybe he was just tired of making the journey to his home away from home. The mice in the city were fat and slow, and Mora brought him a variety of treats, from apple slices to bits of bread, cereal, and the rehydrated peas she loathed but that her mother made more nights than not when she was home. It was a good life for a bird, and if not for the lack of other ravens in the city, he might not have had a reason to leave in the first place.

And then where would she be?

Before school, before she and Jim had stumbled on the raid and seen her mother guiding Shannon onto the Institute transport, before everything that gave her purpose had crumbled around her, she'd planned to get into her newest science fiction short story collection. Now, she couldn't fathom fiction.

They're erasing my city.

She opened the communication application, pleased to see the network setup Jim had done earlier remained steadfast. *We need your help*. The last message stood out to her like a single bloom in a field of weeds, reminding her there was more to this world than the pieces crumbling around her. Before she could talk herself out of it, she typed out the question that had been burning inside of her since their last communication.

> Mora: If I make it out successfully, how will I find you?

She didn't know when she could expect a response. It was late afternoon, and the sun still hung in the hazy spring sky. What did the people on the outside do with their time? Would she have to wait until the end of a work shift for Georgia to check for a message? Was Georgia waiting for her message even now?

A minute later, as Omen settled into the crook of Mora's knees to shelter against the wind, the response came.

> Georgia: What do you mean, if?

Mora wasn't sure if it was because her previous messages had sounded more determined or if Georgia was doubting her abilities, but she felt the question deep in her gut like a growing angst.

> Mora: I'm still working on a plan!

> Georgia: Not good enough. You can't wing this one, kid.

It was a valid observation, Mora knew. She also knew that if she were going to make this exodus work, she'd need to be transparent and accept all the help she could get.

> Mora: I'm planning to leave after the Retest. I've been studying as a diversion and taking things very seriously. No one will suspect.

> Georgia: Always assume someone suspects something. How are you planning to get out?

> Mora: I was going to ask around the Hole to see if anyone had a line on a smuggler who did exports…

It was logical to believe that the Hole was the right place for this sort of communication. The vendors either knew who brought the goods in or knew someone who knew those people. She'd been dealing with them long enough to establish trust and figured making her break was a foregone conclusion.

But that was before the Hole got shut down. Before she'd looked into her own mother's eyes and for that one, brief second, recognized her mother seeing her back.

> Georgia: Trusting the wrong person could get you caught.

> Mora: Yeah, I know. But that's not really an issue anymore because I can't do it.

> Georgia: Why not?

> Mora: The Hole is gone—it was busted earlier today. My mother has been busy.

She'd talked to Georgia before about her mother. It was easy to vent to a stranger about her strained relationship with the DDC communication and transportation liaison.

> Georgia: What's the plan now?

> Mora: The Test is next week. No one will suspect anything right away. I'll have found an exporter by graduation.

> Georgia: careful who you trust.

Mora rolled her eyes. The last thing she needed was yet another parental figure in her life telling her which ways she'd messed everything up.

> Mora: Obviously.

> Georgia: Less obvious than you'd imagine.

> Mora: Let me take care of that part. Once I'm out, how do I find you?

> Georgia: If you get out, we'll find you.

Mora gaped at the message, wondering how anyone on the outside could be so brazen, so bold. Below her, there was some commotion in the street, equipment moving and workers setting up their gear. It was a familiar sound in the cities lately, given all the renovations going on. It barely registered anymore.

> Mora: How will you do that? There are patrols around the City States—especially the capitol!

> Georgia: We know.

> Mora: Well, if you know, then you must also know the dangers of getting caught without documents. How will you find me without someone in your team getting swept up as a Resistee or a volunteer?

There were more issues than that, but the issue of someone showing up outside the city and getting immediately caught or worse, somehow leading the DDC directly to the other people on the outside and making them disappear, too, was on Mora's mind.

> Georgia: Let me take care of that part. We're working on it, so you can consider the details on a need-to-know basis.

Mora considered the message, anxiety spreading through her at the familiar lack of information. Would being on the outside be more of the same? She drafted her next message, aiming to extract more than *tell you later* from Georgia but not wanting to come across as too insecure. Omen snuggled deeply into the groove between her legs, making it difficult to stroke the soft feathers at the base of his neck. As she reviewed her words, the noise from below reached a new crescendo, and the building shook.

"Watch it!" came a shrill command over a comm from the ground below.

Mora rolled her eyes. This must be a pretty rookie team of workers, crashing into residents' buildings and working on the Westside. Omen stirred from his relaxed position, setting his wings out for balance as he scrambled to his feet, then settled into an uneasy stand.

"Hey," he said in his Mora-voice again.

"It's okay," she cooed, returning to her tablet. She held her breath as she sent her inquiry.

> Mora: If you expect me to put all my trust in you, you're going to have to have a little faith in me. Maybe you can't tell me how you'll track me down. Fine. You can tell me why you think I can help you. What are you doing out there?

> Georgia: What are we doing? We're living. We're free.

It was a partial answer at best. Mora was about to call Georgia on it when another message came through.

> Georgia: No one is going to be free until we eradicate the near-dead infection. Aside from living, that's job número uno.

Mora was halfway to interpreting the end of the message—she recognized the phrase but wanted to be certain—when the building shook again and Omen squawked in disapproval. She reached out to comfort him, and he pecked the tip of her finger in disapproval before hopping onto her forearm. She clenched her fist against his weight but held her arm steady.

When the building shook a third time and a sharp, metal-against-metal grinding sound rang out in perfect unison with the vibration of what felt like an engine against the building walls, suddenly, Mora understood what that grinding was, and her heart nearly stopped.

Omen took flight, having had enough. As he flew into the early evening sun, Mora raced to the ledge that separated the roof from the world below. There was a snapping sound. The building continued to shudder, and the fire escape came loose from the side. She didn't have to look to know that was exactly what was happening, but she did anyway. She needed to see it for herself.

Carefully, Mora peeked out over the thick brick ledge, down at the work. She couldn't afford to risk being seen stranded on the roof. She needed to figure out how to get back down. From her vantage point, it looked as though the bottom several flights of the stairwell were gone. There was an elevated platform working on the next portion of the structure. Escaping into an empty apartment would be impossible.

Her heart thundered in her chest as she watched a terrible metal claw rip the next portion of the fire escape free. It was the loose section that made Jim woozy and that she'd refused to admit used to do the same to her. There was nothing attaching what remained to the apartment building, so when the machine got that bit free from the rest, the entire top section of the fire escape collapsed before crumbling down and away from the building.

She almost forgot to hide from the workers, who would certainly be looking up to confirm that their job had truly been that easy.

The fire escape was gone. It had been ripped from the building as though it hadn't clung there, steadfast, for more than a hundred years. She sank down onto her knees, overcome, which was likely the only thing that prevented her from being spotted by the workers below. One portion of the crew was already collecting the twisted metal of the escape as the rest of the workers moved on various lifts to make certain the places where the escape used to cling to the building were mended and whole.

There was no way down. She'd never needed an alternative to the fire escape and had never considered that might change. She was trapped. Mora's vision blurred as panic began to set in.

Forcing herself onto her feet, Mora peered down the side of the building once more—maybe to convince herself the escape was really gone, maybe to search for something she hadn't noticed. The fire escape was gone, and there were no secret passages against the side of the building hiding a secret way down.

She searched each side of the building again and again. No matter how many times she peered down the sides, no escape presented itself. Mora let out a frustrated wail as her panic transformed again into something even more desperate. The sound of her desperation was drowned out by the uncaring wind.

She had to calm down. Below her came more clatter and grinding as the workers scrambled to finish the job. She took in a slow breath, then another, relishing the way the cold air made her lungs burn, making it easier to think.

There was nothing on the roof that might give her some clue of how to escape, but perhaps there might be a secret locked away in some old city schematics, waiting for her to find it.

It was the first sensible thought she'd had since realizing the fire escape was going down.

"Guess I was an idiot to think the Test was going to be my biggest hurdle," she mused, walking back to her tablet. Having a practical next step was making her feel better.

Before she had a chance to close out the communication app, she noticed another message from Georgia.

Georgia: There isn't much time left.

Mora looked up from the message, eyes darting to each corner of the rooftop and the skyline beyond.

Did she know? For a terrible second, Mora thought that maybe Georgia was a planted agent working inside along with her mom in the DDC. But no. That wasn't possible. The tracker had confirmed Georgia's location, and there was far more information that came with Omen's journey than someone could fake using DDC tech. Mora was certain because it was one of the things her mom complained regularly about.

Mora thought to answer but decided the conversation could wait. Right now, she needed to figure out how to get off the roof before the sun set and she was in serious trouble.

She closed out the communication app and opened the city building schematic. There were doors on a lot of the old roofs, but most of them had been sealed off. Maybe she could figure out how they were sealed. If she knew, she might manage to pry the one on this roof open and sneak downstairs before her mom got home.

Mora was staring down at her tablet screen, making her way toward the door near the center of the roof, when it let out a low, metallic shudder and shriek, as if merely thinking about opening it had summoned the hinges to yield and the door to swing open.

Then she found herself face-to-face for the second time that day with her mother.

MORA STOOD, frozen, about twenty-five feet from the door, now a gateway between the building's roof and its interior. She had always thought that door was useless. Soon after she discovered the rooftop, she'd tried to find the access inside the building, but it didn't seem to exist. The interior stairwell stopped on the top floor. Mora had explored every corner of the top floor and found no sign of access to the roof. It was like it had never existed, though she knew it had to have existed at one point. Probably that access had been removed and the door sealed when the building's interior was renovated.

Obviously, she'd been wrong because Morgan Rossi-Stern was standing in the doorway, having accessed it from some interior stairs. Mora tried to suppress the panic surging through her body, making her fingers tingle. She wanted to run, but there was nowhere to go. Her mother had her completely cornered.

"Mom!" The word felt choked in her throat, cut off by the wind.

Morgan stepped out onto the roof, leaving the door to bang against the wall with a gust. Mora cringed at the sound, but Morgan appeared unaffected. They were standing so close together, but Mora had never felt further away. Slowly, she realized she was still holding the old-world tablet. At least Omen was already gone.

"It's time to come downstairs, Mora," Morgan said.

What was she supposed to say to that? *Okay, Mom!* Would she follow Morgan back down those stairs into their apartment as if nothing were wrong? Was that where they were going, or was there a team of officers waiting behind her to take Mora to prosecution? Would her mother do that to her?

"I need to get my bag," Mora said, searching for anything to stall the inevitable moment.

"That's right, dear. You wouldn't want to leave behind any *study material.*" Morgan stood, statuesque against the wind and indomitable in her slim, black suit. Everything about her made Mora feel small and helpless, like a mouse caught in a sticky tray-paper trap waiting for the poison to seep in through her pores.

"Of course," Mora agreed, numb with cold and dread.

Her motions were stiff and automatic, a trained response to her mother's unquestionable authority. It was something Mora thought she'd unraveled during her last three years of secret rebellion, but the obedience came automatically. She had to turn her back to grab her bag from the chair. What was Morgan going to do, shoot her? They might not see eye-to-eye on everything, but she was still her mother. She grabbed the strap of her bag and pulled it toward her, her heart beating so hard it drowned out the wind and made her remember how Jim described doing the last bit of the climb to the rooftop.

She'd never make that climb again, and she was pretty sure she had her mother to thank for that.

Morgan waited as she fumbled with her bag, tucking the tablet under her chin to unzip the larger compartment and slip the black-market tool behind her school tablet. Maybe her mom couldn't tell the difference from where she was.

"I'll take that," Morgan said, reaching her hand out toward the illicit item.

"It's just a tablet." Mora shrugged, trying to look nonchalant. She didn't know if she should proceed with shoving it in her bag or keep it in hand and run at the earliest opportunity she had to make it disappear. Could she be lucky enough to run into Jim outside their apartment? Maybe he forgot something in her room, or maybe he'd come back to say sorry for bolting after the whole thing at the Hole.

"Don't lie to me, Mora. You've always been a terrible liar." Morgan took three slow steps toward her. There was no hurry, no urgency. She had Mora completely trapped.

"I don't know what you're talking about." Mora stalled, searching frantically for something—anything that might get her out of this situation. She absolutely could not let Morgan get her hands on the tablet. She didn't think her mom could unlock all her secret files and the communication program on her own, but there were people in the city department who could do all of that and more.

Morgan closed the gap between them. When she reached out, Mora flinched, pulling the tablet into her middle as if she could stop her mother from taking it. But Mora knew Morgan would have her way in the end. That was how things always went. That was why Mora had agreed to a Retest. She was no match for her mother.

Instead of reaching for the tablet, though, Morgan placed her hands on Mora's shoulders, forcing her to face her. "You aren't as clever as you think, dear. I know about the roof—I've always known about the roof. I know about the research and the tablet and the Hole. Did you think I didn't know what my own daughter was doing? It's time for all of this to stop."

Mora didn't know what to think. Part of her was surprised to realize her mom had known about the roof and the Hole the whole time, but the rest of her understood. To Morgan, knowing and hiding that she knew was power. But Morgan had never used the door before. Mora knew because of the way the paint crumbled away from the broken seam now. So there was a good chance Morgan didn't know about Omen, and if she didn't know about Omen, there was a chance she didn't know about Georgia and the people on the outside either. Jim was the one who encrypted the communication program. Morgan might be able to read Mora like an open file, but what Jim did was special.

"I know you knew," Mora said. She would get as much information from Morgan as possible before things were completely out of her control.

"You knew before or after James told you?" Morgan asked, raising an appraising eyebrow.

Jim? Mora's heart sank, nearly shattering at the possibility that he could be the reason her mom was up here taking everything from her. Was he the reason Morgan shut down the Hole, or was that Mora's doing?

Morgan read the look on Mora's face and smiled. "You didn't know James told me about your little hiding place, or you thought you were safe with your illegal data up on the roof?"

Mora felt tears welling in her eyes and did nothing to keep them from sliding down her cheeks. Maybe it could distract her mother for a few seconds.

Mora had never been shy about using the old-world tablet when in her bedroom. It was easy enough to nestle the clunky thing against her pillow with a blanket over her head. Through that level of cover, the screen's glow could easily be mistaken for her school tablet, and Morgan had opened the door plenty of times while Mora was reading. Jim knew Mora used the tablet almost everywhere, not merely on the roof. But clearly Morgan didn't know that, which meant Jim hadn't told her. If Jim hadn't told her, then he hadn't told Morgan that Mora was planning to run away, and he hadn't told her about the people on the outside. Which meant there was still hope.

"It's time to grow up, Mora," Morgan said, wiping the tear and its path as if she could erase all the distress of this moment.

Mora nodded but kept her eyes down. She needed to look defeated. She didn't want to look up and find Omen circling the roof in search of a place to land and listen in. The workers were still making a racket in the alley. He'd most likely flown out of their range, but still, if Omen was near, Mora didn't want Morgan to see the recognition in her eyes.

The act seemed to work because Morgan continued with her speech, making certain Mora knew what things would be like from now on. Making sure she knew Mora had lost and Morgan Rossi-Stern was victorious once again.

"There will be no more roof. There is no more black market, and you are going to give me that damned tablet. Everything you insist on ruining your life with is gone. You are going to take the Test, and when it's done, you're going to the Institute."

"If I pass," Mora blurted, not able to keep herself from delighting in this one bit of control her mother couldn't have.

The smile didn't change, but Mora could see the anger behind Morgan's cool brown eyes. "I know how hard you've been studying," she said.

"Sure, I've been studying, but we both know it won't be enough." This wasn't a lie. "There is no amount of practice that will catch me up —no little tricks or brilliant strategies Jim could teach me that can make up for all the effort I refused to put in over the years. No matter how hard I study, no matter how badly you want me to succeed, I won't be able to pass."

Mora had expected Morgan's smile to falter. She'd expected her mother's face to fall, to collapse into furious rage, but the smile remained. In fact, Mora thought the smile brightened, touching her eyes with a hint of glee that couldn't mean anything good.

"Oh, I think you'll pass," she said. "In fact, I'm so certain you'll pass that I plan on having your bags packed before dropping you off at the capitol."

Mora had a horrible, sinking feeling. Did she mean…? Thankfully, her mother didn't keep her guessing.

"I'm so certain you'll pass the Test that I've arranged a transport to escort you from the testing facility straight to the Institute."

There it was. Morgan had bribed the testing administration with whatever power or authority she wielded in the DDC to force a pass. Once again, Morgan Rossi-Stern was undefeated.

"I didn't realize how much progress I'd actually made this last month," Mora seethed.

Morgan cupped her face in cool, unfeeling hands, the smile in her eyes still not wavering. "I'm so proud of you, dear. Now, let's go downstairs. I'm making chicken."

She dropped her hands and turned away from her daughter. It didn't matter that she hadn't yanked the tablet from her grasp; there was nowhere for Mora to go. She watched her mother saunter to the door, unable to move.

"What will happen to the people from the Hole?" Mora asked, still clinging to the tablet as if it could shield her from whatever terrible thing her mother had done.

Morgan paused long enough to look back over her shoulder. "We'll talk about that when we get downstairs. You'll hand over that tablet, and I'll tell you everything. Downstairs."

Morgan grabbed the edge of the door and held it open for her daughter to follow.

Mora put her bag over her shoulder, not bothering to zip it closed. She searched her mother, wanting to see some sign of compassion or humanity but not expecting to. All she could see was the heartless instrument of the DDC erasing one more problematic person from the city's landscape.

She wasn't getting off this roof any way but Morgan's way—wasn't going anywhere but their apartment—but Mora would not give her mother the tablet. She took a step toward Morgan, who held her head up in triumph, then another. On the third step, she peeled away from the direct path to the door and lurched to the edge of the roof. The move was so sudden that Morgan didn't have enough time to react. Mora was nearly at the ledge before she could chase after her.

"Mora, don't!" she commanded with all the authority that typically achieved her desired result.

Mora refused to give her the pleasure. She needed to take something from her mother in the same way Morgan Rossi-Stern had taken nearly everything from her. This was a victory her mother would not have.

Once Mora's body touched the ledge, she flung her arms outward, forcing the tablet into a terminal fall. It hung in the air for less than a second, velocity zero at the top of the arc, before accelerating, spinning end over end as it plunged toward the ground. It would not survive this fall. Morgan couldn't have this piece of her. She wouldn't lay a finger on the only thing that had nourished Mora's hungry soul. She would not discover the names of her favorite stories, and she would never unveil the communication with the woman who had tried to save her.

She watched it fall in silence, her mother at her side now, taking in the failure Mora swore would not be her last. When the tablet hit the side of the building and split into three pieces, Morgan gasped. Mora caught a glimpse of a black wing plunging down near the broken thing.

When the tablet pieces hit the ground, they shattered into a thousand bits. Like Mora's heart.

"You insolent, disobedient child," Morgan growled.

Mora relished the look of rage masking her mother's defeat. She could not suppress the genuine smile that touched her lips. "Let's go downstairs and talk about it."

CHAPTER
Forty-Two

REED

THE INTERNS FILED into the clinic for their final physical before graduation with minimal conversation. This was the last obstacle between them and the Northern Laboratories. As usual, the casual ease most felt in the privacy of their dormitories faded quickly in the presence of their observing professors, medical team, and DDC coordinators. This was when Reed felt most at ease, though. The reticence he'd adopted since Park left the intern program blended well with the expected presentation of a scientist. *He* blended well.

"Last men standing, am I right?" Ward said in a voice that shattered the silence like a rusty sledgehammer, slapping him on the shoulder as they approached the waiting benches.

Reed cringed at the gesture, which was more familiar than he typically felt toward Ward or any of the other interns. At first, it was because he had Park. They hadn't needed anyone else to survive the brutality of the intern program. Their alliance lasted long enough for all the other interns to buddy up and find their own social circles. Reed and Park might have been the only couple to arrive together at the start of the three-year program, but they weren't the only couple in the cohort by the end of the first year. Mason and Emery had been hot and heavy until they both dropped out of the intern program, disappearing into energy management. He was pretty sure Brown and Lowell were still seeing each other, too. But he and Park—it had been different.

"You, me, and everyone else in this room," Reed said.

"You think we'll all make it to graduation?" Ward asked, not picking up on Reed's dismissive disinterest.

"You'll have to pass this physical first," an old medic interrupted, guiding them to the benches where three other medics stood by trays with sample materials. He deposited the boys in line and moved on without another word, but Reed caught him looking back their way and wondered if the scowl was meant for them or if it was just the natural set of the medic's face.

"Is that Dr. Garth?" Ward whispered, following Reed's gaze. His voice contained a hint of reverence for the head medic. There were a lot of stories about the research he did at the Institute and what powers and privileges he might have.

"I'm pretty sure," Reed said, looking on as Garth set the scanner and examined Lowe's eyes.

"Did you hear what he did for Dr. Wong's shoulder?" Ward asked, still not noticing Reed's distraction.

"That's the DDC doc, right?"

A medic stepped between them, asking for Reed to put out his arm. He did so without protest. This sort of screening was typical. As the second medic took his samples, Ward continued, "The one that supervised our patient diagnostics with Amos. There's a rumor a volunteer nearly ripped his shoulder out at intake when the patient he came in with got sent to medical."

"What'd Garth do for him?" Reed asked absently, barely wincing at the prick of the medic's needle.

"He gave him a whole new shoulder!" Ward gushed as the needle went in. His medic had a steadier hand, and he didn't even register the draw.

"What do you mean, a whole new shoulder?" Reed asked. Garth was looking at him again, and Reed was sure the scowl was associated with the look.

"Biosynthetics," the medic finishing Ward's draw butted in.

Reed pulled his attention away from Garth long enough to look at the medic. "Biosynthetics? You mean from biotheory?"

"It's not theory anymore thanks to Dr. Garth," she said, a thrilled gleam lighting her eye.

"Functional synthetic tissue, fully integrated into biological systems," Ward mused.

Reed supposed the research and technology to enable biosynthetic systems and procedures would exist at the Institute, but he struggled to believe it was the unpleasant-looking old man scowling at him from across the room who'd done it. But if not him, then who?

"Elevate for three minutes," the medic instructed, rolling their tray back to the next intern. Ward's medic nodded in agreement, but instead of repeating the instruction, she said, "Garth has a hand in everything medical at the Institute."

The statement landed like a lead weight in Reed's gut. Park was in medical. He suddenly understood why the old medic kept staring at him. Ward's medic had already moved on to the next intern, but her words remained: *a hand in everything medical at the Institute...*

Dr. Garth's dark looks became clearer when Reed paired them with Park's final words to him—words so strange he wasn't even sure he heard them correctly.

I'm pregnant.

He'd left her standing in the cold. The second that light came around the corner, he'd bolted into the safety of the intern quarters, leaving her to whatever fate waited behind that light. He hadn't seen her since, and worse than that, he'd lost track of how long ago that night was. Weeks? A month? It couldn't have been more than that.

And now, an angry medic with a bald head and deadly scowl was tracking his every move.

Reed had a lot of questions, like: how could Park be pregnant? They'd both undergone the procedure in the first year along with everyone else in their cohort. That sort of thing didn't suddenly reverse, did it? And if it did, why now? His mind reeled with questions and impossible explanations, but it wasn't until he moved up to the last bench and Garth was only a couple of interns away from doing his examination that Reed realized exactly why the old man looked at him with such disgust. He wasn't asking the right questions.

Where was Park?

What sort of consequence would she have gotten for being out of her room after hours? She wasn't an intern anymore; she was a resident medic, and he had no idea what her life was like. He'd listen to her complain about the patients and entertained her theories about changes at the Institute, but he'd never bothered to ask. He'd forgotten to care.

A sick feeling spread through him as he realized just how much had gone on without him caring. Park had washed from the intern program. She wouldn't be going to the Northern Laboratories with him, and his solution had been to... *tell her they shouldn't see each other anymore?!*

A memory of Park dissolving into his arms in the storage rooms came to him, making his heart race. How could he have forgotten the way she'd made him feel? The ghost of her hand brushing across the day-old stubble on his jaw could erase all his worries.

"He's the one I'm rooting for."

She was right. He'd changed. It had happened so quickly he hadn't even realized it—not even when she'd shown up at the intern quarters to tell him she was pregnant.

Was she still pregnant? Reed suddenly wanted to know more than anything.

"Chase Reed, third year, second ranked." A gruff, disinterested voice interrupted his thoughts, and Reed realized Garth was standing right in front of him, so close the scowl might burn the skin off his face.

"Top ranked," Reed blurted without realizing he was going to.

"That's not what your file says," Garth mused. His voice was deadpan, but Reed thought he detected some sadistic pleasure in it at his expense.

"Probably hasn't updated."

Garth gave him a look that suggested he didn't care if the file was up-to-date or not, then busied himself with the scanner. Reed could feel his heart beating in his fingers. Curiosity, embarrassment and shame coursed through his veins as he tried to decide what to say to the man who almost certainly knew what happened to Park and exactly how responsible Reed was for it.

"Look here," Garth said, pointing the scanner at Reed's left eye.

"You're the head medic at the Institute," Reed said, deciding he had to start somewhere.

"A well-established truth," Garth agreed, switching the scanner to his right eye.

"No. I mean, yes. But that's not what I was asking." The conversation was harder than Reed had expected.

"Identifying me as head medic at the Institute isn't a question. Unzip."

Reed pulled the zipper from the collar of his intern suit, dragging it down his torso to expose his bare chest. Garth ran the scanner there, recording his respiratory function.

"You work with Park—she's a new medic," he said, trying to force their non-existent conversation into territory that was at least adjacent to the one he wanted to have.

"That isn't a question either, Mr. Reed. Deep breath." Garth clearly wasn't planning on making things easy for him.

"Do you know who I'm talking about? Amy Park, third year—or, she was third year up until a few months ago. She's a medic now." At least he'd managed to get a question out that time.

"There are dozens of medics at the Institute, as I'm sure you're aware. This is both a treatment and a research institution."

Reed's heart sank as he realized that there was almost no possibility that the Institute's head medic would know who a washed-out scientific-intern-turned-medic was. It occurred to him that he'd probably imagined the angry scowl situation, too. Garth was just a grumpy old man who'd worked too long at the Institute.

The scanner beeped completion, and Garth pulled it away, gesturing for Reed to zip up his suit. As he did, the old man said, "But as it happens, I'm acquainted with Amy Park."

Reed sucked in a breath as he scrambled for a third time since arriving at the clinic to process a new reality.

"Is she—"

"Fine," Garth said, not letting him finish the sentence.

He was going to say *pregnant*, but the look on Garth's face made him think doing so would be a really bad idea.

"We were close—in the program. We, um… studied together a lot." Reed cringed internally at the euphemism but hoped Garth would get his meaning.

Garth ran the scanner over Reed's hands, waiting for the clearance indicator over each fingernail. "I didn't think it was advisable for scientific interns to get too close to one another. It could cause issues with ranking, among other unprecedented problems," he said.

So he knew. Reed wasn't sure where to go from here. Before he could figure it out, Garth wrapped up the physical.

"Chase Reed, third-year intern, *second* ranked and testing for Northern Laboratories assignment," Garth read from his file. He looked up, and Reed saw something in his eyes. He wasn't completely certain, but he thought it might be rage. "You have a clean bill of health and should be bound for the Northern Laboratories after graduation," Garth said.

"That's a good thing," Reed said, unable to stop the relief that flooded through him at knowing he'd made it through the last barrier. The relief was followed shortly by shame at having forgotten so easily that he was supposed to be trying to find out about Park.

"No, Mr. Reed, it isn't a good thing," Garth said, derailing his train of thought once more.

"What do you mean?" Reed didn't think he could stand another bout of emotional whiplash before he made it out of this medical assessment.

Garth leaned in so close that his face nearly touched the side of Reed's neck. "I mean, Mr. Reed, that it is *not* a good thing that you will be going to the Northern Laboratories. You've got too much baggage. It could get very messy if it spilled. I can't let that happen."

Garth pulled away from him, leaving a cold rush of air where his hot breath had been. Reed tried to grasp what he'd just said. He had to mean Park's pregnancy, which meant she must still be pregnant.

"Which is why you will not be going to the Northern Laboratories," Garth concluded, speaking at a normal volume so that anyone listening could hear.

"Wait—not going?" It was an injustice Reed didn't think he could take.

"As head medic, I have the final say, and I'm revoking Northern Laboratories," he said, closing Reed's file on his tablet, done with him.

"Can you do that?" Reed asked.

"I have already done it," Garth said before walking away from the clinic without a backward glance. One of the remaining medics picked up the discarded scanner and called out, "Next?"

CHAPTER
Forty-Three
ZAYD

THE THRASHING near-dead at the end of Zayd's pole almost looked human. But only almost. Its skin was too raw, its face too snarled and twisted, with a thick foam of saliva smeared down the side. The eyes were grey and cloudy, but the beast kept them wide open, frantically searching for its next victim—its next meal. The monster at the end of the pole may have once been Janice Kilmer of Massachusetts, but it wasn't anymore. None of them were.

"I thought they already had a developed patient for screening today. Did it get loose and nosedive into the force field?" Zayd asked, straining to keep his pole straight ahead so the monster remnants of Janice couldn't tear him open. He was doing his single-volunteer patient-handling qualification. Patients were normally handled by five volunteers at a time, but every volunteer needed to pass the single-volunteer patient-handling module as part of their training.

It had sounded easier than it actually was. Handling an infectious, thrashing monster without backup was terrifying. Failure to make it through single-volunteer patient-handling meant guaranteed infection or death. Just the previous night, three volunteers had failed. He only found out because he'd returned to the dormitory while their belongings were being cleared out.

"These near-dead aren't going to screening," Jemani said, straining to keep her own patient, the former Arnold Tanning from Eastport, Maine, under control. Zayd wasn't sure why she was only just now doing her single-volunteer patient-handling module, but he figured he hadn't been around long enough to understand how everything worked. This was only his second time taking a neurologically developed near-dead patient from cryogenic slumber to… whatever you call *this*.

"Laboratory?" Zayd asked. Jemani was doing a much better job keeping her patient straight in front of her. It didn't help that the monster version of Janice was unbelievably strong. He'd heard that body building was a hobby in the old world but hadn't believed it until now.

"No." The way Jemani said it proved that she was also straining hard against her patient even though he was a slight man who looked like he used to spend his time sitting in front of a tablet. The hallway they walked through was lined with double-plated glass so they could be observed by the DDC trainers as they worked.

"The file said their destination was classified." Jemani gritted her teeth. There was only a little further to go, but each step they took threatened to be the one that ended their control of the thrashing creatures at the ends of their precarious holds.

"You saw the file?" Zayd asked, turning to study Jemani's face through the thick cover of her bio-suit, his arms rigid with the strength it took to keep his patient in position.

"Watch it!" Jemani growled, pushing his arms to the side. Ahead of them, the patients nearly collided, unaffected by each other's presence.

"Sorry," Zayd breathed. His arms burned from the constant pressure of getting the patient to the end of the hall. He'd understood conceptually why patient transport required five volunteers, but now he understood it intimately. He was exhausted from less than ten minutes of work, and couldn't understand how Jemani looked so calm and easy doing the same job when the consequences of failing were fatal.

The barely contained patients reached the yellow line at the end of the hall. Zayd braced with both feet, leaning back against the forward motion of the creature on the other end of his pole until he successfully stopped it. He glanced over at Jemani, expecting her to have done the same, but she let the patient at the end of her pole reach the wall and stop on its own before taking two backward steps to stand even with him.

"Work smarter, not harder, right?" she said when she saw him looking.

Before he had time to acknowledge her words, the lights above the yellow line turned green, and the wall at the end of the hall began to retract into the ceiling. This was the end of the single-volunteer patient-handling trial, and Zayd was relieved to be done with it. Sweat made his hair stick to his forehead. It poured down the sides of his face and the back of his neck, soaking into his jumpsuit.

When the wall retracted completely into the ceiling, he had expected to see suited volunteers with lashing poles, waiting to take over the assignment.

Instead, the wall opened up to a massive, open room that reminded him of the loading bays at the factory. Except where he would expect to see the rolling doors for the transport trucks on the opposite wall, there was nothing but rough concrete, and instead of trucks, there was one disc-shaped hovercraft. Standing next to the hovercraft were two black-suited DDC officers armed with pulsar guns.

"Why is there a hovercraft?" Zayd asked under his breath, arms screaming as he tried to hold Janice back. Why would anyone transport developed near-dead off Institute grounds?

"No good reason," Jemani whispered as the officers approached.

"Take those things to the loading ramp. There are magnetic restraints in the hull," one of the DDC officers said, curling his lip and stepping back.

"Is there volunteer support?" Zayd asked as Jemani took off toward the back of the craft like she'd done this before.

"This is a classified mission. No unnecessary personnel," the same DDC official said.

"That thing more than you can handle, son?" the other official scoffed. He was an older man with close-clipped grey hair on the sides of his head and a widow's peak that nearly reached the top of his head. He wore what Zayd could only describe as a vulgar smile.

"She looks like she really might've been something back in her day," the first official agreed as the monster at the end of the pole snarled and lunged for them.

Zayd ignored both of the men and followed Jemani up the ramp, taking extreme care not to let the monster he was wielding get too close. Both patients were screaming, only it wasn't quite a scream because it wasn't a human sound at all. It was the embodiment of unadulterated hunger and rage. The sound filled the hovercraft, echoing off the curved interior surfaces, rattling Zayd's head until he thought his skull would vibrate off his neck, but he could still hear the DDC officers outside the craft, laughing.

"Give me that," Jemani said, suddenly yanking the lashing pole from Zayd's hands. He wasn't expecting it, and between the lurching patient and her sudden movement, the pole came easily out of his hands.

"What are you doing?" he yelled, his head spinning wildly in search of Jemani's patient. It was bound by wrists and ankles against a magnetic half cylinder in the wall, lashing pole still wrapped around its neck but now dangling loosely in front of what was otherwise a mindlessly furious, wailing monster.

By the time Zayd turned his focus back to her, Jemani had his patient at the top of the ramp, facing away from them at the craft entrance. The patient was straining with everything it had to dive down the ramp.

"Why don't you laugh at this!" Jemani screamed down at the DDC officers, pressing the button to disengage the magnetic lashings and release the patient. She gave the back of its head a shove. The monster once named Janice stumble-ran down the ramp toward the officials.

"What in the…" the older officer yelled.

"Loose patient!" the other screamed.

Zayd did his best not to panic but failed miserably. He stared at the woman who had just set the patient on the officials. "Why did you do that?"

"No unnecessary personnel? A hovercraft? What do you think they're going to do with them?"

Jemani whirled in the craft to face the bound patient, grabbing the lashing pole and searching the side of the cylinder until, to Zayd's horror, she found and pressed the magnetic release. Outside, the sound of discharged pulsar bursts mingled with shrieking snarls. Janice let out a bloodcurdling wail, suggesting she'd been hit, but the continued sound of pulsar bursts and yells meant she wasn't down.

Free, the patient lurched at Jemani. She stumbled backward, struggling and failing to find control with the lashing pole. Watching the patient close in stirred Zayd to action. Without thinking, he wrapped both hands around Arnold Tanning's emaciated waist and pulled him off Jemani, whose arm was up as if she could block the terrible onslaught of teeth and nails.

The second Zayd made contact with the patient, he realized his mistake. He was too close. He had no weapon—no lashing pole. The bio-suit wouldn't stop the thing for long. The patient twisted and wailed within his grip, nearly managing to catch a thrashing arm against Zayd's mask and rip it off, but before it could, Jemani recovered and grabbed the lashing pole.

"I got it!" she said, pulling the patient away from him.

Zayd released his grip on the patient's waist the second he felt the pull, and their bodies separated. With a final, ferocious cry, Jemani whirled the patient toward the hovercraft door, releasing it with the same shove she'd given Janice.

She looked back over her shoulder to study him, chest heaving with the effort of what she'd just done. "You saved me."

Zayd's heart was beating a thousand miles a minute. He didn't think he had the words for the swirling panic and horror, but he managed to say, "He was going to eat you."

She eyed him with something like curiosity, and he noticed the fire burning behind her steely glare. "Like it wouldn't have eaten you? I was ready for what I did."

Outside, the commotion intensified as one of the officers let out a horrified, pain-laced yell.

"Kill her!"

"She won't go down!"

"Another one behind you!"

A hot blast of plasma whizzed past Jemani, singing the bio-suit at her arm before burning into the metal interior of the hovercraft.

"Get down!" she yelled.

"How are we going to get out of here?" Zayd asked. The more out of control things got, the more he realized the trouble they were in. *Why did she release the patients?*

"We don't," Jemani said. That's when he noticed the blood dripping down the side of her protective suit.

"We need backup!" one of the officers said. The sounds of mayhem had died down, suggesting they'd put at least one of the creatures down.

Zayd stooped to retrieve his discarded lashing pole, intent on going down the ramp to see what could be done.

"What are you doing?" Jemani asked. Some of her intensity had diminished.

"I need to get out of here," Zayd pleaded.

Jemani grasped at her side, struggling to keep herself upright. She must have been hit several times while standing in the doorway. "Let those DDC assholes die," she barked through gritted teeth.

"If I do that, I'm dead for sure," Zayd objected.

Jemani was paler now. Sweat poured from her brow. "If you save them, you'll be killing someone on the outside. Every DDC officer that lives—every near-dead they have under their control—is like killing a hundred innocent people. Let. Them. Die." She swayed, her body drooping against the side of the craft as she slouched.

"Why won't you die, you beefy bitch?" The officer whimpered as the power cycled on his pulsar gun. It was a sound Zayd was getting accustomed to at the Institute.

He gave Jemani a final look before exiting the hovercraft. What he saw was worse than anything he could've imagined. Blood streaked down the ramp in thick, wet patches. At the base of the ramp, the patient formerly named Arnold Tanning lay motionless, his head nothing more than a charred mess. Beyond him, the younger DDC officer was fumbling with his pulsar gun with hands that shook so badly he couldn't possibly be doing anything constructive.

The blood and carnage continued to where it pooled in a viscous pile underneath the older man, who looked back toward them with lifeless eyes above his torn jaw. The other patient—Janice Kilmer—was feasting at his middle, greedy hands tearing into the hole she'd made below his rib cage, where his intestines spilled into a torn mess. The patient was so bloody Zayd couldn't tell how many times she'd been shot. He could see one hit where her shoulder met the base of her neck. Her flesh was a charred mess, but everything below that was a conflagration of accumulating horrors.

The remaining officer was quivering still, trying to twist the intensity meter on his pulsar gun and chanting, "Why won't you die, why won't you die?"

Zayd turned one hand over the other on his lashing pole, exposing the blade the way he'd been taught before bringing it up to chest height at a downward angle. The sound of the blade slinking out of its sheath caught the patient's attention, and she turned. Her mouth was too full of the older officer to scream, but a low, wet bubbling sound emanated from somewhere within her. It turned Zayd's insides into jelly. He thrust the weapon down, and it penetrated through her temples, extinguishing the sound she'd been making before she sank off the end of the lashing pole under her own weight.

Red lights flashed overhead as a sea of armed volunteers poured into the loading bay to surround him and the DDC officer.

"Contain the survivors," one of them said.

Zayd was bound by at least half a dozen lashing poles. His skin was hot where the wires made contact.

Another suited officer entered once the area had been cleared. The officer surveyed the carnage before walking past Zayd into the hovercraft.

"Resistee garbage," the officer muttered.

A single shot sounded from the hovercraft as Zayd was escorted out.

Forty-Four

PARK

"I'M NOT FOOLING anybody anymore, you know. I don't even think hiding behind medical carts and wearing a bigger lab coat is working, and none of my pants fit."

Park sat on the examination table with her arms crossed over her undeniably expanding belly, bemoaning Garth's plan between bites of generously buttered toast.

"I'm not arguing with you on the matter; I'm merely saying I can't get you out yet," the old medic grumbled, taking a careful bite of his own toast, on which butter was meticulously spread from crust to crust in an even layer.

Park finished her toast in a final, ravenous bite, then reached across the medical tray that held their breakfast for one of the barely-sweetened muffins that tasted like sandpaper. She didn't care. She'd eat actual sandpaper today if it slaked her undying hunger. Ever since the nausea passed, she'd been overcome with hunger like she'd never experienced. She would eat and eat until it was slaked, only for it to barrel back into her world a couple hours later, typically in the middle of her shift. After washing down a too-big bite of muffin with the coffee that Garth brewed much stronger than the stuff they served in the dining halls, she asked, "Did you expect me to work in the L-wing for the whole nine months?"

Garth set his toast aside, grabbing his coffee mug and palming it in his hand. "Of course not. You were already four months in when I finally got hold of you. I figured we'd be lucky to get a couple months."

"You say it like my body can follow orders," Park scoffed, popping the last bit of muffin in her mouth and chasing it with a mouthful of coffee.

"Unlike disease research, pregnancy can be a bit… fiddly," Garth said, seeming to choose his words carefully. "Besides, I didn't know which way you'd want to go when I brought you in."

Park set down her cup, the most vicious edge of her hunger tamed for the next half hour or so. "That's a fair point."

"And it's not exactly like you've got a small frame," he added, giving her middle an appraising look.

Park gave the larger lab coat a self-conscious tug, meeting his look with a meaningful scowl. "Hasn't anyone ever told you it's impolite to comment on someone else's body?"

"Bodies are quite literally my job here. I am meant to look, study, and discern whatever I can about them," Garth said. He finished his coffee with a dismissive tilt of his head.

Park stood, indignation flushing her skin and making her heart race. "You aren't rebuilding my guts. In fact, you aren't doing any of the work here. I am. I get that you're used to calling the shots and getting away with whatever you want, but that's not going to fly between you and me. If you're not rebuilding it, you can't comment on it. And you need to accept that this lab coat isn't doing anything to hide what's going on."

Garth smirked. It was the sort of tic that came without conscious thought and looked shockingly uncharacteristic on his unpleasant face. "You've gotten quite bossy recently, don't you think?"

She leaned back against the exam table, surprised but not displeased. She considered the merits of one of the dry-looking pieces of questionable protein and decided it wasn't worth the risk. Meat didn't agree with her lately. "Yeah, well, I'm sick of hiding and acting meek all the time. You and I both know this isn't going to work for much longer."

"It's the pregnancy hormones," Garth said.

"What is?" Park's arms were crossed over her middle again. She didn't know if she'd gotten used to doing it to hide what was there or if it was a genuinely comfortable position. The lines between desire and necessity were blurred lately.

"Your gumption. When I first brought you in here, you were so scared I thought you might shake apart, but not anymore."

His observation made Park pause long enough to reflect on the last two months. When had she gone from scared to bold? Was it when she first started doing medic duties on her own? When Reed rejected her? When she'd agreed to help Anika? When the baby she'd never known she wanted started moving around inside of her? Or had she transformed in increments, each incident building a piece of this person she'd become?

"That attitude will serve you well out there. It won't be easy to raise a kid in this world, but in here, it's going to get you killed if you can't keep it in check. I shouldn't have to tell you that."

He shouldn't. Almost three years in the intern program had taught her that lesson. Three years of watching interns get berated for the slightest missteps and cut completely out for anything worse. It made her think of Emery and the way she'd always stood out for being so bold and outspoken. She should have thought it stranger that Emery and Mason hadn't been cut sooner. Emery had been brilliant, but so were many interns. How many of the other brilliant interns were shuffled away to energy management to hide their brilliance?

"What's it like on the outside?" Park asked, suddenly curious about what awaited her at the end of this journey.

"You were last there more recently than me, dear," Garth said, bringing the carafe of coffee over to the tray to refill his mug before offering it to her.

"You know what I mean." She glared but accepted the carafe without protest. "What's it going to be like where you're sending me? With the people doing what you're doing?"

"Nobody does what I do," Garth corrected.

Park had to bite her lip to keep from rolling her eyes. The old medic could be so literal sometimes. She was about to try a rephrase when Garth offered up the answer without making her work for it.

"It's not all that different from in here, except that they don't poke and prod at the diseased, and you won't feel the edges of your humanity fading away. They'll give you a job and a home. If you get infected, they'll put you in cryo—ours, not the Northern Laboratories', so be thankful for that—and if things go our way, we'll be that much closer to shutting this place down."

"You mean the Institute?" Park asked.

"I mean everything they're doing!" Garth nearly wailed, but he brought his voice down to a furious hiss at the last moment. Park suspected whoever worked in these halls was used to his temperamental outbursts and didn't pay him much mind. *He was hiding in plain sight.*

Park's mind reeled. She'd suspected—no, she'd *known*—something was happening long before Garth pulled her into this room for the first time. Even before the L-wing, Park could tell that the Institute's medical facility and donation programs had some greater purpose than medical research. She just hadn't put the whole picture together yet. She still hadn't, but things were clearer from this vantage.

"Will I actually be able to raise this baby?" she asked.

"I don't know. I can only say you'll be given a chance. The rest will be up to you," Garth said.

So literal.

"What type of jobs do these people give outsiders?" she asked, curious even though she knew she was about to overstay her welcome. Much longer and she'd risk being late for her L-wing duties.

"You will, in all likelihood, be assigned responsibilities as a medic, given your current training and prowess, but I suspect you already knew that." Garth studied her with a quiet, knowing sense that made her want to squirm.

She hadn't told him about the patient's husband or how she'd promised to get him out of the Institute when she ran. How the old medic had figured it out was a mystery, but she didn't have time to consider it.

"I will halt this line of thinking by informing you that he will not be traveling with you," Garth said, shocking her further that he'd speak about it.

"I'm not sure—"

"I had the distinct honor of meeting with the young man in question and denying him his final right to transport. He will not be going to the Northern Laboratories," Garth said, only confusing her further.

She didn't think Zayd had ever been slotted for transportation to the Northern Laboratories, given that Anika was meant to stay in the L-wing.

"That being said, I did think your young Mr. Reed was rather handsome, so you may rest fairly assured that the genetics of your progeny —born of two hyper-intelligent, Institute-bound interns—will be matched only by the child Emery and Mason produce. Of course, they're living together on that management facility, so I suppose they'll have an opportunity at more than one…"

Park realized he wasn't talking about Zayd at all. How had she forgotten about the boy who had consumed nearly every waking moment of her consciousness for years?

"He… isn't going to the Northern Laboratories?" Park asked, Garth's words finally sinking in.

"No, I took care of that," Garth said dismissively. He considered, then discarded his last piece of toast before wandering aimlessly to browse the many tools he had out on display in the room.

"That's all he ever dreamed of! Why not?" Park was surprised to find she was absolutely furious with the pompous old man standing before her.

"I told him it was because he knew too much to be allowed to move freely in a place where he could ruin all of our plans. Which is true. But the real reason is much more practical." He stopped his browsing at a pair of what looked like tongs.

Park was about to be sick. Reed wouldn't go to the Northern Laboratories. What did that leave for him? Fighting to keep her breakfast, she swallowed once, twice, a third time. "What's the practical reason?" she asked. She needed to hear him say it wasn't because of her.

"Because you'll be on that transport, and he, of all people, would know the second he saw you that something was amiss," Garth said.

Park shook her head, rejecting Garth's assertion that getting rid of Reed and sending her to the Northern Laboratories was the practical solution. "He's not the only one who would recognize me! Lowe and Brown! Carmen! Ward! Even if they don't all make it, some of them will be on that transport, and they'll know I'm not supposed to be there."

"You will be traveling in disguise," Garth said, waving his hand in her direction as though he were able to remove her anxieties.

"Traveling as what? A patient?" Park didn't want their conversation to draw attention, so instead of getting louder, she was getting quieter. It had the same effect.

"As a volunteer," Garth corrected.

Park froze. It was a good plan. Hardly any of the interns took a second glance at the volunteers. Even she hadn't thought of the obvious solution. But then the rest of the plan fell apart for her.

"I can't go to the Northern Laboratories," she protested. "I can't give birth there or raise a child!" *Zayd can't go to the Northern Laboratories. I promised I'd get him out.*

"I didn't say you were going to the Northern Laboratories. I said you were going to be on that transport," Garth said. He carried the tongs to his medical bag, tucking them in with a series of very fine wire tools that looked painful.

"Well, where is the transport going?" Park asked. Their hour together was almost up.

"I don't know for sure, but the transport and its contents—you, the patients, the other scientists and volunteers—will become property of our cause long before it reaches the road north." Finding the last of his required tools, Garth snapped his bag closed. "Now, you better get to your patients. I have a meeting with Dr. Wong's right shoulder."

Garth left the room before Park could respond.

CHAPTER
Forty-Five
PARK

PARK RUSHED DOWN THE DIM, white-tiled hall, trying hard not to draw attention to herself from the milling medics, professors, and intern groups. The last thing she needed was for someone at the Institute to notice her or her expanding midsection.

She held her breath until she made it to the L-wing doors, then, scanning her ID card, let it out with the sound of the vacuum seal breaking. It was strange that she thought of the L-wing as safe, considering it was likely the least safe place for her within the entire Institute. The L-wing was run by the DDC, whose intentions and secretive nature were damning, but it was also quiet. There were only a few attending medics, and volunteers only ever entered or exited to bring or remove patients. The L-wing patients were never removed. They were the foundation of this refuge.

The patients themselves were probably what Park found most comforting about the L-wing. They were so... human. No one screamed as their body and mind succumbed to the ravages of Zoribiatus. They were infected only by technicality. Their bodies carried the live virus, but its effects were still unseen. And because the patients Park worked with didn't spend their days screaming and sobbing, she'd managed to recognize them for what they were—people.

She didn't know when she'd stopped seeing the patients in the main medical wing as people. That's just what had happened when she started working with David, Anika, Abigail, Gerald, and the rest. The L-wing patients read books, sang songs, watched videos, and craved conversation. They ate full meals, kept themselves washed, and made their areas personal and appealing. Although some of their humanity was enhanced by what the DDC allowed them in their rooms, it was their ability to take those allowances and turn them into something more that struck Park.

David's room was never without the smooth tones of complex music. His decor was spartan, but it never felt barren when she visited him. He liked to sit at the edge of his bed in his fuzzy green slippers and tell her about the movements and composition of each piece they listened to while she worked. Sometimes he sipped tea with an appalling amount of sugar and cream while she worked, but he never ate anything that she saw. This was concerning, of course, because it impacted his bio-markers. She meant to have a good talk with him about that today.

Abigail's room was the opposite of David's. Her floors were adorned with lush, brightly colored rugs, and pink curtains hung on the blank wall behind her bed. She wasn't allowed any candles in her room but had accepted several self-contained light balls, which she'd lined up on her cabinets to cast a warm glow over her space. Her room was silent save for the conversations, of which Abigail was always able to make plenty. She kept a stack of physical books at her bedside, and Park noted how rapidly the bookmark traveled down the spine of each one and into the next.

Gerald didn't have decor or music to speak of, but he had requested a thick pair of sweatpants and an oversized flannel shirt and cap. He looked like an old-world mountain man, sitting upright in his bed watching old films on his tablet. He always had a small plate within arm's reach filled with nuts and thin sandwiches. He said the meat wasn't the same as what he'd grown up with but tasted alright. Not being much for conversation, Gerald always kept the tablet on so he could watch shows during his examination, and no matter how many times Park reminded him it wasn't allowed, he always offered her one of the sandwich slices when she came.

Anika had been late to make her space her own, having held off until she was certain Zayd could be helped. It took a while for Park to convince Anika that begrudging herself allowances wouldn't change her husband's situation. When she'd finally relented, the first things she'd requested were a specific brand of lotion and a red satin robe with slippers. She looked infinitely more comfortable with the robe wrapped around her middle, and her skin, which had looked dry and chapped, was now a glowing rich brown. She'd requested several documents, books, and videos from their tablet library, but the thing that seemed to lift her spirits most was the extensive set of nail polish materials. Since having them delivered, Anika had a different color on her nails every time Park visited. She left a single fingernail bare for Park to scan before trading information—her knowledge from the baby books for Park's updates on Zayd.

The patients in the L-wing reminded Park of the world she'd left behind and the reason she'd wanted to become a scientist in the first place—to help. She knew she would never go to the Northern Laboratories, and she knew going there wasn't what she'd once thought it was, but being in the L-wing, even for this short burst of time, had reminded her of what she'd once valued and how much of it she'd lost along the way. It was ironic that the DDC's top-secret project had done more to unravel the training and conditioning of the intern program than anything else at the Institute. Maybe it was because they expected that she, like the patients, would never leave.

A single medic manned the central monitoring for the L-wing. They looked bored, and why not? The recording devices didn't have sound, and nothing ever happened. Without Dr. Wong to jabber on about what fascinating research potential each individual patient could offer, there wasn't much to do.

This was the perfect opportunity to talk with Anika without interruption, to speak plainly. She didn't know how long Garth needed with Dr. Wong, but at least she could be sure the day would start without his intrusion. This was rare, as Anika's condition was Dr.

Wong's current obsession, although as far as any of them could tell, it was nothing more than a typical early pregnancy.

Park had six patients on her schedule for the day, and Anika would be her first stop. Grabbing a fresh medical tray, she headed toward room twenty-three.

She'd been in the L-wing for two months now but still hadn't gotten used to how quiet the halls were. Nothing could erase the agony of the main medical wing. Should she tell Anika how lucky she was? Was there such a thing as lucky at the Institute? Park didn't know anymore.

The door swung inward, revealing the stunning woman with a luxurious braid piled high on her head, wrapped in her red silk robe with legs crossed over one another as she squinted down at the fine pattern she painted onto her nails. Black on red. The pattern of the swirls and dots connected to something deep within Park, making her wish for something intangible.

Anika didn't look up when Park entered. Likely she was expecting Dr. Wong, or if she had expected Park, she'd expected Dr. Wong to be along shortly.

"Those are beautiful," Park said by way of announcing herself.

"Thank you," Anika said, brow crinkled in concentration as she finished the last touches. "More samples?"

Park let out a heavy sigh. "Yes, eventually."

Anika raised a curious brow at this response, looking up for the first time. "What comes first?"

"News," Park said. Anika needed total transparency at this point. She'd given too much without payment. Their bond needed something concrete.

She replaced the fine-tipped brush into the darker polish bottle, twisting twice to seal it before setting the supplies aside and gingerly replacing her hands on the meal tray she used as a painting surface.

"Those are very good. Have you thought about painting?" Park asked, feeling far too scrutinized under the woman's full attention.

"I am an amateur beauty hobbyist, and I do not require your flattery," Anika said, peering imperiously down at her nails and making

Park feel foolish for having said anything at all. "I thought you said you had news."

"I do." Park stepped forward, not bothering to ask Anika to move into the restraints.

Anika watched her move into the marked perimeter of the bed. "Don't keep me waiting."

It was pointless to keep anything from Anika—she either trusted her or she didn't. She rushed into a full explanation with nothing to lose but the time until Dr. Wong's return.

"There will be a transport—soon. It's supposed to go to the Northern Laboratories, but it will be intercepted. The people who are helping me—the ones I told you about—will take everyone on the transport to a new location. We'll be safe. Zayd will be safe."

"When?" The question was so breathless it was nearly silent.

"No official date yet. I just have confirmation that's what's going to happen," Park said.

Anika's eyes flicked from Park to the door, clearly on high alert for Dr. Wong's sudden appearance. "And you're certain you can get Zayd on this transport?"

Park dug her thumbnail into the palm of her hand to mask the desire to chew her lower lip. "That's the plan," she said.

"Whose plan?" Anika demanded.

Park repeated the action with her other thumb and palm, wishing this were easier.

"The medic helping me set things up," she said. "He's responsible for creating the opportunity, but I'm the one who will get your husband onto the transport."

"And you're sure you will be able to do it?" Anika's voice was quiet and breathless, as if speaking at a full volume might suck the air from her lungs.

"I have some sway among the volunteers," Park promised. It wasn't quite the same thing as guaranteeing she could get Zayd on the transport, but it was the closest thing she could offer.

Anika was quiet for a long moment, as if trying to decide what she would do next. Her eyes flicked back and forth underneath delicate lids as she considered this offer.

"How will I know it's done?" she asked.

"You won't," Park said plainly.

"Not good enough," Anika said in a clipped voice. Park's heart sank.

"What do you want from me?"

"Confirmation," the woman said, her fists balled into pistons on the table, never mind the delicate new paint.

"What if I could send word?" Park asked.

"From where?"

"From the outside!" she snapped.

"I need a guarantee," Anika decided after a moment of staring into the false blue clouds of a painted sky.

"I'll try," Park said.

"Not good enough," Anika seethed. "I said I need confirmation."

Park squeezed her fists so hard she nearly drew her own blood. "You'll have my word. That should be good enough."

It looked like Anika was about to relent, but they were interrupted by an alarm sounding out in the halls. Park had never heard it before, but based on the flashing red lights, she knew it couldn't be good.

Anika saw the light, too, and seemed to instinctively know it wasn't the time to argue.

"I'll be right back," Park said, heading to the door to check on whatever had set off the alarm.

Anika looked between the door and Park, then back again.

"Be back," she insisted as Park tore through the door.

"I will," Park promised, but her thoughts were already moving toward the flashing red light and ringing alarm and what they might mean.

CHAPTER

Forty-Six

PARK

THERE SHOULD HAVE BEEN chaos in the halls, but there weren't enough people in the L-wing to cause chaos. A couple of medics rushed from the stations or their patient rooms toward the alarm's origin—no one she recognized, but that didn't surprise Park. She very rarely overlapped with anyone in the wing besides Dr. Wong. The small current of people flowed toward the front of the hall, where the earliest patients were kept.

Park followed their movement, unable to tell which room had triggered the alarms until she pressed at the edge of the crowd in front of room number eight—Abigail Fitzpatrick.

It didn't occur to Park that it was odd for an alarm to have been sounded from that particular room. In all the time she'd worked the L-wing, no alarm had ever sounded. Only when she saw the white coat of a medic pressed against the door's slim window did she realize that someone besides Abigail Fitzpatrick had to be in the room to set the alarm off. She didn't know who it could be. Abigail was on her list of patients for the day, and Dr. Wong was with Garth. There shouldn't be anyone in the room.

"What's going on?" Park asked the shaved-head medic trying to look through the window.

"Someone is in there that shouldn't be?" another medic asked in a furtive whisper.

"That's not Dr. Wong?" the shaved-head medic asked, trying harder to see what was happening inside.

"No one else can get into the L-wing," Park assured them. But was she sure? Had there been an unauthorized entry? She was confused and more than a little worried for Ms. Fitzpatrick.

"Where is Dr. Wong?" the medic from the central station asked.

"He had an appointment, I think," Park said. This truth seemed safe enough. It couldn't reveal her relationship with Garth.

"It could be Dr. Wong," Shaved Head said. "Whoever it is has short dark hair and is about the same height."

Park tried to decide if a reasonable amount of time had passed for Dr. Wong to meet with Garth and return to the L-wing to start rounds in room eight. There was no sure way to tell. "What set off the alarm?"

"Whoever's in there did. That's what the alarms are for. If something goes wrong with the patient or the sampling. Or a contamination." Park didn't like the way the medic sounded almost excited by the list of possibilities. People at the Institute shouldn't have been excited about anything if they'd been here for any amount of time, and especially not infection.

She stepped forward, badge in hand. "Room eight is on my list today. Move out of the way so I can go in and get things straightened out." She said it with so much authority that even she was almost convinced it was the right course of action.

"Park, you don't have access to an active patient breach room." The voice came from behind the three medics clustered at the door. Park whirled with the others to find Maddoux approaching from the main entrance, her slim tablet tucked under her arm as she strode imperiously toward the door. Park hadn't seen the woman since her first day and had taken her absence to mean Maddoux was more in charge of personnel and operations than anything happening on the ground in the L-wing.

"What sort of a breach?" Park asked, hoping like hell that she wasn't overstepping an unspoken line in addressing the DDC official in such a way.

Maddoux glanced down at her middle before returning her gaze, reminding Park she didn't have her cart to hide behind. "The details are classified, but I can tell you we are dealing with an unconfined neurologically developed patient."

Park's chest tightened at Maddoux's explanation. It could only mean that the occupant of room eight had succumbed. Abigail Fitzpatrick's transformation would have had to have been unfathomably rapid. Park had just been in the evening before to do a series of swabs and sedation in preparation for a scheduled scan. She didn't know the details, lacking the clearance, but she was aware that these trials were primarily neurological.

"Who's in there with her?" Shaved Head asked.

"That's one of our DDC scientists," Maddoux said, not offering any further explanation.

"I've been on shift since midnight, and I didn't see anyone come or go. The camera for eight has just shown the old loon wearing that weird cap all morning, reading a book and eating cookies. I never saw anyone in there with her," the tall medic from the central station said.

"The camera points in at the patient, so you wouldn't have seen the scientist in the room measuring data unless he'd had to do any adjustments, would you have, Jin?" Maddoux said, easily dismissing his concern.

"So he's been in there this whole time? All night?" Jin asked, incredulous.

"Clearly," Maddoux agreed.

The whole thing made no sense. None of Abigail's other trials lasted more than an hour or two. She was an incredibly old woman who tired very easily. Park had prepped her in the early evening the day before. Why would a scientist stay in the room but not interact with her at all? The sedation would have worn off after only a couple hours, and if no one saw him on the monitor, it meant no one had re-sedated the poor woman.

And on top of all of that, she was now being considered a developed patient? What had happened to disease progression monitoring? To cryogenic options? Park had seen her chart on more than one occasion and had never once seen a donation clearance.

"What are we going to do?" she asked, suddenly horrified to realize that all of them had done nothing more than stand outside the locked door and gawk.

"You will do nothing," Maddoux said.

"But… the scientist. The patient!" Park protested, having not allowed herself to think of Abigail as a neurologically developed creature yet.

"A team will be here presently to handle the situation."

As if on cue, the L-wing doors opened, and a group of five bio-suited volunteers and two black-suited officials crossed the threshold, headed directly toward them with Dr. Wong in close pursuit. The doors closed behind them, and Park could hear the vacuum seal cycle as the air pressure in the L-wing normalized.

Dr. Wong pushed past the volunteer and official team, squaring himself with Maddoux, who watched impatiently.

"What's the meaning of this?" he demanded.

"The neurological trials on eight have reached a conclusion," she said as though Wong should understand what she was saying.

"There should be no patient breaches in the L-wing," he said.

His tone was so accusing that Park got the impression that he believed Maddoux might be single-handedly responsible for whatever had gone wrong in room eight.

Maddoux crossed her arms over her middle, looking impervious and unyielding. "That's not your call, Wong."

"I'm in charge of the medical care in this wing!" he insisted.

"Of course you are, Dr. Wong. But I'm in charge of the trials."

"You're in charge of trials and developed specimens. Until a patient has reached the near-dead state, they are within *my* jurisdiction." He pounded his narrow finger into his chest so hard Park was certain it would bruise.

Park watched in stunned silence, her attention only drawn away by the volunteers who cleared them far away from the door as they prepared for entry. Each one of them carried a lashing pole. The officials stood behind them, tablets out, as the door was surrounded. One of the officials swiped a finger over the screen, and the alarms went dark.

"This is a fully developed patient. Room eight is out of your jurisdiction," Maddoux reiterated.

A stab of aching grief passed through Park's chest at the confirmation of what she'd been trying not to think—Abigail Fitzpatrick was gone. She'd developed to the neurologically near-dead state. *So quickly.*

"I did not give clearance for that," Wong seethed.

"Ready on two," a volunteer said.

His team nodded, turning the lashing poles forward to be ready for whatever was happening on the other side of the door.

The nearest official swiped their ID card, and the door swung in. For the first time, Park heard the sounds of grief and agony pouring out of an L-wing patient room, mixed with the gurgle and wail of something that used to be human but was no more. The screams were tearing, gut-wrenching things. The scientist had yelled until his throat was raw and all that was left were the choked sounds of what might formerly have been known as speech.

"H-elp eee. Elp."

Two of the volunteers moved toward the screaming man, whose words had become almost as inhuman as Abigail Fitzpatrick's wails but were still eerily familiar.

Almost human.

The rest of the volunteers approached the bed, and with their movement, Park could see clearly into the room for the first time. Abigail wasn't sitting in her bed anymore. The headpiece and cords had been ripped aside and lay in scattered disarray on the ground, revealing a patchwork of silver hair and angry, red bald spots, some of which were bleeding.

The woman's arms were bleeding, too, as if she'd shredded her own skin in an effort to break free of the confines of the narrow space. When the first volunteer cast out their lashing pole, capturing the woman's face and neck in magnetic bindings, she let out another inhuman wail. The other two were close behind, securing Ms. Fitzpatrick's arms and torso.

Park could see by the clouding in the woman's eyes—and the way she spoke but didn't speak—that she was gone. The woman she'd come to know, the one who had always been so chatty and uncomfortably friendly, was no more. Only this monster remained.

As the three volunteers worked to secure Ms. Fitzpatrick, the first volunteer into the room put an arm out toward the scientist, demanding he drop his tablet and put his hands forward. The man cried in a broken voice that did something to Park she didn't understand. "No. No. I wasn't supposed to touch her."

The first volunteer wrapped his hands in magnetic lashings while the second used his pole to bind the scientist's throat. Park could see the similarity between the way the patient and scientist were bound and suspected it was purposeful.

While Dr. Wong and Maddoux argued over the L-wing and whose prerogative it was to progress patients in the trials, another volunteer used his lashing pole to disengage the wrist and ankle braces from the former Ms. Fitzpatrick, and a fourth bound her wrists. Park and the other medics cleared a wide path for the volunteers to bring out first Abigail, then the scientist with the raw and stripped voice.

"Take me to screening at least. Take me to screening, and I'll be clear. You saw, she was contained," he pleaded.

It wasn't until the volunteers turned him and he was headed out the door, about five feet behind Abigail, that Park recognized the scientist.

Later, she would tell herself that she'd known the whole time. That it was why the ripped voice had struck her. Later, she would relive the moment in her worst nightmares as she tried to make sense of what had happened and why it had gone that way, but in the moment, what Park was most acutely aware of was the way her heart had ripped in half upon seeing Reed's tear-streaked face and haggard expression—and the way that the baby had kicked her for the very first time.

Before that moment, there had been bumps and taps. She'd felt that almost-uncomfortable swirling tension on several occasions. It was their job to grow and squirm and fill her middle so obviously up. But the baby had never actually kicked that she could recall. When Park saw Reed's face, the baby had pulled its leg up against its tiny but rapidly growing body and let 'er rip, right into Park's kidney.

It was her first sucker punch.

CHAPTER

Forty-Seven

JAMES

MORA WASN'T at school again. It wasn't the first time she didn't show up, but James had a sick, sinking feeling about it. She hadn't been at the draw clinic on Friday, and she hadn't responded to any of his messages.

It wasn't unusual for Mora to ignore James.

Sometimes, when she was deep into one of her favorite texts, or if she was busy with Omen, or if she'd stayed up too late the night before and was sleeping the day away… But it wasn't the weekend anymore. She wasn't coming to school, and she hadn't responded to any of his messages.

Something was wrong.

She might have decided to leave. That was the plan, after all, and even though the plan was for her to wait until after she took the Test, he knew that seeing the raid at the Hole had upset her. He knew seeing Morgan there had done more than upset her. She was mad, and when Mora Rossi was mad, she made stupid mistakes.

Having no one to walk home with, James opted to take the tram to the Westside apartments. He swiped his tablet and, after the beep and green light, passed through the threshold to take one of the many empty seats. Only a few students dared use their precious allotted credits for the speedy ride home, and most factories were between shift changes. James didn't mind. He wasn't in the mood for anyone else's company.

The tram stopped just past Mora's apartment building. As he disembarked, James had a sudden impulse to rush into the building. He could follow the woman carrying the overfull sack of market goods and scolding her very young child. So long as he didn't get too close, the woman wouldn't think twice about him ducking into the building behind her.

He decided against it. He didn't know what he'd do if he went up to Mora's apartment and discovered Morgan was still home. What would he do then? Would she watch the surveillance recordings to see who had given him access? Should he just ring up instead? If Morgan was there, what would he say? He would never be able to feign ignorance of what they'd seen.

It was better to wait for Mora to reach out to him. She always did, and since they'd started their study sessions, Morgan seemed complacent about their frequent communication, if not encouraging. He only needed to wait for Mora to reach out.

It was a solid course of action, James decided; nevertheless, he went around the side of the building to see if there was any evidence that Mora had decided to spend the day on the roof instead of in class. It would be a foolish decision, but she might not be above making foolish decisions with the Test coming up. There could have been an important conversation from Georgia and the people on the outside, or maybe Omen had needed something from her—there was that one time when the bird had been ill, and she'd refused to leave his side until he was upright again.

What he found in the alleyway left him utterly speechless.

The fire escape was gone, leaving huge pockmarks and long scrapes along the crumbling brick surface where it used to stand. Some of the metal that used to make up the fire escape lay twisted in the alley like the spine of a broken beast, but the majority of it was gone, likely hauled away by the workers who tore it down. James knew they'd be back for the rest of it. Metal scrap, even rusted, was too valuable to be left to waste.

A sudden and terrible thought occurred to him then. What if Mora had been on the roof when the fire escape was torn out? What if she was stuck there still?

She would reach out, he tried to console himself.

If she were missing, Morgan would've already inquired about her whereabouts.

Unless she was out on business again already. But James knew it was likely too soon for Morgan to be traveling again. It was why he didn't bother to check the apartment.

With the Hole dissolved and Morgan out on business, if Mora were trapped on the roof, he might be the only person in the whole City State who missed her. He and Omen, anyway, but he didn't see the bird anywhere.

There was nothing James could do in the alleyway and no way for him to climb up onto the roof to check for her, so he decided he should go home and try to build a solution. While he wanted to believe Mora would reach out to him if she were trapped on the roof, he knew her tablet had a finicky power source. There was always the possibility that the power had run out before she could react and she was trapped up there. At the very least, this thought gave him a problem to solve and a place to put his worry until he had more information.

He hiked his pack higher onto his shoulder and raced back to the main road, his feet crunching in a spread of glass and shattered black bits. The main road was clear like it always was this time of day, and there was no one else entering his building, so he had to scan in to gain access. He was halfway to his floor, devising a crude remote camera to check the neighboring rooftop, when a message came through on his tablet.

It had to be Mora. But it was just as likely to be Morgan, asking him if Mora was with him. Or had she already gotten the notification that Mora hadn't been at school? He let the strap of his pack fall to his elbow so he could dig his tablet out while he made his way up the last flight of steps. A second message came through as he pulled his tablet out of the pack.

We need to talk.

It was from his mother.

Your father and I are home waiting for you.

Jame's stomach did a halting flip as he digested the messages. His parents shouldn't be home. If they were home, he wouldn't be able to check the rooftop for Mora. Something had to be wrong. What was he about to walk into? James was glad, at least, for the warning.

The door to apartment 346 was unlocked. Richard and Doreen Dunn waited for him in the kitchen, their faces tight and anxious.

"What's going on?" James asked, setting his pack on a hook by the front door before entering the small kitchen quarters.

"How was school today?" Richard Dunn asked, as though the situation wasn't the epitome of abnormal.

"Fine. Typical," James said, opening the fridge to search for a snack or a drink or something to occupy his hands and his mind for whatever was to come.

"What do they have left to teach you with graduation so close?" Richard asked, a hint of his *proud father* voice sneaking into his otherwise unnatural formality.

"We're working through energy conversion models in physics," James said, deciding on one of the thick, protein-rich drinks. They were too sweet and chalky, but it was better than facing his parents empty-handed.

"You were always good at that. Only, you aren't going for energy management, are you, son? You're going all in for scientist." There was the rest of the *proud dad* voice.

James carried his drink over to the kitchen table, sitting in the chair across from his parents and squaring his attention on his mother, who had been curiously quiet up to this point. "What's going on?"

"They sent him home from the factory today," she said, skipping over the pleasantries.

"For the day?" James asked. But if it had just been for the day, they wouldn't be having this meeting.

"We don't know for how long. Rumor has it they're collapsing poultry on the entire Northside," Richard said, rubbing his hand across the back of his neck.

"How many factories is that?" James asked, trying to wrap his mind around it. There was a lot of poultry on the Northside—almost the entire City State's supply.

Instead of answering, Richard said, "We've been struggling with quotas for a while now, but we had a twelve percent improvement this last month."

James' brow furrowed as he tried to process what his father was saying. Hadn't he told Mora they were ahead of quotas? How could the factories produce enough if they were collapsing production?

"James, honey," his mother began, her face looking worn and tired for so early in the day.

"What about you? Did someone send you home, too?" James asked, struggling to keep up with the situation. His mother worked in market distribution for canned goods. Today was a market day.

"I asked for time when your father contacted me," she explained.

James didn't like the idea of her asking for favors she wasn't owed.

Doreen powered forward, not waiting for the scowl to clear from his face. "James, your father and I were wondering how tutoring was going with Morgan Rossi's daughter?"

"You mean Mora?" James asked, realization dawning. This wasn't about his father's job—or at least not in the way he'd thought when he first sat down.

"Yes, Mora. Wonderful young woman," his father agreed, then added as if an afterthought, "Very pretty, too."

"You've been helping her prepare for the Test," his mother added, as though James could forget what he'd been doing this whole time.

"Why does that matter?" he asked, twisting the bottle of protein drink so the label bunched and changed. The motion left a smeared streak of condensation on the table.

"We know you're very fond of her, and it's so good of you to work with her despite her… troubles," Doreen said, speaking very carefully around what James knew she really felt.

"Mora isn't troubled!" James said, feeling hot and defensive at his mother's words.

"Oh, we know. She's absolutely lovely," Richard rushed to say. He'd never called Mora lovely a day in his life before this.

"We just want to know if something—happened?" Doreen said. She said it like a question, like James should know what she wanted from him.

"Something like what?" James asked, wanting her to say exactly what she was wondering instead of making him guess at it like a child. He was seventeen years old and about to go to the Institute, possibly to never see them again, if things went right.

"Did you and she have a fight?" Richard asked.

"Did she decide not to take the Test?" Doreen's voice overlapped.

James clasped the protein shake bottle, squeezing so hard it began to buckle. This wasn't about Mora at all. It was about Morgan Rossi-Stern and the threat she'd made on his family. This was about what his parents thought about Mora and how they didn't see her as anything more than either a means to greater success or a risk to their wellbeing.

"Nothing happened," James insisted, unable to believe his parents would ask this of him.

"If it's something between you—your mother and I would never judge…"

James squeezed until the protein drink sloshed out of the warped opening and all over his hand and the table, too mad to look his parents in the eye.

"I said nothing happened. Maybe you just did a bad job with projections," he seethed, wanting to hurt them. He'd never felt this way about his parents before. He'd felt it about Morgan Rossi-Stern but not his parents. He always thought they'd understood Mora well enough or, if not Mora, at least him.

"Don't talk to your father that way!" Doreen gasped.

"You shouldn't talk about Mora that way!" James shot back, letting the drink slosh onto the table as he stood up. "I'm telling you nothing happened, so if Dad lost his job or the factories are shutting down, it has nothing to do with her. And even if it does, it's not her. It's her mother. It's Morgan Rossi-Stern, and you know it!"

He turned away from them, grabbing his pack before rushing off to his room and slamming his door the same way he'd mentally condemned Mora for when she had argued with her mother. Thanks to her teachings, he hadn't lost his sense of irony. But he worried he might lose Mora.

Forty-Eight

MORA

MORA SAT on the crumpled mass of her navy bedspread, staring at the blank wall above her blank and empty desk, thinking about the research she'd dedicated the last three years of her life to. She'd lived in this apartment with her mother for almost as long as she could remember, but she hadn't done anything to make it her home. Ever since she'd moved in, since Morgan spread the navy bedsheet on the spartan mattress, she'd been looking for a place she remembered but couldn't picture. Not since Morgan Rossi-Stern had uprooted them and brought them to the capitol.

It was for her job, her mother had promised. But Mora thought there might have been more reasons. She had a vague memory of a terrible, smoke-and-scream-filled night and flashes of the man she used to call Dad disappearing into the wild. Every time she began to worry the memories were fabricated, she reminded herself of the odd things she'd had in common with him.

If she tried hard enough, she remembered past the horrible night to old city blocks transforming into residential areas filled with homes—not apartments, but whole homes with porches in front. She could remember running down a road with a group of children her age, laughing and screaming outside a school not so unlike the one she attended now but with smaller classrooms where they painted with real paint on actual paper.

Every interview, every stolen piece of data about recent history—about places outside the force fields—made the memories a little clearer. Mora was certain the memories that crept around the edges of her mind were real, but every time she tried to look at them directly, they dissolved into uncertainty. Could she remember, or were they part of a story she'd read of someone else's life?

The same impulse that made her doubt the reality of those memories had also prevented her from making this apartment her home. For years now, her room had remained bare. Blank walls, blank desk, empty drawers.

Here in the capitol, the roof was her home. The old-world tablet with its rich database of stories and poems was home. The black-feathered raven who knew how to whisper her name was home. Jim was home.

The thought of him made Mora's already blistering heart cry out. What would her mother do to him for keeping her secrets? She didn't think Morgan would punish him too harshly for the roof or the Hole or the Resistee talk. Those things were easy enough for Mora to own, but the tablet was different. Even without the physical evidence, the old-world contraption reeked of Jim's particular skills. Morgan would assume Jim helped her set it up and keep it charged. Her mother was furious with her for having destroyed the thing. Was she furious with Jim, too? Would she punish him? So near graduation, there wasn't a lot she could do, but Mora worried that Morgan might do the one thing that would punish them both.

The only thing Jim had ever wanted was the very thing Mora had spent the better part of the last two years avoiding. Jim was Institute-bound and probably had been since he was old enough to say *scientist*. It was the only thing more important to him than her, and Mora knew it. Unfortunately, she also knew how angry Morgan was. If she somehow took Jim's Institute position from him, it would be punishment to them both, and Mora was terrified her mother might have the power to do it. How else would she be able to get her an auto-pass on the Test? How could she arrange to have Mora shipped off the second she finished?

Mora had been sitting on her bed, staring at her walls, for so long that she couldn't tell anymore if these were wild fears or likely scenarios, but she couldn't stop ruminating.

There was nothing else to do. She'd destroyed her beloved tablet, and her mother had confiscated her school tablet. She couldn't contact anyone. She wouldn't be saying goodbye to Jim before she was hauled off to the Institute. All she could hope was that Morgan would have the decency not to interfere with Jim's placement and he'd follow shortly after.

The idea was comforting, but only mildly so. Not even Jim was enough to make the Institute an enticing proposition. The thought of being forced to go had made Mora consider extreme methods of escape.

Several hours earlier, after Morgan had come to collect the lunch tray with its half-eaten sandwich and chalky protein drink, Mora had tried to remove the screws from her bedroom window. Without any tools, she'd only managed to get the top screws undone. There were about eighteen inches of open air she couldn't reach. Even if she could reach it, she wouldn't be able to safely squeeze through the narrow opening. And besides, there was nothing to cling to on the side of the building, so many stories above stained concrete and asphalt. Mora pictured herself breaking into thousands of scattered pieces like the tablet and knew there had to be another way. She wouldn't give her mother the satisfaction.

She was considering her mother's satisfaction when a tap against the window pulled Mora from her thoughts. The tapping persisted.

Her first thought was Omen. She thought she'd seen a flash of black twinkling in the sunset. But that wasn't it. Omen would fly straight into her room without bothering to manipulate his clawed feet or beak against the glass. Plus, she hadn't seen him since the fire escape went down. When the flash of black appeared again, tapping furtively against the glass, she was able to identify it for what it was and immediately knew the responsible party.

"Jim," she said, launching herself off the unmade bed and climbing onto the surface of her desk so the tips of her fingers barely brushed the top of the open pane. Outside, the little black flier continued to tap against the window, either trying to solicit attention or make its way inside her room.

Unsure what else to do, Mora tapped back, putting her bare hand against the cool glass. She tried to repeat the pattern of taps Jim had used initially. *Tip-tap, tip-a-tap, tap tap.*

The flier stopped for a moment as if trying to assess the response. She repeated it, and the flier lifted, then dropped, then lifted again. He was trying to communicate with her.

Mora tapped the glass again before pointing up at the top of the window where the gap remained out of her reach, but not out of the flier's.

Jim understood, like she'd known he would. The flier moved slowly upward, occasionally tapping the glass in search of the opening. Mora didn't know what sort of visibility Jim had on the flier or what other abilities the hastily made machine had, but she could guess he'd planned for at least a few contingencies.

Finally, the flier made it through the opening. Once inside, she could hear the hum of its little blades spinning wildly in the air. Then she heard Jim.

"What happened?"

Her eyes widened. "You put speakers on a flier?" *Of course he had.*

"Speakers, a camera, and a little tracking chip like the one we put in the paper. Mora, I thought you were trapped on the roof!" Jim cried with clarity, only barely distorted by the wiring of the blades.

"I was," she admitted, unwillingly recalling the sensation of watching the fire escape crumble away from the building. "My mom opened the door from the inside."

"Oh. Oh, no!" She could almost picture his expression as he realized the implications of what she said. "Did Omen get away?" he asked.

"He did."

"Did she get the tablet—"

"No," Mora snapped. "She will never have the tablet or Omen or any proof of what she must suspect I was planning to do—*am* planning to do still."

"You're still planning to run away?" Jim asked.

Mora told him she was. She told him everything, from the conversation she'd been having with Georgia to the impulsive decision to throw the old tablet off the roof. She told him she'd lost the other tablet, too, though he'd already known that after days of no communication. She spoke in low, furtive whispers, afraid Morgan might be on the other side of her door, trying to listen in.

"What will you do now?" James asked, matching her low, quiet tones.

"The Test is tomorrow." Mora shrugged.

"Are you going to take it?" he asked.

"If she takes me to the capitol, I won't have a choice." She couldn't believe she was saying it—that she was admitting defeat. Not when she was always the one to have another answer, an infinite selection of options other than compliance.

"I suppose we better not let her take you to the capitol," Jim said.

His response was so un-Jim-like that Mora nearly did a double take. "What do you mean?"

"Mora, you said yourself that if you go to the capitol building, she's sending you to the Institute. So if you don't want to go, you can't go to the capitol building."

She was listening, barely able to believe Jim would make such a dubious proclamation or that he might put his brilliance to such illegal intentions. "Even if I could get out of here, where would I go?" she asked.

"Outside," Jim said so swiftly she was sure he hadn't had to think about it.

"How? I never had a chance to get a ride…"

"I can get you out," Jim said. "If you want to go, I'll get you out of here."

Mora looked at the little flier hovering and buzzing in her room, wishing more than anything that it was Jim in the flesh so she could throw her arms around him. "Don't you want me to go to the Institute with you?" she asked.

"More than anything," he said. The confession made hot tears burn her eyes.

"Sometimes I wish that, too," she said.

Outside the room, footsteps approached, then faded as Morgan walked from the kitchen to her room, her voice muffled by thin walls and total distraction. She was on conference again, and from the sound of it, things were going her way.

"No, you don't. And I don't want you to," Jim said, buzzing close to her as if to brush the hair from the side of her face. She wished she could see him the way he could see her.

"Jim…" It was all she could choke out.

"Enough. Are you ready to leave?" he asked.

Mora's stomach did a flip. Was she ready to leave? *Right now?* She knew it was a practical question with only one answer, but she struggled to get the words out, so instead she nodded.

"I have a bag under my bed. It has a bunch of survival gear and a few things of water in case I ever had the chance," Mora said, realizing that the bag was probably a foolish idea. What if Morgan had wanted to search her room?

"Is there enough in it for you to run?" he asked.

"For a while," Mora said, fear gripping her despite her determination. She thought she'd have more time.

"You said they'd find you once you were on the outside," Jim reminded her.

She nodded, knowing this was true. "But how will I get outside? How will I even get out of this room?"

"I have an idea," he suggested.

"To get me out of here or to get me out of the city?" Mora asked.

"Both." If Mora could see him, she was certain he'd be smiling.

"Are you sure you want to do this?" she asked, feeling guilty for dragging him into this insanity. James wasn't a rebel like her. He wasn't a Resistee or an outsider. He was an Institute-bound future scientist.

"More than anything," James said.

"You've got to quit saying that," Mora said, suppressing a giggle.

"What would you rather me say, something brilliantly clever from one of your books?"

Mora thought about it for a second. Originally, that was exactly what she'd meant, but now it seemed silly. "How about just *yes*?"

MORGAN ROSSI-STERN WAS SITTING in the small main room of the apartment, going over the finishing details of her report, when Mora's door creaked open. It was the sort of almost-silent occurrence parents grew attuned to after several years of children trying to sneak things around them. Though the report was all but finished, she paused to listen, certain Mora was up to something. She'd been far too quiet for the majority of the day, and the window of hours left for her to try something was rapidly closing.

She thought she might hear the creak of floorboards as Mora snuck through the hall, but that wasn't it. There was a strange buzzing sound, first present, as if shifting the air in the whole apartment, then faint. It wasn't enough to prove she was up to something, but Morgan knew if she waited, that part would come. She let the tablet screen turn black in her hands, determined to remain undetected until it served her.

Other than the faint buzz, there was no further indication of what Mora was up to. That didn't sit well with Morgan, who prided herself on being several steps ahead of everyone around her at all times. Her daughter was no exception. That was how she'd deduced her activities on the roof, and while she hadn't yet discerned the purpose of Mora's involvement with the merchants at the Hole beyond the purchase and exchange of illegal goods in service of her illicit learning habits, she would. She had theories about the function of the Hole in Resistee groups, but she meant to transform those theories into provable activity.

After Mora left for the Institute.

Morgan sat still for so long that the overhead lights turned off, drowning the apartment in nearly absolute darkness. The only light, a dim grey, filtered through fine particles of dust in the hall from Mora's room, confirming her door was open. If she moved now, she'd spoil whatever confidence Mora had gained while waiting.

There was a tapping sound from further back in the hall.

Or was it the far wall in Mora's room?

The tapping was irregular and intermingled with a rustling sound. It was coming from Morgan's room. She was certain of that—almost as certain as she was that she could hear the faint sound of whispering.

Confident now that Mora had somehow snuck undetected into her room, Morgan tilted her tablet, awakening the screen and sliding a careful finger across the home controls so the overhead lights would remain off even if she moved. That done, she stood and took the first of several silent steps toward the commotion in her room. There was more whispering, which was unsettling because there was no one in the apartment for Mora to whisper to. Morgan had possession of her school tablet, and the other one…

A dark feeling threatened to well up, and Morgan shoved it deeper down. She would deal with it later—after she watched the transport carry Mora out of the city toward the Institute. Maybe she would make the Dunn boy pay the price for that misstep. Maybe it would be his parents. But she had time to figure that out. The Dunn boy might even share what was on the tablet with her openly after Mora was gone—if she played it right. If she could appeal to his clearly evident feelings for Mora.

It occurred to Morgan that Mora might have a second tablet or one of the communicator devices—something acquired at that damn black market. But Morgan had searched Mora's possessions thoroughly. She had clothing and survival gear, but nowhere to go and nothing to use it on, and no additional means of communication.

The whispering continued as she made her way silently down the hall, nothing more than a shadow passing the doorway to Mora's empty room. She could discern the voices now but not what they were saying. One of them was Mora, of course, and the other was the Dunn boy. She didn't like that. It would be impossible for him to have snuck past her vigil in the main room, but that was a more likely explanation than Mora having a third means of communication. His voice was clear, carrying no electronic tinge or distortion.

"...find it in the dark?" came his meek, tentative inquiry.

"I know she keeps it with the rest of her secrets!" Mora hissed.

Morgan stood at the door, listening to them argue while they searched, certain she knew what they were looking for.

One upon a time, she and Mora had lived somewhere else with a man she never spoke of. They were a family living in a village with other families just outside the force field barrier. And then Morgan had ruined it by trading the whole community for a chance to be great. When he'd tried to take Mora... There was nothing Morgan wouldn't do to keep her daughter safe. But Mora didn't remember any of that. At least, she'd thought Mora didn't remember.

But if they were in her room, then Morgan had failed to keep their past hidden. If they were in her room, then they were looking for Mora's identification and transportation cards. It meant Mora had finally realized that if *he* was still out there, she would be granted rights to travel outside the City State.

Knowing what they were looking for was nearly as unsettling as the realization that the Dunn boy had managed to somehow sneak past her into the apartment. If Mora left tonight, she would circumvent Morgan's plans for the Institute; she would make it out and see what had become of the communities beyond the wall—what Morgan had done to the people living on the cusp in order to secure the City States and their future.

Morgan stood at her door, which was only open a crack, as if the children had swung it closed but it hadn't latched. How would she handle the two interlopers? She would send the Dunn boy home, of course. She might call his parents and have them come retrieve him. Then she could bask in their shame. But what to do with Mora? Send her back to her room and endure a sleepless night keeping watch until she could escort her to the capitol.

But should she destroy the forms?

Morgan was a shrewd and sometimes cruel woman, but what she did, she did out of necessity, to keep Mora safe. To protect her from herself. When it was all done and Mora looked back at everything Morgan had done, Morgan wanted her to see it was necessary. If she destroyed those documents, Mora would never be able to see that she'd done it all out of love.

Morgan Rossi-Stern was so preoccupied with indecision—something that almost never happened to her—that she didn't notice the shadow that momentarily crossed her own as it moved down the hallway, as silently as she had but in the opposite direction. The lights stayed off in the main room as Mora crossed the open space, taking painfully slow steps so the zippers and clasps on her back wouldn't rattle against each other. She stopped at the apartment door and waited. She would run from here if she had to, but she wanted to make a clean break if it was possible. She wanted her escape to be so complete that it left Morgan humbled. *No.* She wanted her devastated.

CHAPTER

Fifty

MORA

MORA WAITED until she heard Jim's signal—three short taps. They'd agreed anything more might be disrupted, and if Morgan said anything, Mora wouldn't wait. The moments seemed to stretch on forever as she waited, wondering how long her mother would stand outside the door listening to the recorded conversation. Would she listen long enough for the recording to loop around and play again? But then it happened.

All at once, she heard the squeal of the door hinge as Morgan swung it open. She heard the taps of the flier against the wall in rapid succession, Morgan's gasp, and the thundering of her own heartbeat as she yanked the door open and slipped into the hall. It took everything she had to ease the door shut before sprinting down the hall toward the stairwell.

When she reached the ground floor, Mora forced herself to walk. She risked drawing too much attention running out of a building at sunset. It was still too near the last major shift change to trust that no one would be lingering. The oversized backpack felt ridiculous strapped over her jacket, and her hair was wild, sticking to the sides of her face from panic, sweat, and exertion.

Flop sweat, she thought, recalling it from one of the stories.

She passed a small man with thick glasses as she made her way to the exit. She had to shove down the notion of greeting the man as they passed. Instead, she kept her head down and her hands close to her sides the way everyone else did—afraid that coming too close to someone unknown might spread a disease that hadn't existed in the cities as long as she'd been alive. The only part of the disease she'd ever experienced was the way it slowly robbed her of everything that mattered.

When she finally made it out the door, her whole body was shaking. She was free, but only free of the apartment. Morgan might still be able to find her, and she didn't know where she was going or how she would escape.

"Mora!" Jim called from the shadows under the awning.

She ran to him, wrapping her arms around his neck in relief. "It worked!"

"She's already destroyed the flier. We've got to go," he said, taking her hand.

She clasped down on it, grateful it was just as clammy as her own. "Where are we going?"

"North," Jim said without hesitation.

"No. There are too many workers. We'll be seen," she protested, stopping short so her hand jerked out of his.

"Not anymore. Something's happening. The DDC is consolidating the factories, and everyone got sent home," Jim assured her, giving her hand a firm tug.

"What is going on around here?" Mora asked, falling in with him, moving at a fast but not urgent pace. She wanted to run, but she knew it wouldn't look good for two children to be running up Main Street after sundown.

"I was actually hoping maybe Morgan had told you, because I don't know."

"You called her Morgan," Mora said, curious that he would do it now, when he'd resisted her prompting to do so for the last two years.

"That woman doesn't deserve to be your mother," he said.

They moved in silence past a group of shoppers making their way on foot toward their homes, bags in hands and heads down. People were always so jumpy when the sun set. Mora waited until they'd gone another several blocks without seeing anyone before she spoke again.

"What are we going to do when we get there?"

"We're going to get you out," he said, as if it were a stupid question.

"I know, but how?"

"I made something," he said, slowing his pace and dropping his voice. "It should disrupt the electromagnetic signal of the force field so you can pass through."

Mora looked over at him, marveling at his ingenuity. Behind his flopping sandy blond hair and wire-framed glasses was a brilliant mind. "How did you do it?"

James blushed. "Do you remember that guy who broke my tablet?"

"He gave you all those credits that you refused to spend on a new tablet!"

"That's right. I… I went to the Hole," James admitted.

"When did you do that?" Mora moved closer to him as they walked. All around them, night was falling.

"When you told me your plan to find a smuggler. I thought it'd be a good idea to have a backup in case things went sideways."

Mora couldn't see his face anymore, but she knew he was blushing.

"How did you do it without your parents finding out?" she asked.

"I put the credits in a dummy account." She felt him shrug.

"You are way too smart. The Institute doesn't deserve you." Mora placed her head against his shoulder as they walked. It almost felt like she wasn't about to leave him for the rest of her life. She almost felt like she wasn't panicking.

"Or maybe I'm exactly who the Institute deserves," James said, wrapping his arm around her.

"If anyone could find a cure and stop all my mom's bullshit, it'd be you," she said.

They walked like that until the buildings were behind them and the roads turned to unkept gravel and dirt. Mora had never been out this far. She'd walked to the force field boundary on the Westside once before, but when the DDC border officer had threatened to call her mom, she'd run away. There was no border guard here.

She reached her hand out, feeling for where the air turned hard as glass.

"Can you see it?" James asked.

"Not without a light," she said.

He produced one without hesitation, shining it ahead of them until they found the shimmer of the force field barrier. He handed her the light and got to work, placing a small device with two wires sticking out from either side against the force field.

"I put a magnet on the back like we did in class," he said.

Mora grinned despite the mounting tension. "What if it doesn't work?"

"It's going to work. We learned the exact same principles this quarter," he said, putting one wire into the little circle that now stuck to the force field and appeared to hover in midair. The other wire went into the force field, suspended in space by electric forces neither of them could see.

For the first time, Mora didn't feel as lost as she usually did when Jim explained something technical to her. Maybe it was always this simple, and she'd just been too lost in her own mind to realize it.

James pushed a button, and a small hole appeared, just large enough for Mora to crawl through.

"I told you," he said.

"You sure did," she said, looking between him and the hole. This was it.

"Georgia said she would find you on the other side?" he said, making it sound like a question and a statement at the same time.

"I don't know how," she said, counting the seconds she had left on this side of the barrier.

"It doesn't matter if you know how." He took her hand into his. "You're going to be okay. This is your dream."

It was her dream. It was only the fear making her forget it now that she was finally here.

"I don't know how to thank you for this, Jim," she said. This was their goodbye.

"You don't have to thank me. I love you, Mora." He squeezed her hands. His were dry now.

"I love you, too, Jim," she said, forcing the tears back.

"That's not what I meant," James said, glancing away.

Mora grabbed his shoulders, forcing him to look back. "I know," she said, keeping her gaze steady on him. "I know what you meant."

"You don't love me like that," he said.

"I don't," she agreed. She couldn't read his face in the dark, but she didn't need to. She knew him. "But that doesn't mean I don't love you, James Dunn, and it doesn't mean I don't understand your love for me," she said.

"But—"

"But nothing! You never have to apologize for loving someone. Not when you do it like you did," she said.

There was a commotion somewhere far off that drew both of their attention. Mora felt the panic trying to rise up again inside of her to ruin this moment.

"You better get going. I want to be back to the capitol when Morgan finds me so you have the best possible head start," he said.

"I'm going to miss you, Jim," she said.

"I'm going to miss you, too."

There was nothing left to say. She gave him one final, fierce hug before crawling through his miraculous little hole. He left it up long enough for her to wave once she was on the other side, then he disappeared. She looked out into the open world around her, not sure what was next. She'd only been walking for a minute when a black bird swooped low before landing on her shoulder.

They continued out into the world together.

SIMONS CRACKED the bedroom door open just enough to see Terni asleep on what he liked to call *her side* of her own bed. There wasn't supposed to be anyone else in the bed with her, and he knew that was the crux of the problem. Though her middle had grown an undeniable and impressive amount, he couldn't believe it was real. He didn't feel like he was about to become a father. Wrapping his newborn baby in a warm blanket and walking out of this place wasn't something he could wrap his mind around.

Thankfully, he had a bit of time left to get used to that reality. In the meantime, he'd gotten a new assignment.

He pushed the door the rest of the way open and entered, loving the way the morning sun shone in through the slits of the window cover, basking his love in golden rays, making the short, dark curls peeking out the sides of her skewed bonnet shine and warming the smooth skin of her sleeping face. He wanted to watch her sleep like that for hours, pretending she was resting late into the morning as a luxury and not because it had taken her more than half the night to get comfortable. The thought of waking her was almost too much, but he wanted to tell her as soon as possible so they could spend their last day together knowing it was their last—until the baby was due.

She stirred but didn't wake, her twisting motion pulling the cover from her middle so he could see her stomach, skin pulled tight over her rounded belly. He wanted to touch her, to place his hand over her middle and feel the both of them together, as if doing so might convince her to change her mind—that the three of them belonged together. He would hold on to that fantasy until she forced him to let go.

He sank down into the space below where her feet curled up against her body, placing his hand on her thigh instead and rubbing gently until she took her waking breath—that sweet, soft sigh of awareness before she ruined the moment.

"I need coffee or I'm gonna puke," she said.

"I've got you," he said, handing her the mug he'd prepared only moments before entering the room. He'd made it shortly after receiving the message about his next assignment, both as a peace offering and an act of love.

She sat up, taking the mug and shaking it at him. "Don't speak until this is at least half gone," she said, smirking despite her harsh words.

He was ready for this. It was their ritual, just as much a game as it was truth. He watched her take her first sip without hesitation, trusting it would be the right temperature, the right strength, the right amount of sweet. She breathed in the fumes with satisfaction, pulling her feet away from him and putting them on the ground so she could sit completely upright. Her shirt rolled up as she moved, and she didn't bother to try and tug it back down. Instead, she took another long drink.

"Better?" he asked.

She put a finger up to his lips to silence him. Simons closed his eyes, relishing the feel of warm, gentle pressure. "Not yet. But getting there."

He waited. She took another drink before resting her head against his shoulder, her empty hand curling up and around the inside of his arm. She let out a satisfied sigh.

"What time is it?"

"A little after ten," he said, kissing the skin at her temple. "Am I allowed to speak now?"

She finished another drink of coffee. "You told me what time it is, and I let you live, didn't I?"

"You're a woman of infinite mercies," he agreed.

"It's a miracle considering how little sleep I've gotten lately." She stretched, setting the nearly empty mug on the table next to the bed.

"I know. I was there, too," he said.

Terni stopped mid-stretch, giving him a sideways look. "Your snoring is half the problem, so if that's what you mean by being there, yes, you were there, too."

"I wish I could take some of the trouble from you, seeing as I'm the one that caused it," he said, running his hand up her arm then down her back, letting it linger in all the right places as he went. She offered him a grateful *ohh* as he went, assuring him he still knew how to do it right. When his hand made it the whole way down her back and rested at the top curve of her thighs, she turned, crawling onto his lap and never minding the space her middle took up between them. She put her hands on either side of his face, cupping just behind his ears before bringing him down into her.

Their lips met, and he pulled her the rest of the way into him, feeling every place her body curved and tucked into his. He tasted coffee and her, and for the millionth time, he thought about forgetting it all and begging her to run away with him. The dissenters would recover from their loss, and the two of them would find some place to be together without running.

She broke away, leaving him breathless as he rested his forehead against hers, at a loss for words.

Go with me! Run with me!

"You're about to take all of it," she said, trailing kisses along the smooth surface of his freshly shaved jaw and sending thrilling chills down his spine.

"I don't have to, you know," he said, trying not to lose all reason as she continued her painstakingly slow trail down the side of his neck.

"Are you backing out on me, Moe?" She smiled into his shirt collar.

"I hear shared parental duties are all the rage in the cities," he said, trying hard not to pant.

She stopped, pulling back from what she'd been doing to look up at him. "We agreed. We have to do it this way to keep from being found out."

"The dissenters can cover our tracks," he begged.

Terni eased off his lap, reaching for the mug. "We would *hope* they could cover our tracks. We would hope my running wouldn't be the thing they needed to figure out what we're doing with the energy management facilities and the network of people on the inside."

"And we'll never know if we don't try!" Simons said.

Terni looked at him over the top of her mug. "If we ran, we'd spend our whole lives looking over our shoulders, always running, always worried someone might catch up to us. If you take this child, you'll have a chance at a life—a *real* life. And the dissenters will have a better chance of doing more than just getting this resistance going. We could make a real difference."

Simons was silent. She'd talked him into a corner again, and he didn't have a response except that he didn't want a *real* life if it wasn't with her. He still wanted to be a part of the difference the dissenters were making, and he was scared out of his mind of being a father.

Terni finished her coffee and said, "So what did you come in here to tell me?"

She had him there. Simons never woke her up unless it was something like this. Since the beginning, their agreement had been to always spend the whole last day together.

"I got an assignment," he said.

She stood, finally yanking the shirt down over her belly before carrying the coffee mug toward the kitchen. She stopped at the door to ask, "Where's this one got you going?"

He followed automatically. There were a couple of cold sandwiches waiting for them. "I'm supposed to drive a team of dissenters to intercept a Northern Laboratories delivery," he said.

She placed the mug on the counter, shaking the electric kettle to see if there was enough water left. "A shipment?"

"Personnel," he corrected.

She filled the kettle about half full before returning it to its cradle and setting it to boil. He'd left the used coffee grounds in the filter, and she was disposing of them now in the countertop bin, reaching for the can that held fresh grounds. "That sounds a little high risk, don't you think?"

"I'm only dropping the people doing the intercepting. I'm not involved in what happens from there," he said.

She added three scoops of grounds into the filter as the kettle sighed its first breath of steam. He pulled out a chair and sat at the table opposite the sandwiches.

"Will you be doing standby for the job?" She plucked his mug from the sink, giving it a rinse before setting it next to hers.

He eyed the sandwiches, wishing he'd made two more.

"Standby, then escort once the job is done." He picked up one of the sandwiches and took a hungry bite. If he needed to, he could make a few more.

"Where are you escorting them to?" She added two spoons of sugar into each of the mugs as the kettle began boiling in earnest.

"There's going to be another intercept down south," he said. His mouth was full, but he took another bite.

"How far south?" she asked. The smell of coffee filled the room as hot water penetrated the course grounds.

He chewed for a moment too long before swallowing the mass of sandwich, leaving his mouth too dry. "Below the southmost City State."

"You mean the Deadlands," she said.

"Just at the border," he assured her.

"That's going to take days. Maybe weeks!" She turned, eyes wide as realization struck.

"About a week down if nothing goes wrong, then maybe two weeks back, depending on transports and search activity," he confirmed.

"What if you don't get back in time? What if we're wrong about the due date?" He could hear the panic in her voice.

"You did the math. We pinpointed the visit it happened on, remember?"

"Babies come early all the time," she said, setting his mug in front of him. He took it without really wanting what was in it and winced when he swallowed the too-hot beverage.

"If you tell me to stay, I will," he said.

She picked up the other sandwich, studying the thin slices of highly processed meat and pale greenhouse tomatoes before taking her first bite. He waited while she chewed and swallowed, washing it down with a careful sip of coffee.

"Go. I'll send notice to keep the DDC away until you get back if something happens."

"You can't keep them gone forever," Simons said, twisting the coffee mug in his hands.

"You aren't going to be gone forever," she said. He knew she was putting on a brave face. He wouldn't make her unmask.

She took another bite of sandwich, and he followed suit, both of them eating in near-complete silence, waiting for the other to speak next. Terni took another bite of her sandwich. While she was chewing, her hand went to her lower back, resting there as she suppressed a grimace.

"Everything okay?" Simons asked, finishing the last bite of the sandwich.

Terni set the other half of her sandwich down, the grimace easing as she shifted in her chair. "It's just those practice contractions I told you about. They've been coming a bit more often lately."

"Are they supposed to hurt like that?" Simons asked.

She shrugged. "Everything I've read about it suggests labor isn't pretty, so why would the practice be any different?"

He nodded. That made sense at least. "I'm going to make another sandwich. You want one?"

Terni eyed the uneaten half of her sandwich. "No. I'm good. I'll finish this one up in a bit."

She watched him fish two more slices of bread from the delivery bag before retrieving the meat from the cold box. If anyone ever did an audit on her food supplies, she'd have a lot of explaining to do. "When are you leaving?" she asked.

"Late tonight. I need to have the transport moving by dawn," he said.

She stood, taking a long pause to massage at the base of her back in the same place she'd asked him to work on the night before. "I better go check the reactors so we can enjoy each other as much as possible before you go, then."

"You better," he agreed, dropping an extra slice of meat on the already-large stack.

She kissed him a final time before ducking into the mudroom to pull boots onto swollen feet and waddle out to the reactor room. Simons watched her go with an uneasy feeling, suddenly realizing he didn't want the second sandwich after all.

Simons would never be able to say if he'd actually intended to leave. Part of him completely believed he'd meant to go. People were depending on him, and he wasn't the sort to leave anyone hanging. But his heart only belonged in one place, and when Terni's practice contractions turned into full-blown labor, he completely forgot he needed to be anywhere else.

There might have been a moment, before Terni panicked, before things got too intense, when he remembered he needed to send a message to his contact to tell them he wasn't going to make it, but that moment was so small and so fleeting that there wasn't any time to act on it. Everything happened too fast.

One moment, they were lying side by side, basking in the late afternoon quiet, and the next, Terni was on her feet, racing to the bathroom. She moaned as he rubbed her lower back, and when he suggested it might be labor, she dismissed him and his efforts. When the pain got too intense, she began to cry.

It's too soon!

But there was no stopping what had started.

He stood with her, then he sat with her. When she was too tired to do either, he held her, and when she swore she couldn't breathe and he thought she might die from not trying, he breathed for her. There was no roadmap for this journey, and neither of them had finished packing, so they did what they could to make their way.

CHAPTER

Fifty~Two

REED

REED WAS BEGINNING to accept that he would not make the graduation ceremony. He'd been in quarantine for days now, and no one had been to see or update him. He was beginning to think he'd been forgotten—or worse, that he was on the fast track to becoming a patient himself.

There was no explanation for what had happened. One day, he was Northern Laboratories-bound, and then he wasn't. Garth denied his health clearance, and he was sent to the main DDC office for reassignment. When he begged for a reevaluation, he was sent to another office and, once there, met an official he'd never seen on campus before.

"I need someone for a side project," the official said, his dark eyes glinting.

"The L-wing?" Reed asked, forgetting he wasn't supposed to know about it.

"Exactly," the officer confirmed. "Do this for me, and I will submit the paperwork for a reevaluation myself."

It was a no-brainer. Reed would do anything to get back into the Northern Laboratories program. He didn't even ask what the project was. He was given an ID badge and one of the medics' white lab coats to replace his navy intern coat, along with a small, square device that fit in the palm of his hand. His instructions were simple enough, although they didn't make any sense.

Go into the L-wing and act like you belong there. Grab one of the sample medical trays and choose a room—any random room will do. Once inside, note the line on the ground and stay well back from it.

Talk to the patient. Ask them what they did in the City States, if they have any family, what they had for lunch. The questions aren't important. What you're doing is confirming they're cognitively cohesive. Yes, these are patients, but they're different in the L-wing. In order for this experiment to work, you will need to establish that the patient you are working with is completely whole and well. There should be no sign of disease progression beyond whatever was initially reported upon admission to the L-wing. If this isn't the case, simply exit the room and move to another.

Once you have established the patient's mental status (mind the lines on the floor), press the button on the device and initiate the frequency repeater. If this test is successful, you will know what to do next.

There hadn't seemed to be anything nefarious about the instructions at the time, but Reed now realized how naive he'd been. He was just as much a test subject as the patient, if not more. The officer had been searching for someone disposable, and he'd fallen right into their lap.

He'd done what was asked of him—gone into the L-wing, pretending like he was supposed to be there. He grabbed a sample cart and pushed it to a random door. He double-gloved before entering, expecting the patient in the room to be like the ones in the main medical wing. Yes, the officer had told him they were different, and yes, Park had, too, but he hadn't really realized it until he was standing across from the old woman in a neuro-cap wearing eccentric clothing that clashed with the many lights adorning her shelves.

Reed did what he was told. He asked the old woman her name.

Abigail Fitzpatrick, but he shouldn't have to ask, because her name was right there on her chart.

How was she feeling today?

Just fine, boy, for a prisoner in this medical facility.

And what was she doing?

Reading a book, but of course he could see that, so why was he asking?

What was he doing, showing up with a medical tray and asking such asinine questions to waste her time? She might be old, but she had plenty of time and energy left for what she had stacked at her bedside (a monumental stack of ancient tomes) and didn't want to waste any of it if he didn't intend to ask earnest questions or remove the confounded headpiece.

It was around that time that Reed had decided the old woman did indeed have all of her mental faculties and was using them to be insufferable. He pulled the device, which he'd been palming the entire time, out from his pocket and pushed the button without any further thought.

He wished he'd given it further thought because what happened when he pushed the button was…

Reed had become a lot of things since starting the intern program. He was shrewd and analytical and had the ability to do terrible things without hesitation because they needed to be done. He could pull a flesh sample from a living specimen. He'd grown callous to the cries of the patients in the main medical wing and could do an assessment in under three minutes without even acknowledging them. He'd refined his skills in the area of cellular metabolism and had been looking forward to having his own research specialty, which Professor Hugo had suggested he would excel at. He'd done so much to prepare himself for the Northern Laboratories, but nothing could prepare him for what happened to the old woman sitting upright in her bed, scolding him for being stupid.

Her body went slack, like someone had severed the line that held all her muscles and tissues together. She slumped into a pile on the bed, reminding him of a rag doll as the book she'd been holding so primly in her lap slid to the floor. The collapse was instantaneous and deceptive. If the old woman's head hadn't slumped forward, he might have seen the way her eyes had clouded. The vessels at the surface of her skin contracted all at once, leaving her so pale she almost looked blue, and if she hadn't been dressed, he would have seen the more obvious greying of the skin more directly connected to her lymph system. It was classic ZCC strain, but there was nothing classic about the way she'd transformed.

Progression of the disease into full neurological development—

what was colloquially known as the *near-dead* state, as it was the last phase of the disease before the patient deteriorated to the point of death—took time. Sometimes it was days and sometimes weeks, but all strains of Zoribiatus had predictable patterns of progression that, whether fast or slow, were traceable. Nothing that happened to Abigail Fitzpatrick was either of those things.

She'd been mid-sentence, saying something about how she expected better from a medic at a facility of this caliber. The word "facility" died in her throat, but it wasn't the quick death of a thing being shut off. It started like a regular word but seemed to get stuck in her throat in the middle, causing her to make this terrible hissing sound that sent chills up his spine.

"Ms. Fitzpatrick?" he asked, referencing her name against her medical chart.

The woman's head snapped up at the sound of his voice, and she stared at him from that terrible position—half-slumped but head turned, body contorted. The hissing had transformed into something more like a growl, and the formerly frail-looking woman was moving at an alarming rate, righting herself on the bed before stumbling off. She was quick but clumsy.

Reed had his back pressed up against the door by the time she'd righted herself, but when he tried to open it, nothing happened. He wasn't thinking right. He was trying to turn the handle without scanning his ID card. The door didn't budge. Reed was trapped in the room with a developed patient.

The patient shrieked and pressed against the line around her bed as if caught in a net or behind glass. She screamed and charged, but each time she tried to cross the line, an invisible field held her back. Reed realized it was the cuffs on her hands and ankles and relaxed a little. Then he remembered the instructions he'd been given. *If the test worked out, he would know what to do...*

Reed whirled around, searching the wall frantically for the alarm before pulling it and signaling for his rescue. He'd done everything that had been asked of him.

He'd seen Park just before the volunteers hauled him off into quarantine. In that moment, whether it was because of the terror or just seeing her scared, horrified face, he'd wanted to tell her how sorry he was.

But he hadn't seen anyone since that had happened. He'd just sat in quarantine, waiting.

What if that wasn't what was supposed to happen?

The time alone was getting to his head.

They'll put those cuffs on you and stick you in one of those beds.

Reed was all but convinced. He was drinking the last of the bottled water that had been shuttled into the room with him by a remote-touch flier when the door opened and the DDC official appeared.

"You're good at following instructions."

"Was that supposed to happen?" Reed asked.

The official looked lazily at his watch, as if Reed were making him late for an engagement. "I'd hoped, at least," he said, giving the boy in the medical lab coat a meaningful look. "Of course, I'll need to play around with the frequency strength. No one has reported if the patients in the adjacent rooms reacted the same or measurably similar."

"How did it change her?" Reed asked, catching the shrewd way the man assessed him. "I mean, what does the frequency repeater do that causes the change?"

The officer smiled, and Reed thought it was a wicked look. "It activates the virus," he said.

"How?"

The officer brought his hands together in front of him, his malevolent grin taking on an uncomfortable edge. "A virus can stay dormant for years if adapted to do so. There are all sorts of biological signals that can flip the on switch, but this one is a bit more mechanical. All we needed was time. Time for the virus to spread throughout the patient's system so that when activated, the development could be instantaneous. I thought it was very effective."

Reed understood, and the realization caused a sinking feeling in his gut. Park had been right.

"Am I done now? Will I get to go to the Northern Laboratories?" he asked.

The officer wrapped his arm around the boy's shoulder, bringing him in close. "I have a better proposition for you—a position in *my* laboratory," he said.

"But I want to be a scientist," Reed stammered, not sure why he was uneasy but more certain than he'd ever been that whatever this man had to offer was wrong.

"Oh, you will be," the officer said.

Reed was quiet for a moment, his mind racing to decide what he would say next. He was in quarantine for a reason. If the job was done and the Northern Laboratories were an option, he'd already be free. This was it.

"Will I have my own research?" he asked.

"Of course!" the officer gushed. The sound was the sickening, cloying sweet of a poisoned trap.

"Okay," Reed said. Then, realizing his response was too weak, he shifted his shoulders back, lifting his head. The man was watching him with shrewd discernment. From this close, he could see the name carved onto his scientist's emblem. *Orman.* "Alright. That's great. I have a lot of ideas—especially about that transition. I study cellular metabolism, you know. I think we could reduce that reaction time by quite a bit."

Orman studied the boy with a hungry gaze. "I'm going to like you, I think."

The statement made Reed smile despite himself.

Orman gave his shoulder a shake. "Let's get you to graduation."

Fifty-Three

PARK

PARK HAD until the end of graduation to find Zayd and get him on the transport. Inside the Institute, she wore her white lab coat, buttoned to cover her stomach, and walked with her tablet in front of her, trying to look busy. But outside, she shed the lab coat and wore an oversized volunteer uniform, blending into the background of the facility like she didn't exist.

She walked quickly across the wheel of converging paths toward the volunteer quarters. It was late in the evening, and the intern quarters were empty. Scientific interns were either at graduation, in the academic laboratories, or doing rounds with Professor Hugo. It was the same every night, save for the graduation, and thus the safest time to move like she did out in the open. If Zayd was doing an evening shift, she might have some difficulty pulling him off duty, but she had the lab coat and false orders pulled up on her tablet if it came to it. She hoped their egress would be easier than that, though. She hoped he was resting in the volunteer quarters after a long shift.

According to Benji, last time she checked—which was longer ago than she cared to admit—Zayd was doing morning training rounds with development and delivery. It was a logical choice since he wasn't scheduled to go north while Anika was in the L-wing. With an active patient on site, he was disqualified from being a medical volunteer. He would remain a volunteer at the Institute, limited to patient developing and handling. It was a miserable and ultimately lethal sentence, which was why Anika wanted him gone so badly she was willing to risk never seeing him again.

Thinking of Anika made her feel sick. Could she lie to Zayd about his wife's safety after what she'd seen? Would she lay that down next to the one about Anika's already-uncertain pregnancy?

Anika would be alone for the rest of her life. Until recently, Park had believed the rest of Anika's life was a fairly extended proposition, but after what happened to Abigail…

According to Dr. Wong, the transformation had been instantaneous and unexplainable. The video footage showed her there one moment, then collapsed, and the next moment, she was gone—fully neurologically developed. Gerald in the room next to her succumbed to disease progression two days later.

It didn't matter what consolation Park had to give her because it now seemed that her life could be over in an instant. There were no old-world comforts that could change the discomfort of this reality. So when Park told her the transport was scheduled for graduation, Anika had been glad.

"Get him out of here," she said.

Park intended to. She and Zayd were going to get out. They would both leave behind more than they ever thought they could stand to leave, but they were getting out.

The volunteer quarters were quiet. Most of the volunteers off shift were either dining or resting. There were only a few people visible through the window to the little recreation space and only one that she recognized. She knocked on the door to draw the young man's attention before cracking it open.

"Vang," she whispered.

He scurried to the exit, his slight frame blocking the view of anyone else who might try to see.

"Is this about Benji? Is he okay? What are you doing in a volunteer uniform?" Vang demanded, worry etching his typically stoic face.

"Benji is fine. He's on shift in medical, and there's nothing high risk happening," she assured him.

Relief flooded his countenance, and his narrow shoulders relaxed. "You can't scare me like that."

"I'm sorry, really. But you know Benji. He's always fine," Park said.

Vang gave her one of his charming half-smiles. "You give him too much credit. He's charmed you, too, hasn't he?"

Park shook her head. "We both know where his heart belongs."

Vang sighed, and there was a quiet moment where they both acknowledged the difficulty of caring for anyone at the Institute. When the moment passed, Vang cocked an eyebrow at her. "You look ridiculous, you know."

"You don't think I look good in blue and brown?" she asked.

"A wolf in sheep's clothing," he said, forcing her to remember the risk he and all the other volunteers took when they worked with her— every time they agreed to help her with anything.

"I need to speak with Zayd," Park said, deciding not to waste any more of the volunteer's time.

A look of genuine surprise crossed Vang's face at that.

"What is it?" she asked.

"You don't know?" he said as if she should.

"What am I supposed to know?" she demanded.

"Zayd's gone," Vang said. The words struck like lightning in her gut.

"What do you mean, gone?"

"Last week. He did his single-volunteer handling lesson and didn't come back. Him and Jemani," Vang said.

Park could feel the world turn out from under her as she grasped for the door. Vang was at her side before she could stumble.

"Hey! What's wrong? Are you okay?"

She righted herself, embarrassed. "I'm fine. I just… are you sure he's dead?"

Vang's face twisted in confusion. "I didn't say he was dead; I said he was gone. Jemani—she's dead. We've got confirmation on that. Rumor is she went rogue on a couple of DDC agents."

Park tried to process what he was saying. A volunteer attacking

DDC agents was unheard of, despite being exactly what scientists were warned about. "What happened?"

"Nobody knows for sure, but it involved near-dead. Benji says Jemani was really fixated on city infection rates. He said she was 'Resistee-adjacent.' But you know how Benji is; he thinks all the city recruits are Resistee-adjacent."

Park's heart sank. She didn't have the context to unpack Benji's theories about the city recruits and Resistee activity. Her whole life, Resistees had felt more like the zombie under the bed than a real threat. But she knew how she felt about near-dead. Nothing good ever came of incidents involving patients. "Did Zayd go to cryo?"

"No. We'd know about cryo. You know how things work with the volunteers. He's not dead, and he's not in cryo, so we thought maybe you knew where he was."

Park considered this. The volunteers were very good about keeping account of themselves. Between them, they covered the entire Institute on any given day at any given time, so it wasn't hard for them to keep track of what was going on. They knew about every death, infection, and transfer, so for Zayd to just be gone was strange.

"What about quarantine?" she asked, her mind racing to find an explanation. People at the Institute didn't go into quarantine often, but it wasn't unheard of. Most often, it was for other infectious illnesses. The Institute wasn't the place to let a flu virus run rampant.

"Only person delivered to quarantine was out of the L-wing. That's where you work, right? Volunteers don't usually go in there, but a medic was in there with a developed patient. Can't wait to hear the full story on that one if it ever gets out," Vang said.

Park's mind was working overtime. She knew exactly who he was talking about, but why Reed was wearing a medic's uniform and was trapped in a room with Abigail, who had been fine just the day before, was beyond her. At least she knew where one missing person was.

"Which room?" she asked. She had to find Zayd first, but there was a part of her that needed to see Reed one more time. That part of her that couldn't let go—wanted to believe he was still in there somewhere. If she could find Zayd in time, she would go to him.

"Dunno. But since it's a quiet month, I'd say in the front," Vang said.

Park stood straight, pulling away from where she'd been leaning against the door. "Thank you, Vang. I'm sorry I scared you about Benji."

"No problem. Benji does plenty of that without your help, if you know what I mean," he said.

She turned away from the door, intent on continuing her search elsewhere, when Vang stopped her.

"You never said why you're wearing a volunteer suit."

She considered whether or not she should tell him, then decided that since she was dressed like a volunteer, she'd act like one and tell the whole truth.

"I'm getting out of here."

Vang let out a low whistle. "Well, let me know if that works."

"Sure. I'll send word." She had no idea how she'd do that, but Vang didn't question it.

She rushed on, not knowing where she would look next but determined to figure out something. As she passed the intern quarters, she'd all but made up her mind to go to Garth next. He was just as likely as anyone else on campus to know where a volunteer might be. It was the fastest way to get to the bottom of the mystery, and if he didn't like her throwing someone else on the transport, he could just deal with it because neither of them would be his problem once they were out of here.

She was walking fast and not looking. There wasn't supposed to be anyone to look out for, so she didn't see Reed rushing toward the intern quarters. They collided so suddenly that she only barely kept her feet, and she didn't realize it was him until their eyes locked.

"Reed," she gasped.

He froze, his hands still on her arms and his mouth open in an imperfect o, clearly not expecting to see her or anyone else on his way. The most striking thing about it was that his touch was unfamiliar, like the embrace of a stranger rather than her longtime love.

"What are you doing out here—in a volunteer uniform?"

"I was trying to find someone," she admitted before realizing she risked disclosing too much. She corrected quickly, asking, "Weren't you in quarantine?"

It was his turn to be caught off-kilter. He glanced away like he always did when he searched for the right lie. She decided she didn't want to hear it. "I saw you with Abigail Fitzpatrick."

His face told her he hadn't expected her to know about that, and it gave her a modicum of satisfaction to know that she was putting him through a portion of the same discomfort he'd put her through when he left her out in the cold.

"I was released in time for graduation," he said, looking between her and the intern quarters.

"I didn't think you were going to the Northern Laboratories," she said. Her mouth was running away without her, but it felt good. She wanted him to hurt.

"I'm, um… I'm not." He released her arms as if he had only just realized he'd been holding them. Lifting his chin, he said, "I've got a research project with another laboratory for the DDC."

"There are no other government laboratories," she said, wondering why he would lie about this.

"You said yourself that none of the L-wing patients go to the Northern Laboratories. You're the one that told me something was happening here. *You* said there was something going on!"

"But you didn't believe me until you saw it with your own eyes," Park snapped.

"I didn't just see it. I caused it!"

A jolt of understanding ripped through her. She stepped back, observing the way Reed's chest heaved as he thrust his hand through almost-nonexistent hair. The action drew her attention to the side of his neck below his jaw where his skin flushed.

"You couldn't possibly understand. This is too far above your position. I shouldn't have said anything," he said, trying to dismiss her, to regain control.

"You shouldn't have," she agreed. She knew him so well. She could read his frustration and the edge of fear. He was distracted. But he wasn't sorry. Did he still know her well enough to see her heart was broken?

"I have to get going," he said, trying to move around her.

He didn't ask her where she was going. It was like he'd forgotten the volunteer uniform that had thrown him so completely off guard to begin with.

"I wish they'd left you to rot in quarantine, Chase Reed," she spat, unable to help herself. Seeing him this way was worse than she'd thought it could be. He was fine. He was so utterly and completely fine with everything. He was fine with Park's swollen middle and whatever she was doing here. He was fine with the old woman who'd transformed so suddenly before him. He was fine, and she wasn't.

It didn't matter that she was about to leave this place. She didn't know where Zayd was or how to begin searching for him. She would never get him onto the transport in time. She would fail Anika. She would fail them all! Reed was on his way to put on a black suit and graduation gown, and he didn't care. It was like the pieces of her heart were falling away from each other.

"Get over it, Park," he said, walking away from her. He pulled open the door to the intern quarters, but before going in, he looked back at her one final time. "Besides, I think you'd fit in quarantine better than me in that volunteer suit."

The remaining pieces of Park's heart ignited.

YOU'D FIT *in quarantine better than me in that volunteer suit…*

Reed might have broken her heart, but he'd also given her the key piece of information she needed to get out of the Institute.

Vang said nobody else was in quarantine, so if Reed saw a volunteer in quarantine, there was a chance it might be Zayd. A good chance.

She hurried toward the door adjacent to the main medical wing, thankful the clearance that granted her entrance to the L-wing was a grade higher than what she needed to enter quarantine without an escort. Under normal circumstances, she'd worry about using her ID card somewhere like this, but it didn't matter now. By the time someone checked the entrance records and questioned why she'd been here, she and Zayd would be gone.

Though she wasn't afraid of anyone coming for her once this was done, she wasn't foolhardy enough to think she couldn't ruin things in the moment by not being careful. Running headlong into Reed was a sobering reminder of that. She moved cautiously through the narrow hall of the quarantine section. It was nearly identical to the residential wing of the main Institute building except for the white-tiled halls and windowed doors that locked from the outside.

Park considered the layout of the wing, not wanting to waste any time. Reed would have been brought in through the interior doors from the L-wing, but he'd exited the way she'd come. If he'd seen a volunteer, it would have been along that direct path. She went from room to room, looking through the large, one-way windows that granted views to the miniature rooms with their sparse decor. Each one had a low bed with a dark brown blanket, a sink, and bathroom facilities. It didn't take her long to find the only occupied room and the defeated man sitting within.

She flashed her badge on the security lock, and the light flashed green, granting her access. Swinging the door partway open and taking care not to step over the threshold, she met his gaze as he looked up.

"It's time to go, Zayd."

He stood, straightening the top of his volunteer suit, which hung loosely over his shoulders as though he'd shrunk since it had been assigned to him. He followed her out, looking furtively over his shoulder as if someone might appear from within the walls to chase after them.

"There's a Northern Laboratories transport waiting. We both need to be on it before the scientists board," she explained in a hushed voice.

"I don't want to go to the Northern Laboratories. Not without Ani—"

"We're not going there," Park snapped in a quiet growl. She knew the man was a reluctant partner at best. She stood in the hall, considering. She'd meant to take him right back out the doors through which she'd entered and onto the transport, but now, as the events of the week coalesced and condensed around her, a different idea occurred. She glanced toward the interior-facing doors. There was a soiled laundry bin perched immediately next to the exit as she'd expected. Institute policy dictated minimum contamination spread from area to area. If laundry hadn't been collected yet, there ought to be a lab coat in the bin—maybe even the one Reed had been wearing on the day he was dragged out of Abigail's room.

Zayd looked as though he was about to mount further protest.

Before he could begin, she instructed, "Follow me. Don't say anything to anyone. Keep your head up, and do what I do."

She approached the bin, ignoring the way she struggled to bend and pry the lid open due to the size of her middle and the way it threw her off-balance. She retrieved one of the two white lab coats, handing it to Zayd.

"What's this for?" he asked.

"Put it on," she said, not wanting to explain. If she did, he probably wouldn't be able to keep it together, and their success depended on him looking at least a little like everyone else at the Institute.

After another moment of hesitation, he did. She was relieved to see it was a near fit. Flashing her ID against the exit, she reminded him, "Don't say anything to anyone."

Zayd nodded, and she was grateful that at least for now, she wouldn't have to fight him. Maybe he hoped for what she was trying to give him.

They moved quickly through the mostly empty halls, passing the entrance to the main medical wing as a door closed, cutting off the hopeless wail of a patient. Zayd glanced nervously her way as they moved.

"Head up, look forward," she hissed, keeping her clip quick and her face neutral. She would be less nervous if the halls were full and there were more moving bodies to distract anyone they might come across.

What if Dr. Wong was back on shift? He hadn't been since the incident. Garth said there was changeover happening in the DDC administration. He seemed to think it was directly related to what had happened in the L-wing—or rather, from his perspective, what happened in the L-wing was a result of changeover within the DDC.

"I'm being recruited," he'd said.

Park didn't know if that was a good thing any more than she knew if Dr. Wong's disappearance from the L-wing floors was better or worse for her. It was better to get out than worry about it. Her current plan threatened that, but she hoped the gamble would pay off.

She brought Zayd up to the L-wing doors and flashed her ID card. If he hadn't figured it out by now, he would. She glanced over at him to see he was following her instructions exactly. His head was high, and his face was relaxed. He looked like he could be anyone else at the Institute. He looked like he had no idea he was about to see his wife again.

There was no one at the central console, which was good. There hadn't been anyone at the central console since the incident day, which Park considered completely counterintuitive.

Not my problem, she reminded herself.

"This way," she whispered, taking Zayd down the hall toward room twenty-three. When the light turned green, she turned the handle and held it there. "If you don't want to get caught, wait until I say."

All that was left was trust. She opened the door and let him enter, following closely behind him.

Since Zayd was in front of her, she saw the look on Anika's face first. She'd expected glee or perhaps relief, maybe even shock. All she'd ever asked for was Zayd. Every concession, every bribe was done in an effort to bring him to her. And now, finally, he was here. Anika's face was blank.

Zayd stood rigid at the doorway, either too stunned to move or following her instructions to wait. Park didn't hesitate in case it was the former. She grabbed the lashing pole hung adjacent to the door and thrust it up at the ceiling surveillance. She was out of practice since leaving the intern program. Finally, she managed to get the wires around the little camera over the doorway and yank it down so the wires stuck out of the ceiling like pulled sinew and the blue light went dark.

"Go," she said.

Zayd didn't need further prompting. He rushed to his wife, stepping over the barrier line painted onto the floor. "Ani! Ani!" He was crying.

She caught his wrist before he could touch her, grabbing him with perfectly manicured hands and pushing backward. "What are you doing here?"

She sounded angry. By the expression on her face, she was furious.

"We're leaving. I told you I would let you know," Park said, surprised by her reaction. Zayd stood frozen just outside her grasp, wounded.

"You shouldn't have brought him here!" she shrieked.

"I thought this was what you wanted—"

"That was before!" Anika wailed, splitting herself between anguish and fury.

Before. That meant she knew about Abigail and Gerald. "There's a reason it hasn't happened again, and it won't—at least not to you," Park said, drawing both of their attention.

"I don't want him to get infected—"

"If he wasn't infected when you came, then it means you can't transfer it to him. At least not by touch, or—" She thought of the pregnancy Anika insisted on hiding. "You've already tested the limits of transferring dormant Zoribiatus."

"Ani, please!" Zayd begged. He lifted her hand free of the second cuff, caressing her wrist.

"It's inside of me." Her voice shook as she whispered to him, eyes too large and glistening with unshed tears. "If it comes out, I'll tear you apart."

"I would rather let you tear me to shreds than never hold you again." Their hands were entwined now. Her resolve was breaking. They were like two halves of a whole, the ocean and the shore being pulled together by an unrelenting tide.

"I want you to live," she choked.

He pulled her into him. Their bodies intertwined. Park ached at the perfect fit of them, but the ache was good. Zayd whispered to his wife as she quietly wept on his bent shoulder. He kissed the top of her head near the beginning of her braid, then her forehead. Their bodies trembled with barely suppressed grief. "I love you."

Something shifted in Park as she watched them. She was done fighting Zayd. She didn't want to leave Anika any more than he did. It wasn't right. She wouldn't be safe.

"Anika, there's something I need to tell you about what happened to the other patient," she said.

"I know she progressed, and the man in the next room," Anika said, wiping her eyes as Zayd caressed the top of her head. She looked up to meet his gaze. "They were patients like me—"

Her voice caught in her throat.

"I know. I'm sorry. No one deserves that," Zayd comforted her.

"But that's why I need you to go. Because I couldn't live with you staying here only to have to know that I—know that I became like that," Anika sobbed.

"You don't have to," Park said.

"What do you mean?" Anika asked.

"I mean you don't have to succumb to the disease. Not if you come with us," Park said.

Zayd gripped Anika's hand so hard she winced. He gave Park a hard stare. "Are you saying—"

"None of the other patients have succumbed again because the medic who caused it hasn't come back to do whatever he did to make it happen again. There's something about this strain of the virus in the L-wing. If I'm right, Anika won't succumb so long as she stays away from whatever trigger that medic used to make it happen. She's not safe here. She has to come with us," Park explained. She didn't have proof, but she was certain nonetheless.

"Did you hear that, Ani? You're coming with us," Zayd gushed, barely containing the overwhelm of emotion. He pulled her into him, hugging her fiercely, not bothering to mask the fresh stream of tears.

Anika let him hold her, contemplating Park's supposition. "What if you're wrong about there being a trigger?"

"Where we're going—they have their own cryo," Park said. "If the disease progresses, they'll put you in, same as here, only I'm certain your odds will be better on the outside."

"It's still too much of a risk," Anika insisted.

"Well then, you're not going to like this next part," Park said, stepping over the indicator line on the floor and positioning the lashing pole over Anika's ankle braces.

She repeated the action she'd watched the volunteers do when they'd taken Abigail. The ankle cuffs fell to the mattress with a dull thunk.

Anika stared, stunned.

Zayd looked from Park to Anika, trying to decide if he could hold on to the hope exploding out of him. Park wedged the lashing pole between them, releasing the first wrist cuff. "We have to hurry."

Park glanced nervously at the door, wishing this new, dangerous, and potentially damning addition to her plan was even partially developed. "We need to find an intern suit."

"Can we go back through quarantine?" Zayd asked, urging Anika to her feet.

"That's a good idea. My bags are hidden on the side of the building anyway," Park said.

An alarm bleeped on her tablet. She nearly jumped outside of herself at the sound. She'd set it as a final warning for boarding in case things went sideways. "We need to go now."

"I don't have shoes!" Anika gasped.

Park's stomach dropped. "You're going to have to wear the slippers and hope no one notices," she said.

The couple exchanged terrified, incredulous looks.

"There isn't time!" Park hissed. She took one last glance at the couple, knowing they didn't blend in even a little, but there wasn't time to come up with another plan. She took a final, deep breath before flashing her badge, but before she could compress the lock handle, the door swung inward, and Park found herself staring at a very perturbed Garth.

"LET ME GET THIS STRAIGHT. I arrange a highly risky and tenuous exodus from the Institute for you—YOU. A very stupid, vulnerable, powerless, and extremely pregnant-even-though-she-shouldn't-be first-year medic, and you decide to take it upon yourself to include not just a volunteer who is currently enmeshed in a sordid and gory DDC incident, but you also decide to throw an infected L-wing patient in there, too? Am I getting that right?" Garth fumed.

Park stood just to the side of Zayd and Anika, who held each other, cowering under the old medic's fury. She refused to cower.

"You missed the part where it's your fault I'm pregnant in the first place," she said, hoping she sounded cool and authoritative.

"I fail to see how that impacts the current circumstances," Garth said. He had his back pressed against the door so no passing medics could take in the disaster of a scene playing out in room twenty-three.

"Why can't they come with me?" Park demanded.

"The volunteer can go. It would be easy enough to absorb him into the multitude of incidents on campus." Garth waved a dismissive hand in Zayd's direction. "But I'm afraid the patient would be missed."

Park knew Anika would be missed. She knew it would cause a

multitude of problems further down the road for everyone on the inside. She'd known the whole time, which was why she'd fought the idea of saving her, even when her hypothesis about the L-wing's true purpose began to bloom in her mind. That respect for Garth and his *group of like-minded people* only went so far, though. She wouldn't defer to them on this matter. Not after seeing Zayd and Anika together. Not after Reed had shattered her heart so completely. Someone deserved to win.

"Can't you just make her disappear?" Park asked, trying not to stare too hard at the way Zayd held Anika.

"She's a patient. She's not just any patient. She's a patient of extreme interest in the DDC's most experimental and most highly classified medical wing. She can't just disappear without things falling apart," Garth said.

"Maybe things need to fall apart, then," Park hissed.

Garth opened his mouth to refute her, but she wasn't done. "I mean, look at this!" Park placed her hands out around her middle, putting it on display. "How much collateral before you question the means to your end? How many more people have to be manipulated? Who else has to suffer for you to do anything besides celebrate your position within the system you swear you're trying to destroy? How much can you sacrifice before you become just like the people you're trying to destroy?"

"I'll stay here. Just let Zayd go with Dr. Park," Anika pleaded, pulling away from Zayd to confront Garth.

Zayd held Anika close, frantic and possessive, as though keeping her close might shield them both from the inevitable outcome. "No. Please. Let her come with us. Say she had a heart attack. Say she turned like the others. Anything. Just please—don't make me lose her."

"I'm sorry, son. We've got extensive data on her health metrics. We can't claim she just dropped dead," Garth explained with an unusual level of empathy.

Anika reached for Zayd's face, pulling him into her. "It's okay. Go. I will be fine."

"I won't leave you!" Zayd's voice tore into Park's already-eviscerated heart.

She looked into Garth's sour, expressionless face, her own brows turned down with disdain. "What justifies their suffering? Who decides which person is worth fighting for and which ones become statistics?"

"It's not a matter of deciding who is worthy of action. This is a matter of logistics!" Garth protested.

"Then change the logistics!" Park insisted.

Garth stared wordlessly. A part of Park was aware of the passage of time narrowing the possibility of her successful escape.

"You kept an entire intern group from getting sterilized. You hid me in the L-wing in plain sight amongst the highest-ranking DDC officers. If you can do that, then you can make Anika disappear." She watched his unmoving face as he processed her assumption. "I know you can. You can rebuild a person from the inside out. You can infiltrate the DDC so completely that they're putting you in charge of their top-secret project. You can make her disappear."

The only hint of Garth's inner workings was the shift of his lower lip as he chewed the inside of his cheek, thinking. Computing the odds of success. "There's a lot of risk involved."

"They're worth the risk," Park insisted.

"She might still succumb, ultimately," he ventured.

"Your people have cryo," Park countered.

Anika used the sleeve of her robe to wipe at the side of Zayd's tear-streaked face in the silence.

"They're just as worth it as I am," Park said.

Garth scowled, reaching with his left hand to the top of his lab coat without looking. "You understand how many things have to come together for this to work?"

"I do," Park said. "Which means you must understand how completely I believe you're capable of making the effort to ensure they do. That's all it is—prioritizing someone other than you."

Garth worked the buttons on his coat until they were loose, shrugging it off his shoulders before extending his arm toward Anika. He looked at Park. "You overestimate my capabilities," he said.

Park smirked. "We'll see about that."

Zayd helped Anika into the coat, buttoning it over her robe with inefficient, trembling fingers.

"Keep your hands in your pockets," Park said, glancing at Anika's fingernails.

"There should be intern suits in the laundry of the main medical unit," Garth said as they completed their disguise. "There is a chance, thanks to the persistent passage of time, that you might not make it."

"We'll hurry," Park promised.

"Nevertheless. I only have so much power. This was the chance I provided, and this is how you've chosen to spend it," Garth said, sounding more like himself than the man who was letting them escape. He flashed his badge, compressing the door lock.

Park made eye contact with him on her way out, taking care to actually see his eyes through the thick lenses. "Thank you. For everything you've done."

"I think, given the circumstances, you're responsible for the outcome of this situation," he said. Then, picking up the communication connection next to the door, he compressed the speaker and said, "I need medical 401C to L-wing twenty-three for a DOA. Send a team of volunteers for transport to postmortem exam."

There was a pause. Park pushed Zayd and Anika through the door. There would be time to deconstruct the import of Garth's words later.

The group moved silently out the L-wing doors, following Park through the entrance to the main medical unit. Once inside, they shed their lab coats. Park retrieved a volunteer suit for Anika from the laundry bin. She changed quickly, discarding the red robe before they made their way together to the exit.

"Aren't they going to think it's strange—three volunteers boarding the transport last minute?" Zayd asked, reeling from the unbelievability of their scheme.

"The only folks out there to think it's strange are volunteers. Everyone else is rounding out the graduation ceremony." A door opened, loosing a gut-wrenching shriek that drowned out the last of her words.

Anika's face transformed into a mask of horror. "What was that?"

"A patient," Park said, urging them toward the exit.

"But—"

Park scanned her ID before forcing the door open. The bite of the cool night air met her burning face with startling contrast. "That sound? That's their hearts breaking again and again as they face the reality of what's happening to them. It's the agony of lost humanity."

There was more commotion on the open grounds than when Park had last been out, and for a moment, she feared they were too late. Then she realized the ceremony must have ended, meaning they only had minutes. "This way," she said.

The transport was waiting, engines running to keep the cryogenic support online. She ushered Zayd and Anika around the back to the cargo entrance. They followed her up the short ramp and into the dim interior of the vehicle. There were others inside, but as she'd expected, they didn't pay them much mind. Volunteers kept to themselves. She pointed at the seats near the exit, tucking Anika into the one nearest the cold metal of the cryogenic cell. Zayd sat next to her just in time for the sound of voices to rise above the engines. The scientists were coming. Park reeled around to sit in the space across from Zayd and Anika just as the first scientist boarded from the front.

Fifty-Six

MORA

MORA HAD EXPECTED the world outside to be a wild place. From the rooftop, it had appeared to be nothing more than rolling hills and rampant greenery, but that wasn't what she'd walked into. She was traveling down a street—crumbling and overgrown, but it was a street all the same. All around, buildings were crumbling into oblivion as nature overtook them.

It was a neighborhood, not so unlike the murky memory of her childhood, except that this one was empty and dead. She wondered how likely it was that this ruin of a place was the same one she'd grown up in. If it was, then she and her mother weren't the only ones to abandon it. Something in her gut told her that this wasn't it, though. It was similar—maybe one of dozens—but not it.

She wondered where all the people were.

There isn't anyone left on the outside.

That's what her mother had said.

The City States are the only remaining safe haven.

So came the battle cry at school.

But it couldn't be true. Though she passed building after dilapidated building—*homes*—she didn't see any evidence that the disease had ravaged this place. There were no wandering sick. No remains lining the streets. There was no evidence that anyone had fled this place in a hurry. There were no overturned vehicles in the street or supplies strewn wildly about. The buildings themselves were the only evidence that people had been here at all. This place didn't look abandoned; it looked evacuated. It looked like a ghost town.

"This place is spooky," Mora said to the bird splitting its time between her shoulder and the collapsing rooftops.

"Hey," Omen said, swooping low on the street and making her heart stutter.

"Hey yourself," she grumbled, trying to force a brave face. How was she supposed to find anyone out here?

Ahead, the world opened up. Whatever once stood there was nothing but rubble now. For the last several hours, Mora had walked through a tangle of structures—mostly homes—and nature. The destruction progressed in proportion to the natural regrowth. But ahead, something different was happening. Both structure and nature seemed to have been destroyed.

It looked like something had gone through and leveled the earth in a way that reminded Mora of how the workers tore down the fire escape. This was an unfinished job with pieces of the old buildings left to be picked up. As she crossed the threshold from the overgrown neighborhood into the ruin, she realized this was the outside version of what was happening in the city. This was the crossover from the Westside into the East. She had come from the way things were and was entering what they would become.

To what end?

Who was tearing down these old communities, and why were they doing it? What purpose was there in leveling the remains of outside life if there was no one to witness it?

Mora kept on, trying not to let the shadows of destruction creep into her psyche. It was late, and she was tired.

Or was it early?

She was disoriented from exhaustion and needed to stop for a drink, but every step she took convinced her she needed to go just a little farther before it was safe to do so. There were signs of life. She'd seen wild dog tracks, or coyote. At this point, they were likely one and the same, Mora mused. A number of other animal tracks speckled the trail, from rodents and birds all the way up to deer or maybe even elk, according to her old-world atlas. She told herself she wasn't afraid, but at the same time, she didn't know what she would do if she suddenly encountered an animal more than half her size.

Omen, who had been staying close since she'd crossed through the force field, lifted suddenly into the sky, flying out of Mora's line of sight and leaving her feeling exposed.

"Hey," she hissed, hoping to trigger a recall.

The night responded with eerie silence.

She waited a moment to see if she could hear where he'd gone, but she couldn't even hear the beat of his wings in the distance. He seemed to have evaporated into the darkness.

Mora knew that if she continued walking, Omen would have no trouble finding her in the night—if he chose to—but she convinced herself she needed to stop and wait. She pulled the pack from her shoulder and grabbed the circular canteen that came with her black-market gear. She untwisted the cap and drank greedily. After several seconds, she lowered it, gasping for air and feeling the change in weight. She'd drunk too much at once. If she was going to manage out here on her own, she would need to work on restraint.

"Tomorrow," she said. Rules and structure were so much easier to follow in the daylight. At least the word sounded good in the empty, crisp air.

Mora replaced the canteen, turning her focus to the bird and hoping to pinpoint his location. She let out a long, low whistle, something she used to do to call him up from further away when he was younger. There was a moment of silence, then the sound repeated back, eerily not bird-like.

"Hey," she whispered, waiting to see if Omen would respond in kind. If he was near, he almost always did.

There was no response.

A bold part of her wanted to whistle again in case the first time had been her imagination, but the rest of her was scared of the looming shadows and the little voice at the back of her mind whispering, *what if?*

She didn't have to whistle again. The sound repeated after another minute of silence. It came from the darkness ahead.

Not knowing what else to do, Mora stepped into that dark, toward the sound. Every few steps, she paused to listen. Less often, she whispered into the darkness, hoping Omen wasn't far.

"Hey."

After several minutes that stretched out like hours, the thin sliver of a moon rose into view. The night was overcast, and clouds scattered what dim light the sky offered into a hazy glow, making the shadows darker. It was quiet. So, so quiet.

Mora knew there should be some sound—the skitter of rodents, the buzz of insects that permeated even the most populated corners of the City States—but their absence was undeniable. She also knew, based on her reading and preparation for the outside world, that their absence was a bad sign. Something else was here.

"It's people," Mora said, keeping her voice low and to herself. "Near-dead don't whistle. People are predators. Wild dogs spend all their time talking to each other."

She had no way to know what of her reading was actual truth, but it felt better to believe she knew something about this wild outside world than to believe she was stumbling blindly into it.

There were shadows ahead, larger than the rubble lining the crumbled road. When she stared too long, she was certain some of the shadows moved. Maybe she was becoming delirious with exhaustion and terror. She almost hoped so.

Inside the force fields, the workers were systematic. They started renovations on the Eastside, right up against the force field, and moved toward the West. It was more efficient that way even though it meant they had to wait until half the city was redone before they renovated the capitol building. Mora supposed they were doing the same thing on the outside. But if they had started from further out and were moving in toward the force field, there had to be a reason. The dark shadows ahead weren't buildings.

A third whistle broke the silence, and this time, Mora saw the motion of the caller's arm as they brought fingers to their mouth to make the sound.

Mora responded, acting on instinct to draw the caller's attention. She could make out their shape and the rough outline of a large black bird perched atop a larger structure—a vehicle.

Omen responded to her call. He was close enough now that she could hear his whistle, almost human while still very much something else. It was like the way he said *hey* or called her name.

"I told you I would find you," the woman said, and though she'd never heard her voice before, Mora knew it was Georgia.

"How did you?" Mora asked.

"Your bird left the city, but he didn't fly out. He was waiting for you. That's how we knew it was time to move in," Georgia said. Her voice was deep and rich, full of humor and an ill-defined thing Mora identified as beauty.

"That's nothing more than a lucky guess. I was trapped. It was just as likely I would have been shipped to the Institute, and someone would have caught you out here," she said, closing the gap between them.

"We don't get caught," Georgia said. "And yeah, I might have made a calculated guess or two."

Omen flew to Mora's shoulder as she stopped in front of the woman and her rusted old-world vehicle. Georgia was very short with broad shoulders and thick arms. The top of her head was level with Mora's mid-torso, but she was imposing as she studied Mora in return. She wore her long, greying red hair in a thick plait that ran down the top of her head and draped over her shoulder, stopping at her waistline, just above her jacket hem. Somehow, this woman was exactly what Mora had pictured.

Georgia shifted away from the vehicle's door. The action made Mora jump.

"I'm not going to bite," Georgia said.

"I'm sorry. It's been a long day," Mora said, trying to explain away the tension that coiled around her.

Georgia's face softened. "Relax, kid. Nobody here's going to hurt you. We're just happy to have you on the outside—on our side."

Mora looked beyond the woman and her vehicle, noting the distinct lack of other people. "Where is everyone?"

Georgia glanced around at the crumbling structures and leveled ground. "Do you mean my people or the ones who used to live here?"

Mora's chest tightened in anticipation. "I meant your people, but… I used to live out here, you know? A long time ago. And I thought maybe your people might be the same people who used to live out here…"

She was rambling. She could tell Georgia was waiting for her to get to the point, and Mora didn't mean to be taking so long. "I thought someone from before remembered me and maybe that was why you wanted me?"

Mora's face burned from the sloppy explanation. She hadn't even managed to get the words past her trembling lips. *I want to know if my father is with you. Is he looking for me?* She hoped Georgia was as good at reading between the lines as she was at calculated guesses.

"Ah," Georgia said, tipping her head back to look into the blanket of clouds blocking the starlight. She held her gaze there for a moment before letting out a long breath. "The DDC started clearing the outlying communities years back. They used a mix of tactics: outbreaks, near-dead, raids… They wanted the people on the outside gone. Some folks, like your mom, made bargains and moved into the cities. It helped the DDC tell the story they wanted. People won't clamor to get out of the cities if refugees come in crying about the dangers outside the force fields, you get me?"

Mora nodded, wondering where this was going.

Georgia didn't keep her waiting. "Most of the people from the outside communities scattered. The DDC wants this land for something. We don't know what yet, but we have our guesses. Factory production in the City States is down. Whatever they're planning, it's not going to be good."

Mora agreed. Nothing the DDC did was good. They'd swept through her life like a storm, leaving nothing but loss in their wake.

"If there was someone out here—"

"My dad," Mora blurted, finally managing to get it out.

Georgia uncrossed her arms and nervously kicked at the rusted truck's front tire. "I hate to disappoint you, but I don't know your dad."

Mora felt the shock of disappointment course through her. She had to look away to hide the tears stinging her eyes. "I always knew it was a long shot," she said.

"I'm sorry," Georgia said. She took two awkward steps forward to pat the top of Mora's hand. "It's not like that means he isn't still out here somewhere. There are a lot of scattered communities on the outskirts. We're working on finding everyone, but it takes time. We can't find people who don't want to be found. That's why we've got to get rid of the virus."

Mora considered. She hadn't immediately found her dad outside waiting for her, but she hadn't truly expected to, had she? He wasn't even the entire reason she'd left. She wanted to be outside, and now she was. She wanted to learn about the people on the outside and be free, like Georgia and her people, and now she had the opportunity to do so.

Georgia gave Mora a little shake. "What do you think? Are you ready to go?"

"Let's go," Mora said, hitching her pack higher up on her shoulder.

Georgia opened the vehicle door, gesturing for Mora to enter.

Mora hesitated, glancing up at Omen.

"Don't worry, he knows the way."

The vehicle's interior was short, dark, and smelled like dust, mold, and partially burnt hydrocarbons. Georgia swung into the driver's seat and pulled a belt over her shoulder, clicking it into place in the same motion. After watching her, Mora did the same with the strap hanging above her own right shoulder. The vehicle growled to life with an obscene amount of noise.

"Just because I'm the only one here doesn't mean the others aren't happy to have you," Georgia nearly shouted as she eased onto the road.

Mora watched as they moved through rubble and leveled land where homes used to be. The further they went, the more thorough the job.

Georgia continued. "I'm aware that this is a lot. I wanted there to be more of us when you got out. I can only imagine how it must feel—a kid on the outside getting into an old lady's vehicle and heading to unknown places."

"I knew what I was getting myself into," Mora said.

The speakers on the old truck crackled, and a voice blatted through the static.

"We're set to intercept the target."

Georgia grabbed a slotted black square that dangled from the end of a coiled wire. The device made Mora think of the walkie-talkies from one of her books. Georgia compressed a button on the side.

"Copy. Do you have eyes on the dissenter interceptor?"

There was a terrible squeal as static rose and fell through the speakers like a doppler storm. Mora covered her ears reflexively.

"Negative. Something must have happened. We sent a crew to investigate."

Georgia pressed the button, cutting off the crackling sound. "The intercept is the priority. We can figure the rest out later."

"Copy. We'll stay on target."

Georgia replaced the device into the holder on the center console.

"What's that about?" Mora asked.

Georgia gave her a half-glance, keeping her eyes forward as she navigated the crumbled earth. "We became aware of an opportunity we couldn't pass up. That's where everyone else is."

"Are you always this elusive or just when you're picking up random runaway teens outside the force field?" Mora asked.

Georgia smirked. "We get in the habit of only saying what needs to be said. You can't squeal what you don't know if somebody catches you, but since you're new and you can't say much else, I'll tell you. There's a Northern Laboratories transportation headed out of the Institute that we want to get our hands on, and we've got good intel that it's not under surveillance, so the group went west to intercept it."

Mora felt a thrill at the revelation. The DDC was doing raids outside the force fields. They were *stealing* government property.

Georgia gave Mora a sideways glance, eyebrow raised as she shifted the truck into another gear. "Don't freak out on me, okay? This is just part of what we're doing out here. Nobody's free until everyone's free, right?"

"I won't freak out," Mora promised.

The vehicle was quiet now that they were on the maintained road. It was quiet for a long time. The sun crept over the horizon, the low angle of the light catching the force field and refracting to turn the sky a brilliant orange.

"You said we'll never be free until the virus is gone. Do you really think there's a way to get rid of it?" Mora asked.

"Like I said, that's the number one job out here," Georgia said.

Mora hadn't known anyone besides the Northern Laboratories was working on eradicating the virus. Perhaps the DDC was more effective at telling stories than she'd realized.

"Where are we going?" she asked.

"Home," Georgia said.

Mora watched the city recede, marveling at the disappearing shimmer of her old life. Not far behind them, a black bird lifted into the sky, followed by another.

CHAPTER

Fifty-Seven

ANIKA

ANIKA'S HEART pounded so forcefully in her throat it was hard to breathe.

Less than an hour ago, she'd been sitting in her room, trying and failing to read a firsthand account of an early war outbreak while ignoring what was happening in the L-wing.

Park hadn't come back to her room after racing out, but she'd figured it out quickly enough. Someone had transformed. A patient, previously unaffected by the disease raging inside of them, had become a monster. It had only made her more certain that Zayd must leave the Institute.

Zayd was on his way to freedom now. He would be free, and she would be with him, and if Park was right about the disease being dormant until triggered, they might actually have a chance at a real life on the outside with these people.

Anika studied the young medic as she took in the other passengers. There were ten scientists and fifteen volunteers—eighteen if she included herself, Zayd, and Park, but doing so seemed like a joke. They were seated amidst twenty-two cryogenic cylinders containing treatable patients, meaning there were a total of twenty-three patients aboard the Northern Laboratories transport. Anika hoped the number didn't mean anything.

Park gave up her constant vigil of the scientists at the front of the vehicle, seeming to accept that none of them recognized her. She placed a hand on her stomach in a gesture Anika suspected she didn't realize she did so frequently. She rubbed her stomach, and Anika wondered if it was to alleviate some persistent discomfort or if it was a soothing gesture. Was she comforting her baby from the outside? Anika yearned to know exactly what Park was experiencing. She resisted the urge to mimic the gesture on her own, not yet visibly growing stomach.

Zayd didn't know. Whether or not the pregnancy was viable—or possible—she would have to tell him. She couldn't justify keeping the secret now that there was no risk of him forsaking his freedom.

As if sensing her thoughts shift to him, Zayd reached for Anika's hand. She jolted at the brush of his skin against hers, mind racing with images of infection and transmission. He placed his hand on her leg, soothing with gentle pressure.

"It's okay. Remember? Park said we're good," he whispered.

What did Park actually know about the infection? How much could a first-year medic truly understand about a new strain of Zoribiatus?

"I just want to be cautious," she breathed.

"We're way past cautious, Ani. It's you and me on the outside. If you go, I go, and they'll have to put both of us on ice because I'm not gambling the rest of our lives together on a risk that doesn't exist. We went to the Institute. We got our answers, and we're where we're supposed to be with the right people to help us." He grabbed her hand and held fast.

She squeezed back. He was right. They couldn't live the rest of their lives with a barrier between them. Thoughts of the L-wing and patient transformation rushed forward, but she forced them back. She wasn't a patient anymore, and she wasn't a monster. The people running the Institute were the real monsters. She let a few tears run freely down her face, not wanting to draw attention to herself.

Zayd kept her hand in his, resting in the soft space where their legs met. He ran his thumb idly across her knuckle as Anika retreated back inside herself. The transport buzzed with quiet conversation. Several tablets glowed toward the front of the vehicle where scientists did their best to pass the time. In the mask of ambient noise, Zayd leaned forward, daring to ask, "Do you know how long we have to wait?"

Park shook her head, thumbing nervously at the edges of her tablet. "I didn't get a lot of details. I don't even know who's doing the intercepting. Just members of the dissenting group."

Anika glanced at Park, turning over the limited information. "What's going to happen to everyone else?" she asked.

Park's cheeks reddened at the question. "I didn't ask," she admitted. "I was so busy worrying about someone noticing me. And getting Zayd out—I don't think they would do anything terrible."

Anika studied her, taking in her pale face and pregnant stomach. If she were any indication, these people didn't put much thought into the casualties of their decisions. The transport interception could be yet another example of questionable practices.

"Are we working with the right people?" Zayd asked after a long silence. "Ever since Jemani let the patients loose, I've been wondering what sort of people we're dealing with."

"Garth is sure the dissenting group is making the right sacrifices, but that's hard to reconcile with how he made me feel like a means to an end," Park added.

"I always thought it was eerie how excited Dr. Wong was about—" Anika stopped herself.

"There is no good solution. I think we're trusting the right people for now," Park said.

Anika sighed, thankful for the distraction. "You think?"

"Did you hear those screams in the medical wing?" Park asked.

Anika shuddered. "I heard them."

"I listened to those screams every single day for months before I moved to the L-wing. I learned to ignore them as part of the scientist program." Park gestured toward the other scientists. "All of them learned to ignore those screams. We call them patients, which I think used to mean something before the Institute. But now the only thing *patient* means is something less than human. Something you can ignore or experiment on or put in chains and let die behind a force field to keep everyone safe. And now, Reed said he caused Abigail to develop—"

"Abigail?" Anika's breath caught. A sick chill ran down her spine as she connected the pieces.

"The patient that turned. Her name was Abigail Fitzpatrick. She was an old woman who didn't deserve what happened to her," Park explained.

Anika felt a new rush of grief. Of course it had been Ms. Fitzpatrick. Of course they were both in the L-wing.

"I knew Ms. Fitzpatrick," she said.

"You knew Abigail?" Park asked, her face pale but her eyes bright.

"From before," Anika clarified. "She was a client at our clinic. She was there every other week for as long as I worked there."

"I'm so sorry," Park whispered. Zayd put his arm around Anika, pulling her close to absorb her grief.

"It's interesting, though," Anika continued, "because Cora called her a patient. She called all the clients patients."

Park blinked at the information.

"Cora was from the Institute," Zayd explained.

"They're infecting them at the clinics," Park breathed, almost inaudible. Her face darkened.

Anika considered the statement. "It's possible," she said, slow to be certain of anything anymore. "It's possible it wasn't on purpose. Perhaps a chance in the infusions—"

"It must be on purpose. There's no way something like that would make it to the cities without being tested," Park said, keeping her voice low so they didn't attract any unwanted attention. She looked as though she were grappling with the idea still. "It would explain how they were able to develop so fast."

"You're saying they flipped her switch. Why would they do that unless they wanted to use her like a weapon?" Zayd asked a little too loudly.

"I think that's exactly what they're doing. The Institute uses the same word for the people they're supposed to be helping and the near-dead," Park said, raising her voice just loud enough to draw a volunteer's attention.

They were quiet for a long time, waiting for the crush of road below them to return their conversation to obscurity.

"What did Jemani do with the patients?" Park asked when enough time had passed.

"We were supposed to load them onto a hovercraft, but Jemani set both of them loose to attack the DDC officers," Zayd explained.

"You said she set patients free. Do you mean sick people?" Park pressed.

"I mean monsters," Zayd replied without hesitation. "They tore those DDC guys open like they were meat pies. One of the officers died, and the other went to cryo. After the volunteers cleaned up the mess, a third officer shot Jemani. He called her *Resistee garbage*." Zayd shuddered, clearly distressed by the horror of it all.

"Was she a Resistee?" Anika asked. She was feeling as if she'd missed quite a bit shut behind the L-wing doors.

"Jemani came to the Institute from a city volunteer program. A lot of the volunteers who came with family think the city volunteers are connected to Resistee groups. Clearly, the DDC agrees," Park explained.

"Does it matter if she was a Resistee? I didn't think they were around anymore," Zayd said.

Park shook her head. "I don't know. The volunteers take issue with the Resistee movement," she said.

"But that could be because of the anti-Resistee sentiments in the City States," Anika observed.

"Maybe," Zayd agreed. "But if I'd thought someone was going to set a couple of near-dead loose on somebody innocent, I'd probably do what Jemani did. I don't think that makes what the Resistees do particularly radical."

"I don't think the Resistees are a part of the dissenting group. I think they're separate but have the same goal," Park suggested.

"Like two branches of the same tree facing in different directions. They're both reaching for the sun," Anika mused. It made sense that the pushback against the DDC would be coming from more than one place.

"Seems like a lot of folks have a problem with what the DDC is doing at the Institute," Zayd said.

Anika's stomach turned with the magnitude of everything happening.

"Can we maybe get to safety before we figure the rest of this out?" she asked.

"That's the best idea I've heard all day," Park agreed.

"I beg to differ," Zayd said, pulling Anika's hand onto his lap.

Park rolled her eyes, making Anika blush at Zayd's obvious affection.

"I think we can all be mature volunteers for a little while longer before our lives completely change," she said, hoping to remind him anyone could be watching.

"I'll show you a mature volunteer," Zayd teased, tilting his head toward her and making her squirm.

Anika tried to keep a stern face, but a deranged giggle threatened to dismantle her calm exterior. She was still terrified about what was to come but couldn't help feeling triumphant. She was infected but would not turn. They were fleeing the Institute together, hand in hand, waiting for freedom.

The vehicle slowed as Zayd settled under Park's serious scowl.

Fifty-Eight

PARK

THERE WAS no way to determine if this was a natural part of the journey or if this was it. The vehicle was definitely stopping. Around them, other scientists and volunteers were looking around, trying to make sense of it.

"Welcome to the Northern Laboratories!" one of the scientists joked. Was it Ward?

"Why do you always have to be an idiot?" another scientist, Davenport, hissed.

Definitely Ward.

The engines died, drowning the vehicle in silence. Underneath the rustling of bodies, Park swore she could hear the collective sound of their heartbeats.

"Where's the backup power?" one of the volunteers asked.

The backup power cells hadn't activated when the engines died, meaning the cryogenic tanks weren't being cooled. Would the patients be collateral in this, too?

Outside, metal clanged. Someone shouted, and a few other voices rose above the din, not clear enough to distinguish their words. More banging, followed by the surge of a pulsar gun.

"Something's happening!" someone yelled in a voice pitched with fear.

"Why aren't the power cells running?"

"Lowry, get around and check that out." The last one was a command. From outside came three quick bangs, like boards slapping against a hard surface.

A volunteer—ostensibly Lowry—made their way to the back of the vehicle, shining a light on the control panel for the load door.

"I can't get the door up without power."

"Are we trapped in here?"

Park could feel the tide of rising panic threatening to overtake her. She glanced at Zayd and Anika, hoping they would remain calm. Their faces were frozen in stoic terror.

The door opened suddenly from the outside, filling the transport with misty, grey morning light. Three people stood outside, their chests level with the interior floor. They wore thick jackets of varying colors. Their hair was long and swept back from their faces with thick pieces of cloth. Each one of them had a weapon trained at the people inside.

"No one move," the person in the middle commanded.

Park hadn't expected this level of aggression, but she had every intention of following orders. Possibly the dissenters had to put on a good show to get away with what they were doing.

The person on the left climbed into the vehicle, then waited for the one on the right to join before advancing. No one moved. Park didn't even think they breathed.

Outside, someone shouted, "We've got what we need. You and Louisiana need to finish up in back so we can move on out!"

"Give us a few more minutes, Del," the man still standing outside the vehicle shouted back, then said to the people inside, "Do you have eyes on them?"

"It's us," Park said, indicating to herself, Zayd and Anika.

The woman standing just past them turned to study the trio, pointing her gun in Park's direction. Instinctively, Park put her hands over her stomach as if they could stop an errant burst of energy. When

Zayd saw where the gun was pointed, he rose from his seat, placing himself between the woman and Park.

"Get back in your seat!" the woman commanded.

"Lower the gun from the pregnant woman's stomach," Zayd snapped back.

The woman's eyebrows rose at this. She pointed the gun at Anika, and for a terrible second, Park was certain Zayd would attack.

"There. Now sit," the woman said.

"Waving guns around at unarmed people is a great way to get somebody killed," Zayd seethed, lowering himself back into his seat so his body blocked the weapon's path.

The woman watched him do it, keeping her gaze on Park, clearly curious. Park took this curiosity as an opportunity to explain. She kept her voice low enough that the others wouldn't hear. "I'm the medic, and they" —she crooked her thumb at Zayd and Anika—"are coming with me."

"Alright, medic," the woman said, still eyeing her up and down. "Go ahead and hop down with your boyfriend."

"Her, too," Zayd said, reaching for Anika.

The woman shifted her aim to Zayd, but Park could tell it was more bluster than intent. "You're an insistent bunch of hostages, aren't you?"

Park turned her attention to Zayd, trying to give him a reassuring look. Zayd kept his eyes on the gun as he stood, bringing Anika with him and backing up until they were against the edge of the transport's elevated floor. Park followed.

"Why don't you sit, and I'll help you scoot off the edge?" Zayd suggested, looking between Park's stomach and the large jump.

"I'm plenty fit," she said, wrinkling her nose at his suggestion.

"You're top-heavy. Do what he says if you don't want to end up on your face," the woman said.

"I've got two here that fit the profile. Do you know which one we want, Lou?" the man inside the vehicle asked.

"Bring them both," the woman—*Louisiana*—instructed.

Park lowered herself, struggling more than she wanted to get her legs out from under her. She accepted Zayd's hand, then the left side of his body as she scooted over the edge, barely managing to keep her feet below her on the landing. By the time she recovered, two scientists were being escorted from inside the transport.

Park remembered seeing them board, wearing their black suits and white lab coats with freshly polished scientist emblems. Both women were about the same height with light-colored hair clipped into the same short cut. One of them looked scared enough to faint, while the other scientist only appeared mildly curious. Her reeling mind couldn't pluck their names from the rest of her jumbling thoughts.

"Ready to move out!" Someone—*Del?*—called. Park looked around the side of the transport to see two flatbed trucks filled with people and gear. Each of the people was armed with either a pulsar gun or a smaller weapon that looked like it had come out of Gunther's old films.

"I've got space for these two in front," Del said, accepting the scientists.

"Utah, Kansas, take care of the rest of them," Louisiana instructed the two people standing nearest the Northern Laboratories transport.

Two men jumped into the transport, pointing their weapons at the volunteers on either side. When they fired, small darts with red tips embedded into the volunteers' legs, making them cry out.

Del pushed the scientists into the waiting hands of other members of their group before saying, "Make certain they all go down. We can't have anyone calling for backup before we get out of here."

Utah and Kansas continued moving through the transport, embedding a dart into each passenger's leg as they went. To Park, Louisiana said, "If you're coming with us, you better follow me."

Park looked back at Zayd and Anika with wide eyes, willing herself to act more confident than she felt before following Louisiana. They made their way, stepping over deep cracks in the asphalt until they stood before the second flatbed. Del was loading the scientists onto the first vehicle. One of the waiting personnel on the flatbed reached out a hand to Park.

"Can you boost her from behind?" they asked Zayd.

"I'll keep my hands on your hips," Zayd promised, stepping behind Park to help hoist her up.

She didn't have time to protest. Everyone was moving with efficient urgency. Together, Zayd and two other people hoisted her onto the platform, creating space for her amidst what looked like large pieces of the transport's engine.

After helping Anika, Zayd jumped up to sit beside her, putting a reassuring hand on her knee.

As Park tried to orient herself, Louisiana crouched down in front of her. "What's the deal with the scared lady in the volunteer suit?"

"She's from the L-wing," Park said, sensing she shouldn't start her relationship with these people with anything other than honesty.

"What's the L-wing?" Louisiana asked.

"Didn't Garth tell you?" Park asked, alarm threatening to upend her.

"Honey, I don't know who Garth is. Nobody sent us," Louisiana said.

Shock rocketed through Park's arms as her heart rate quickened. Her stomach clenched, and her bladder threatened to give way as the baby bore down against her rising anxiety. "You aren't dissenters, are you?"

The woman shook her head. "We're not associated with anyone from the Institute. Your intercept isn't coming."

Park swayed.

"Take a breath," Louisiana said, putting a steadying hand on Park's shoulder.

"Did you do something?" Zayd demanded, giving Louisiana's pulsar gun a disgusted glare.

Louisiana swung her gaze to him. "No. We don't harm innocents. The intercept didn't show. We don't know what happened."

"Maybe they're running late?" Park asked. Her voice wavered. Everything was going wrong.

"I don't think so, and we can't wait around to find out. You're either coming with us or taking a dart and staying with them," Louisiana said.

Park followed her gesture back to the transport filled with sleeping scientists and volunteers. There was a low rumble as the backup power cycled on to cool the patients' cryogenic cylinders.

"How do we know we'll be safe? Who are you?" Anika demanded. The sureness of her tone bolstered Park.

"We're citizens of this place just like you. Difference is, we're on the outside," a man—*Kansas or Utah*—said as he climbed into the flatbed to sit next to Zayd. The truck rumbled as the engine came to life.

Going with these people was their only option at this point, but Anika and Zayd pushing back reminded Park that she didn't have to be complacent ever again. It didn't matter that these people weren't Garth's. They had wondered anyway whether trusting the dissenters was in their best interest. All that mattered was that they were together. They'd gotten out.

"We'll go with you for now. I need a safe place to have this baby —*We* need a safe space. If you can give us that, I'll offer my services as a medic to your people," she said, certain this was the right choice.

"We don't barter," Louisiana said, crossing her arms as she settled on the truck's floor. "We'll give you a safe space because that's the right thing to do. We don't need you to trade your services, but if you decide you want to help, I hope you'll do a lot more for us than work as a medic."

"What do you want me to do?" Park asked, curiosity blooming as the trucks moved away from the Northern Laboratories transport.

The sun was breaking through the fog now, painting the forest in vibrant greens. Louisiana turned away as it rose over the trees, meeting Park's gaze with a crooked grin.

"Help us change the world."

CHAPTER
Fifty-Nine

JAMES

JAMES' pack was light. There wasn't much to bring to the Institute, and he didn't have anyone to give him a send-off gift. His parents would be in detention until after he was gone—Morgan Rossi-Stern's doing.

Still, he figured, it could be worse. He graduated and was headed to the Institute. He could send word later. His parents being detained was a small price to pay for getting Mora out.

His insides felt warm despite the cool morning air. All around him, people were milling. There were only a few families waiting with their interns. Everyone else was going about their normal business, living lives that didn't include the same monumental transition.

James had dreamed of this moment for most of his teen years. There had been several different iterations of the dream, of course, as his vision of his own future had developed and matured. Since he met Mora, all of those dreams had included her in some capacity. Sometimes she was going with him. Sometimes she kissed him goodbye. In some, they had been together, boarding the transport hand in hand. He'd done his best to correct those images since her admission, forcing himself to keep the moments platonic. His mind had even managed to keep her in the vision after he knew she was leaving, replacing her physical presence with a message painstakingly typed out from her old-world tablet. In reality, he had none of those things. He didn't even have his own parents to wish him a good trip.

It didn't matter. He told himself it didn't matter. He'd done right, and wherever Mora was, she was grateful for him. The transport pulled up, moving through the thin stream of people walking down Main Street. His heart rate quickened. He could see the silhouettes of other interns from other cities darkening the windows. This was the last stop before the Institute.

"This is it," one of the men standing with Naomi said.

"More than five hundred students took the Test this year," Naomi gushed to her appreciative crowd.

A woman in a black suit stood on the capitol building steps just behind them. Her presence drew all of James' attention away from the scene. He thought about ignoring her. The transport vehicle had stopped in front of him. He could walk onto it without looking back, and there wasn't a single thing she could do to stop him.

He stepped back from the curb and made his way around the other families readying their goodbyes as the transport doors opened. He didn't have any reason to run.

"Did you come to wish me a good trip?" he asked, stopping at the step just below where Morgan Rossi-Stern stood.

"Just making sure you get on that transport," she said, not making eye contact.

"Don't worry. After today, you'll never have to see me again," he said, cinching his pack tight across his shoulders.

"I'm counting on it." Morgan kept her gaze just above his head. Even though he was on the step below her, she had to tip her chin up to do it. It was curious how he'd never considered how much taller he was. She was such an imposing figure in his life that he'd always assumed he was the smaller one.

He turned from her, meaning to walk away, but a thought occurred to him. He looked back to catch her looking at him instead of over him. Seizing the opportunity, he said, "You might as well say goodbye, since it's the closest you'll get."

He held her dark, icy stare for a second longer than necessary before turning for good. He knew what she must think of him—knew she was glad to be rid of him even if he was the one who would receive the prestige and accolades and not her. He wasn't sure who between them was the victor in her eyes, but he was at least certain that he'd taken the one thing that mattered. Morgan Rossi-Stern was no longer in control of Mora's destiny.

His hand was on the rail when Morgan called out to him.

"You didn't actually help her, Dunn. She won't be safe."

He gripped the cool metal, feeling the heat pour out of him through its conductive surface. She was trying to take this victory from him.

"She's safer now without you," he said, swinging his legs up the steps and into the vehicle.

The door closed behind him, shutting out any attempt Morgan might make to respond. He found a seat by the window just behind an intern with short hair framing their very high cheekbones. Like him, the intern was wearing their school uniform shirt—maroon instead of red. He tore his eyes away from them to watch Morgan disappear as the transport pulled away, rounding the block to head west to the city boundary. His stomach did a flip as he considered the fact that he was about to pass outside the force field for the first time in his life.

What would it look like on the other side? Was it possible he would see Mora? He hoped not. He hoped she was long gone from this place now, having found Georgia and her people from the outside.

"What do you think the Institute will be like?" the intern ahead of him asked.

"I don't know." James shrugged, watching the city pass by with increasing speed. The renovations were well underway on the West-side, and pieces of the city he'd grown up in were unrecognizable. He wondered how much longer before he wouldn't recognize his own home.

"Do you think it will be as competitive as the city programs?" It had only been a few seconds, but he'd already forgotten he was in a conversation with another intern.

"Probably more competitive," he admitted. Ahead of them, the border guards waited to scan the manifest for the transport. His name would be officially stricken from the city records and sent to the Institute roster.

"I only barely passed the Test, you know." The intern was watching him with wide eyes.

"I think all of us lagged in at least a few areas," James said. He'd struggled with some of the psychological portions and had a few low marks in logic and ethics, which had surprised him at the time. After helping Mora escape, he thought maybe he understood.

It was difficult to quantify what was right and what was wrong.

"My name is Sam. I'm from 42SE."

"James."

They were both quiet as the transport drove through the force field barrier and out onto the main road, James in awe of the moment and Sam out of respect for the moment. The outside looked both like and unlike what he'd expected.

The road stretched out ahead of them through a densely grown area. It was difficult to see past the trees and greenery that hugged up against the road. It was so unlike the city.

"It's strange to go from such a peaceful, organized space to something so wild, isn't it?" Sam asked.

James thought about Mora moving through this dense greenery and tried to suppress the nagging panic the thought conjured. It would be difficult for her to see Omen in this level of growth.

"It is," he agreed.

"Some of the interns in the back said they saw near-dead when we were on our way into the capitol."

James tore his eyes away from the window long enough to study Sam, who had an arm draped over the back of the seat to face him. They looked casual for such a serious conversation.

"Did they really?"

Sam shrugged, offering him a charming smile that lifted their whole face. "Who knows. I think everything that moves outside the City States looks like near-dead. But at least it makes a cool story for when we get to the Institute."

The last thing James wanted to think about was wandering near-dead lurking near the city boundary.

"There one is!" someone shouted from the back of the transport.

The entire transport shifted from one side to the other to catch a glimpse. James made it just in time to see the bent human form disappear into the forest and wondered if Morgan had known what he'd see when they left.

She won't be safe.

"How many is that total?" someone asked.

"That's four," an intern responded.

"Six for me, but we were the first pickup," another said.

Clearly, near-dead sightings weren't an uncommon experience.

"Do you think they round them up and ship them to the Institute for us to study?" Naomi asked.

"They have some on-site already."

"But they're constantly looking for new developments for innovating the research."

The conversation turned to analysis of Institute research and education policies. James had to admit he found it comforting. For the moment, at least, he was in good company.

He wondered what Mora would think of these fellow interns. Would she be interested in their upcoming research and understanding of Zoribiatus, or would she want to argue about the inconsistencies in disease treatment and management?

Resistee attitude, he could hear their professor say.

Ahead of them, a black bird swooped low over the road before disappearing above the trees. James had no idea if it could possibly be Omen and hoped he and Mora were long gone, but the sighting lifted his spirits.

There were more birds out here. *She* was out here.

"Do you think there's hope for the future?" Sam was asking.

"I do," he said.

SIMONS LEFT the management station at the break of dawn on an early winter morning. He kept the baby tucked tight against his chest, pulling his jacket over her little body to keep the chill out but looking down constantly to make sure her perfect little face was clear of any obstruction. The baby slept peacefully, her perfect black curls plastered to the top of her head and sides of her face.

His pack was nearly bursting with more supplies than he probably needed, but he had a long journey ahead of him and had no intention of being caught unprepared. It was about a half day's walk to his transport if everything went well, and he knew it wouldn't. Trudy had a habit of stirring every two hours like clockwork. If he didn't get a bottle in her mouth fast enough, stirring would transform into something much more disruptive and, if she needed a change, a lot noisier. Simons figured they'd be doing good if they made it to the transport before nightfall.

They had stayed at the energy management facility as long as possible. Long enough for Simons to get comfortable doing impossibly delicate things with his massive hands. Trudy was small—smaller than he'd even tried to imagine—but she was also tenacious.

And opinionated.

She was the absolutely perfect miniature of her mother in a way that made Simons' heart swell. He didn't know he could feel that way about such a tiny, fresh human.

But he did. He felt that way and then some.

He kept the baby tucked snug against him with one hand and the lashing pole out ahead of him in the other. He didn't intend to have any surprises.

"We'll be back to visit soon enough," he'd told Terni, who cried freely as she kissed the baby's tiny hands and feet, sucking in her smell like she'd be able to keep it bottled in her lungs long enough to sustain her until they returned.

Terni had been advised by her inside contact that there would be a series of audits and a grid changeover on the schedule, which meant it wouldn't be safe to return for some time.

"We'll head into the cities. I'll get work in repairs for a while."

He asked her one more time if she wanted to run with them, but Terni had refused.

"Letting her go makes me feel like I might die, but everything inside of me wants to keep her safe. She isn't safe here, but if I stay, she's safe with you," she'd said.

Trudy grunted, shifting her head against his chest. He moved his hand up to support her, marveling at how little the sounds she made were now, when he knew what her tiny body was truly capable of. Already, he had a bottle waiting in his front pocket, bumping against his leg as he moved soundlessly through the brush.

It was strange how fast he'd changed. It took almost nothing for him to send the message letting his contact know he'd need support.

He was still a dissenter, but for the time being he was on hiatus. He would be heading into 42SE to stay with another dissenter—someone with kids—who would help him learn the ropes. He could offer help on the inside while he got the help he needed for his new role. Then, when Trudy was older and things were clear, he'd start his runs again. He would take people where they needed to go. They would go together to be with Terni. They'd be dissenters, but in between, they'd be a family.

He could see it all play out in his mind. He knew it wouldn't be perfect, but he wanted it more than anything. He knew it would be worth it.

Together, they would change the world.

Acknowledgments

Writing a book can feel lonely sometimes, but it takes a village to make it happen. The village of Hearts of a Vanishing City was vast and well-populated, and I will forever be tied to its residents in the bonds of community.

To my early readers and developmental editors— you were there for me when I was certain this story had nothing to offer and had the grace to tell me I was being an insecure idiot in the nicest possible way. You made me realize all the important pieces and encouraged me to do the work to make this book the incredible story it is.

To my husband, who not only let me read him every sentence I found clever but also read the book in its entirety and picked up all the slack when the schedule got rough— thank you. I hope this book earns us 17 million dollars because you deserve it.

To my copy editor— I'm sorry I still don't have commas figured out. I think that part of my brain doesn't work right. You were very patient with me, and you also left one of my favorite feedback lines of all time: "Girl, your bird talks!" I appreciate you more than you know.

My children aren't allowed to read my books yet, but they're getting close, and like Mora, they will read them whether I'm ready or not. They're determined and headstrong and I love them dearly for it. So, when they read this, I intend for them to know how much they're loved and how incredible they already are. We can laugh about this when you're ready to tell me you looked.

And to my readers and life-supporters. You might think that because I mention you last that your role was somehow less but that couldn't be further from the truth. You, my dears, matter so much.

You're the reason I write these books. You give me my voice, and together, in this world of story, we are whole. Thank you the thank-you-i-est.

About the Author

Jill N Davies started out as a chemist working for a pharmaceutical manufacturing company. After several years working in development she moved on to become... a high school science teacher. (You see where this is going, don't you?)

Before she went full *Breaking Bad*, she took a sharp left turn at Albuquerque and decided to dedicate her working time to creating stories. She now writes in the quiet moments of her life, squeezing novels into life's nooks and crannies that act like the pauses between heartbeats.

Her debut series combines much of her acquired knowledge and experiences with the fascinating dystopia of a science-driven world.

When she's not writing, you may often find her running the trails near her home, hiking the national parks, or reading the same book over and over to her two daughters.

Find more at www.jillndavies.com

instagram.com/jillndavies_books
tiktok.com/@JillNDavies_Books
threads.net/@jillndavies_Books
amazon.com/author/jillndavies

Also by Jill N Davies

Due North

Into the Deadlands

Darkling Project (Book 3) Release Date TBD

Extinction Event (Book 4) Release Date TBD